AWOKEN

Book One
Shadowed Veil Series

Billie Jade Kermack

All characters and events in this publication, other than those clearly in the public domain, are fictitious, and any resemblance to actual persons, living or dead, is purely coincidental.

Contact the author at:
bilbo86@hotmail.co.uk

Acknowledgements

Jimmy Hughes for all his love and support. My brother James for all that he has taught me and for being my role model. My father who can no longer be with us but watches over us from above. My beautiful babies, Noah James and Aavie Mae, who continually inspire me to never give up. Last but by no means least, to my mother, who introduced me to the magical world of books and taught me that anything is possible. I am forever grateful.

ISBN: 9781795835190

PREFACE

ꟾ

The sound of a screeching three hundred and sixty degree handbrake turn, raucous laughter and the bright white lights from a speeding car on the road outside my window woke me, not as suddenly as they had the past seven nights in a row, but then my sleeping body did very little to note it as an expected wake up call. The neon green numbers on my alarm clock informed me of just how absurdly early it was, the pitch-black sky outside confirming it. I kicked back my covers dramatically, mumbling a curse word or two under my breath, as I hobbled over to my open window. The lights danced around the walls of my room, the unseasonably warm June air billowing in past my curtains, the smell of burnt rubber an unpleasant after taste in my mouth. Within moments everything around me was starved of that light, the flickering street lamp below my window about as useful as a lit candle on a boat at sea. Manoeuvring around in the dark, across the Minecraft assault course that was my bedroom floor, I edged my way back into bed, nearly breaking my ankle on my laptop cable and landing in a bowl of something squishy was karmas way of agreeing with my mother's protests that my room was in desperate need of a clean. 'you'll break your neck one day.' Her words were clear in my head as I side stepped a half-drunk bottle of coke.

I must have tossed and turned for what seemed like an hour, with every passing minute my mind was that much more awake, the idea of getting the sleep my body so sorely desired, was more like a pipe dream. The beeping begun slow and out of sequence at first, each ping slightly different from the last.

Fumbling around in the dark for the second time that night I had decided sleep was overrated and anything was better than lying in bed alone with only my thoughts for company. Even coursework had to better than this torture, and if I'm honest I wasn't even sure I was sold on the idea of higher education. At this point in my life, doing the things people my age considered normal, was just my way of fitting in, each task followed through with just the right amount of enthusiasm necessary, to stride under the radar of my mother. I rubbed my eyes and instead of allowing them to adjust to the darkness, I stupidly tugged on the cord to my desk lamp. All 60 watts seared into the protective film covering my eyeball, there was a far worse smell then burning rubber it seems. I shuffled about aimlessly with my eyes closed tightly. Cursing wildly at Mary, Joseph and either God or the holy ghost as I fought to right myself, I finally made contact with the panelled wood door that led into the hallway, I reached up to grab my dressing gown from the hook, rummaging blindly for the comfort of my hands meeting its plush faux fur; no hook, no dressing gown.

I opened my eyes apprehensively, even though my inner child, sensing that uneasy trickle climbing our spine was vehemently against it. All I could see in front of me was a dirt speckled cream wall with a patient's clip chart attached at eye level. I ran my hands over the wall aimlessly, that scared little voice inside screaming 'I told you not to open your eyes!', Praying a door handle would magically present itself but realising quickly that I wasn't living in a Harry Potter novel, my panic level escalated quickly to at least a six.

'Inoperable', 'risky', 'cancerous', 'sickness' and *'blindness'*. The words levitated off the chart and ingrained themselves in my subconscious. I knew where I was now, but even that couldn't lull me. Knowing where I was only provided me with a deeper level of fear. That faint beeping sound emanated from behind me and as the sound grew louder, I took a deep breath, rubbing my shaking hands into

submission, turning ever so slowly to face what was behind me. My heart plummeted to the pit of my stomach with a thud and all the strength of an unexploded bomb. There, in front of me, was the manifestation of a memory that I had desperately tried to forget. He lay there motionless, his frail body invaded by tubes and needles. The repeated bleeps of the monitors and machines mimicked the beat of my fragile broken heart. With his gaunt face and bony arms, he resembled an ancient man in his late nineties, not the strapping, six foot three, handsome man in his early thirties that I knew.

What am I doing here? I screamed in my head, as the child within me cowered away in the corner, her hands covering her eyes. I turned back towards where my bedroom door should have been, but a wordless and uncomfortable groan from the man behind me made me turn to face him again. I took in a deep breath and clenched my fists until my knuckles were white, in an attempt to settle my nerves. With his emaciated finger he beckoned me towards him. Unsure of what to do, I reverted back to my six-year-old self and moved slowly towards his hospital bed, climbing up beside him and tucking my face into his chest. I desperately searched for some long-lost warmth. Where once his affectionate soft hands had cupped my face and his lips had tenderly met my forehead, now laid a frozen, clammy hand, that he could barely move an inch without a surge of excruciating pain. His lips were dry and cracked, almost colourless, his breath passing through them in laboured wisps. One thing remained the same though - his aroma. The scent of Mum's lavender comfort and the sweet redolence of his favourite aftershave washed over me, its familiarity holding me momentarily in happier memories. A darkness quickly engulfed those memories, any joy lost.

Somehow, while lying close to him, I came to the realisation that it was all a dream, but I didn't care. The fear in me had now settled and whilst in his loving arms, I was at peace. This memory, this dream, whatever it was, meant that I was one step closer to him, closer to my Dad again, and soon enough I would have to go back to an existence without him. I snuggled into his side as best I could and closed my eyes. I wanted this reality, however heart-breaking it was to see him this way I felt a wash of contentment seep through me, until something suddenly and cruelly ripped it away. A darkness quickly engulfed those memories, taking with it any semblance of serenity that I had allowed myself to feel.

I opened my eyes, and then he was gone. I was alone. I pressed my hands into the bed to steady myself and sit up, or at least that was what I told my body to do. I couldn't move. Why couldn't I move? *OK, Grace, whatever you do, don't panic!* I told myself.

Of course, I always did have a problem following instructions, even if they were my own. I looked down and saw that my hands and feet were secured with tatty old leather straps that pinched and tore at my skin as I struggled. The pain felt real, each tug biting at the nerves in my wrists, straining my ankles cutting off the circulation in my toes. I cried out ferociously and continued to tug at my restraints but all I could hear was the slow beeping sound of the monitors. I soon realised that my screams would not be heard. I was stuck in a silent nightmare and there was no way of getting myself out of it. *OK, now you can panic* my inner voice advised unhelpfully and a little late. I arched my back and pulled at my restraints hysterically, not knowing whether to scream or to sob. After a few minutes of tirelessly trying to get free, I gave up and collapsed back onto the bed. Only now it was not a bed beneath me, but a cold steel table. The temperature in the room lowered dramatically, the hairs on my legs standing to attention as a wisp of air circled my lower half, drenched in sweat from struggling but the air around me frigid, the confusion only heightened my panic. I glanced down apprehensively. The shabby hospital gown I was now wearing was torn at the clavicle, shredded around the hem and caked in dried blood; blood that I was almost certain wasn't mine. On the ceiling above me, the cracked and peeling paint appeared to move, cautious black smoke filtered through the cracks, tendrils moving almost animal-like as they stalked me, apprehensively approaching my skin as it assessed its prey. I was a rare steak all trussed up and ready to be devoured. Something was gravely wrong here, something very strange and something I was powerless to fight. This was unlike any other dream I had had of my father's death. Fear of losing him, fear of living without him; these were fears I knew, the fear of never coming out of this alive, was brand spanking new. The smoke that had approached me had a presence about it, not one I had come across before but yet there was a familiarity to it. Its movements were somewhat hypnotising as it danced around in the air, each dip and dive fluid in nature. With my lungs full to the brim, my chest high, my extremities taught like boards, I felt it grip my throat. Amongst the black swirls of smoke, I could see them; a pair of eyes; piercing white eyes with tiny black pupils. The strain around my throat released and my whole body shuddered, fighting to right itself and remind me the natural process of breathing. Before I had time to comprehend what I was seeing, the smoke smashed full force into the ceiling with a deafening pound. Dust and paint shavings rained down on me, making me cough and splutter as they invaded my mouth. Then came the silence - dead silence.

Instead of the comforting aroma of my Dad's aftershave, the sharp stench of disinfectant and stagnant blood stung my nostrils. However tightly I closed my eyes and wished for the comfort of my bedroom, the reek held me rigid. Then something warm grazed my exposed collarbone. I nervously opened my eyes and there, about an inch from my face, were those piercing eyes. They no longer glared at me from within a cloud of black smoke but from the face of a tall and willowy man with snow white hair. He was robed in a dirty, blood smeared, doctor's jacket and the rusted stethoscope that hung from his neck felt crushingly heavy as it lay on my chest. He floated horizontal in mid-air with little effort and his stale breath made my eyes water. My gag reflex jumped instinctively into action and the water cascading down my cheeks tasted bitterly of salt as it traced over my trembling lips. I soon realised my eyes weren't just watering, I was crying, strangled with sheer fear. *Don't cry, don't cry, please, don't cry!* I pleaded with myself, determined that I could keep in my grasp at the very least a semblance of sanity.

I struggled frantically to get free of my bonds and it was then that his right hand came into view and I saw my impending fate beginning to loom. The bright fluorescent light from overhead reflected off the razor-sharp scalpel that was gripped tightly in his hand. A sinister smirk played on his lips as he moved it towards my face. He traced the cold steel lightly over my cheek, his hesitation not a sign of his sense of guilt at my predicament but rather a sign of his depraved enjoyment at watching me squirm. With that final flash of joyous menace in his eyes, there was darkness. I struggled again, this time praying with everything that I could muster that the darkness wouldn't be my forever place. I fell out of my bed and onto the floor, taking my bedside lamp with me. Scrambling up to find the light switch I flipped it on. My throat was sore, my breaths fast and ragged. I gazed into the mirror, horrified at my reflection. There, on my flushed cheek, was a small and precise, crimson cut. This was not the first time I had experienced a nightmare like that. As I cleaned the blood from my face with the back of my sleeve, I knew for certain, that it wouldn't be the last time either.

~~~
~~~

Love is hoped for, life is a trial, and death is inevitable.
My name is Grace O'Callaghan.
I am daughter to James and Catherine and sister to Cary.
I was a person who loved and was loved in return.
But none of this matters now.
As he walks towards me with his skeletal fingers curled around a sullied blade, the only thought that pierces my petrified mind is 'How in the hell did I get here?'

ONE

I glanced towards my window from under my warm duvet, still half asleep and trying desperately to ignore the noise of my alarm clock. After my nightmare last night, I had managed only two hours sleep. Waking up on the wrong side of the bed as they say, wasn't the only reason I wanted to stay in the cosy confines of my bed. I could see the overcast grey sky and an incessant downpour of rain rattling on the glass; the heavens were well and truly open. *'Alarm clock - meet floor.'* It landed on my rug with sufficient force to stop the ringing. I did not want to get up. First day of term or not, I was feeling wildly uninspired.

In the bathroom, after I had showered and cleaned my teeth, I stood looking at myself in the mirror, assessing the long, thick waves of my unruly chestnut brown hair, which more often than not had to be pulled up into a ponytail. As I pulled on my tight blue t-shirt that showed my pale midriff, I remembered how I had decided around the age of fifteen that I was never going to have the body of a model. I had hips, I had boobs, I was a size 12 and finally proud of it. My height was just under five foot six now and maybe I would grow even taller – and maybe not. I glanced at my reflection again, at the small nose, rosebud lips and the heart-shaped face I had grown into and I suddenly saw a younger version of my mother. Those features were my heritage, passed down from my Irish ancestors. They were the maps that showed the world where I had come from. My eyes though, were my father's eyes. They were a deep cerulean blue and the only feature I possessed that could spark a thousand memories; a constant reminder of what I had lost. My aversion to my reflection was because of those eyes, the skip of my heart and sinking feeling in my stomach that reminded me he wasn't here by my side. Trying to dispel the thoughts that would inevitably take me back to last night my senses were suddenly heightened. My mouth was filled with a metallic taste that lingered on my tongue and the stagnant smell of decay mixed with the sterile odour from the hospital, as I had known they would come despite my fight to ignore them it dragged me back to the night my Dad died and to the brutal nightmares that tormented me. I shrugged off the feeling as best I could and grabbed my camera from off my desk and unhooked my backpack from the back of the chair. I made my way downstairs, as I did most days, with a sombre expression and what I thought was a lifetime of pain already packed high on my shoulders.

~~~~

I walked in and glanced around at the same faces that had greeted me last term. We all felt as sorry for one another as we did for ourselves. Tutors were the pick of the draw and all of us residing in this room felt as though we'd picked the dud ticket. I quickly found a vacant seat at the back and sat down; the back seemed the safest option. Mr Sanders had not yet arrived and for that stretch of time, everyone could enjoy the last moments of their ever-dwindling holiday break, he was sure to squash any and all happiness that may be ruminating when he arrived. The class started to fill and as usual, two minutes before the bell was due to ring, Amelia dashed in and threw her tiny pink handbag on the table. The oversized, cream, leather 'I love NY' bag only made an appearance on days she had homework or
~~~~

assignments with her and this was rare. When I voiced my concerns on her usual choice of clutch bag, which was a teeny, crystal-drenched Prada bag that could surely hold nothing important, she replied *with 'as long as a girl has a compact and a full tube of lip-gloss, she will never have a problem'.* Funnily enough, not one of her teachers agreed with this theory.

'So how was the drudgery of slave labour then?' she questioned, as she removed her jade studded compact and cherry lip gloss from her bag. Lining up her a powder pot and a brush next to her notebook. The Kardashian 101 morning routine, her most sacred of all beauty regimes, was how Amelia vowed to start every day.

'Well we don't all have rich parents Amelia. I'm what you call working class.' I smiled, but it was dripping with sarcasm, a tone that Amelia often missed. Amelia didn't work, full stop.
I suddenly felt like a bitch for saying it, even if it was true. She may have acted like a spoilt princess at least once a day but she didn't ask to be born into one of the richest families in Gallows Wood. Way down deep she did have a heart, even if it wasn't always visible.

'Grace, it's not my fault your parents aren't as successful or thrifty as mine. For example, it's like my parents own the building and your parents clean it, that's just life.' Her condescending tone was coupled with a pat on my shoulder which made me chuckle. *GOODBYE GUILT!* If it was anyone but Amelia, I think I would have taken offence but after so many years of friendship, it was utterly pointless holding a grudge. Even with all her flaws, Amelia never pretended to be anything other then what she was and I liked that about her.

'So, you aren't thinking of making this summer work thing a

permanent career then?' she added.

'I don't think you could call it work' I laughed, still keeping one eye fixed on the door. `Slave labour is a more apt description of what I had to endure, so you're right there.' The moment I decided to relax and take my eye off door watch, Mr Sanders burst through it, his arms filled with files and folders. He dumped them onto his desk and ran his hand through his hair, straightening what little of it he had left.

'So, we're all ready for a new year of learning then?' he asked with an uncharacteristic chirp. Everyone was unsurprisingly unresponsive. 'No answer. A response I've come to hold dear from my students.' he wailed sarcastically. As he raised his voice the chatter settled. He scanned the room like an eagle hunting out its weakest prey. 'I want Lucas and... Grace' he said, his voice sated with torturous glee. 'Can the two of you hand out these class diaries and without dropping them please Grace?' He indicated at two small boxes on the floor at the foot of his desk. I hadn't done anything wrong yet and still he had it in for me.

'Without dropping them please Grace!' I repeated caustically under my breath, like a disobedient child. Apparently, Mr Sanders had the hearing of a bat. Just my luck.

'Sorry Grace, is there a problem?' He practically spat the word sorry at me as it rested unfamiliarly in his mouth. 'Some uninteresting drivel you would like to share with the rest of us?' he coaxed. 'Handing out a few measly books too much like hard work?' He chuckled, glancing around at the rest of the class; a delusional man waiting for the roaring applauds of his doting audience that would clearly never come. He obviously had no idea how in tune I was with the ways of hard work. I threw him an artificial smile laced with aversion as he concentrated on the papers in front of him. To my dismay he looked up and caught me - his glare said it all. *This year really was going to be exactly the same as last year,* I thought dejectedly. I'd come to expect nothing less. That first week was a blur. The second week became more bearable and by the start of week three, I'd sunk right back into my college life, exactly as I had done each term previously. By week three my expectations at enjoying college had completely vanished, *don't get your hopes up*, that was officially my college moto.

TWO

ꕥ

'Hi, is this beef or lamb?' The selection of animals my burger could have been sourced from was endless, but with very little else on offer it was a dicey decision I had now committed to. I held it under the counter warming lights, so the lunch lady could get a better view. The thing was still just brown sludge, only now it looked like it was sunbathing.

'It says chicken sweetheart, but your guess is as good as mine.' I took my chicken/surprise meat burger from the canteen and went and sat outside on the grass. It was always beautiful this time of year. The flowers were blooming and it made a brilliant backdrop for a perfect picture; calming sky blues against vivid fire reds and oranges, the forest green leaves encasing them as tall trees lined the border of the grounds. A few of the students had come outside, all tucking into their lunches and gossiping, but I had my own special place in the huge gardens, masked from prying eyes by the close littering of four trees that stood away from their lined friends. I sat in my usual spot beneath the colossal oak tree,

behind the gym. As though hand carved especially, a concave crescent section in the middle of the trunk provided a warm and inviting place that shielded me from the predictable British weather and any unwanted visitors. I wasn't much of a people person.
I enjoyed the tranquillity of having only my thoughts for company. I put my camera to my eye, adjusting the lens to focus and in the distance stood a lone figure; a young man. A student? Teacher maybe? I wasn't sure. He was strapping and lofty at about six feet tall. His shaggily cropped sandy brown hair blew in the wind, his unlaced combat boots with light denim jeans tucked into the tops and pristine white short-sleeve t-shirt set him aside from the others. In Gallows Wood most of the guys liked a more polished appearance, boat shoes, collared shirts and tank vests were in fashion. I got the sense this guy liked to create his own identity. Oddly though, there was something familiar about him. I was utterly engrossed, gazing at him but not fully understanding the emotion he had stirred in me. My heart beat a little faster, my palms were sweaty, a strange whirling deep in my belly.

'Hey, Grace, how's life treating you?' I jumped erratically, nearly dropping my camera.

'Jack! You scared the living crap out of me!' I seethed; my tone harsher than I had intended.

'Sorry' he muttered apologetically.

'I forgive you.' I didn't. When he sat down beside me, I smiled and slapped his back jovially with as much force as possible, without making him suspicious of my real intention. Unfortunately for Jack, on most occasions, he was just one of those people you wanted to slap. With my raging inner bitch leashed, I put the camera back to my eyes, scouring between the trees trying to spot the lone young man again. 'He's gone' I sighed disappointedly and with little regard to Jack's presence.

'Sorry Grace' Jack said again. 'I didn't mean to.' He said whilst fluffing his ornately sculpted hair, the wind whipping it out of shape.

'Mean to what?' My camera was still firmly fixed to my eye as I continued my search. Jack waved his hands in front of my lens in an attempt to grab my otherwise engaged attention.

'Hellllooo! What's up Grace? You've got your head in the clouds again.'

'What?' I snapped. I wasn't invested in this conversation and Jack was finally realising it. Jack gazed down at the English textbook hanging out of my bag.
'Are you worrying about Mrs Crayman's English essay? If you are, I can help you.' I finally lowered my camera and glanced at him with the undivided attention he craved. I know he didn't set out to drive me insane, he just did it without even trying. It was too obvious that he was seeking more than a mere friendship, but it was something that could never happen, mainly because I had always thought of Jack like a brother. He did not get this memo.
'Listen, Grace, I finished my essay yesterday, so if you want to come over to my house one night...I could give you a hand with yours.'

'Oh, I appreciate the offer Jack, but I can handle it. I've just got to get it all down on the computer and then it's pretty much finished, but thanks' I lied. I had not nearly finished it; in fact, I hadn't even started it. 'Look Jack, I really have to go.' I said politely, I didn't want to hurt Jacks feelings, but there's only so many ways you can tell someone you aren't interested.

'I'll walk you to class then. I was watching a programme about Andy Warhol last night; I've got a few questions for you.' *Oh, goodie* my inner bitch teased. I began to feel the slight hint of a fever boiling in my forehead. I took a deep breath and tried to compose myself. 'You okay, Grace? You look a bit flustered?' I had to think fast. I had to make him want to leave.

'Ahhh....well, actually, my period came on today.' I indicated to my stomach and gripped it animatedly, as though wincing with pain. I wasn't the best actress but when the moment called for it, I could definitely give the Sex and the City cast members a run for their money. Thank you, NBC, for the re-runs. 'I just need a few minutes of peace and quiet on my own in the toilets.' A faint queasiness swept over Jack's face and within seconds he had remembered an appointment he just had to keep and rushed off behind the tech building. As I made my way into the main building, I looked back over my shoulder into the distance, where I had seen that handsome stranger walking. There was nothing now but the green trees and the empty spaces between them as the bell chimed signalling the start of the next class.

THREE

ᘓᘐ

I took my seat in photography class and casually threw my coat and bag under the table, as though I had just arrived at home. Mr Geddes' class was my all-time favourite. His laid-back approach meant that the stresses of registration with Mr Sanders were immediately forgotten. He was running some students through the developing chemicals in the darkroom when I sat down. Amelia strolled in a few seconds later with her limited edition, oversized, red Stella McCartney shoulder bag that complimented her skinny jeans and off the shoulder boho top perfectly. She ran her fingers through her coiffed blonde locks, making sure the invisible strays were still controlled by the entire can of hairspray that held it in place.

'Let's have a look then' Amelia said brightly, pointing at my camera bag. I apprehensively handed it over. 'So, what button do I press to make the TV screen thingy come on?' Amelia had taken this class because she thought it would be a great way to meet hot photographers when she started modelling, the fact that she could copy my coursework also sweetened the pot.

'Slide over the switch to the left' I instructed, leaning over to make sure she was handling it properly.

'Who's that?' Amelia questioned inquisitively, tapping her manicured nails on the camera screen.

'I don't know, he must be a new student. I saw him earlier, when I was taking pictures of the flower garden.'

'WOW!' she emphasised, smiling seductively as she stroked the screen.

'Wow, what? He's barely distinguishable. He could be butt-ugly for all you know.' We both seemed a bit confused by my hostile reaction but luckily, Amelia had the attention span of a fish so within a second or two she was back onto the photo.

'He's definitely a hottie - without a doubt' Amelia insisted. 'Look at his figure. Tall, fit and strong, looks the sort that works out at the gym, I would definitely take a slice of that man pie.'

'Another five minutes and you'll be telling me you know his mother.'

'Jealously doesn't look too pretty on you Grace.'

'Why in God's name would I be jealous?' I chimed defensively.

'Just saying is all, touchy much!' she blanched. On some level I knew she was right, but I didn't know why I was so bothered. Questioning my sanity was a path I didn't much want to go down right now. As she continued to flick through the pictures; at least ten or so, she peered at the screen with a quizzical look in her eyes. 'What are all those weird lights around him?'

'What lights?' I grabbed the camera from her and stared intently at the screen. *Please, please, please, don't be broken!* I thought. 'I've no idea what they are. There better not be a problem with this camera, I only got it a few weeks ago.'

'Wow, overreact much?' As you can probably guess I wasn't amused by her comment and my expression conveyed my feelings. 'Maybe he's an angel' Amelia cooed whimsically like a misguided Disney princess.

'Or maybe he's as ugly as sin' I added, not believing one word of it.

'Don't be so silly' she seethed. *Who's being hostile now?* I thought.

'Everyone into the darkroom please!' Mr Geddes called.

'Angel or not, that boy is all kinds of fine. Those arms, those legs, and don't even get me started on that tush!'

'If I haven't said it already, you have a beautiful way with words Amelia.' Amelia sighed, before turning and mincing over to the darkroom curtains, her patent heels tattooing on the wooden floor as she went. I moved to follow her, still deep in thought. *What were those lights behind him? Could he be an angel?* It's official, I've lost it; my sanity has finally evaded me! At that moment the door at the back of the classroom swung open and a young man entered. I gazed at him and nearly choked on my own saliva. He was utterly stunning! Tall and toned, ruffled, cropped sandy brown hair, white t-shirt and royal blue denims tucked into a pair of scuffed black military boots. *'It's him'* my inner bitch squealed excitedly. His intense, piercing, electric blue eyes scanned the room and met mine, each of us unmoving.

'Is this the photography class?' he asked, his voice almost melodic. *OK, breathing may be a good idea at this point* I thought. I soon realised the silence between us was being drowned out by the sound of my uncontrollable thumping heart, that threatened to explode from my chest.

'Eh, urm, huh, sorry yah, yup, yes. Yes, it is.' I answered finally sounding like an absolute moron. *Great one Grace, could you be any sadder at this moment? Kill me, kill me now!*

'Ah!' Mr Geddes exclaimed in a welcoming tone as he exited the darkroom. 'Our new student has arrived. Would everyone please take your seats? Come in, Beau, come in. Welcome.' As his eyes caught mine for the second time I glanced away swiftly. I then realised that I hadn't taken a steady breath since he had entered. I was all yah's and yup's but had forgot the most basic of human functions.

'We weren't expecting you for another couple of days Beau.' He smiled at Mr Geddes. My heart continued to batter incessantly against my ribs. I had never seen someone who could encapsulate the phrase tall, dark and handsome better than him. He ran his hand through his hair leaving it settled at the base of his neck for a moment as everyone looked on in awe and hung on his every step.

'Everyone, this is Beau Milner. He is joining our class and I hope everyone will make him feel welcome. Is there a seat for him?' We all looked around in an excited flurry; every girl who already had a desk mate hung their heads, disappointment swamping them. It quickly became clear that the only seats available were next to me and next to Amelia. I shot a glance at Amelia who was quickly laying some more cherry-red lip gloss on her rosebud lips in anticipation. *God, she plays dirty!* I had no lip gloss at my disposal, tightening my ponytail was about as tarted up as I got. Answering every prayer that had been running through my frazzled head since he had walked into the classroom, in stomped Michael Patterson with large black headphones hung over his ears. His hands busy plucking at the invisible strings of an air guitar. He apologised loudly and unconvincingly for his lateness, strolling over to take his usual seat next to Amelia, gazing at her adoringly with those puppy-dog eyes that were reserved only for her. Amelia instantly huffed, sulking with a perfectly polished pout. I, on the other hand, was the cat that got the cream. I blushed and bit my lip as I surveyed his Adonis form, my thoughts for a moment blazing and explicit, every nerve in my body alight.

'There, the seat next to Grace' Mr Geddes remarked jovially. I could not take my eyes off of him as he approached my table. A quiet bustling of conversation vibrating around the room. The heat radiated from my face and my mouth was bone-dry. *What about this guy made my hands sweat like this?* 'Now, are we all here?' Mr Geddes asked clapping his hands together. His attention now fixed solely on Michael, who was still nodding along to whatever drum and bass tune that rung loudly from his headphones. Every girl in the room had fixed stares on Beau. Everyone but me. The close proximity made it impossible, even though I longed to glance at him. The nervousness that bubbled up inside me made me tap my fingers on the wooden bench frantically. My vain attempt at acting casual.

Throughout the lesson Beau made no attempt whatsoever to have any kind of conversation with me. Even the slightest slip of eye contact seemed to be a definite no-no as far as he was concerned. I tugged at my starched shirt collar in response to every slight movement that he made, as my temperature fluctuated under the stress of his presence. The way he twiddled his pen between his fingers skilfully, drumming his palms on the seat of his stool to a silent beat, turning the pages of his textbook; every move he made led my thoughts deeper and deeper into parental advisory territory. His eyes were dazzling; they were the exuberant colour of the sea, and were not talking Bogna sea, a crystal-clear blue sea in the Maldives was more like it. With just one passing glance they made the blood course through my veins at an alarming speed. The hairs on my arms prickled in response. The fluorescent lights above us hit his chiselled jaw, reflecting off his flawless honey-toned skin. I made my way down his body, slowly drinking him all in. His muscular arms heaved beneath the cotton fabric of his top with every breath he took. *Please talk to me, please, please, please! Hi, my name's Grace. What do you like to do in your spare time?* My brain tortured me as words, any and all words, threatened to explode from my mouth! After my earlier issues with a simple yes, I didn't trust anything that might fall from my lips.

As my eye line made its way back up his ripped torso, I encountered a problem. His eyes, his beautiful, mesmerising eyes that I would happily drown in, were watching me, watching him. *Hello awkward moment, oh how unwelcome you are.* It was by far the most uncomfortable situation I had ever endured in a classroom; scrap that – the most mortifying experience ever! I spluttered a little as I attempted to speak. Obviously against my better judgement. He responded by edging his seat a few inches away from me, a confused smile resting on his face. A sack full of willpower and sheer determination would be required from now on, if I had any hope at surviving an entire term with him as my desk buddy. Something about this guy was different, something I couldn't quite place. I thought about it for a while – no, a while is wrong - I thought about it until Mr. Geddes called time and the bell above the door rung. I shook myself out of my daze and watched as Beau collected up his books and slung his rucksack over his shoulder. He even did that with finesse. The delicious combined scent of his fresh aftershave and fruity shower gel lingered in the air as he walked down the aisle beside me. I could feel myself running my hands through my hair and patting down my clothes. I felt like a woman possessed; I felt like an Amelia clone. I glanced down at my shabbily put together ensemble of skinny, ripped denim jeans, black vest and unbuttoned tartan checked shirt. My stare wandered over towards

Princess Amelia as she wound her blonde tendrils around her manicured fingers. Who was I kidding? Why would Beau be interested in a girl like me? Amelia was more of a strawberry and chocolate chip surprise ice cream with sparklers and sprinkles. You know, the fun exciting treats with bubble-gum at the bottom. The only ice cream that could describe me was vanilla, and not even the good kind; more like that half fat, organic crap, no cone and a plastic spoon that breaks the second you dive in too deep.

'I think a change in your style is a necessity Grace' Amelia whispered over my shoulder, as we both watched Beau shake Mr Geddes hand and then leave the class. 'That boy is all kinds of fine but at the minute you just look so...' She looked me up and down and mulled over her next word choice, not in an attempt to spare my feelings, of course, but to ensure I understood completely, just how terrible I looked. 'Vanilla!' she exclaimed. I did question whether it was possible that Amelia had the gift to read my thoughts. I soon shrugged off that mind-bending impossibility and put it down to her close relationship with the devil. Amelia had all kinds of evil living in her closet; the difference was, she considered them friends!

FOUR

ꕥ

As the days turned into weeks, I still hadn't found the courage to speak to Beau. Every day without fail he would sit next to me in photography class; the hovering silence between us was unbearable and severely hindering my ability to concentrate. It didn't take long for Beau to become the talk at our lunch table. Everyone had their own theory about him and it didn't surprise me that Jack just downright hated him.

'There's something not right about him' Jack insisted.

'I think he's dreamy' Amelia said to no one in particular picking like a bird at a cheese cracker. Every girl at the table nodded in agreement and sighed as their thoughts wandered. 'Hey and there he is!' Amelia said, arm outstretched pointing out towards the gardens. So, there we were, a table of weirdos, all staring intently at Beau. He was dressed casually in those army black lace-up boots with military green cargo pants tucked into them. His chest, which I noticed was clearly toned, was only barely masked by a thin, crisp, white, long-sleeved top with the cuffs pushed up to his elbows, showing various leather and beaded bracelets on one arm. His other arm had a worn, black skull-patterned headscarf wrapped tightly around it and tied in a knot. He strolled with an air of coolness surrounding him. All the girls, including me, swooned and sighed, while a wash of unmistakeable jealousy rushed around the boys at the table; they watched on, critically analysing and trying desperately to find an obvious fault with him. Not that the girls would have listened if they found one. I stared at him closely, there was safety in

numbers, shamelessly wishing those arms were draped around my waist. Those fingers running through my hair, those lips smashing passionately against mine.
'Grace, you look hungry.' Amelia said, interrupting my daydream. So, my longing face could be mistaken for my hungry face; always good to know. Amelia and I made our way to the food station through the hordes of students and gazed over the undesirable dinner options that lay like dead animals in metal troughs, bathed in icky brown muck. No change there.

'Chips?' we said decidedly in sync.

'See something you like girls?' Landon Earl Bogstean was the biggest creep in our college and as we scooped the chips onto our plates, the trough of brown muck at the other end of the canteen stand suddenly looked appealing. Poisoning ourselves would be like a holiday in Barbados in comparison to a conversation with Landon Bogstean. Landon flashed us a dirty yellow smile that made my toes curl. What we all saw when we looked at Landon was definitely not the image that he was faced with when he looked in a mirror. His greasy, dirty, blonde hair fell onto his face and as he used his grubby, stick like index finger to brush it out of his face, his moss green bug eyes worked over our bodies, causing an explosion of disgust to penetrate my stomach. Landon was one of those people who had always been filthy in both appearance and personality. Not even a chemical peel, a number one head shave and a yearlong turpentine infused bath would help him. He was every girl's nightmare and every psychiatrist's wet dream. As Landon licked his lips suggestively, my breakfast of warm Weetabix and banana threatened to reappear in a grey gooey mess on the floor. I swallowed the bulging lump in my throat and quickly made my way back to the table as fast as my legs could carry me. Taking a seat, I glanced lazily around the canteen and stopped as my eyes reached the far end; I saw Beau on his own, reading a book. I had never wished I was a book before, but in that moment I did. I sat gazing at him for a while, probably for longer than was socially acceptable, heck, I was never one for conforming to the social norm.

'You know stalking is illegal right?' Jack muttered with an obvious edge of attitude, interrupting my train of thought and making me jump, in one swift motion my plate and its contents tumbled to the floor with a deafening crash. The hum of the entire cafeteria died out and became silent as everyone's eyes turned to me. I jumped to the floor and tried to scoop up what I could of the mess. Mrs Dayton, the greying cafeteria lunch lady, was promptly by my side wielding a dustpan and brush. I glanced in Beau's direction, hoping for the first time ever that he wasn't looking at me and that his book really was just too riveting to ignore - but he was of course looking at me, as was everyone else within ear shot. My luck congealed among the mess on the floor; daunting embarrassment now my only ally. A little smile appeared in the corner of his mouth, which sent my situation hurtling from embarrassing to soul destroying in the blink of an eye. I went back to helping Mrs Dayton clear up, successfully hiding my face underneath the table.

'I'm really sorry, Mrs Dayton, it was an accident...I didn't, it wasn't....' I spluttered. I shot Jack a stern and much deserved glare. It grated on me even further that he looked so pleased with himself as he continued tucking into his food, a sly smile never leaving his mouth.

'Sweetheart, it's not a problem, it's not like they're made from gold' she soothed, whilst patting my arm. I felt awkward and uneasy as I returned to my seat and not just because I was the klutz of the dining room. I could have kicked myself and kicked Jack even harder. He could see it too, the anger on my face, as my glare sat firm in protest. Reading the situation and my mood expertly now, Jack cleared his throat, lost the smile and promptly moved around to the other side of the table. *Wise move buddy!*

After a few minutes I turned my attention again towards Beau and to my amazement, he was still looking at me. His smouldering, electric blue eyes tore into me, instantly tugging at my insides and causing an unexpected surge of heat rushing through my entire body. What was happening to me? I felt out of control, unable to access the most basic of bodily functions. My thoughts were a flurry of excitement, pleasure, anticipation and nervousness. This guy had me hooked.

Blimey, the way he had looked at me, as if he was interested in me. Interested in me! I looked down and tried desperately to keep my eyes on the empty table in front of me but after a few more excruciatingly long seconds, I looked up to see him packing his books into his backpack, a small smile for me as he looked up melting my insides and then he was gone. The sky darkened as a sudden storm cloud of gloom swept over me, as though all the light left with him. Nothing but the rest of a dull and dreary day ahead for me now, and an even duller and drearier weekend. I think it was at that moment that I realised, I was falling for Beau. Truly, madly, deeply falling. Whether it was lust or love, the feeling was addictive and intoxicating.

~~~~

At college on Monday, I took my usual place at the table and waited anxiously for Beau's arrival. I was a nervous wreck. I spent my weekend contemplating just how sad I had allowed myself to become over the past few weeks. I had decided that his long-withdrawn silences were no longer tolerable. I couldn't stand it anymore, sitting so close every day and never speaking to each other. It was strange and unusual, and what's more, it was daft! I mean, I know I am shy but I didn't see him as being shy; just evasive and strange. Gorgeous, sexy, delectable and just the right
~~~~

amount of strange.

He strolled in with his usual laid-back demeanour. As soon as he took his seat next to me, I could hear the words rushing out of my mouth like vomit before I had a chance to stop them.

'How's it hanging handsome?' *That did not just happen. What the hell is wrong with me? That's it, I've ruined it. I doubt he wants to date a crazy person*! I felt the blood rush to my face and knew I must have resembled a ripe raspberry. That was not what I had intended to say. I wanted the floor to open up and swallow me whole. Beau laughed at my expense briefly and rightly so. His smile was intoxicating. Once again, my heart fluttered aimlessly in my chest in response. I would take that embarrassment for that smile any day. I almost jumped out of my skin as he held out his latex, glove covered hand to me and said in a cocky and endearing tone 'It's hanging nicely, thanks beautiful. Great to meet you at last.' There was a warming twinge in my stomach as his words repeated in my head. The smile that stretched from ear-to-ear was unstoppable. At first, I just sat there staring at his hand until my inner bitch popped up with some helpful advice. '*Take his bloody hand*' So I did. Some long moments later he grinned as he eased up his grip, trying desperately to retrieve his hand. Struggling to use my brain to operate standard motor functions I smiled awkwardly, finally letting it go.

'Sorry.'

'Don't be. It's just that I need both hands to hold my camera.'

'Yes' I chimed. My brain only allowing for one-word answers.

'So, Grace, I know you really want to ask me some kind of question, so go ahead, what do you want to know?' Within a second and with my lame well rounded answer of 'yes' behind me, my apprehensions had fluttered away and I was drawn willingly into his world, with no backward glance at what I was leaving behind.

'How come you didn't start here at the beginning of term?' I probed.

'Well I travel a lot.'

'Really? Lucky you. I wanted to travel but my Mum forced me to start college. I had my mind set on a yearlong trip around America but unfortunately what Mum says goes!'

'My parents died when I was small.' His words sounded heavy and pained. 'So, I've been lucky enough never to have had anyone to force me to do anything.' A small and unsteady smile formed on his face but it was merely to cover the pain behind his revelation.

'Oh, your parents died? Oh, Beau, I am sorry.'

'Don't be. I'm not keen on people feeling sorry for me.'

'But when you were small, who looked after you?' He shrugged.

'I've been in and out of more foster homes then you've had hot dinners.' He laughed uncomfortably, not meeting my gaze, but his expression mirrored mine and I suddenly realised how much of himself he was sharing with me. He shook his head as though under a spell, ridding his memories of their demons. *Damn it, he's going to make an excuse and run* I thought. I decided to bite the bullet and lay myself uncharacteristically bare.

'I lost my Dad a few years ago.' The words stuck in my throat.
And he looked at me intently.

'Oh, so then you know.'

'Yes, I know. I still have upsetting dreams about it.' I looked away for a moment, not wanting the sadness of thinking about my Dad right now.

'Are you okay, Grace?' We threw each other an understanding yet painfully awkward smile as we each questioned our outbursts of unfiltered emotions.

'Why did you move in and out of so many foster homes?'
He thought about his response for a long moment, and then smiled at me. 'I like change.'

'What? No, seriously. Were you difficult to handle or something?'

'No, I was just misunderstood. At least, that's how my care-worker labelled me. Misunderstood. She thought I was a lovely boy.'

'And were you?'
'Of course I was.' He smiled cryptically. 'Were you a lovely girl?'

'No' I admitted honestly. 'I was misunderstood too, all the time. Especially after my Dad died. One teacher even told my Mum I was bordering psychotic.' I laughed.

'Right everyone!' Mr Geddes yelled as he walked into the room. 'Now, what are we are going to do today?' Beau and I glanced at each other, knowing our minute of intimacy was over.

'Another time?' he whispered with a soulful grin.

'Yes' I cooed, wanting desperately to reach out and touch him, but adamantly calling on my better judgement and deciding against it. After my conversation with Beau I found myself questioning him. I couldn't put my finger on it but there was something off about him. I'm not talking a wooden leg or the fact that he was a serial killer or anything but it did seem like he was keeping something back. The way he made me feel, scared me almost. I hadn't spoken to anyone as freely as I had him, I certainly never spoke of my father. The pain was softened with him, thoughts of my father that would usually reduce me to tears, more bearable when I was sharing them with him. After class I walked through reception, knocking shoulders with a group of students heading in the opposite direction. As usual, Amelia was twiddling her hair and chatting suggestively to Mr Geddes. Oblivious to it all, Mr Geddes conversed comfortably, recounting his photography filled weekend adventures in the Midlands with his wife Mandy. The shiny gold wedding band on his finger was no deterrent for Amelia. It was like watching Hansel and Gretel follow that line of breadcrumbs; you know that nothing good will come of it and it will most definitely end unpleasantly. Except in this case there would be no little witch, just an infuriated headmaster, and a very angry wife. As I approached her, our eyes locked, the crazy eyed glare she threw my way was a warning, so I continued on outside to wait on the steps for her. Watching her hit on a man twice her age was not appealing. About twenty minutes or so later, Amelia graced me with her presence. Mr Geddes was the hot topic of conversation for the entire drive home. I'd learnt with great skill how to stage an interest with Amelia and react successfully without her catching on. To be perfectly honest, I hadn't taken in a word she had said. I caught key words and phrases like affair, older man fantasy and arse that won't quit, beyond that I was happily dancing along to the Maroon 5 track that was quietly spilling out of the one working speaker.

Suddenly all the hairs on the back of my neck stood up and an icy shiver made its way down my spine. My heart felt as though my body could no longer contain it. A rush of panic filled me as the beating grew out of control. My lungs swelled and my breathing became short and sharp. I quickly pulled the car to a screeching halt as I slammed both feet down onto the pedals with great force. Resting my forehead on my hands that were gripped tightly around the steering wheel, I breathed as deeply as my lungs would allow, which wasn't as much as I needed them to.

'Grace - what the bloody hell are you doing?! Are you okay? Is there something I can do?' I took another deep, steadying breath, in through my rounded mouth and out through my nose, waiting patiently as my heartbeat slowed down to its normal pace, thankfully the heaviness finally felt as though it was easing.

'I'm fine. I just felt a little light headed.' I resumed the ten to two hand position on the steering wheel; a manoeuvre I hadn't done since actually doing my driving lessons. I slowly pulled away from the kerb, trying my very best to ignore the short, sharp pain that still tickled in my chest. I rolled down my window halfway, a broken felt tip pen stuck below it stopping it from going any further. Amelia had resumed her conversation about Mr Geddes, but I no-longer had any energy to feign interest this time. I picked up my speed, subtly cranked up the radio and soon enough Amelia's voice faded into the background. A breeze blew through my hair, pleasantly taking my breath away for a moment. The familiar scent of aftershave, soap and motorbike oil wafted in through the open window. Beau's striking face flashed in my head, that face with that mesmerising smile. With my senses stolen and my heart still oddly ready to leap out of my chest at any given moment, I couldn't help but dream only of him that night. I was bewildered by him; conscious or not, he had me enthralled. Finding out the secret behind that brooding gaze of his was a challenge, a challenge that I would accept without question.

FIVE

DAILY GLOBE
Lift Plummets into the Afterlife
By Cameron McKellen.

Today's tragedy has left a community feeling bewildered and distraught. At 8.15am on Tuesday, September 15th, an event occurred which has bemused officials, with no explanation as to how it occurred. The high-rise offices on Berkley Road, in the heart of London, held the scene of a monstrous accident that resulted in the death of four people, all of which are yet to be identified.

An elevator, last seen on the 21st floor, plummeted at a record speed to the lobby with no warning. Its occupants had no way of escape and we can only assume how terrifying this experience must have been for them. It took fire fighters forty-five minutes to prise open the doors of the lift and help the people inside. It wasn't clear at the time how many people had lost their lives but the rescuers remained hopeful. Bystanders watching through the large floor to ceiling windows that surrounded the lobby spoke to the news crew: *'I could see so much smoke and rubble, the whole wall surrounding the lift was demolished. All you could see was the top half of a large metal box.'*

Sky News were the first media channel on the scene.

The employees of Ryland Maintenance reported that there had been no problems with any of the lifts and two weeks prior to this tragedy all lifts had been serviced to an excellent standard. Police are still unable to determine the cause of this horrific disaster.

The cries of a small child trapped helplessly within the steel metal enclosure could be heard by the fire fighters, once recovery was under way. Fire-fighter John Simms was first on the scene and had this to say: *'All we could hear was a little child crying for his mother. Repeatedly my colleagues and I could hear the child yelling for his mummy. This spurred us on to work as hard as possible to retrieve the child and get the other people to safety. Once we had successfully prised the doors apart, we could see the dim red power light engulfing the lift. It was all a little hazy at first. The bodies of the victims were piled on top of one another. It was immediately clear that two of the occupants were dead; an elderly woman and a young man in his late twenties. One woman in her sixties, who was lying nearest to the lift doors, appeared to be suffering from multiple and critical wounds, including both of her femurs protruding awkwardly from the skin on her legs. The child we had heard screaming was a little boy, still secured in his pushchair, lying on its side. He appeared to be about two to three years of age and seemed unharmed, apart from some minor scrapes and grazes. There was a young woman lying unconscious beside the pushchair and the boy was frantically trying to grasp her hand, so we determined that this was his mother.'*

Having since been taken to hospital, it is said that the young boy is doing as well as could be expected; his cuts and bruises were surprisingly minor and with time they should heal. I regret to inform my readers that the woman presumed to be his mother was not as fortunate, she passed away shortly after arriving at hospital. It is reported that she suffered facial contusions, had broken several ribs, broken both legs and a hip, and that the impact had caused an irreparable bleed in her brain. After numerous efforts to save her life it was eventually clear there was nothing more the doctors could do for her. This is an immeasurably tragic event and my heart goes out to the families of the people who were lost. The two survivors of this unfortunate incident will never forget the impact today's events have had on them.

Letter 6 of 15
Dear Miss Jane Wells,
I regret to inform you that when you placed Beau in our care, we were unaware of his status. He has continued to present problems for me, my husband and the other children who reside here and I honestly don't believe this arrangement can continue. On numerous occasions, Beau's odd behaviour has been unexplainable and he refuses to talk about it. I can't imagine how he is feeling and to be perfectly honest, I don't believe I am supposed to. He is clearly very troubled and an impending bad influence on the family. I asked for permission to baptise Beau and on two occasions your office agreed that if Beau had no problems with it, it was possible. Beau has shown no desire to conform to our religion which saddens me. I was hoping that bringing him closer to God would enable him to cease his questionable behaviour. His desire to play practical jokes has become tiresome. This is a house of respect and honesty, but Beau seems to grasp neither. If you could get back to me as soon as you can, it would be much appreciated.
Mrs G. Hanne

Letter 13 of 15
Dear Miss Jane Wells,
I unhappily write this letter. Beau's disruptive behaviour has become too hard to handle and I have four other children that need my time and attention. His behaviour at times is very strange. I really don't think this is the family for him but I do wish him all the luck in the world with the next

family he is placed with. Hopefully they will be more equipped for his needs.
Sincerely,
Mrs Lucile Jones

Letter 9 of 15
Dear Miss Wells,
For your files, I am sending you a transcript of Beaus interview with the child psychologist, Dr Fathom; I hope it helps in getting him reassigned.
Kind regards
Janey Humphreys

DOCTOR'S OFFICE

Date: - May 11th
Time: - 3.13pm
Patient: - Beau Milner, aged thirteen.

Dr Fathom: "Beau do you understand why you are here?"
Beau: "I have a pretty good idea."
Dr Fathom: "I was wondering if I could ask you some questions today. Would that be okay?"
Beau: "Why not? It's not like I haven't been in this position before."
Dr Fathom: "Can you tell me what happened?"
Beau: "What happened was nothing to do with me."
Dr Fathom: "Just explain what happened please."
Beau: "I was sitting in the living room. We had just finished dinner and Mrs Merchant was washing up in the kitchen. I was doing my homework on the sofa when I heard the noise.

I looked up and all the furniture was upside down, stacked in the middle of the room. Then in walked Mrs Merchant who blamed me for everything... (patient paused) ...and once again I got sent back."

Dr Fathom: "What furniture exactly Beau? Be specific."

Beau: "There were the six dining chairs, the dining table, the coffee table, the TV bench, the footstall and the shoe rack by the door, I think."

Dr Fathom: "And how did you get all this furniture stacked up so quickly?"

Beau: "Have none of you listened to a word I've said? I had nothing to do with it! I'm thirteen for Christ's sake. How could I be strong enough to lift and rearrange a whole dining room set in the space of five minutes with no one hearing a thing?"

Dr Fathom: "I think we should calm down for a second Beau. All we want to know is why you did it. Were you not happy at the Merchant's house? Has it been difficult adjusting to your new school?"

Beau: "I really don't see the point in this! It's the third time you people have asked me these questions and I've told you all again and again, I didn't do it!"

Dr Fathom's evaluation:

This patient appears to be relying heavily on his emotions. It seems that he creates situations in order to get the attention he desires, but if he receives an unfavourable reaction, he fabricates a lie as an explanation. I recommend further studies.

I am fairly sure that Beau genuinely believes he isn't responsible for these happenings, but with no other presentable explanation, he clearly is responsible, so I think it best that he resides at this facility until we can get to the bottom of his problems. I will be conducting another question/answer session with Beau Milner on the 23rd of next month. As his social worker, Miss Wells, I do hope that you can be present to view his progress.

SIX

ꕥ

Beau was never really far from my thoughts, no matter what time of day it was, but when I saw him in person, the longing I felt to be close to him, was that much stronger. Propping up my locker with ten minutes to spare before registration, I allowed myself to daydream, until I saw Beau approaching me from the other end of the hallway. I smiled and naturally expected him to return the favour, but his eyes were diverted to the floor, his earphones clouding his hearing. I watched him pass me and descend a flight of stairs to the maths building, without even a head nod of acknowledgement.

'Come on, we're going be late and I'm not in the mood for one of Mr Sanders' rants.' Amelia interrupted nudging my shoulder, her nose parked in a copy of heat magazine. I followed behind her as she headed towards the classroom. Glancing back to where I had last seen him.

'One minute, I forgot my grammar book in my locker. I'll catch you up.' With her eyes now fixed on me Amelia had caught sight of my apparent forgotten 'grammar book' approaching us, she dipped her head and animatedly winked, which was about as subtle as a slap to the face, returning to her magazine with a smile.

'Good luck. I'll see you in class' she whispered with a grin. Did I say whisper? I meant hollered, as she sped away in the opposite direction. I turned around and Beau was closer than I had anticipated. I put my hands out to stop him from walking straight into me, a gut reaction that made me jump back.

'Beau, is everything OK?' His face was solemn, his eyes hooded. As he pulled his headphones down around his neck, I realised I had my answer, everything was definitely not OK. A more apt word from the dictionary to describe the look on his face would be furious.

'Look, I really can't do this right now Grace.' Each word hit me like a bullet.

'If I upset you, I'm sorry.' I didn't know what I was apologising for but the words flew out of my mouth without hesitation all the same. My inner bitch shaking her head in disgust at my lack of self-worth. 'Did I do someth...'

'Just stop!' he interrupted brashly, with his hands raised out in front of him. I took a wary step back, not recognising the guy in front of me as his expression grew darker. 'To be honest Grace, I'd rather not discuss it, I've got to go.'

'I better get that book then.' I gestured towards my locker, realising that the lie about my grammar book would now work perfectly, to get me out of this uncomfortable situation. He pulled his headphones back up over his ears and strolled down the hallway sluggishly without a backwards glance. 'Bye then' I muttered into the growing distance between us. I was like a little girl with an uncontrollable crush. Let's just say if he had pigtails, I would have pulled them by now. I couldn't understand why I was beating myself up and reacting this way. He was so rude, I had apologised and he had stubbornly rejected me for no reason; my inner bitch agreed with a stern and unwavering nod.

~~~~

The day was young, my mood wasn't great, but I held onto
~~~~

the hope that it would all get better. Positivity was literally all I had in my arsenal right now. I jumped into my tired old beetle that I had affectionately named Bob; now there was a guy I could depend on. Yes, he was old and falling apart, but I loved him. I convinced myself he was both vintage and retro, my friends agreed with neither of those descriptions. The truth was, it was more than probable that one day I could be driving along the motorway and the floor of the car would just drop away. I'd be forced to Flintstone it to school; a painful and embarrassing thought but an all too probable outcome due to its state. For the fortieth time that morning, I tried my hardest to push Beau out of my mind. This was a chore with difficulty rating nine. He may not want to be in my life but my imagination didn't seem to get the memo. College was like the Hunger games right now, a lengthy tournament of avoidance between Beau and I. But then there were times where that just wasn't possible, mainly when one of the participants in this game realises what an absolute twat they've been. Beau walked towards me with his proverbial tail between his legs and a repentant expression on his face. I held my composure that threatened to topple over at any given second, like an unpredictable game of Jenga. 'I won't cave, I won't cave.' I mumbled to myself to boost my courage.

'Grace, I am so sorry about yesterday. Being a jackass comes a little too naturally to me sometimes.' I won't cave, I won't....' I thought. Secretly I had accepted his apology the moment he had smiled at me, but being the girl that I was, I went with my instincts and decided to feed that courage. I'll make him sweat!

SEVEN

ꕥ

'So, what's new then?' Mum hollered from the kitchen as I made my way to the stairs. 'I know you, Grace, and I haven't seen you smile like that for a very long time. Add that to the fact that you've started fussing about with your hair, so my conclusion is, that you have a new man in your life.' She coaxed as she whipped her tea towel around and attempted what can only be described as a *Mum jig*. Like mother like daughter, we both pretty much sucked when it came to dancing.

'I've run a brush through it! Kill me for trying out a new look' I retorted defensively.

'You have beautiful hair, I like the way you've been doing it lately, but that is not why you're so happy. I'm old Grace, not stupid' Mum laughed. 'Now tell Mummy all about it.' She pulled at my cheek like old Aunt Flora used to and pursed her lips mockingly. I batted her hand away and rubbed at my face. She was clearly in a quizzical mood. She had the same glint in her eye that she always had on a Saturday night when who wants to be a Millionaire was on the TV. I had every intention of fobbing her off and retreating to my bedroom, but I couldn't get rid of the blinding smile glued into position on my face.

'Come on Grace, you can't even force a frown you're that bloody happy.' She teased me with a poke.

'Would you rather I was upset?'

'No, I like the new you, it's very becoming. I'm just curious as to why you look like a five-year-old whose been let loose in a sweet shop' she giggled. *Who was acting like a five-year-old now?* I thought.

'School's just going well, I got an A in my English assignment' I fibbed, it was barely a C.

'Wow. Just to let you know sweetheart, us O'Callaghan girls are useless at lying, so give up the goods...and stop trying to change the subject! We will also be addressing what you really got on that assignment another time.' The unrelenting interrogation continued at full force. 'You barely touched your food and prawn curry is your favourite.'

'I had a big lunch Mum, there's no great mystery.'

'Okay, so how about the fact that in the past three days you haven't once smacked your brother around the head?' I was stumped on that; she had a point there. Usually it's a matter of minutes before Cary's annoyingly incessant nattering will cause me to overload and lash out. Over the years it's become a reflex of mine. I glanced at Mum and the Ronald MacDonald grin on her face. She knew she had won and she had loved every second of it.

'Well, you going to share?' she prompted again, neatly folding up her black, scissor embossed, work shirt and placing it on the dryer.

'Okay Miss Marple, fine. There's a new boy at college, we've become friends, he seems really nice. There. Happy?'

'Nice? Is that all you're giving me?' Disappointment hung from her words. 'I mean, Grace, I just thought that Orlando what's-his-name had a new calendar out or something. I never thought it was about a boy at college.' She was clearly enjoying tormenting me, maybe a little too much. 'I've got some questions about this boy.' She smiled devilishly as she pulled out the chair opposite me. Her questioning raised eyebrow set high on her face.

'Before you even start Mother, NO, I am not bringing him home. YES, I'm pretty sure he's against guns, drugs and gangs. He's a photography major and NO, Dad probably wouldn't approve, but apparently Dad was going to keep me locked up until I was twenty five, so I don't think even Prince William would have been acceptable and for your information, while we're here, the actor's name is Orlando Bloom.' I took a deep breath and stared at my Mum's surprised face' Her jaw was wide open but her eyes; her eyes were screaming *'well done'* which made me chuckle. 'So, did I forget anything?' I asked.

'Yes, actually. This boy, his name, what is it?' At that moment it occurred to me, that since my Dad had died, my Mum and I hadn't done anything girly together at all. We hadn't spoken personally like this and especially not about boys. For the first time in a long time, everything felt like it was going to be okay. Something that had broken between us finally felt as though it was on the mend.

'His name is Beau.'

'Beau? That sounds like an American name.'

'No, he's English.'

'Are you sure?' She pressed. Well, no, if I was honest, I wasn't sure about anything when it came to Beau.

'Of course, I'm sure' I said with surprising conviction and then turned to make my way out of the kitchen and up the stairs.

'Grace' she called from the foot of the stairs.

'Yes, Mum?' My voice spiked, as I stopped halfway up the staircase.

'I'm really happy that you're happy again. It's been too long.' Her smile was warm and comforting. 'Do we need to have the birds and the bees talk?' There was not one ounce of unease in her question. I, on the other hand, was bathed in mortification.

'I think you might be a couple of years too late but if I need a refresh, I'll let you know!' That was the biggest lie I had told to date, but then this wasn't a typical conversation that I would usually have shared with my mother.

~~~~

It was a new day and although the inky sky above encouraged a usually sullen mood, the pep talk with Mum the night before only made my smile greater and my mood lighter. I glanced out of my car window waiting for the traffic lights to change, while the downpour pelted at the glass incessantly. Although it was dreary, there was something calming about it. I had so many questions floating aimlessly around my head. Beau was constantly in my mind, accompanying me everywhere. BEEP, BEEP!! I didn't know how long the light had been green but judging by the driver's enraged face behind me, I had been daydreaming much longer then I should have been.

~~~~

As I entered the classroom with Amelia, Beau's eyes immediately drew me in. They seemed darker then when I had last talked to him, troubled in some way, and a tight expression that I was sadly too familiar with, etched over his brow. He gave me a slight smile and I felt my heart start to race. I smiled back at him as casually as I could, but I hadn't noticed the new light machine someone had stored on the floor in front of Mr Geddes' desk. With my eyes still on Beau and my head bouncing giddily in the clouds, I went flying and I am not talking about the good kind, with the complimentary pillow and a packet of salted peanuts. I travelled in slow motion, there one minute and gone the next. I was certain that gravity was pulling me hard and fast towards the grubby, linoleum floor beneath me as Beau sprung off his seat and reached out to catch me. Little did I know, this gesture would be our undoing. Staring into those eyes, knowing that he was there to catch me, I gave myself over to the pulling sensation and hurtled towards him willingly. For a brief and fleeting moment, we were locked into each other, oblivious to everyone else around us staring.

'Arghhhhh' Beau cried out in excruciating pain. I was no-longer cradled in the comforting confines of his strong arms. I hit the floor with a thud, using the hard shell of my elbows to support my weight and watched forlornly as Beau clutched at his head in sheer agony. His breaths were ragged and hasty, his body buckling beneath an unseen pressure. His neck taught, the blue veins bulging and throbbing as something unseen ripped through him.

'I don't know what I did, I didn't mean...is he OK?' My questions fell on deaf ears as everyone was silent around me, watching the terror unfold. With a dull thud Beau's knees hit the floor as Mr. Geddes rushed to his side.

'Are you okay mate?' Mr Geddes asked as he offered Beau his hand.

'Please, just leave me alone' he muttered almost silently. 'Don't touch me, I'm fine' Beau pleaded further as everyone took another step towards him, his face red and pained.

He stretched his shaking hands out as a warning to stop any and all contact kindly offered from his band of fellow students, who had thoughtfully already removed their camera phones from their bags in case Beau had another attack - or whatever that was. The optimist in me hoped the phones were in the event they would have to call 999, the pessimist that ultimately didn't trust people, knew that in this YouTube age, it was more likely they would record his reaction to post on the internet. Beau stumbled uneasily to his feet like a baby deer, batting everyone away, the force of his full weight on his muscled arm clear as he rested on the desk for support. Trying his best to compose himself, sweat drenched his furrowed brow and the blue veins in his neck continued to bulge under the stress. I could tell that the uncomfortable stare from around the room was one not unfamiliar to him. He knew their looks, he knew what they were thinking about him.

'Beau, are you sure you're okay mate, I can go and get the nurse?'

'No, honestly, I'm fine. I just knocked my head Mr. Geddes.' I ran to Beau's side once my shock had subsided and the feeling had returned to my legs. 'I'm so sorry, did I hurt you? I feel awful.' He rubbed his arms anxiously, taking a quick step back from me. My presence hadn't proved to settle him any.

'Grace, I'm fine, really.' he pressed, trying to muster a small smile for me that never really reached the corners of his lips. His annoyance at everyone's concern left him ruffled. As the empty space between us grew, my heart fell.

'Really? You're sure? You looked like your brain was on fire' I called after him. I was riddled with guilt and concern, and I didn't even know what I had done.

'Look, I said I'm fine, so can we just drop it and sit down on the bloody stool already.' he retorted abrasively. My whiny concern clearly grating on him, the legs of his stool scraped along the floor as he slumped down onto the desk. His back arched from exhaustion, his forehead visibly clammy, his hood now up and his hands tucked down into the sleeves of his hoodie. Not overly keen to sit beside him, I played along and participated in trying out the new light box with everyone else, but I was relieved when Mr Geddes announced textbook reading time. I must have read the same page at least twenty times. If the polarising components of a 350 lens ever comes up in a test I will be sorted. What had I done to make him react that way? He touched me briefly when he caught me, but that was it. I folded my arms on the table and laid my head on them, ensuring I was facing the window and not Beau; I couldn't bear to see the agitated expression on his face. Fairly soon, I had drifted off into the muddied sea of my own thoughts. I awoke to the incessant ringing of the bell above the door. I turned to Beau, but much to my dismay, he had already left. I was always sure to be the last person to collect up all my stuff and awkwardly struggled under the weight of it, as I either hobbled to class or towards the lockers. This also always inevitably ensured lateness to my next class. As I threw my bags over my shoulders and cradled three hefty text books in my arms, I made my way to the door with a slight cramp in my left calf. I was officially sunk deep in what could only be described as emotional hell.

I glanced up at the clock and suddenly realised how late I actually was. I broke into a brisk power walk that would have made Mari Winsor proud. Luckily, I was only meeting Amelia for lunch and she had become accustomed to my lateness, but today was different. She was trying to avoid Bobby Sherman, waiting at the front steps for me meant she was a clear target.

I stopped to readjust the ample weight of my books, fighting the urge to childishly drop them on the floor and walk away, but then I unexpectedly heard a voice coming from Mrs Teeters' English class, someone purposely trying to be as quiet as they could be. A bright yellow poster depicting the upcoming school Shakespeare production, was plastered over the small rectangular window in the door, I took a few steps closer. My nosiness momentarily making me forget the weight of the books in my arms. I heard a voice talking, just one, and I knew that voice. I was sure of it, but I couldn't for the life of me place it. I tiptoed closer towards the door, my ear making contact with the battered wood; my intrigue once again taking over my better judgement. It was a man's voice and boy was he angry. The one-sided quarrelling must be some sort of roleplay.

'I can't do it, not yet. She can't know yet!'

How can you argue with yourself, where's the other voice? I thought. I lifted the piece of paper hiding the identity of the rogue voice. At that very moment my arms gave way, sending the books tumbling to the floor with a thunderous thwack. I heard footsteps inside the room rapidly moving towards the door, but there just wasn't enough time to scoop up all the books and make a run for it. The door opened and whoever it was, wasn't stepping around me to leave. I could feel the heat of their stare ingraining itself into my back as I collected the books from the floor. Clearly losing this stand-off I glanced up at the stranger. In fact, not a stranger at all. I knew I had recognised that voice.

'Beau!' Why couldn't I just have minded my own business and kept walking? Damn it! His expression was not as light and dreamy as I would have hoped. Funny thing hope; it has a way of stabbing you in the back when you least expect it. Curiosity had officially killed any chance of romance. 'Who were you talking to?' I inquired. Before he could obscure my view completely, I glanced behind him into the empty room, trying not to buckle under the weight and drop the books again. He swiftly pulled the door shut behind him, edging me backwards into the hallway.

'What do you think you're doing eavesdropping?'

'I was running late and I wasn't eavesdropping! Your split personality disorder is seriously messing with my head. I never know what Beau I'm going to get!' Who was I kidding, I was totally eavesdropping?

'Sorry Grace, I didn't mean to jump down your throat. Here, let me carry those.' He took the shoddily arranged books from my arms and began walking towards the stairs. My inner bitch was now wide awake and determined to make my life a living hell. *Is it wise to just roll over and accept all of his apologies without a second glance? Whatever happened to playing hard to get? Let's remember he's just been caught having a conversation with thin air...hello, nutjob!*

'Are you coming then?' I couldn't say no to that smile. I don’t know what it was about Beau that made me immediately drop my guard but for now my only option was to go with the flow. I caught up with him and we walked down the stairs together. I was still desperately trying to shake off the uneasy feeling of confused suspicion that lurked beneath the cloud of absolute desire that I had for Beau. It niggled at me just enough to invade my thoughts. *Why was he talking to himself in an empty classroom?*
We walked to my locker in silence. Although I had a rush of questions I wanted to ask him, I wasn’t sure if I should. As we reached my locker, I loaded my books into it, then returned the rusting keys to the front pocket of my satchel.

'Do you want to get some lunch? With me, I mean?' I asked with only a smidgen of confidence behind me. *Hello awkward silence! Has it been only twenty minutes or so since your last visit?* I thought. 'You know everyone's got to eat' I smiled uneasily.

His mesmerising cobalt eyes were locked on my face, but he still wasn't saying anything. I flicked my car keys casually. That's a lie, there was nothing casual about my body language. I looked exactly how I felt – TENSE. My red, battered knuckles, sore from the mental beating.

'I'll take that as a no then. See you next period.' I literally wanted to die as I turned to walk down the corridor, my inner bitch chastising me as I did.

'Okay then.' He yelled after me.

Suddenly, those two small words were the sweetest words in the history of the English language. Excitement, longing, apprehension and sheer desire swelled in my chest. I turned to face him and he was closer than I had anticipated. I glanced up at his perfect half smile, those eyes of his sparkling and not a hint of darkness visible. I took in a breath to steady myself as the scent of his aftershave, soap and motor oil filled my nose. He was close, much closer than he had ever been before. My cheeks flushed pink and my legs threatened to give way beneath me. *How does he have this effect on me? What would it be like to have those beautiful lips on mine?*

EIGHT

ꕥ

It was becoming clear that when Beau had entered my ordinary and mundane life, it wasn't just my heart that was experiencing a sudden change. I had tunnelled unknowingly into a world that was bizarre, a world I wasn't altogether sure I wanted to be a part of.
'Morning all. Our aim of the day? Exploring the historic myths of a hidden town and discovering the forgotten legends of an abandoned community. The houses that reside deep in the vast Gallows Woods hold secrets but what secrets? Today we will discover those secrets.' Our tour guide, Fred, dressed head to toe in a bespoke Victorian outfit was overly enthusiastic to say the least. He clearly loved his job as tales of times past rolled off his tongue in riddles. We strolled up a cracked, red brick path towards a ramshackle house that had seen better days. I picked social studies as one of my core subjects for this very reason, it was the only class where you got to visit off campus locations.

'This is one of our actresses. Much like they would have done in the 1800's, women often washed their clothes in big tin buckets. Cool huh?' The actress, clearly didn't agree with Fred's love of the past. She glared at him and plastered an overzealous fake smile on her face, a smile plastered there just for the visitors. Her blue Nike air trainers that poked out from beneath her torn, layered, soot covered skirt dragged me swiftly back into the 21st century. 'Well let's move on.'

We stepped over the threshold of a rundown cottage, that stood alone from the other houses circling the worn, grassy exterior. Most were now just disturbed, yellowing, grass plots, where hand-built homes once stood.

Fred noted with glee that 'this was once the home of Miss Luan Lesney; she was cast out of the village in 1872 and branded a witch. It is said that Miss Lesney was forcibly removed by her fellow villagers and sentenced to live her life in solitary. If you have a look at the carved markings on the walls surrounding the cottage you can see that they are containment spells. In my opinion her crimes befitted a crueller punishment, but after a series of attempts on her life the townspeople did the only thing they could think to do. Hanging Luan proved fruitless; no weapon forged could stop her evil heart from beating. After numerous attempts on her life, Luan's patience was pushed further then it should have been. It wasn't long before children in the town started to die. Some deemed them accidents, some knew the truth, and some played blind to the curse befalling their small settlement. Over the years and to this very day, many visitors have disappeared from this house, never to be heard from again.' I didn't know if this was a marketing tool to scare us, but if it was, it worked. I edged up the stairs behind my classmates listening intently to every word that left Fred's mouth.

'This house has claimed the lives of eight people in its past; eight which we know of anyway. After the death of Luan in 1889, it was noted in the archives to have been from a serious bout of influenza. This theory is widely criticised amongst historians. The townspeople would steer clear of the derelict cottage. What is unclear, is that one windy day in early February, in the year 1901, a group of travellers bound for Gallows wood came face to face with an abandoned village; this village. It was as if everyone in it had just vanished into thin air. Washing was still hung on the lines and pots of food were found still warm on smouldering log fires but the people of the village were nowhere to be found. Strange huh?' Sheer and unwavering excitement shone brightly on Fred's face as his eyes widened. He ushered the first ten of us into an upstairs bedroom with its greying, chipped, stone walls and a small cast iron fireplace. It was sparsely decorated with a single, handmade, wooden bed and a set of high cabinets that had one broken foot rest causing it to lean drunkenly against the window frame. I stood back as the others foraged around through draws, letting their imaginations run away with them. I don't know whether it was because I believed Fred's stories or because everything looked extremely dirty but I was happy to stand in the centre of the room, keeping my hands to myself.

'So, you like this tour guide stuff then Fred?'

'I absolutely love it! It's a shame that today is the last time I will get to do it.' The giddiness in his face quickly dissipated.

'Why?' Something told me I didn't want to know, but as always, my mouth reacted quicker than my brain.

'Last year we misplaced a young girl from Mother Mary's catholic school. They weren't too happy, as you can probably guess. With a 15,000-person petition from the community and a council that cave at the first sign of pressure, they demanded its closure. Luan Lesney's cottage is the last to survive.'

'May I ask what you mean by misplaced. She turned up eventually right?'

'She turned up, eventually. Unfortunately, she wasn't in exactly the same condition when she was found as she was when she was lost.' Fred's words sent an icy shiver down my spine. I didn't want to know any more but I couldn't just leave it there, could I?

'What condition Fred?' He edged a little closer to me and

lowered his voice, softening his tone.

'She was discovered at the bottom of the well, outback. She had apparently hit a few rocks on the way down. I didn't see it for myself, but the word is, she had razor like cuts to either side of her mouth. I have no idea how we are meant to believe that rocks did that.' As he spoke the words *'razor like cuts'* Fred ran his index finger over his mouth simulating the gash.

'I didn't need that visual Fred.'

'If you go in there you can see the garden from the window. But don't wander off!' His voice was stern and filled with worry. He made his way into the bedroom to stir up the crowd with another legend. I gazed through the slated wooden door hanging off its makeshift hinges into the room opposite me. Well, what would you have done in my position? Curiosity may have killed the cat but as I tiptoed into the sparse and dilapidated room, I prayed that in this instance, I wasn't the cat. Through the window I could see the battered well, with missing stones and cracked fillers to the point that is didn't even look like a well anymore, at least not a functioning one. It was surrounded by yellow tape and there was another actress resting up against it. She was wearing a blood stained, beige cardigan, a black skirt and white knee-high socks. It didn't take me long to realise it was a Mother Mary Catholic school uniform, which personally, I thought was in very poor taste. I could understand now why the organisers were getting stick for their little horror parade. A creak from behind me made me jump, fortunately there was nothing there, just my imagination at play. I tried to laugh it off and returned my gaze to the blood-soaked actress at the weathered well, her vacant eyes met mine. Even at this distance they had the power to evoke a feeling of dread. The gory makeup brilliantly executed, like something right out of a Romero horror film. The creaking noise in the room returned but this time from beside me. As I peered into the open closet to my right, a force pushed me forwards and the door swung closed behind me. I was trapped. The door knob stuck, no matter how hard I tried to force it. It took me a good few seconds to calm down. My breathing was laboured, my heart was racing uncontrollably.

'OK, whoever is out there, open the door. I mean it. I am not in the mood for this crap!' Silence was my only response. The air around me cooled considerably and my breath wafted out in clouds of white smoke. The panic returned in unsettling, rippling waves that unbalanced me. I heard a pained gurgling and spluttering from the darkness behind me. I didn't want to turn around, I didn't want to investigate further, but it soon became clear, what I wanted, didn't matter. The cracks in the wooden door allowed for smidgens of light to creep in, enough light that meant whoever or whatever was behind me, hiding in the darkness, would surely be visible, whether I wanted to see them or not. A woman dressed in 1940's attire greeted me as I turned on my heels. *Another actress? Is someone playing a trick on me?* Her throat was brutally slashed from one side of her neck to the other. Pieces of her anatomy that should have been on the inside plunged out of the jagged wound. I watched on, horrified, my body immobilised and fixed to the spot. With every gasp and gurgle she made, blood pumped out of her wound and onto her blue and white tea dress. With my stunned brain finally catching up I stumbled backwards and fumbled again for the doorknob, unable to take my eyes off her wide stare. I screamed, the noise a strangled prayer for my escape. I pounded on the door incessantly as her fingers traced through my hair, then there was a wash of light flooding the cramped closet. I fell forwards to the floor with a thud.

'Excuse me; do you know how old this house is? What the

hell do you think you are doing in there? You have ruined this door.' Fred's rage was surprisingly comforting.

'I'm sorry, someone locked me in. Then one of your actresses scared the crap out of me. I think she should take some of the blame.' My breathing still hadn't returned to normal as the flash of her image in my head made my heart hammer in my chest.

'What actress?'

'The dead woman in the 40's dress, you know the chatty one with the slashed throat.'

'What are you talking about? Have you been smoking something in there?' He craned his neck forward, inspecting the now empty closet.

'No, of course not!' I screamed as Mr. Sanders entered the room. After sniffing for evidence in the closet Fred turned his accusing eyes back my way. 'OK, well what about the actress you have out there by the well. You do know it's morally wrong to profit off that poor girl's death? Do the school know you are using their uniform?' I pointed my finger accusingly and a little too close to his face. I don't know where it came from but my anger was out there, laid bare, as naked as a new-born for the entire world to see. Fred pulled me towards the window and lowered his voice.

'What are you talking about? I never said she was wearing a school uniform.' His words were sobering. 'Look I think we should all move on with our tour.' He chipperly remarked addressing the people who had flooded into the room to see what all the fuss was about. As Fred led everyone downstairs, I glanced back from the decaying well outside, to the dank closet that moments ago had held me hostage. I left Gallows Wood settlement that day shaken and confused.

I did see them, they were there, but no one believed me. I tried to leave what I had seen that day where it belonged - in the past. That memory, if allowed to remain, would surely rob me of my sanity.

NINE

ꕥ

As Beau and I sat in the cafe, opposite the college, safely away from prying eyes, it was as though a new side of Beau had broken through. He was chatty, enthusiastic and attentive and he had the politeness and manners of a 1920's gentleman. The cheeky twinkle in his eyes was the icing on the cake.

'So how was the trip yesterday?'

'Please don't even get me started. It was an absolute nightmare. If I believed in ghosts, I could have sworn I met a couple there. It was just a really weird day; one I wouldn't mind forgetting if that's OK?'

'Of course. No problem.' His words agreed but his eyes did not. I didn't know why but he suddenly looked uncomfortable. I shuffled past it and moved on with a more socially acceptable topic of conversation.

'So, what made you choose to come to Claynor?' I asked, my voice now brimming with feigned happiness, the craziness of yesterday still lurking in the back of my mind.

'Well I've been in care for longer than I can remember and they finally gave me a choice. I had to go into hospital last year'

'Hospital?' I interrupted brashly. 'Sorry that was rude of me, you were saying?' I shoved a complimentary bread roll from the red gingham basket on the table into my mouth quickly to stop another outburst.

'Yeah, well it was nothing very serious. I get these really violent nosebleeds sometimes, my foster parents used to take me into hospital in frantic hysterics. Gwen, the foster mother I'm living with now, was working there at the time. We clicked instantly and for the first time in a long time, I made a connection with someone I liked. Gwen's been fostering children for the past twenty-five years. When you meet her, she'll tell you that our meeting in that hospital on a cold November morning was fate - predestined'. His boyish chuckle and closed lipped smile showed his age as his fond memories of Gwen played out in his head.

'So you met Gwen, moved here, and are you happy now?'

'Yes, I'm happier now than I ever imagined possible actually.' Behind his positive words was a pained expression.

'That does not look like the face of a happy man' I teased.

'I have a lot going on that I'm not going to bore you with. I don't know what it is about you Grace, but you make me feel free. I can just be me. I don't have to act a certain way when I'm with you, and that's very new for me'. The honesty in his words hit me hard and my desire to comfort him was tearing me up inside. *Right I'm going in for the kill; don't ask-don't get. I want to know everything and anything, so this is my chance.* I thought. 'If you don't mind me asking, what happened to your parents?' I lowered my head innocently in a bid to disguise my nosiness.

'To be perfectly honest, I've never got the full story myself, just a few random bits and pieces. I'm still trying to get hold of the rest of the puzzle.' He grinned, putting his cup back onto the table. His moment of unfiltered honesty taking him off guard.

'Well, if I can ever lend you a hand, I'm pretty nifty when it comes to puzzles.'

Oh my, shoot me now. Embarrassment swelled in my stomach and flushed at my cheeks. Why don't I just go all out and ask him why he behaves so strangely and talks to thin air. He looked at me quizzically, unable to stop the smile on his face. My thoughts as always wandering in a completely different direction. A curvaceous woman, dressed in a low cut, pink, lace top, eye-wateringly tight jeans and a sea scene embossed apron strutted towards our table. With a slapped on sultry (or in my opinion smutty) smile, she glanced into the six-foot long mirror on the far wall opposite her and adjusted her curly long blonde hair around and over one shoulder.

'Can I get you another drink, sir?' she enquired hanging onto the word sir seductively as her eyes bore into Beau.

'Yeah, could I get a Fanta please?' Beau turned his eyes to me questioningly, awaiting my order. She was the deer and he was the headlights and as she fixated longingly on Beau, a surge resembling the green-eyed monster stirred uncomfortably in me. Was it wrong to close my eyes and imagine that this particular deer was being mowed down by a Russian military issue tank?

'Can I have a bottle of water please?' I requested, as politely as my inner monster would allow. I couldn't have told you our waitress's eye colour, she would have had to have looked at me first. With a cheeky smile from Beau, my jealously took a back seat. 'Hey I've got something that will make you laugh.' I mused. He just grinned, waiting on my next words. 'Right what was the name of your first pet?' I asked playfully.

'Lionel' he replied quizzically, one eyebrow settling higher than the other.

'OK, and what was the name of the first street you lived on?'

'Stamford Crescent'

'Well, usually that information tells you what your porn name would be, but Lionel Stamford sounds more like an accountant then a porn star.'

'Fair enough, what's yours then?' I hesitated for a second, realising the awkward, self-inflicted position I had got myself into. I whispered my response incoherently as I took a sip of my water.

'Sorry, I didn't quite get that, what did you say?' He chuckled a little too loudly.

'Bubbles Laroue' I said clearly, soon realising how loud I had spoken. I glanced around and everyone had their eyes fixed on me. Beau continued his muffled chuckling. I punched him on his arm playfully, still smiling. I pulled my hand to my face, wishing with every bone in my body that I had the power of invisibility. No such luck! I bet if I were dating Harry Potter I wouldn't have this problem. Where can you find a fictional wizard at short notice to get you out of a sticky situation? Once the dust of sheer humiliation had settled around me, we continued chatting, swapping stories from our past, and then more hesitantly sharing our dreams for the future. I noticed he spoke adamantly, as though it was a speech meant for many others beside myself. He spoke like his future would always be in the distance, like he would never get there no matter how hard he tried, or how fervently he believed in its existence. Without making him aware of it, I starred wistfully into those beautiful, crystal, blue eyes of his and watched as a glazed darkness appeared in them, as if an element of our conversation touched him unnervingly. His lips danced as he spoke, every word silently commanding of my attention. His light hearted chuckle when he said something amusing was music to my ears and the slight dimpling of his cheeks, as his eyes locked onto mine, made my knees go weak – my body's silent approval at my choice of lunch date. Losing track of time was not unusual for me, but I knew that appearing back in class with Beau by my side would begin a whole load of questions that I just wasn't ready for. I didn't want this, whatever it was, to end, I could have happily sat across from this guy for hours, listening to anything and everything that he decided to share with me. Time however was not on our side today. I raised my watch and tapped the glass. Tapping his iPhone home screen, he nods in agreement.

'Oh yeah, definitely time to make a move.'

I reached deep into my pocket, through the handful of chewing gum wrappers and bits of old yellow notepaper. I finally delved deep enough to reach the dishevelled five-pound note screwed up at the bottom. I glanced up at the busty blonde waitress at the till, who was clearly oblivious to my presence. I coughed loudly into my hand and moved into her eye-line to grab her attention. Almost instinctively she shuffled a step sideways, her eyes still fixated dreamily on something behind me. She let out a fanciful sigh from her perfectly formed glossy lips. *What the hell is she looking at?* I glanced around and ruled out the robust, leather clad, hairy biker, sipping a caramel mocha in the corner. Chances are she wasn't staring at the withered old man either, who was using a fork to clean the spinach out of his teeth. Then I saw him, Beau, with my camera bag slung over one shoulder, holding the door open with that cheery half smile directed straight at me. I glanced back at the waitress. *Back off love, if I have it my way, he will be mine and mine alone. My vote goes with the biker - enjoy!* I thought, a sunny smile now etched across my face.

The sunlight flooded into the cafe from behind Beau, creating a heavenly haze around him. I dropped the five-pound note on the side Infront of the waitress and although she appeared unaffected by my presence, I thanked her for the service. I grabbed my bag from the back of the chair next to my seat and hurried after him. Walking side by side, our bodies mere inches apart our conversation had calmed, the need to be close to one another however was like a thread of electricity invisibly connecting us.

'Grace, do you fancy coming to mine for lunch one day next week?' His eyes never left the pavement as he spoke.

'I'd love to,' I gushed, trying desperately and failing horribly to hide my enthusiasm. 'Well, actually, I've got this work party thing I've got to go to Wednesday night. I don't know whether you'd be interested in coming. It won't be that much fun, a bunch of old fogies probably.' I saw an opening and I tried to grab it forcefully with both hands. The reality was somewhat lacking in force though, with me blushing a bright fuchsia colour. Beau took charge and put me out of my misery. He smiled that smile, his welcomed gaze meeting mine.

'I'd love to go.'

TEN

ꙮ

I slammed the car door behind me, threw my bags on the passenger seat and buckled my seat belt. As soon as I turned the key in the ignition, deafening music blasted out from the only working speaker. Fumbling frantically, I managed to turn it off. My radio was somewhat temperamental; it seemed to have a mind of its own, but at that precise moment I had more to worry about then my dodgy radio. The light drizzle outside was quickly building up into a full-on rainstorm and much like everything else in this car, I only had one windscreen wiper that worked. Thankfully it was on the driver's side. I made it home without mowing anyone down and pulled onto the cobbled drive, reached over for my bags.... what was missing? *Damn it, my camera!'* I must have left it behind. One windscreen wiper or not, I had to head back to college and get it. With the rain picking up speed, I hoped my zero fatalities stayed at exactly that.

As I pulled up to the college gates, under the cover of the now black night sky, I could just about see that the car park was almost deserted. Only three cars remained. I pulled up as close to the school as possible. I didn't condone parking in a disabled spot, but there were seven others available and the idea of parking any further away in the poorly lit carpark terrified me. I took the wide stone steps quickly and two at a time, aiming to leave the black night and the eerie silence behind me. I walked through the twenty-foot high Romanesque pillared entrance and towards the empty receptionist's desk. There was something eerie about seeing a familiar place in darkness and out of context. The large, granite, marble desk felt out of place. It was surrounded by 19th century animated cherub mouldings positioned high on the walls in each corner of the room. The hefty and hideously dark-wood framed oil paintings of past headmasters lined the walls, each one seeming just as aged as the last. Usually planted behind the desk was a minuscule framed woman named Judith. Her presence was austere and she came across as painfully timid. Without her glaring stare, my eyes were drawn to the portrait on the wall above her empty chair, which was about five times bigger than her. Sitting on an enormous, deep red, stilted chair was a mature, podgy gentleman with short, greying hair and piercing grey eyes. Standing behind him was a younger, lofty, sinewy man with combed back, jet black hair and deep brown eyes. His wiry hand rested on the older man's shoulder and he had a slightly irritated look about him. Claynor Ray's founders appeared as complete opposites. As I circled round the desk and advanced up a step towards the Great hall entrance, I felt their eyes grinding down into me, following my every move.

'It's a bit late for you isn't it?' His booming voice made me jump. My heart skipped a cautionary beat, causing all the fine hairs on my arms to prickle up. The six-foot five security guard towered above me. With his arms as big as boulders and his body-builder like stature, only one word leapt to my mind - *STEROIDS!* I fumbled nervously in my bag for my ID and found it burrowed away in the bottom corner but in my haste to pull it out, I failed to notice the Tampax packet wrapped around the end of my ID chain. No matter how bloody discreet the adverts claim they are, it was still blatantly obvious what it was. As the blood that coursed through my body rushed rapidly to my brain, I flushed a bright crimson cherry colour; I was officially mortified. The Tampax had swung loose and dropped to the floor. I bent down to retrieve it, I could feel his eyes burning into the back of my head. I stood up, desperately trying to avert his stare.

'I've left my camera in class 102, it's really expensive, my Mum will murder me if I lose it. Could you maybe unlock the door for me? I'll be literally two minutes.' His imposing stare never wavered. I was desperately hoping my angel face would soften him. 'In and out, I promise!' I added solemnly. His glare broke, suddenly he didn't seem as scary as I'd first assumed. I think the Tampax incident, plus my obvious mortification, may have helped a little.

'Okay, just this once. Come with me and we'll get the keys. Stay close.' I followed him as he led the way to the art department. Each corridor looked the same; dreary, peeling, magnolia walls, with posters for student president elections plastered on them. If I were on my own, it would have only been too easy to get lost.

~~~~

The impending blackness of the stormy night sky flooded in through the windows. Anything beyond the glass was now shrouded in the shadows. We finally reached the door. As I entered the classroom, the strong odour of developing fluid hit me with an intoxicating rush that made my head swim. The room was crow black and it took a few seconds for my eyes to adjust. I had never been in there when it was empty - or when it was dark - and I suddenly realised, even though I had been in and out of this room at least a hundred times, I had never paid attention to where the light switch was. The shadows that stretched onto the far wall from the corridor lights were creepy, water like stretches of bright white light. I had a strange feeling of being watched, and it wasn't by the security guard pacing about impatiently outside the door. It
~~~~

really doesn't matter how old you get; the dark can still make you feel like a vulnerable five-year-old hiding from the bogeyman. I took a deep and steadying breath. *Right, find camera and leave quickly. Might be a plan to find the bloody light switch though Grace. What's this switch do?* A rush of welcomed relief surged through me as the fluorescent lights overhead flickered on and came to my rescue. 'We have light!' I bellowed theatrically, turning to the security guard who was now resting against the door frame nursing a scowl.

'You've got two minutes. Don't make me regret this.' he warned with a chubby finger as he exited the doorway to wait in the hall. I began my arduous search, fumbling around cluelessly. His pacing footsteps outside the room reminiscent of the countdown TV show clock.

'Hey Mr. Geddes, ever thought about cleaning this room?' I said into the empty room to no-one in particular. There was mess everywhere. I reached under the front desk, immediately regretting it as my fingers met with something foreign. 'Urghhh, please, please don't be what I think you are' I said quietly, sluggishly retracting my hand. There it was, a wad of old chewing gum attached firmly to the end of my fingers, with bits of god only knows what embedded in it. I unceremoniously shook the gum off my finger and kicked it back under the table. I decided to change course. I glanced at the door and threw the guard an awkward smile; the gesture was unsurprisingly not returned as he grunted at me in response. As soon as I began my search underneath the tables, his radio went off with a low hiss, he swiftly removed it from his belt.

'Hey Winston, are you anywhere near block B, the alarm has been playing up and I can't tell whether it's gone off accidentally or them graffiti artists are back again?'

'I'm on my way' Winston said as he answered the strong, Polish accent of his colleague. 'DO NOT LEAVE THIS ROOM!' he ordered. I nodded at him obediently. He pointed his sausage like finger at me again and threw me a bug-eyed glare to emphasise his point. *Holster that finger big boy. I've got KFC waiting for me at home. I don't actually want to be here.* I thought the words, I didn't dare say them out loud.

As I made my way around the classroom, wishing I had customised my camera bag with bright pink fabric and sparkly sequins, the vacant stillness of my surroundings became uncomfortable. I did the only thing that sprung to mind - singing. 'Build me up Buttercup' was the cheeriest song I could think of and for a short while it did its job, even though I only really knew the chorus. I finally found my camera bag underneath a stack of photo paper, nestling snugly between two large bottles of developing fluid. Winston still wasn't back to escort me out, so I made myself busy arranging some of my contact sheets.

BANG!
I must have jumped five feet in the air and catapulted back onto a nearby table, my feet now clear of the floor. 'Winston is that you? Winston?' Every fibre of my being wished it was Winston.

THUD!
In the silence that followed, I began to hear a faint whistling sound coming from the darkroom, behind the plush purple curtain. In no scary movie ever did I shout at the television, *yes, why don't you look behind the curtain?* 'Hellooooo?' I called out, my voice breaking. *Damn you smidgen of courage.* Fear pricked in my throat as the hairs on my arms stood to attention.

I edged towards the curtain apprehensively. Against my better judgement. With a breath of preparation, I hesitantly drew back the bulky fabric, not knowing what to expect. In the stillness, the rail on which the curtain was attached sounded like a shower drape as the loops scraped against the metal bar, creating a soft chiming. The potent aroma of developing fluid hit me hard and stung the sensitive lining of my throat. I began to cough and wheeze, the fumes almost visible white puffs of smoke in the air. Looking just ahead of my feet the floor was bathed in the clear liquid, masses of contact sheets floating atop it. Nearly two hundred sheets I would have guessed, that crinkled under my feet. In the corner, was a large, upturned, empty, brown box. I edged closer and the negatives, which had been in the box, appeared to contain the image of a slight and pale man, his face a contorted glare; he had a sly smile with a mouth full of crooked, discoloured teeth.

I edged backwards towards the door to the hallway. The makeshift darkroom may have been bare, but I couldn't take my eyes away from it. In an instant, I felt a great surge of energy vibrating around the room, the air solid, for a moment, the walls seemingly brushed with a flowing liquid. Every machine and light fixture blew with a deafening crack. A second later something or someone pushed me hard back into the darkroom, a stabbing pain piercing at me way down into my stomach. I fell onto the floor amongst the sodden contact sheets. I was dazed for some time, maybe even unconscious for a minute or two. I felt my hand react and eventually move to the back of my head. I could feel that my hair was matted and dripping wet, soaked in developing fluid and my blood.

The smell was stringent, but luckily the acidic liquid had not gone anywhere near my eyes. Thankfully the stinging of my head wound didn't match the wash of confusion that I now wallowed in. I felt the sickness bubble away inside of me. My head was whirling. Using a metal bench, I climbed uneasily to my feet, the sticky fluid mixture sliding down the back of my neck. I stood shakily for a moment; my weight now supported by the wall. There was that muddied confusion again. The smudge of blood on a metal photography case by the door sent my mind racing. The last thing I remembered was a shimmering grey light and what looked like charcoal black smoke dancing in front of me. As my brain fought to clear my confusion of thoughts a flash hit me, I saw them; a pair of transparent hands, slim and calloused, with black fingernails. They were reaching for me. Then there was nothing. Darkness swallowed me and I was on the floor again, now bathing in my fear, my blood and some pretty toxic chemicals. My weakened knees were barely able to support my weight.

'Did you find it?' I looked around into a blinding torchlight and my focus began to clear on Winston's disapproving face. 'Really?! I've left you alone for two minutes, are you trying to make my job harder?' His anger didn't go unnoticed, as with every syllable the shooting pain in my head went into overdrive. He turned on a huff and led the way out of the darkroom into the now blindingly bright classroom. His grasp on my forearm was bordering on abuse. I staggered mutely under his grip, my eyes watering and my head pounding painfully. *Hello? I'm in pain here! I guess a little sympathy is out of the question?* My inner bitch piped up to *help* the situation. *Should have waited and picked your camera up tomorrow* she mused. I gritted my teeth and followed Winston tight lipped. I was sure nothing I could say would alleviate the situation anyway.

'I'll call for Agnes, she should be here soon. What the hell were you doing in there?' Winston handed me a wad of tissues as he gestured around the car wreck of a classroom. If he had been concerned at all, he was hiding it very well.

'I heard a noise' I replied hazily, as I applied the wads of Kleenex to the throbbing wound on the back of my head.

'Really, was it a massive dump truck that caused all this

mess by any chance?' Sarcastic annoyance dripped from his words. 'I knew I shouldn't have let you in after hours. I think a shelf must have collapsed on you or something.'

Wow Sherlock, did you come up with that theory all on your own? I bitched. The immediate feeling of dread wouldn't shift; it lurked in the pit of my stomach and for a brief second it overshadowed the pain in my head. I just wanted out of that classroom, fast. The nurse arrived, first aid box in hand. She was a lonely, frail, old woman and luckily for me this school was her life; always the first to arrive and the last to leave. The idea of depending on Winston to patch up my wounds was laughable. 'It doesn't need stitches; I can see that.' She lulled after her inspection of my head 'but I'll bandage it for you to stop the bleeding. Here, drink some water honey.' She handed me a large salty glass of warm water and a miniature packet of energy boosting maple crackers. I pushed away the crackers. My throat felt coarse and strained from the developing fluid. The last thing I could do was eat. 'Please eat them dear, at least try, the sugar will kick-start your blood pressure, you need to help it return to normal.' She placed the crackers in my hands and I slowly nibbled at them, wanting nothing more than to be in my car and on my way home. Winston stood directly next to me, breathing impatiently down my neck. I was grateful as his monstrous size was blocking out the overhead fluorescents that were engulfing my sensitive eyes.

'I need to know exactly what happened. I'll need to make a full report. I found you mumbling about it being 'foggy' and you kept repeating 'his hands, his hands.' He performed his statement theatrically, as though he was ready to condemn me to an insane asylum. 'I couldn't get any bloody sense out of you. Do you have any idea how much all that equipment's going to cost to replace?' The severe throbbing in my head pulsated beneath my skull. This was where my manners and sense of decency completely dissipated.

'Put it on my tab bell boy!' His disgust and shock were inaudible. 'Look, I didn't do it on purpose! Scrap that, I didn't do anything at all. Someone else did it and someone else screwed with the lights and pushed me over!' I shouted, the noise of my voice making the pain worse in my head.

'What someone else? There's not been anyone else in here since I let you in and boy was that a mistake!' I saw him looking at the nurse as if to say I must be some kind of loon. I brought my hands up to my head and winced in pain. This really was the last thing I needed. Mum and I were finally getting on and now her excuse of 'she's just misunderstood' would rear its ugly head again. Winston glared at me again and pointed that finger at me accusingly. 'I've called your mother. She's coming to pick you up. I don't think she's going to be too pleased with you.'

'I've got my own car, I can drive myself home' I protested, trying desperately to convince them, as I attempted to climb off the table and not wobble like a drunk person. I inevitably stumbled and threw my hand onto the nurse to steady myself. *Man, I wish I was drunk. Mortification would roll right off me now if I was.*

'I really don't think you should be driving sweetheart, not with a head wound, and your eye-sight seems a bit misty to me.' She said, placing a comforting hand on my shoulder, guiding me back onto the table. I was still too shocked and emotionally exhausted to argue.

'Thank-you, I really appreciate it.'

'I wouldn't worry about her eyesight, the fact that she has about as much spacial awareness as a blind drunk who can't stand on her own two feet, I think is proof enough.' He didn't take his hollow stare from mine. 'You will have to fill out an incident report tomorrow and then the headmaster will decide what to do with you.' This was mean Winston. Not too different from nice Winston. This man had the emotional range of a dung beetle.

'Well, Winston, I'm lucky you were here to get all the paperwork in order, aren't I?' A hint of annoyed acrimony plagued my voice and Winston picked up on it. He wisely decided to leave me be and walk out into the corridor. A few minutes later he reappeared, with my Mum pushing past him. She raced towards me, saw my bandaged head, and hugged me.

'Oh, Grace, what have you been doing?'

'I'll tell you what she's been doing...' began Winston.

'Oh, shut up you intolerable man!' *Whoa, go Mum!* A small smirk curled at the corner of my mouth. Her mothering instincts took over with a nice chunk of fiery chilli. 'You've already told me once in the corridor and I don't believe a word of it. Come on Grace, let's get you home.' A small part of me felt tremendously bad for Winston. He did let me in and it wasn't his fault I got hurt. It also wasn't his fault he had some major personality defects; working at the school could have been partly to blame. *Everything will blow over and I can make sure he doesn't get in trouble tomorrow. I want my bed; I NEED my bed.* Mum cradled me against her shoulder as we walked slowly down the deserted hall to the reception area. As we made our way to the exit, I looked longingly at my beloved car and dreaded the lengthy walk to school the next day. By the time we pulled into our drive I had already began to drift off to sleep, and within minutes my Mum was tucking me up in bed and lightly laying a worried kiss on my forehead. There had been no conversation; no questions at all.

AWOKEN *Billie Jade Kermack*

ELEVEN

ꟹ

I took the container of Ibuprofen and the bottle of Evian out of my bag and fumbled with the childproof lid. The two tablets that looked more like horse tranquillisers than painkillers stuck in my throat and felt like razor blades as they coursed down my gullet. I guessed from the hushed gossip and obvious stares that I was getting from the other students, that my *'accident'* in the photography classroom was now on everyone's radar. One person whose radar I was desperate to stay clear of was Lucy Appleby. Luck definitely favoured someone else that day. I passed the girl's toilets and out strolled Lucy, followed of course by her pack of loyal, skimpily dressed minions. 'Hey Grace, we heard about your little freak-out last night. You forget to take your crazy pills or something? What are these then?' Before I knew it, Lucy had grabbed my bottle of Ibuprofen and emptied it onto the floor. 'Grace I am so sorry, complete butterfingers.' Her face said sincerity - her sarcastic tone said a cloying 'screw you'.

I had taken only a few steps inside when Mr Geddes approached me and all eyes in the room assessed me. 'Grace, can I have a word with you?' I nodded solemnly and followed him outside into the corridor. It was 9:45am and I was already regretting getting out of bed that morning. 'I heard about what happened last night.' He looked with genuine concern at the rim of the bandage edging out from under my hat. 'Are you okay?'

'Yeah, I'll live.' I smiled uneasily. My hand instinctively flew to the cricket ball sized contusion, still throbbing on the back of my head.

'I've been complaining for months about the wires and electricity problems we've been having here. Maybe now they will actually listen and do something about it.'

'Yes,' I agreed meekly. 'Do you want me to help clean up? From what I remember, the darkroom was in a right mess last night?'

'No, no, don't be silly Grace. I think you've had enough to deal with in the darkroom.' His eyes were now on the red scrape on my forehead just above my eye. 'Are you sure you should be here today?'

'I'm fine, it looks worse than it is.' I lied.

'Are you sure?' He pressed. I turned to push open the classroom door. 'I'm sure Mr Geddes, thanks though, for your concern.' As soon as I entered the classroom and walked towards my seat, I saw that Beau's seat was empty and a huge feeling of relief washed over me. He was the last person I wanted to see. Luckily for me, I spent the rest of the day being quizzed at every break by Amelia, who seemed more concerned by the fashion faux-pa of my hat. Unable to deal with it any longer she removed the diamante slide from her hair and clipped it onto my beanie. 'There' she said, looking satisfied. 'Even a homeless man's hat can be dressed up. But you do look pale, Grace.' She reached into her bag. 'Here, have some of my lip-gloss.'

'No' I said irritably, 'I don't want any lip gloss, I'm fine.'

'No, you my friend, are not fine' she insisted, 'you look half dead and you need a nice bit of slap on your face to liven you up. Don't forget you have a date tonight.'

Oh, holy crap! I had completely forgotten. It's Wednesday.

~~~~

Once home, Mum removed the bandage and inspected my wound, decreeing that it was not too bad; not bad enough to need stitches anyway. She dabbed at it with antiseptic and shoved all her medical supplies back into the sink cupboard.

'What actually happened last night, Grace.'

'Mr Geddes said he's been complaining about the wiring and electric problems for months.' I used the lie, even though the truth tugged uncomfortably at my lips.

'They're lucky I don't sue them' she replied angrily. 'Here, drink this cup of herbal tea, it'll do you good.' I hated herbal tea, but I drank it thankfully, because now I knew, that as far as Mum was concerned, I was off the hook.

~~~~

I stood outside Mr Luigi's Pizza Parlour where I worked, waiting for Beau. The six-foot neon sign of a fat chef juggling pizzas above my head, rained down strobes of red, yellow and blue onto the pavement in front of me, with the letter G blinking as the bulbs died. I gazed down at my sore hands. Scrubbing the cramped toilet floor for an hour after closing had left the stench of disinfectant embedded in my red, blotchy skin. I soon realised that even a pair of trusty marigolds could not protect my hands. My Mum had assured me that everybody's first job was a complete let down. Apparently, until you are no longer a teenager, all your CV says to an employer is UNTRAINED, LOW WAGE, SKIVVY.

The wind whipped against my face and filled my nose with the aroma of baked anchovies and Gorgonzola cheese. I smoothed out my clothes and worried instantly about my casual jeans and pink flowery strap-top combo. I prayed Beau hadn't forgotten our date. I contemplated going inside and out of the wind but that evoked worries of its own. *What if he can't find me in there? What if he turns up, sees I'm not outside and leaves? Bigger worry, what if he doesn't turn up at all?* I braved the cold night air for another ten long minutes. My smile was shatter proof and my sore head a distant memory. Everything faded as my eyes met his. He wore a crisp white shirt with the sleeves rolled up to his elbows and a pair of dark blue jeans tucked into his beaten-up military boots. Oh yes, there was my man! The sight of him took my breath away, as it always did. He waited for the traffic to pass and jogged across the road towards me, a warm smile on his face.

'Hi, sorry I'm late.' He bent his head and kissed me on the cheek. An unexpected move that for a brief moment brightened his face and showed his age. I was so surprised I almost fainted.

'Beau, you do remember what I said, that it will be all old fogeys inside?'

'No, it won't' he grinned, 'not with you and me in there. We're not old fogeys.'

'Oh, yeah, right.' I beamed like a schoolgirl. My breathing was now more laboured as his eyes met mine, he clutched my hand tightly in his, stroking the back of it with his thumb. I pushed the door open, the low hum of an Elvis track and the chatter of strangers filling my ears. Mr Luigi had moved all the furniture to the edges of the large restaurant to create a black and white tiled dance floor.

'Grace, I'm so glad you have come, the men's toilets are blocked up again.' *You have got to be kidding me!* My composure faded, utter disbelief the only expression present on my face. 'Only joking!' Mr Luigi laughed loudly, as he grasped his large belly jovially like Santa, loving his own joke. My laughter was forced and uncomfortable. *I really want to hit you right now funny man* I thought with a tight upper lip. 'So, who is this Grace, your new boyfriend?' He teased.

'No, just a friend' I muttered awkwardly. *What was this between Beau and I? What should I call him? He did kiss me, so were we dating?* Beau extended his arm politely to shake Mr Luigi's bulky hairy hand.

'Hello, sir, I'm Beau.'

'Sir? Oh, you've got a proper young gentleman of a friend here Grace.' He smiled, clearly approving of Beau as he shook his hand enthusiastically. 'Please, call me Mario.'

'Any relation to Super Mario?' Beau asked with a grin. Mr Luigi sniggered loudly.

'Everyone asks me that! I had to buy a Nintendo to find out who this Super Mario was. But no, he is not as super as me. Now come, have some wine.' He looked at Beau. 'Or for you, some beer?'

Beau nodded. 'A beer will be great, thank you.'

'Oh Grace, I don't think you've met my wife Claudette, have you?' He reached out, clasping the arm of a beautiful, svelte, olive skinned woman with straight black hair that trailed the entire length of her slender back. Her sparkly, grey and black chiffon knee length dress hung on her slender hips as she moved lovingly to Mario's side. She was way out of his league, a complete mismatch. I felt guilty at my judgemental thoughts. As she fell into his bulky arms and pecked him on the cheek, the look in her eyes was that of pure devotion. They were clearly in love and from what I could gather they had been in love for a very long time; the signs were clear, however small and discreet they were.

'It's lovely to meet you Grace, I hear you're one of Mario's most valued employees. He speaks very highly of you.' She sung, her words light and whimsical.

'Well he's a joy to work for.' I lied.

'And this is Grace's friend Beau.' As he took Claudette's outstretched hand in to his, Beau just stood there, looking grave stricken, unable to break the bond. His face was pale and he was staring at Claudette intensely. With her eyes panicked and confused, running wildly from Beau's face to his tight grasp on her hand, I knew something was wrong. Beau's expression was clouded and torturous. I tightened my grip on Beau's other hand dragging him back to reality.

'Sorry' Beau muttered to Claudette, his words brimming with contrition. He expertly shook off the uncomfortable atmosphere with a light hearted laugh. Claudette responded with a gracious smile and appeared flattered by his attention.
Something is wrong here. There's something I am just not seeing. My gut was screaming at me - *Open your eyes woman!* He edged backwards away from Mario and his wife which I took as a sure sign that we should make our way across the room, away from my uncharacteristically jovial boss and his stunning wife. Claudette went to extend her hand towards Beau's shoulder to make sure he was OK and with that, you would have thought Beau had just been bitten on the leg by a tiger. He swiftly edged back a step and stumbled back into one of the buffet tables, decorating the floor with a tray of fresh shrimp.

'Sorry about the mess. Nice to meet you both, but I really need to use your toilet. Too many beers and not enough time.' He chuckled, the laugh not meeting his wide eyes.

'Beau, are you okay?' I asked shakily as I chased after him across the dance floor. I laid my palm on his chest without thinking and his heart vibrated fiercely beneath it, it's humming bird speed alarming.

'Yeah, I'm fine, do you want a drink?' And with that he was off, propelling through the crowd towards the bar. Oh yes, something was wrong. Something was very, very wrong and it had something to do with Claudette.

TWELVE

ꕥ

A week or so later, with my suspicions of Beau's behaviour hidden away at the back of my mind, I drove my car into the driveway to park, my nearly bald tyres unable to cushion me from the uneven cobbles. With only a few minutes to spare before Beau was due to arrive, I could hear the buzz of his motorbike approaching from around the corner; it was the familiar hum of the engine that caused my heart to skip a beat. I took a deep breath and swallowed the bulging lump in my throat. As I brushed through my hair with my fingers, trying in vain to remove the tangles, I caught a glimpse of the living room curtains fluttering. I peered around and there was Mum, nervously waiting for Beau's arrival. She raised her thumbs and mouthed *'Good Luck'* with a silly grin on her face. This was the last thing I needed; I was already on edge. I waved awkwardly, shooing her away with my erratic hand gestures. Finally, she closed the curtain, what she didn't realise was I could still see her staring through the white floral nets. I jogged towards the huge maple tree in next door's front garden. The crisp yellow leaves rustled in the cooling breeze and I was sure that this tree provided sufficient camouflage from my mother's gaze.

He stared at me intently, grinning broadly. I hadn't realised until this moment how much I had missed that smile. I had to remind myself it had only been twenty-four hours since I last saw him at college. I hopped onto the back of the motorbike and forced the shiny, metallic, black helmet onto my head. It hugged snugly to my ears shutting off any and all interruptions. My thoughts on the other hand barked at me louder than ever. I buckled up the strap under my chin and threw my arms around his waist, gripping tightly and laying my head on his leather clad back. This was officially my new favourite place to be.

~~~~

'That took longer than I would have expected.' I said, while shaking out my bad case of helmet hair.

'Yeah, well I took a bit of a detour. It's your first go on a motorbike, I thought I'd really get some speed under ya.' *Should I let him know now that motorbikes scare the crap out of me?* 'Hey I'm not complaining' I fibbed, while ungraciously checking my teeth for dead insects. 'I feel so relaxed, no wonder you like just riding about.' That was yet another unnecessary fib to leave my lips, having my arms around his waist and being so close to him was amazing, the actual riding part – less so.

'I aim to please' he replied. 'It would be a pleasure to take you with me any time Miss Gracie.' His warming smile melted my heart and in that second my anxiety drifted away, as his sweet, poetic voice lulled me. I followed him up the ash gravel drive towards a hefty, tawny, stained stable-style door with large black hinges. The Alice in Wonderland style garden with its colourful overgrown daisies and ornately trimmed bushes reminded me of a scene from a fairy-tale. The sloping willow trees were decorated with pale pink flower led lights. These trees encased the fairy-tale cottage, it evoked the sensation of childhood bliss and innocence once lost. A part of me felt the impromptu desire to skip like I did when I was little. Draped up the left side of the cottage, from the pebbled pathway to the thatched style
~~~~

roof, was mounds of intricate climbing ivy. It weaved around the white-wash window frames, hanging down over the front door. Connected seamlessly onto the right side of the cottage was a renovated barn. This was no ordinary home. I didn't have long to gape in awe at my surroundings before pangs of tenseness once again plagued my already butterfly filled stomach. Before Beau could even get his key into the lock an older woman appeared and swung open the top section of the door.

'Hey, come on in! I'm Gwen by the way.' She protested kindly as I passed by her. Gwen was a slim woman with reddish, cropped hair, which made her look a lot younger than I guessed she must have been. Her deep russet eyes were friendly, knowing and oozed compassion. Her peachy coral skin was flawless, apart from the laughter lines around her eyes that highlighted her years of experience. Like Beau, Gwen took my breath away. They both possessed beautiful features on the outside and an inner allure that captured people. They shared agreeing, unspoken glances and warm half smiles; I could tell immediately they connected on a level that was foreign to me.

'Grace, I've heard so much about you from Beau. I've so been looking forward to meeting you.' She took both of my hands in hers. 'It truly is a pleasure to have you here'. I relaxed instantly, my nerves washed away by her sincerity. 'Let's go and sit down. I've made some lunch for us.' She gestured towards the large timber archway. I ran my fingers over the ink-marked lines that crept from top to bottom.

Daniel, Luke, Amy, Paul, Mark, Dotty, Robbie, Beau.

Beside each name was a height, a date and an age scrawled in delicate cursive. *Beau only just moved here?* I thought.

Beau placed his hand on the small of my back to guide me into the dining room, causing a warming surge of energy to flicker up my back to the base of my neck. Hanging high above us were black, bulky, beams and above them stretching all the way through to the kitchen were skylights. In the far corner of the converted barn there was a constructed level with a spiral staircase. Even at ground level I could see a vintage padded rocking chair, a black velvet matching futon, a dark wood side table and upon that, a silver twisted lamp. The white wall behind the overstuffed chair was decorated with a lime green mural of a gnarled tree and falling leaves. Beau ushered me over to a light oak settee and matching armchair with lime green and cream stripped scatter cushions on them. My eyes fell on the oak, glass-topped coffee table in front of me which had a set of tarot cards on it. *Tarot cards*? *Was Gwen a reader...a psychic?* Gwen walked in front of me and cleared away the cards wrapping them in some purple silk material and leaving the parcel on the edge of the table.

'I will be right back, OK?' Beau whispered wide-eyed, while standing up and entering the kitchen. I nodded; my eyes still fixated on the colossal room around me. Every angle a treat for the eyes. The gigantic stained maple wood bookcase that reached from floor to ceiling was situated next to the white Georgian fireplace. It was filled with dictionary sized books titled *'Calming your Chakras', 'Your Inner Being'* and *'Spiritual Healing'*, along with a few old, leather-bound classics for good measure. Gwen came in holding a large tray. On it was a plate of sandwiches cut into perfect triangles, a plate of cookies, a jug full of orange juice and a steaming china teapot. Beau moved and took the tray out of Gwen's hands and placed it on the table. As Gwen reached to open the bay window-curtains wider, the loose sleeve of her long-patterned dress fell back exposing her arm. An engraving of a star on her wrist caught my eye. It was odd, because it didn't look like a tattoo, but more like a burn under her skin. *I wouldn't have guessed Gwen was into body modification?*

'Grace, Beau tells me you also study photography?'

'Yes, amongst a collection of other subjects. I'm more of a fan of portrait photography though.' She assessed me with an attentive gaze, the silence growing in length and making me fidget. 'This is a lovely house, Gwen.'

'Why thank you.' I tried not to look at the wrapped cards on the table, fearing that my questions about them may be considered rude, but it was too late.

'Do you read tarot cards, Gwen? Is that what you do?' It was immediately clear to us all that the silence, however short, was making me uncomfortable. Beau cleared his throat, which stirred an answer from Gwen.

'There are many names for what I do Grace, medium, clairvoyant, tarot reader, psychic. What I offer is a form of emotional therapy. People can find life very difficult at times, unexplainable moments can alter their lives forever. I aim to help others in finding peace. People are convinced that feelings and emotions are personal, they don't like to share the heartache which is causing them to suffer. My aim is to try and ease as much suffering as is possible, with healing.'

'It must be very rewarding,' I said with genuine admiration.

'Is it weird for you, I mean the medium stuff? I can't imagine the people of Gallows Wood being very understanding.'

'You would be surprised. If only people knew the real history of our sleepy little town. My gift, as it is, is only a nibble into the actual cake. You should meet old lady Doris, who lives on the colourful little houseboat just off Tanner Dock. She's a witch. Her power reaches far greater than mine.' She took a sip of her tea and offered me a biscuit, allowing me a second to take in all the new information.

'You will have to come along to one of our...gatherings.' Her pause fed my curiosity, but caused Beau to roll his eyes.

'Really Gwen, she's only been here for ten minutes and you're already planning on introducing her to the nut job nine.'

'Don't sass me boy.' She tried to sound stern but instead laughed which made him grin.

'Gatherings?' I mused.

'You know, Wicca, prayers, spells. Our version of wine night. We cover quite a lot. I think you should come. It will mean Beau has to think up a new nickname for us, inevitably fuelling some much-needed brainpower. *'Gwen – 1, Beau – 0*

'Ha, ha, ha' Beau said slowly, oozing sarcasm.

'Gwen, how long have you been a foster mother?' I asked between sips of my home-made orange juice.

'Well, my first son Daniel arrived when he was just eight months old, and now he's twenty-four.' Gwen smiled, memories tickling at her laughter lines around her eyes. 'He's all grown up now with a young wife too, Jenna. They moved up to Scotland with their baby daughter Megan a few months ago.' She gestured towards the hallway table behind me; the oversized swan-shaped lamp was propping up a delicately embellished silver frame with a picture in it that must have been Daniel and his family. I scanned over the numerous silver frames that sat around that one.

'There are so many pictures. How many children have you fostered Gwen?'

'Beau is my twelfth. I've been very lucky with my kids; all have made me proud – this one especially.' She nodded towards Beau.

'Do you get to see them much?'

'Not as much as I would like. We do get together twice a year though and I'm constantly getting updates, cards, pictures and letters. The kid's gifts are the best though. Robbie's little girl Ava is destined to be an artist.

'How did you manage it on your own?' I questioned lightly.

'Well, it was hard at times, exhausting even...but I felt my kids came to be with me for a reason. It was destined that I should become their mother at that awful time in their young lives.' She pondered her words silently for a moment with a faraway expression.

'Anyway, just when I thought I was getting too old and useless, I was blessed with Beau. He's been with me for...I think...four years now.' Beau confirmed her remark with a nod and a warm grin.

'Now....I think that's more than enough about me Grace, how about you, do you have any siblings?'

'Just one, my brother Cary.'

'Grace and Cary, interesting names.'

'Yeah my Mum and Dad had a thing for the film *To Catch A Thief,* it was their favourite, they saw it every time their anniversary rolled around.' Suddenly an unmistakeable stab of sadness pierced my chest. Since meeting Beau, I had barely found time to stoke the flames of my sadness.

'What about your parents, what do they do?'

'My Dad...' I felt myself choking up with a tear teetering in the corner of my eye. My throat was bone dry. *Liquid, any liquid would be great right now!* The air I inhaled scrapped along my bare windpipe as I fumbled with my words. Over the years I had had a fair bit of practise when it came to not crying about my Dad, but on some occasions, today being one of them, the sadness just crept up on me out of nowhere. Beau, who seemed to be growing even more attuned to my feelings, could sense the change in me, so he quickly changed the subject. It was a habit he was developing, saving me from emotionally painful situations. The day flew by. As the warm sun crept in through the bay windows, splaying itself across the beige wool rug beneath my feet, it finally descended behind the grassy hilltops of Gallows Woods and out of sight. Our lunch was coming to an end.

~~~~

'I'll see you again soon sweetheart, I hope.' Gwen smiled broadly, hugging me tightly. Her light comforting taps on my back as we embraced only further fuelled the feelings I had been experiencing; it was as if I had known her for years rather than hours.

'If I promise to bring her back will you let her go?' Beau teased.

'I'm sorry my dear' she chuckled, as she took a step back on a long sigh. 'Sometimes we just need a hug I guess.'

'I'll drop you home' Beau said softly, his fingers pushing some stray curls behind my ear, his fingers resting on my neck a little longer than they needed to.

'It's OK, I can walk, and it's really not that far'. Being able to breathe properly when I was with Beau, wasn't the easiest of tasks. At the best of times, it only took one of his smiles to throw me off balance and send my heart racing. I certainly didn't need another bike trip.

'I'll leave you two to it. I've got to get the washing in, looks like rain.' Gwen mused as she passed me an umbrella from
~~~~

under the coat rack. As I looked up at the calming sky, which was flushed with the last remnants of yellows and reds, I glanced back at Gwen, who responded with an astute wink. She made her way through the kitchen to the back door and shut it carefully behind her, a wicker washing basket propped under one arm.

THIRTEEN

ജ്ഞ

'I really don't like the thought of you walking back alone.' he said, worriedly peering out into the night sky as the street lamps pinged to life. The stress was clear on his handsome face as he struggled internally against his need to make sure I was safe at all times and allowing me to do as I please. His concern vibrated through his body, raising his hand up to the base of his neck whilst he contemplated how to get me to see sense without appearing overwhelming. I climbed onto my tiptoes and moved in to kiss his cheek. Before I could comprehend what had happened, I was cradled in Beau's herculean arms. I could no longer feel the floor and everything around me swept into a blur. His face was the only thing that was clear. Well, that and his need for me. His lips were soft and warm. I felt the nerves around my spine tingle in a sensation overload, my jelly legs threatening to buckle beneath my weight. As though my body had relayed the trouble it was having to him, Beau's left hand supported my back, intensifying the quiver as it reached the base. His right hand slid provocatively up my neck and his thumb stroked my chin. As his touch lingered, he pulled his lips briefly from mine, panting deeply as he considered his next move. His cool minty breath grazed my face as I too fought to control the pounding in my chest. Even in this heady state, we couldn't bear to be separated. He dipped his head back down to me, silently asking for permission to once again place his lips upon mine. No words were necessary. I placed my arms around his waist settling my palms along the middle of his back, pulling his body into mine and closing the space between us. His hand made its way behind my ear and into my hair, tousling it.

The strong urge to rip his clothes off was looming; I didn't know how much more I could take. He pulled his lips away from mine, my oxygen filled freedom unwanted but necessary. I kept my eyes shut tightly as I lingered in the moment, held there by an invisible force. My lips continued to push forward for a second, following his, the deep need to close the cold growing space between us. Fighting to quench his own needs, his yielding lips found my neck, as he began to pull me upright. His balmy, sweet breath caressed my skin. As I felt the ground beneath me and the tingling subsided, he pulled me close into his chest. His heartbeat was frantic. As I peered up at his face, I was greeted with a smile that I would always fondly remember as *'my smile'*. His eyes sparkled like diamonds, hypnotising me, the ability to look anywhere else but in those beautiful blue pools impossible. I composed myself enough to stand on my own.

'If you think that's going to convince me to accept your lift home, you're mistaken. After that, I need the walk home.' His smile was unmoving, as was mine.

'Don't be a stranger.' he chortled softly as he caught his breath.

'Very doubtful.' I agreed. I put one foot in front of the other down the path, my movements hesitant as I strolled away from him. Once I was sure the warmth from his touch and the spell he had me under had subsided, or as much as it ever could I turned and smiled. Walking away from him was hard but I knew that however much I wanted to stay bound in the comfort of his hold, I needed time; time to allow my emotions to steady, for my thoughts to return to normal.

One thing I was sure of though; a kiss like that meant forever.

I strolled home without a care in the world and a skip in my step. As I turned the corner leading onto my road, I felt something hit my cheek from above. I glanced up above me, within a moment the heavens opened up and a waterfall of rain pelted at the concrete around me, hard and fast. All I could do was grin and picture Gwen's knowing face as the lukewarm rain soaked through my clothes. I smiled and picked up my once leisurely pace and ran towards my driveway with Gwen's unopened umbrella still clutched in my hand. Nothing could spoil this mood, not even torrential rain.

I rushed through the front door with little regard as to the racket I was making. Mum was washing up in the kitchen and Cary was sitting crossed legged, propped up against the sofa, intently reading the dictionary – crazily for fun it seemed.

'Hey honey, you look happy' Mum stated as she threw a mauve stripped tea towel over her shoulder.

'I am actually.'

'Well, I don't think I even have to ask why you're so happy.' We exchanged a look of understanding.

'Do you fancy telling me why you look like Santa Clause on speed, because I haven't got a clue?' Cary added with a smirk as he barged past me towards the sink. I ignored his remark and headed straight for the stairs. Not even Cary could ruin my mood it would seem.

FOURTEEN

ഌ ര

I took my usual seat next to Beau. Mr Sanders was doing his usual thing and babbling on incessantly, oblivious to everyone doing their own thing. *'WE NEED TO TALK. LUNCH?'* I scribbled onto the page of my workbook. I ripped the corner free from the page and folded it in half, sliding it across to Beau. *'Sure x'* was his reply. Today is the day, I will find out what makes Beau tick. However strange and extraordinary it is, I want to know.

'Hey you.' Beau whispered into my ear from behind me. His proximity like a needed drug for my soul. My body suddenly awake and interested.

'Do you want to go and sit behind the PE hall...so we can talk?' I asked, my voice stumbling towards the end. I never was one for bluffing. My poker face looked like I had learnt it from a Barney prime time special on how to play snap.

'Yeah, sure, I think it's about time we had *a talk*. There are a few things I've wanted to tell you.' Beau grasped my bag strap and threw it over his shoulder. 'Lunch lady?' Beau held out a wrapped quarter pounder. Never one to say no to free food, I of course accepted.

'Thanks' I beamed. We sat down underneath the big oak tree alone, with only the distant, chaotic noise of Claynor Ray's finest football team, The Eagles, as a mood filler. I had initiated this meeting, but I had absolutely no clue how to kick off the conversation. *Hello awkward moment!* I shoved the burger in my mouth and looked like a horse chewing on a carrot as my lips smacked together unpleasantly.

'You finish that Grace, and I'll start.' He giggled, but sadly this didn't last. In a matter of moments his mood had catapulted past carefree with a one-way ticket to conflicted. He searched for the words, his hand fumbling through the hair at the nape of his neck as his brain went into overtime. 'I trust you Grace, more then I think you know. I don't usually get this close to people. I know you understand what Gwen does, but do you believe it?' He rushed his words and kept his stare fixed on the grass beneath us as he tugged nervously at the fraying denim patch on the knee of his Levi's.

'Look at me.' I placed my thumb and forefinger on his chin, forcing him to look squarely into my face. His shoulders sagged and with a deep breath his apprehension disintegrated. I smiled and edged closer to him. 'It's all very new to me. When my Dad died, I wanted nothing more than to believe he was with me.'

'Well, that in a roundabout way is exactly why I don't get close to people.' His eyes again assessed the grass beneath us.

'Beau, what are you getting at? You can trust me, just tell me what it is.' I pulled his face up to concentrate on mine again. Our eye contact didn't last long. Whatever it was that he feared to tell me must have been big. This cat and mouse game had me confused. When I touched him, I could feel the connection build, a reminder of the happy place he had found with me, but as soon as he broke free of my hold, apprehension swamped his handsome face and his toned body heaved, fraught with the stress of his untold secret. 'I am here, I am listening. Talk to me Beau, please.'

'I can see sp....s' he mumbled.

'Speak up' I urged.

'I can see spirits.' He blurted, watching me for a response, his face filled with sadness now. I definitely heard that one. All I could muster was a daft look of amazement and utter disbelief.

'Huh?' was the only word my perplexed brain could manage as I debated whether I had in fact heard him correctly, maybe it meant something else entirely.

'Spirits, ghosts, you know dead people!' he shouted at me as he tore lumps of grass out of the ground. His secret was no longer a secret, every moment that it hung there in the air between us appeared to further torture him. I couldn't watch him like that, it hurt me at my very core.

'OK. In an odd way this probably explains a lot.' I answered as cheerfully as I could. It took a few moments for me to piece together all the questionable instances that I had experienced with Beau. *Light bulb moment!* 'So, your conversation with mid-air in the English class?' I prompted. He nodded silently with his eyes focused anywhere but on mine. 'My very painful encounter with the thing in the darkroom?' He nodded again mutely. I trailed off after that and before Beau could confirm my question with another nod, I put my hand up to stop him. 'So, you're like a superhero, with some voodoo mind trick thing going on?' I laughed uneasily, trying and failing to mend the break that was threatening to part us.

'I'm no superhero, more like super weirdo.' For the first time Beau's age and vulnerability was shining brightly in front of me. He was scared.

'Right, let's slow this down a bit. I wasn't expecting this. Do they look like extras from Dawn of the Dead? Or maybe they are more like Amityville Horror. Maybe they just look the same as usual, just see through, like Casper?' I was now just enthusiastically chatting away to myself as the possibilities came in their hundreds.

'I've just told you I can see ghosts, like real dead people and you're more intrigued about whether Hollywood's visual effects teams were accurate when making some low budget horror film!'

'Whoa! Hold your horses, low budget is a bit of a harsh statement! I think Classics was the word you were looking for. Would you rather I had no interest at all and ran about calling you a nut job?'

'You wouldn't dare' he grinned slyly. The tension was slowly fading. He was relaxing finally. He was coming back to me, slowly but surely.

'Oh, you know me too well Beau, of course I wouldn't do that. If you say that's what you can do, I believe you, unconditionally.' I was surprised how much I truly meant what I was saying. It freaked me out a little sure, but if anything, what I felt most was a case of morbid intrigue.

'When someone dies, they appear how they looked when their soul left their body. You die in the Antarctic; your spirit looks like an ice-pole. Car crash, bloody mess, for example.'

'I'm guessing that would be the same case if someone was bludgeoned to death or hacked into pieces?' I added a little too enthusiastically.

'Well I don't get floating body parts visiting me asking for my help, if that's what you're getting at.'

'What do you mean asking for help?'

'I've never really known how it works. I'm connected with their thoughts, feelings and emotions somehow. I sometimes get impressions and mental snapshots that not even they are still in touch with. Over time I became more sensitive to all this and it got a lot easier to interpret. Not as easy to explain to an outsider though it seems.'

'I don't know, you seem to be doing a pretty good job.'

'There is a very thin barrier separating our world and theirs. We are bound by time, morals, rules, laws and so on, they are not. They have no concept of time, they can decide and do whatever they choose to with no ramifications. Most spirits want to give a message to a loved one, but there are a few that have other ideas.'

'How comes you can see them?'

'I'm what you call awoken.'

'You're what now?' I queried, scooting closer to him and lowering my voice as people passed us.

'When my parents died, I was surrounded by death. I was tainted by it, imprinted with something that would enable spirits to be able to talk to me - for me to help them. When I was awoken it took me a while to understand and accept my gift. As I got older, especially when I met Gwen, I realised how very different I was. Very few people can see and talk to spirits like I can.' He searched for my expression.

'So, to be awoken like you, someone has to be touched by death?'

'In my case, yes. But there is a lot that I don't know. Some people are born with their gifts, some people steal others gifts, some people inherit their gifts. It's all very complicated.' There was a long deafening silence. Now was the time to decide – to stay or to go?

'What are you thinking Grace?'

What wasn't I thinking? My brain was like a washing machine, muddled jumbles of information continuously circling, around and around. 'Where do I come into all this?' I urged uneasily, plucking it from the sodden pile of questions that I had, although I did secretly fear another mind-altering revelation as silence engulfed us once again.

'Grace, don't you find it a little strange all the things that have happened to you since we met? Your mind has opened and that means they will use you to get to me. At this point you are safer knowing my secret. Spirits, much like us, evolve; the stronger they get, the more they can affect you. Like us there's good and bad. When a spirit is ripped from their human existence without warning it can cause them to become increasingly bitter and tormented, they feed off our fear and energy.'

'Does this mean that witches, vampires and werewolves exist then?' The shock had clearly set in. My sanity had officially packed its bags. I was completely delusional!

'I don't know about any of that Stephen King stuff but if my gift has shown me anything, it's that nothing is impossible.'

'Beau, is this why you've had so many problems with your other foster homes?' I was enjoying this openness side of Beau, with every question I asked he visibly relaxed a little more. His face light, his eyes no longer hooded and coloured with despair.

'Yeah, the spirits used to ask me to do things. They were desperate for me to finish off what they didn't get to do before they died. Word spread and got back to my foster parents. Hearing about what I'd been doing did not make them happy. So I just stopped listening – I learnt the hard way that this just pisses the spirits off. I didn't know it then, but it was my job to help them crossover.'

'Crossover?'

'Yeah, like send them into the light, escort them to the tunnel of life, pass them over into heaven. There really are a lot of terms for it.'

'What about what happened in photography class, when I fell over and you went to catch me. Was that a ghost thing?' My memories whizzed by on fast forward as I recollected those strange, questionable instances that we had shared again; the unnatural things that I had experienced.

'Well not so much ghost related as emotion related. Sometimes when someone has experienced devastating heartache and I touch them; a sort of ripple effect starts. It's like electricity, it burns through me - all their pain, the torture they have felt and hold on to passes through me - sometimes its unbearable.' he said while rubbing his temple at the memory. It really was my fault he was in pain, I did that to him because I *felt* too much; my sadness was to blame. Reading my grave expression, he placed his hand in mine and stroked my palm with his index finger.

'How come you can touch me now?'

'I understand your pain and grief a lot more now. Sometimes I still feel a twinge but it's not as painful....as before.'

A twinge, so being with me is still hurting him? I retracted my hand quickly. I was hurt but I didn't know why. It wasn't his fault I had a mountain of emotional baggage. 'So, it's like you're allergic to me?' The sadness stuck in the back of my throat uncomfortably like a trapped boiled sweet.

'I'm not allergic to you, I'm just in tune with your emotions and my body reacts.'

'Like an allergy then!' I continued pushing my point like a petulant child. Beau took my hand in his and pulled it up to his soft lips.

'Definitely not allergic' He beamed and with that ever so smooth move so did I, wholeheartedly. I glanced out onto the empty gardens and suddenly my face fell. With Beau's disclosure, a haunting realisation hit me. Everything around me slipped into complete darkness. She was all that I could focus on. I tried to assure myself that my eyes were lying to me - surely it was a figment of my imagination. Her troubled stare bore into me as she moved towards me, her heels clicking unsteadily on the pavement. Her body contorted with every laboured step. One moment there, one moment gone, until the space between us was filled. The severely jagged gash on her throat streamed rouge blood down her dress as she attempted to speak – this was a sight I wasn't overjoyed to see the first time let alone the second.

Then there was nothing.

'She's free!' she whispered from behind me, her voice pained and hoarse. Then there she was, before my very eyes. She threw her head back exposing her slit throat and screamed, emitting a gargled sound that rung in my ears incessantly, shaking me to my core.

'Grace, are you OK? Grace what's going on?' His voice was distant for a second or two. Using it as an anchor I swiftly slipped back to reality, to him.

'I'm fine' I assured him. I was in fact anything other than fine.

'You're as white as a sheet, you're sweating. What's wrong? Tell me!' He demanded rubbing at my arms to get some heat into me. Usually his concern was welcomed. It was a side of him that fuelled my attraction for him, but for now, at this moment, I needed to leave and fast!

'Is it OK if we meet up tomorrow, I'm really not feeling too well?'

'Of course. Are you sure you're OK?'

Before I spilled the beans and let loose my crippling neurosis, I kissed him on the cheek, heading down the hill to the main building. My legs felt cumbersome as the incline of the hill changed. My head was a complete mess as a torrent of emotions and thoughts chipped away at my composure.

AWOKEN *Billie Jade Kermack*

The once beautifully blue, serene skies were now shrouded with morbidity and apprehension. I pushed what I had seen to the back of my mind. I couldn't explain it. If I was honest, I didn't *want* to explain it.

Where did normality end and the unthinkable begin?

FIFTEEN

ᘓᘐ

Once Beau had opened his world up to me it was hard to switch it off. Although an air of trepidation surrounded me, I was curious to know everything. We sat in my car with chicken wraps in one hand and a Styrofoam cup filled with scalding tea in the other. The steam on the windows cocooned us in and the low hum of the radio gave the atmosphere a homely feeling, like something right out of an advert for good living. 'If you think I'm prying, tell me to shut up, but what's the strangest encounter you've had with a spirit?' Beau looked at me and laughed. There was a short silence. 'Well you haven't told me to shut up yet so at least that's a start.' I said under my breath as I took a sip of my tea. *Whoa that is bloody boiling, my tongue is on fire!* Fighting the urge to spit the hot liquid all over the windscreen, I made sure Beau wasn't looking at me then uncouthly dribbled the tea back into the cup.

'You are much pushier then you were yesterday!' Beau teased. I glanced at him doe-eyed from beneath my long lashes edging for an answer.

'Right. My strangest encounter' he mused, visibly sorting through what I would assume was a lifetime of crazy stories. 'I must have been about fourteen. I was on my third secondary school by then and I was well on my way to learning how to ignore the spirits...for most of the time at least. They can be really adamant when they want to be. I was making my way to class and I heard barking, but I couldn't see a dog anywhere. I shrugged it off and went about my business. Throughout the day I heard it everywhere I went. No one else seemed to be able to hear it. I looked down at my feet and there was a young girl, she was about eight I'd guess.'

'Was she the one barking?' I asked transfixed as I edged in a little closer to him still snacking on my wrap.

'Yes. She couldn't talk and she was running about on all fours. I was completely baffled. She was wearing a long nightshirt with dancing clowns all over it, like a hospital gown. Her hair was tangled and dirty. She looked petrified, so I backed off a little.' I couldn't help but notice the distress in his eyes as the memories came back to him thick and fast. His soft inviting lips as they recounted each thought and feeling. 'She stayed by my side for the rest of the day. Usually I'd give anything to block out the voice of my science teacher but the barking soon became unbearable. I scoured the net for two days after that and used every search engine and information file I could think of. Before long I got lucky. I found a medical report attached to some random site about England's strangest happenings.'

'The young girl was found abandoned in the north region of the Scottish Highlands by a couple on a nearby nature walk. She was unresponsive and clearly frightened as they approached her. The female civilian was later treated for a severe bite wound from the girl at Mercy Crown hospital. It is not clear when or why the girl was abandoned. With reference to her feral behaviour and lack of communication abilities we can determine that this is the only life she has known.

Our studies and a select few of the UK's best psychologists have discovered, through the use of various tests, that this girl had no comprehension of the normal day-to-day life.

The girl has been named Maisy by our staff here at Clover Hill. Maisy spent her first two days sleeping on the floor of her room and was found on two separate occasions rummaging for food in the cafeteria waste disposal.

What our staff did not know unfortunately led to the untimely death of Maisy. An autopsy by our medical examiner has confirmed what we had feared. Before being discovered Maisy had ingested a high quantity of rare poisonous berries aptly named 'locan murderana'. This led to her passing. Sixty-two hours after arriving at our facility Maisy was found huddled under her bed with no heartbeat. Her liver temperature indicated that time of death was in the early hours of June 12th.'

'There was also a photo with the article. Once I had put two-and-two together it was pretty straightforward from there.'

'So how could you help her? You can't talk dog language as well can you?' I smiled cockily, but for a brief moment considered it as a possibility.

'Ha, bloody ha Grace. I did the only thing I could think to do.'

'And...' I prompted. Beau smiled, tight-lipped, enjoying my desperation to hear the end of his story, quenching my hope for a happily ever after.

'I led her to the RSPCA.' He was calm. I was utterly perplexed.

'You are joking, right?' I nudged hoping for a happier ending to Maisy's story.

'I'm not joking but it isn't as cruel as it sounds, I wanted to help her. I knew she wanted to be in an environment she knew, that was the only place that made sense. I went back after a few weeks and Maisy was still there but this time something was different. She acknowledged me with a beaming smile. She sat on the floor cross legged stroking a black Labrador. She approached me, her smile firm. She said thank you and put her arms around my waist. She told me she understood what had happened to her and that she was ready to begin her new life as this person. She asked me what her name was and that was it. As quick as she had come into my life, she was gone.'

'That is amazing.' I sat in awe of him and his gift, dreamily smitten for a few moments. The bell rang for fifth period and shocked me out of my dazed state.

'I'm late for English, but do you fancy going over to the café later?'

'With you Miss Gracie, any day. I'll meet you over there.' He stepped out of the car and gestured towards the science building and loaded my books from the back seat into his arms.

'Ladies first' he said as we approached the white pillared entrance.

'Do you want to give me my books then? I doubt they'll be of any use to you.'

'Now what sort of gentleman would I be if I didn't escort you to your class?'

Something was up. I'm the first to admit that he is brilliant, gorgeous and considerate but that was a little too Jane Eyre for my liking. Then.... *light bulb moment!*

'Your class is right next door to mine isn't it?' I questioned suspiciously.

'Yes, but I would have done it anyway' he chortled. I slapped his back playfully, grabbed the remainder of my tea and continued after him.

SIXTEEN

ꕥ

I strode down the bustling hallway with a jovial skip to my step, the mundane world of my fellow students around me a blur of indescribable colours and actions. I searched for his face and found it almost immediately. Suddenly the ability to walk evaded me, stopping me in my tracks, my feet now firmly planted on the grubby yellow floor. He rested his foot on the lockers behind him and greeted me with that smile that made me melt. A surprising concoction of over-confidence and self-assurance consumed me and charged my leg muscles back to life.

'Hey Superman, missed me much?' I smiled as I mischievously tugged at his shirtsleeve.

'Firstly, I always miss you Miss Gracie and secondly, I'm more Forest Gump then Superman, but thanks for the ego boost.'

'Why are you waiting here?' Beau pointed towards his locker; I could see exactly why he was giving his locker a wide birth. Sandra Mason was the loosest girl in college and was now on her eighth boyfriend of this term. Unfortunately for Beau, it was in front of his locker that they were forcibly sharing their feelings. They locked lips in a way that reminded me of a scene from Alien. In a blink of an eye Sandra had dragged her unsuspecting victim towards the girl's toilets and Beau's locker was clear. Beau broke out into a light jog fearing Sandra's return.

'Run Forest, run!' I shouted out in my best southern American accent. It was lucky I had humour; accents were most definitely not my thing.

'Ha, ha, smart arse' he retorted loudly above the noise of the stragglers passing us by in the hallway. I strolled through the crowds to get to Beau. By the time I had reached him everyone had dispersed and with the pound of classroom doors closing around us, we were finally alone. Just how I liked it. I pulled at his t-shirt closing the space between us with a cheeky grin on my face. For the first time, it was Beau who looked surprised. *Kiss him, kiss him!* my inner bitch demanded as she crossed her legs on her high-backed wicker chair. *I think I need a cold shower* she added fanning herself with her hand.

'Well Mr Gump, you are my Superman.' With that, Beau placed his hand on my back and pulled me into the comfort of his body. Every kiss with Beau felt like the first. A heady, intoxicating feeling surged aimlessly through me, fuelling my desires as our lips met. Every breath in my body evaporated as my stomach flew into my chest and my knees weakened. I opened my eyes and swooned slightly like a love-struck teenager idolising a superstar. Beau was everything to me and all I needed as proof was that unusual skip that interrupted the natural rhythm of my heartbeat.

'Well Superman's hungry, fancy grabbing something to eat?' he said whilst running his hand down to my waist. I flicked my hair animatedly and threw him my best heroine pout.

'Well Superman, get your cape and those fetching little yellow boots because Lois Lane could murder a bacon sandwich.'

'Well Lois, just so you know, Superman's boots are actually red, and before you start, every man in the world knows that fact.' The seriousness of the subject crept at the sides of his smile.

'If you say so' I teased. What is it with boys and comic book heroes? The image in my head of his muscles rippling beneath Lycra, with a mask shadowing those beautiful crystal blue eyes, caused a jolt to stampede a little south of my stomach, an aching that I knew would only grow the more time I spent with him.

~~~~

As he strolled towards me his presence commanded the attention of every woman in the room; luckily, I was used to this now. I watched his lips closely, hanging on his every word as my mind begun to wander. I blushed as that nagging ache throbbed. My need to touch him was all I could think about and that southward tug in my stomach was not helping me to relax.

'Are you OK, you look flushed?'

'Yeah, fine' I said, dabbing my napkin at my forehead.

'Grace, fancy playing twenty questions? It's a brilliant way for me to get to know absolutely everything about you. You know all of my deepest darkest secrets. The only rule is, you have to answer them truthfully. Deal?'

'Right, so what do I get out of it?'

'I'll buy you the biggest chunk of Tottenham cake on that stand.' He gestured gingerly towards the seven-tiered
~~~~

shelving unit that had about thirty different varieties of cakes and cookies crammed onto it.

'What makes you think I like Tottenham cake?'

'Well do you?'

'Yes, actually it's my favourite, smart-arse. You're pretty good at this guessing malarkey. Are you sure you need twenty questions?'

'I probably don't NEED twenty questions but I know I WANT them' he emphasised smirking at me.

'Go for it!' I prompted as I tried to arrange my best poker face, you know, the one that I don't possess.

'Firstly, what would you say is your honest opinion of me?' I suddenly feared this line of questioning and we were only on question one.

'Well I think you're handsome, smart and easy to talk to.' He was clearly chuffed at my answer. I was just as pleased I had come out of question one unscathed.

'Question number two. How much do you wish you hadn't agreed to this game?'

'A LOT!' I answered. It was impossible not to laugh along with him, even when I was the butt of the joke.

'Question number three.' He held on to the letter *e* for a second as his next words hung uncomfortably in his throat.

'How many boyfriends have you had?' He grinned at me squirming in my seat with way too much pleasure. I revised the answer in my head.

'None.' I jumped in quickly, trying my darndest to bring about question four.

'Isn't it strange that I don't believe you? Remember the rules of the game Gracie.'

'Is that question four?' I asked. He scowled a little with a wry smile etched on his face.

'OK, OK. Now that I come to think about it there was one, Jason Adams, he was my first boyfriend. If you can call him that, it lasted all of four days. I was about thirteen, I think. My strongest memory of him was the fact that he had a mouth full of shiny metal bars. He moved away a year or so later to Devon, no wait, Cornwall, actually come to think of it maybe it was The Isle of Wight, I'm not too great with the details. I really should pay more attention to what people tell me. After that I never really met anyone I liked, I mean Jason, the half boy, half terminator, was my first kiss, which would probably put any girl off dating.' *And breathe!* 'So how many girlfriends have you had?' I toyed.

'These are my twenty questions Grace, not yours.' he replied playfully, dodging the subject entirely. The questions continued. By the end he knew my favourite food, colour, animal, month of the year, film, actor, my shoe size and a load more information that he stated was imperative, *need to know information.*

'Last question Miss Gracie. Firstly though, have I told you how stunning you look under pressure?' Here came the dreaded blushing again as my top felt three sizes too small, the all too familiar skip in my chest catching in my throat. 'Right question twenty, are you in...'

My phone rung loudly as I fought with the buckles on my bag. I searched frantically through the mess, internally chastising the interruption. I finally grabbed the phone and ***MUM*** flashed up on the screen. I looked up and beyond the floor to ceiling glass window, the weak light of day had set and the sky was now engulfed by sable, murky clouds. The luminous yellow glow of the street lamps bounced off of the café windows. *How long have we been talking?*

SEVENTEEN

ꕤ

'Hiya Mum.' I tried desperately to sound as relaxed as was humanly possible. In no way did it soften the blow.

'Don't you *hiya Mum* me, where the hell are you?' she screeched down the phone penetrating not only my eardrum but also the eardrums of the surrounding patrons. All of which now had their eyes fixed squarely on me.

'I'm just out with a friend, we just had some lunch. Time just kind of ran away from me. I'm so sorry I worried you.' At that very second it occurred to me that I was being sincere, I really *was* sorry that I had worried her. All I could hear was silence. It must have blindsided her that I wasn't arguing back, or resorting to hanging up on her as I would usually.

'Well OK.' she mumbled, unable to think of a response. This was unfamiliar territory for the both of us.

'I love you Mum; I'll be home soon.' It felt calming just to say those words to my mum, she deserved to hear it every once in a while.

'Oh, OK love, see you soon.' I put the phone down and returned it to my bag. I felt like me and Mum had finally moved forward a step. It was a warm but unknown feeling.

'She really does worry about you.' I glanced over at Beau. I felt deflated. I didn't want to be apart from Beau but my eyes were heavy and I could have passed out there and then. Beau took my camera bag off my shoulder placed it over his head, grasping my hand tightly in his. As I peered up at him, I felt tremendously content.

'Hey spaceman.' Beau waved his free hand in front of my face. 'You always seem to be at war with your brain, what goes through that head of yours all the time?'

'Wouldn't you like to know' I teased.

'I reckon I could muster up another twenty questions, if you're game?' he said cheekily with his eyebrows raised. As Beau lifted his rucksack, he ended up pulling the chair along with it, sending his bag and its contents onto the floor. Helping him get his stuff back into his bag I saw something that stopped me in my tracks. It was clear by how fast Beau reached my side that he realised what it was I had noticed. I rushed to the A4 graphic print sketchbook and held it tightly to my chest as though it was made of gold. The DC comics that still littered the floor made Beau's temperature rise and his blood rush to his sheepish face. 'Wow, I'd never have guessed you were into comics Beau.'

'They are not comics, they are graphic novels!' he enthused as he shoved them back in his bag.

'Hey, don't be embarrassed, I played with Barbie's until I was fourteen.' As soon as the damning words left my mouth, I regretted them. *There should be a medicine to cure this - speaking before you process a thought will always get you in trouble.* In an effort to console Beau I had released a secret that I had managed to keep to myself for three long years; not even Amelia knew about my prolonged Ken and Barbie phase. At that moment I felt like curling up into the foetal position and dying right there and then. Mortified didn't feel like enough of a word to even come close to describing how I was feeling at that moment.

'Well it seems my graphic novels aren't so funny now, huh?' Beau was elated, the smile across his face that stretched from ear to ear with glee and satisfaction. Another thing I loved about Beau, even when he was teasing you (and enjoying it a little too much sometimes I might add), he still made you feel special. He still let me know with his smile that he cared for me, which made the torture fun.

'Hey Superman I may have enjoyed the odd time of dressing up Barbie...'

'And Ken, don't forget him.'

'Yes, and Ken, thanks for that Mr. Memory, helpful as always' I jeered oozing sarcasm. 'They also had a luxurious dream house and a pool if we're getting into details' I smirked. 'But I think that we have to get you over your delusions, they are comics and usually enjoyed by eight-year olds.' I placated condescendingly like an adult would a child, the happiness on my face firm and unmoving. *Grace-2, Beau-2*. As though locked in a fierce battle on a chessboard, we both waited in silence for the other to make a final blow move that would crown one of us the champion.

'Call it even?' he whispered with a coy wink. I nodded and agreed. In that moment I hoped there would be many more of these battles. I helped load the other comics (*sorry, graphic novels*) onto the table and realised I still had Beau's sketch book clutched securely in my hand. I flipped it open to the first page and then on through each page gazing at Beau's work. 'Beau these are really great.'

'They're just sketches.' He tried in vain to grab the book away from me.

'The detail is amazing.' I gently ran my fingers over the indentations the pencil had made on the paper and mused in awe at the in-depth detail.

'What would you know?' This was the first time I had ever seen Beau so defensive. His face was taught and unresponsive. I handed the sketchbook back to Beau willingly and after a second or two he relaxed back into himself and the despondent expression that had plagued his beautiful face disappeared. He pulled me towards him and kissed my cheek fervently as his hand settled on my neck. 'Thanks'. The cool night breeze through the open door woke me up instantly as it lapped at my hair and wafted in my face. 'After you madam.' I looked at him and curtsied. We took the short walk to my car through the dimly lit car park and the black cast iron security gates of the college grounds. He kissed my head lightly, not letting go of my face. I glanced up at him longingly, desperately and silently pleading with him not to let me go. Leaving him was getting much harder to handle. 'Until tomorrow' he cooed.

'Do you want a lift home?' I asked, hoping for just a few moments more with him. He shot a quick look into my back seat and took a wary step back.

'No thanks, I can walk, it's a nice night.'

'It may be a bit of a mess but...' I began defensively. *Beau the materialistic type – who'd have thought?*

'It's not that' he interrupted.

'It's only just occurred to me that you've never been in my car. It's like it's radioactive to you or something' I said.

'I've been in your car...yesterday in fact, if I remember rightly. If the rubbish on the floor didn't bother me then it wouldn't bother me now!' he retorted with an unwelcome snigger.

'So why don't you want a ride? Somewhere better to be maybe? What, my old rust bucket isn't good enough anymore?' My voice was a high-pitched squeal and left little precious breathing time. A crazy and unsuspecting mottled green wash of bunny boiler jealously appeared to pounce on me from out of nowhere, taking both Beau and I by complete surprise.

'Hey Annie Wilkes, how about you dial down the crazy a couple of notches.' Beau reached out and rubbed my arms. The tension dissipated into a cooling pool around me as his skilful fingertips kneaded out the tension in my shoulders. *Why do I react like that around him?*

'You see something, don't you?' I glanced at Beau and then into the back window of my car. My face fell along with my stomach. *Why hadn't I thought of this before?* He looked at me intensely, battling with the choice of telling me the truth or fabricating a lie that would be easier for me to handle.

'I'm guessing you got this car second hand?'

'How did you come to that conclusion. Was it the rust that's covering pretty much every visible speck of metal or the fact that it's being held together with duct tape?' I retorted sardonically. I had subconsciously realised the truth and my not so witty attempt at sarcasm was my defence mechanism.

It wasn't making me feel any more at ease though, realisation hit me with a blow that resembled a tyre iron to my head.

'Well the previous owner didn't really...'

'Didn't really what?' I probed, hesitantly taking a few steps away from the car. Beau was silent. 'Beau, didn't really what?' I pressed.

'Leave' Beau answered finally in a hushed voice. I began to whisper, suddenly very aware that someone or something else was with us.

'You mean to tell me that whoever owned my car before me, is still in it? You're kidding me, right? There is no way...How can I drive? What the hell am I going to do now?' I yelled. So I was a little shook up – shoot me!

'Yes, he is definitely in the car and he definitely doesn't want to leave.'

'Well make him leave, I love this car!' It occurred to me that I sounded like a five-year-old who wanted her favourite teddy bear back. It was a natural gut response.

'He hasn't stopped you driving it so far has he?' Beau chuckled.

'Do you honestly think I can drive it now?' I cleared my throat and took another few steps around the car, grabbing Beau's arm as I did and pulling him round so our backs were facing the car.

'Why hasn't he gone to where he's supposed to be, you know, the light, the tunnel, heaven?' I urged quietly and tight lipped. 'If he's worried about the car, tell him I've looked after it and I wash it every month.' Beau glanced at the car then back at me with a disbelieving smirk. 'OK once every two months, but I still do it! And on the note of Casper the friendly ghost in there, how comes you haven't told me about him before?'

'Well the first time I saw him in there I didn't even know you. The second and third time you still didn't know my secret and then on the last three occasions we were having such a great time, I didn't want to freak you out.'

'There was more than one occasion and you didn't think it necessary to mention I was ferrying around a hitch-hiker? What makes you think I would freak out?'

'You're seriously asking me that, and with a straight face no less?' He laughed. OK so maybe, (a big MAYBE), I was overreacting, slightly. Beau strolled towards the driver's door and slipped inside. Watching Beau having a conversation with thin air was a little hard to swallow. As the seconds passed my nerves settled.

'Beau, what's he saying?' I approached the passenger side cautiously, leaning in on the window frame. I peered hesitantly into the vacant back seat.

'He says that when he passed away his wife was evicted out of their house. She couldn't find the deeds. He wants to know why you haven't taken the car in to get the radio repaired.' *OK this bizarre Mystic Meg crap is freaking me out.* I looked at Beau stunned and unable to talk. 'I urm...just...just thought because the car was old, that it didn't really work. I'm really sorry, really, really sorry, please forgive me.' I pleaded with our invisible guest. Beau sniggered. 'What's so bloody funny?' I scowled.

'Grace, he's not going to curse you, relax. He understands that you couldn't possibly have put it all together. He says he was trying to get you to take the car into a mechanics, so they would have to pull up the front passenger seat floor panel to get to the wires.'

'Why the wires?' I asked confused. I don't remember the kids in the Enid Blyton novels having so much trouble deciphering the clues. *Am I really this dim?* My inner bitch for once decided to help. *Wait a second little lady, leave the question alone, lock it away and throw away the key, no good can come from that question.* I did as I was advised and returned my attention back to the task at hand.

'It's not about the wires Grace, underneath the floor panel is a storage area, that's where the documents are.' I opened the door nervously. A part of me was half expecting Beau to jump around laughing at my expense and reveal that it was all a big joke. I apprehensively reached for the panel and pulled it up. I pulled out an A4 crumpled brown envelope that was wedged securely in the space exactly as Beau had predicted. It was brick heavy and stuffed full with all different coloured papers. I replaced the panel and with my other hand I turned the envelope over. In large black capital letters were the words *WALTER HANSON*.

'Is this what he wants?' Beau looked into the back seat and shouted 'Hey Walter, what do you want us to do with this? Walter wants you to take them to his wife.'

'Does he have a specific woman in mind? A name, address maybe? I don't know his wife' I stumbled.

'He says she lives with their daughter two streets from here.'

'Can you ask Walter if his daughters name is Louisa?' I couldn't believe how frustrating it was talking through Beau, everything took twice as long and the suspense was killing me. Beau didn't even have to ask Walter, he immediately nodded in response.

'Grace how did you know that?' It was my turn to surprise him. It was a shame I couldn't enjoy the moment for longer.

'Ahhh Beau, we all have our little secrets, don't we?' I revelled at the curiosity in his eyes.

'Louisa is the lady who sold you Walter's car isn't she?' Now Beau was the only one smiling.

'You're not funny! How the hell do you do that? You're like some freaky mind magician. Just once it would be nice to be a little elusive for longer than five seconds.'

'Well Walter laughed' Beau uttered under his breath. It was oddly eerie knowing spirits still had a sense of humour. With some inside knowledge that Sixth Sense film would have been in a completely different isle in Blockbusters. I climbed into the driver's seat, turning the key in the ignition, giggling to myself as a dull rumble emanated from the radio. 'What's so funny?' Beau asked.

'Nothing. Is Walter smiling by any chance?' Beau peered over his shoulder into the back seat.

'Yes actually'.

AWOKEN *Billie Jade Kermack*

'Hey Walter, this is for you, for old times' sake.' I turned the radio on and set it to the station Walter obviously liked. The 21st century passed by outside the window in a grey haze, whilst inside the colourful melodies of George and Ira Gershwin filled the car.

EIGHTEEN

ꟙ

As we pulled up to Louisa's house my stomach was doing somersaults. I slammed the car door shut behind me and made my way up to the red-brick stone patio, grasping the envelope tightly in my hands. The elaborate and beautiful flowery stain glass inserts in the white door shimmered in the moonlight. As I reached out to knock on the grainy varnished door, I realised I hadn't even considered what I was going to say. I glanced back at the car and Beau was staring at me, egging me on to knock. He stuck his thumb up and a cheesy grin was spread across his face. I took a deep, steadying breath. *You can do it Grace, just reach out your hand.*

'Hey Grace, what's up? If you're looking for your Mum, our appointment isn't until Thursday. Really I should have booked her for last week.' She pawed at her long distressed brown hair, frowning at her split ends. My Mum and her hairdressing shears were definitely needed. My eyes shot towards the hallway table, which was covered with family photos. A photo of a man I assumed was Walter stood pride of place next to an extremely large silver and mauve lamp. It was nice to put a face to my mysterious hitch-hiker. His crooked smile hung slightly on the left, his pearl white dentures and his jet-black headpiece dipped uneasily to the right and his brown eyes were slight and framed by fuzzy grey eyebrows. 'Grace, is there something wrong?' Louisa asked suddenly concerned.

'I'm fine thanks. Is your Mum here? I have something for her.'

'OK, I'll just get her. Mum, can you come here for a second?' Louisa yelled down the hall. Light slipper clad shuffling footsteps and the tapping of a walking stick approached us. As Louisa stepped to one side, I saw her - Walters' wife. She was stunningly beautiful, with a head of silvery grey hair cropped around her long face, her eyes a deep brown.

'Hi. I was sorting through my car and I found something that I think belonged to your late husband Walter.' She just stared at me perplexed. 'I had a feeling it might be important, so I wanted to drop it over.' I handed the envelope to Louisa. Her face alight with happy shock. Louisa turned the top piece of paper round to show her mother. The old lady dropped her walking stick on the floor and threw her withered hands up to her mouth as tears welled in her eyes.

'It's the will, the deed papers. Everything's here!' Louisa exclaimed as she rummaged through the envelope.

'Thank you, Grace, you really don't know how much this means to us.' She pulled me in her arms and held me tightly.

'I think I can guess. It wasn't just me though, my friend Beau was a big help. We're just glad that we found it for you.' I gestured towards the car and both Louisa and her mother waved fervently, beaming. I made my way back down the stairs with a merry skip to my stride. As I shut the car door behind me, I rested my arm on the open window seal and standing in the doorway, still in an embrace was Louisa and her mother. 'How do you do this all the time? It's exhausting.' I started up the car and pulled away from the curb.

'Exhausting, but rewarding. For so many years I ignored my gift. I tried to fight it, to push it to the back of my mind. I was alone and really confused pretty much all of the time. I only begun to accept it when I met Gwen, after years of trying to ignore what I can do, I can say without a doubt this is not nearly as draining as the other spiritual situations I've encountered. Gwen told me I would meet someone who was special, who would understand and accept me for who I was. I didn't believe her at first but then I met you.' I pulled up outside Gwen's house and turned off the engine.

'I think it's more probable that you're the special one, but thanks, I'll take what I can get.' He leant over towards me and stopped, mere inches from my face. His sweet warm breath grazed my neck as he lent in closer and kissed my cheek softly. Right on cue my heart skipped a beat. Without a word, just a cool, kind smile, he opened his door and jogged around the front of the car onto the pavement. Our eyes were locked the entire time. The warmth I felt when I was with him left me slowly as he walked up the path, it was a feeling that I couldn't possess alone, a warming sensation I could only feel when he was by my side. He stepped inside the front door and then closed it behind him. Watching him leave, even if only for a short time, was getting harder and harder to handle. I regained the use of my now cold body and started up the car. As I glanced into my rear-view mirror and into the back seat, I caught a glimpse of Beau's backpack. With what little energy I had left I made my way up the yellow brick path to Gwen's door. Before I could tap at the wood, Gwen opened the door and greeted me with a huge and welcoming smile. I held up Beau's bag and without a word she ushered me in. 'Go up the stairs there, it's the first door on the right.'

'Thanks Gwen.' I crept up the wide wooden staircase and followed Gwen's directions. As I extended my hand to knock on Beau's already ajar bedroom door, I stopped. Beau's reflection in his wardrobe mirror mesmerised me, transfixed me into a state that took control of all my bodily functions. I felt utterly powerless. The warmth he ignited in me was slowly building as my body recognised his close proximity.

He removed his black t-shirt over his head and threw it in a wicker basket next to his bed, my breathing became arduous. A few pale pink scars that donned his Adonis like body was a roadmap to his past, a part of him that I was yet to discover. His beautifully crafted body that appeared as smooth as moulded clay resembled that of a GQ magazine model. His rippling, sculpted muscles heaved as he took a deep breath in and ran his hands through his hair, the muscles in his back stretching to their limit, the feeling of pure want and desire coursed through me and with that, I was a chained slave to my body's jerk reaction. I stumbled against the door which made it creak. Instinct made me cower out of view. I soon realised, as Beau's footsteps got closer to me, that this wasn't a fool proof plan, hiding was useless. The light from Beau's room beckoned the darkened hallway as he pulled open his door. I stepped out into view with a stupid smile on my face. Before he could say anything, or think something a lot worse, I held up his backpack. My cheeks were painful as my awkward smile grew. He took the bag and I darted for the stairs. To no avail, if I'm honest I don't think escaping was really what I wanted. He reached out for me, tugging on my arm. I turned slowly and after a few seconds I realised I hadn't caught anything he had said. His bulging chest was all I could look at. He too noticed this and his grin said more than words could. 'Huh' I said as my gaze wandered slowly from his chest to his face.

'I said thanks' he chuckled.

'OK, well I'm going to go.' My embarrassment engulfed me. My desire to have his lips on mine almost painful, especially when he pulls his bottom lip between his teeth.

'Was there anything else Miss Gracie.' He knew what he was doing to me, the fact that he was enjoying it so much was an extra little kick. I shook my head, the only response I could manage. With his hand still clasped around my wrist he moves his fingers down so he is now clasping my hand. He pulls my fingers up to his mouth, kissing each one. I pulled my hand free, breaking the bond was about ten seconds shy of making me throw myself into his arms.

'I've got a car, got to go.' I shot down the stairs and out of the front door in one fell swoop. *What the hell was that? I am happy to admit to my fair share of stupid things that I have done, but that just takes the biscuit.*

I parked Bob up as usual next to my Mum's 4x4 and with a bounce in my step I put my key into the front door. It was nice to see Mum donning a happier expression as she made us some hot chocolate and I ran through the whole story. The envelope in the car and my lunch with Beau. I obviously left some specific details out though; telling Mum that my new boyfriend, the boy I was desperately in love with, could see and talk to ghosts would probably have gone down like a lead balloon. I really didn't need any excuse for her to believe I was insane. Besides, it was mine and Beau's little secret. I also left out everything that happened outside Beau's room, the thoughts alone still made me blush, I wasn't ready to share those with anyone.

I fell into a death like sleep rather quickly that night. I drifted off easily, glancing at the shadows from the trees that rapped on my window. The last thing that stuck in my mind before I was sucked into unconsciousness was him. It just felt wrong to think of anyone else.

NINETEEN

ꕥ

I sat in Mr Sander's registration class drumming my fingers on the oak table; it was branded with every imaginable rhyme, limerick and graffiti you could think of. Crippling anxiety tore at my stomach, the anticipating of Beau's arrival the only thing I could think about. Time ticked by – no Beau. The lunch bell rang – still no Beau. The day dragged and my constant worry and that persistent niggling feeling of dread lingered. I sat at the lunch table with everyone else silently, trying desperately to mimic their optimistic faces. I just didn't belong there. I knew where I wanted to be and whom I wanted to be with. I picked at my food like a bird, lost in thoughts that debilitated my already limited skills of interaction. As everyone started to leave the table I didn't even notice, I was officially in a world of my own.

All I wanted to do was get home and bury my head in a pillow. With the final bell of the day bellowing, my freedom was welcomed. I joined the hordes of students racing for the exit, celebrating that I was one step closer to getting home, but as I fought for freedom against the masses, I slowly lost the battle. I eventually gave in. Once I started to get dragged in the crowd the wrong way, I pushed my way into an alcove and waited for the stampede to retreat. I finally got through the double doors and to the top of the stairs. Everything was silent and I only had my thoughts for company. *Where the hell is my iPod when I need it?*

'Hey Grace, wait up!'

Amelia was running up behind me towards the double doors. Her pink and gold embellished Prada handbag was flying in the air and the succession of taps from her pink high heels on the badly scuffed wooden floor, only plagued my already forming headache. I took a deep breath and finally mastered the art of mimicking, plastering a full-on fake smile across my face with a surprising amount of ease. Luckily, I had had the entire day to practise.

'What's up?' I asked still keeping the smile as firm.

'Grace, what's wrong with your mouth? You look like the joker. Have you had Botox or something, you can tell me?'

'No, of course not, oh and thanks for the joker remark.' I quickly dropped the smile and resumed my normal expression; she wasn't buying it, what was the point? It was futile doing something that just continued to make my face ache.

'That's better. Christ Grace, for a minute there I thought you'd been taken over by them...umm...Pea people' she said waving her hands about as she searched for the right words.

'Pod People Amelia. But close enough...and I don't know whether your shock is a good enough excuse to use Christ's name in vain.'

'Grace, how was your date?' she asked hurriedly, pretty much ignoring every word that had left my mouth; no change there then.

'What date?'

'I rang your house last night to cheat off your English lit assignment and your Mum said you were out with some boy. I tried to dig for details, but she didn't seem to know anything.' I had no time to prepare a good answer. *Think Grace, Think!*

'Come on, I want all the dirty details' she winked suggestively. She reached for my hair and tousled it in her fingers trying to pretty me up. I batted her hand away snappishly trying desperately to invent something. It wouldn't have to be smart or believable just satisfying. All Amelia ever wanted was some juicy niceties. The urgency to think fast was causing a bad case of brain freeze. 'Who is he? Do I know him? How far did you get?' She beamed like a Cheshire cat. Her questions blindsided me. Once I was sure she was finished with her interrogation I went with the only thing I could think of that would stop her incessantly pestering me.

'He's just some boy I met in the video shop last Saturday night. We both reached for Friday the 13th.'

'Trust you to spend your Saturday night in a video shop.' she judged.

'Amelia, do you want me to tell you the story or not?' OK so I was a little quick with her but the lie was lingering on my lips and I just wanted to get it out. There was more chance of a slip up with all her interruptions.

'Sorry go ahead. You were both reaching for some boring horror flick and...'

'He looks a little like Justin Timberlake, minus the moves, the clothes and the money. He likes cricket and he lives about twenty minutes away.' I stopped myself took a breath and waited for her reply. I had basically just described Amelia's idea of the complete opposite of a good catch.

'Right, so what your telling me is that you have met some guy, who has bad taste in films, can't dance, doesn't have a life on a Saturday night, has no money or taste, likes a sport that is meant for balding old men, and lives so far away that you couldn't walk there. Well done Grace got yourself a right catch there.' she replied bitingly while patting me condescendingly on the back. I was quite surprised with how successful my lie was. The grin on my face now, was definitely not forced. With every word I uttered you could see her interest waning. Like a programmed robot she immediately changed the subject to something that revolved around her. Surprising as it may seem this was one of the reasons why I loved her. It's hard to get bogged down with all the unhappiness in your life when you have a crazed – OK, sometimes selfish – shopaholic chatting loudly over your every depressing thought and misplaced emotion. She could be deep and caring, I had seen it, it was just a rarity. We made our way down the stairs. Amelia's persistent nattering became an annoying octave higher and she was unrelenting, suddenly making me question my earlier thought.

'Did you see David Peters eyeing me up at lunch? I know he's going out with Vanessa Harley, but he's not a bad catch. Definitely worth a try!' she mused as she eyed at her reflection in her compact. I knew I wasn't there for guidance or my opinion. As usual I was there as a mere venting aid.

'So the girlfriend part doesn't faze you then?'

'Minor detail Grace.' I made my way down the chalk stone stairs, picking up my pace as I neared the pavement below. With Amelia and the worry of Beau forcibly jumping through my mind, I just wanted to be in my car and to be alone.

'Amelia, I'll call you tomorrow.' I shouted out of my window as I started the engine.

'OK, but remember your Casanova probably wants to call you to discuss the depths of an LBW.'

'Ha, ha, Amelia, how long did that one take you to think up?' Amelia had already sought out David Peters who was unchaining his bike at the sheds. She waved at me in acknowledgement but I was pretty sure she didn't catch a word I had said. Flirting was like a world sport for Amelia and she was always determined to reach for the gold, at any cost. I drove home making a point of passing Gwen's house. The sun was already setting and the dull but strong orange glare emanating through the buildings was blinding.

Gwen's yellow, rusted, old VW camper van sat in the driveway with Beau's motorbike chained up right beside it. Only the porch light was visible as the rest of the house was still and now shrouded in complete darkness. All was silent apart from the low humming tune of some nearby crickets. I drove home solemn and disheartened. I walked through the front door, heading straight for the stairs. With every step the smell of freshly washed sheets, the scent of fuchsias and Mum's vanilla tumble dryer sheets was uncontrollably inviting. All I wanted to do was curl up in my duvet and listen to my iPod. I ploughed on and was almost at the top of the stairs, almost to the comfort and isolation of my room.

'Hey honey, how was your day?' Mum beamed from the foot of the stairs, her arm resting on the banister.

'I'm not gonna lie Mum, it was complete crap! Why are you asking?' *Wow, don't sugar-coat it or anything!* my inner bitch snapped.

'No reason, I was just wondering why my daughter looked ready to give up on life. You've got a face like a slapped arse.' *My mother everybody! So eloquent when she wanted to be.* My inner bitch was stifling a giggle now.

'Cheers Mum, it's not as drastic as completely giving up, I just feel a little deflated. Honestly, I'm same old, just got a load of assignments due in, very hectic.' I prompted a laugh, which felt awkward, but believable enough. I made my way up the rest of the stairs, dragging my feet as I went. 'Night Mum.'

'Night love, sleep well.' my mother's voice echoed up the stairs. I closed my door behind me with a kick and collapsed face first onto the bed. Now I had no distractions, a question grappled to the forefront of my mind.

Where the hell is Beau?

TWENTY

ꕥ

I set my CD player to disc five and pushed play. I threw the remote on the side table, switched off my lamp and wrapped my duvet around me. Snuggled in my flannel pyjamas I quickly began drifting off. So I'd had a crap day, so what? As the comfort of my duvet fenced me in, my Dad's lullaby cradling my senses from the stereo, my mind felt soothingly clear. If only for a few minutes, it was better than nothing.
Thud!

My clock said three am as the light from the hallway crept underneath the gap of my door. I threw my covers off me, grabbing my dressing gown that was slung over the end of my bed. I prayed for bravery! Where the hell was my bravery? I apprehensively reached for the door handle. I pulled open the door with one swift movement and as much courage as I could muster.

Crash!

Shattered glass from the light bulb above rained down on me as I pulled my hands up to protect my head. It settled around my bare feet and glistened in the moonlight from my bedroom window. *Screw being brave!* I thought and ran back into my bedroom, tugging on the lamp cord beside my bed before the darkness could swallow me whole. I approached the hallway cautiously and after manoeuvring around the diamond shards of glass on the carpet, I jogged to the bathroom and pulled the dolphin shaped light toggle on. I grabbed the dustpan and brush from underneath the sink and as I was about to shut the cupboard door, I heard faint footsteps approach me from behind. I knew that creak on the stairs. I had memorised that squeak on the seventh stair from the bottom when I was eleven; it was the only way I could get to the kitchen in the middle of the night for a snack without my Mum knowing. Thinking rationally at this point was the last thing I had expected. By my logic I had a maximum of three very precious seconds before whomever or whatever was on the stairs would reach the bathroom. The footsteps picked up pace and all that was left to do was ***RUN!***

As I faced the stairs below the footsteps had ceased. There was no one there. With the dustpan and brush shaking in my hand, I wielded it as though it was a twelve-inch machete and crept along the hallway, my back skirting along the turquoise and silver swirl decorated wall paper. With my eyes never leaving the top of the stairs, I searched wildly for the handle to Cary's room. He was sprawled out on his bed with his Star Wars covers strewn on the floor and a University textbook on Quantum Physics perched on his chest. I pulled his blanket up to cover him, bookmarked his page and placed the book on his side table. (Easily the nicest thing I had ever done for my brother.) As I peered into Mum's room, she was also fast asleep, with one arm hanging from the bed and her cheek nestled in her pillow, low hums of wistful dreams emanating from her mouth. *So who was on the stairs? How did the bulb shatter?* I tried to abolish the feeling of dismay that rotted away in the pit of my stomach. After I had cleared up the glass and discarded it in my bin, I shut my door and tried desperately to banish the thoughts that were causing my skin to crawl with fear.

The wind was wailing like a banshee now and the calloused finger like branches of the leafless maple tree scratched at my window. The dim light of the moon masked my room and as the shadows that were created twisted and contorted, the blackness engulfed my every sense. As though I was being trapped in a coffin, my world was getting smaller by the second, the walls of gloom suffocating me. I don't know how long I had been asleep, but I awoke suddenly. My breathing was arduous and I felt a crushing pressure on my chest. I couldn't move my hands. Panic and pain raced through my head, when suddenly a searing twinge ripped through me as though someone or something was tearing me apart from the inside out. I screamed with every trickle of breath I had left in me. I was trapped in a hellish silent movie, I couldn't make a sound. My lamp flew off my side table and hurtled towards the far wall, I didn't even hear it shatter. I was paralysed.

My room began transforming. It was at least a hundred times the size of my bedroom. Through my tear-soaked eyes I could make out a Vaudeville style theatre with luxuriously draped blood red curtains. They billowed eerily, masking a grand, wooden floored, crescent stage in front of me. Row after row of red velvet covered chairs filled out the space around me and I was all alone, with just the confusing weight on top of me for company. I couldn't move. As the room began to expand and evolve before my very eyes, I soon realised my lack of mobility might not be my only pressing matter. A sea of pulsating coal tickled around me, swarming creepily up my legs and over my chest. Against my better judgement I glanced down. A thousand black spiders with their fangs as shiny as a butcher's cleaver ready to carve at my skin made their way up my body. I closed my eyes tightly. With the last smidgen of hope I had left, I prayed for the scratching of tiny spindly legs on my skin to cease.

Right. Grace. Get a grip! Within a few seconds the weight on top of me began to subside... *but if this is a dream shouldn't I be back in my room?* I sat up and looked around at the black, ornately painted walls. The sad, chubby faces of little cherubs glared down at me, wailing as they began to warp and move. The dim lights that shone down on me from the huge, diamond draped chandeliers above, and the creepy cherub statues that were by all means alive, faded into the midnight background. The room felt glacial, every breath that left my mouth appearing as a blast of white smoke, that wafted through the air. The chairs were no longer red but now gravestone-grey as the darkness swamped them too.

I could still feel my heart beating rapidly beneath my pyjama top as it tried to escape my chest. An icy chill running down my spine. The space around me was crow black now and nothing or no one could be seen. The weight was back on my chest and forcing me back onto my bed.

'What do you want? Who the hell are you? Please, please let me go.' I whimpered uncontrollably into the vast darkness. The pain was torturous and unrelenting. My heart felt as though it was being squeezed with a tremendous force, the grip tightening with every tainted breath I struggled to take. The feeling in my fingers and toes dissipated as every bit of blood tried to rush to my brain. As though a rubber band had been secured around my windpipe, the lack of air was unbearable, my throat burning as the last remnants of bitter air slid in to my mouth. When the sheer determination to survive took over my fear, I finally found the power to move my hands and grabbed out frantically for anything that could help me. My arms weakened and every strained, desperate breath felt painful. I closed my eyes. It was clear that what little will I had left to survive was dwindling and fast. I did the only thing I could, I gave in. The unnatural darkness swallowed me whole. Then there was nothing.

TWENTY-ONE

ꕥ

Knock, knock.

I shot up. Finally able to move and breathe, coughing and inhaling as much air as was humanly possible. My throat was ablaze, every breath I took licking at it like flames. My head was an uneasy mess as it fought to right itself, my eyes hazy and fighting to focus.

Knock, knock.

'Hey Grace, do you want to keep the noise down? I've got to write my thesis tomorrow?' I could hear Cary's feet trail off faintly down the hallway, his door slamming shut behind him. I warily laid my head down on the pillow, arranging myself into the foetal position, grasping my legs tightly. Fear and pain were emotions that were easy to describe; my experience however, was not. Whoever or whatever held me hostage would be back. I was sure of it. I laid my reservations to rest as best I could and fell swiftly into a dreamless sleep.

~~~~

I donned my fluffy leopard print dressing gown and the lame kangaroo novelty slippers Auntie Petunia had bought me for Christmas. So, what to do today? Clean my room? No. Gym? Definitely not. Coursework? Laughable! *Some breakfast and a lazy PJ day in front of the TV it is then.* I could hear the radio blasting from the kitchen as I moved down the stairs, sloth style. *'This is Mr Melody Maker. For*
~~~~

all you lovely listeners out there, here's a little bit of Broadway, especially for you. ***'Fame, I wanna live forever....'***

'Hey Grace, may I say sis you look exquisite today, you literally take my breath away.' Cary beamed uncharacteristically as he eyed my attire.

'Ha, bloody ha, ha, Cary.' With no comeback in sight he pulled his yellow raincoat from off its peg and made his way to the front door. Slipping into his green wellies caked in yesterday's mud on the doormat, before opening the front door. All the while having a large smile plastered on his face. *Now that is strange, what the hell is he up to?* I wondered. He slammed the front door behind him running full pelt out into the rain. I danced over to the cooker, got on my slipper clad tiptoes, reaching for the cupboard door. As usual the coco pops were wedged between Mum's Bran Flakes and a yellowing box of oatmeal; which was about as old as I was. As I pranced around a memory of my eight-year-old self at my dance recital flashed before me. I may have been slightly older, but I still had the moves. *Jazz hands. Check. High kick. Check. Arabesque. Check.* 'Mum, can you make sure you put cereal on the shopping list, this box is nearly empty' I bellowed through to the wash room, shaking the box in my hand, using it as a maraca along with the music. The tumble dryer in the outhouse was going full pelt thanks to the rain. The scent of Mum's lavender dryer sheets filling the kitchen. I turned around to grab a clean bowl off of the dish rack, ending my little dance show with a running man-moonwalk combo straight out of the eighties.

'SHIT!'

The cereal box, along with my jaw, hit the floor. *Hello Hell! It's been a while.*

'What are you doing here?!' I stumbled through my blanket of despair. Beau was sitting at the dining table trying with all his energy not to laugh hysterically at my expense. He had one hand across his mouth and the other resting around a mug of steaming tea. *Embarrassment? Check! Kill me. Kill me now!* Mum strolled in from the garden dripping wet with the washing basket secured under her arm. With one look at me and a glance in Beau's direction, Mum realised her error. Even she had to double take in my appearance it was that bad, and she hadn't even witnessed the dancing.

'Ahhh...Grace, Beau popped over to introduce himself, and to see you.' Mum rushed towards me. Her pointless attempt to shield me an epic fail.

'A little heads up would have been nice Mum, look at me!' I whispered angrily through gritted teeth tugging at my pyjamas.

'I sent Cary upstairs to put a note next to your bed' She whispered back, emphasising each word so I could read her lips. The realisation of Cary's plan hit my Mum, a little slower than it had occurred to me, but at least she got there in the end. Her wide eyes were pleading, letting me know just how guilty she felt for unwittingly aiding his dastardly scheme. Nothing could possibly make this any worse. Wrong again – My footwear choice and scraggy top bun hairstyle ensemble were the icing on the cake that was my soul. I glared at my mother as she moved out of the way, backing into the safety of the wash room, nudging the door closed behind her.

'OK...I'll be back in...urrr...one minute.' The awkward smile plastered on my face was all that was stopping the cries of shame from flooding out. I switched off the stereo as I passed. Never again would I be able to watch *Fame*, sing

Fame or even mention the word *Fame* around Beau. Once I reached the first stair Beau broke his silence, giggling hysterically. His hand thumping the table as he tried to contain himself. I slipped on my clothes, taking my time, searching for the note Cary had apparently left for me. *No note. No surprise there!* Once back downstairs, I could hear Beau and my Mum chatting as I approached the kitchen's double doors. I reached out for the door handle but every time my hand got close enough to grasp it, a pulsing heat radiated from it. I took a deep breath, arranged a pleasant smile on my face and mustered what little courage I had. My smile soon faded along with the last shred of dignity I possessed.

'Mum, what are you doing?' I whined, glancing at Beau, his response a taught jaw and apologetic furrowed brow. I stood there, my entire childhood laid bare, desperately trying to not make direct eye contact with him. *Is it humiliate Grace day?* Open in front of Beau, in all its pink, lacy glory, was my worst nightmare. My baby photo album.

'It's OK sweetheart, I just thought Beau would like to have a quick look.'

'Good thought Mum. I've got the date when I stopped wetting the bed upstairs, shall I bring that down?' My words were drenched with sarcasm.

'Don't be so silly Grace, I know you were six.'

Is this woman serious? Mum, please just SHUT UP!

'I think you were a beautiful baby Grace, especially this one of you and your Dad.' I relaxed a little and took a seat next to Beau. The damage was done. Crying over spilt milk never did the cow any good, or whatever that saying was.

'Grace, this one of you eating ice cream naked is so adorable.' My mother gushed as she waved the photo in front of me out of arms reach, passing it onto Beau. *Goodbye relaxation! My weekend is officially screwed.*

'Yeah, really adorable!' I replied humourlessly as the word NAKED rushed through my head. Beau covered my hand with his, stroking my fingers, an attempt to placate me. He was still smiling, but this time, not so much at my expense.

'There's no need to cringe Grace, I like finding out about your past and who you were. Your Mum told me when you were little you wanted to be a ballerina. It's a real shame you didn't follow that dream through, because those moves earlier were rocking!' He swayed his hips in his chair and did a little jazz hand move, mimicking my earlier performance. Even now, I couldn't help but be happy. His laugh was infectious and that smile could make me melt, even in the most embarrassing of situations.

'How much did you see?' I cringed, covering my eyes slightly with my free hand, wishing the floor would open up and swallow me whole.

'Oh Grace, I saw EVERYTHING!' He emphasised wide-eyed with great glee.

'You are so funny Beau, ever thought about being a comedian?' I retorted as I punched him in the shoulder.

'Who's this?' Beau interrupted as he turned the page.

'Oh, that's my aunt Lindsey, she died of cancer. It was a few years back now. I was really young at the time.'

'You look so much like her, the same hair, exactly the same dimples in your cheeks when you smile. Even your eyes are a perfect match. If you were a few years older I could swear that this was a photo of you' he laughed, the beautiful noise not reaching his eyes as it normally would.

'Yeah, well even though photo time has been awesome I'm sure we can think of something else to be doing today!' *Please God – anything else than this!*

TWENTY-TWO

'Catherine, what have you done with your life? You have a silly little job where you fiddle with people's hair. I always told you there was no substance in the beauty business. People are either pretty or ugly, you have no right to meddle and mask that. I can't believe it, nothing I taught you has stuck. It's that silly dead husband of yours that warped your brain and led you down this path. Those infantile views of free speech, loving communities, FRIENDS! He had no idea about the real world. You have two bastard children who were born out of wedlock, a dead husband, no future prospects of a reliable partner and a mortgage, that if you're honest, you can't afford. You were a disappointment when I was here and now, you're still a disappointment now I'm gone' the greying old lady whined. Although she had a frail body of at least seventy years, she had the poise of a teenage ballet dancer. Her expression was disapproving and astute. Her lips were two, thin, pencil like lines. They looked as though they had never experienced a smile.

I crept over towards Beau, who was oblivious to my presence and was peering around the living room door, his neck craned awkwardly to one side to allow for a better view. *Do it, go on. You – know – you -want – too!* my inner bitch sung. I agreed with her instantly as I side stepped the creaky floorboard at the foot of the stairs. I did what felt natural and pinched his bum. He jumped and his bag tumbled to the floor. I'm not going to lie. It felt good!

'You're very jumpy, what you spying on?' I eyed him suspiciously as the living room was silent and empty. 'Beau, what's going on?' My voice dropped to a concerned motherly tone and my laughter subsided as his eyes remained transfixed on the floor as he knelt down to retrieve his study books. 'Beau, what is it?' I pressed, the worry washing over me as I dropped to my knees next to Beau. I placed my hand under his chin – our eyes finally met.

'Follow me outside.' His words were disconcerting and his face anxious. He put his bag and books at the foot of the stairs and took my hand, dragging me quickly through the kitchen. We stepped out of the white, paint chipped, bay panelled doors into the garden. Beau eagerly shut them behind me, taking care not to make too much noise. He paced fretfully the length of the tiny yellow paved garden, his hand across his mouth. The burnt orange leaves of the bindweed against the back fence draped down onto the dishevelled wooden shed that had seen better days. I recognised that look in his eyes; the ice water blue shade that usually lightened his entire face was masked by a hollow mottled cloud that made my stomach sink.

'Ghost?' I queried apprehensively, secretly already knowing what the answer would be. Is it just me or is this job relentless? Every which way we turn we are faced with the afterlife. I should ask Beau when his holiday dates are.

'Not just any ghost.' He paced fretfully up the cracked pavement and ran his hand through his hair, his hand settling on his neck.

'So, do you plan on telling me who it is?' He was silent, his expression pensive. 'Hey, Derek Acorah, fancy sharing?' I pressed, overjoyed at the successfulness of my own joke.

Don't slap it out of him – he will spit it out eventually! I thought whilst squinting at him, gauging just how long *eventually* would actually be.

'It's your grandmother!'

Wow. *eventually* was in fact three seconds.

'OK, Nanna Jean was lovely. What's the problem?'

'I've got a pretty good idea that it's not Nanna Jean. The only words I would choose to describe this woman are angry, bitter and extremely evil.' The penny dropped.

'Noooooo. Not Nanny Devlin, or Nanny Devil as I liked to call her. This is really bad news, she made my Mum's life a living hell. Does she know you can see her?' I whispered tight-lipped like a ventriloquist, the real fear of her eavesdropping never far from my mind.

'Thankfully not. I thought of not telling you, but her ramblings are incessant. I figured if I spaced off into my own world while I was here, you'd start asking questions. After your reaction to Walter, I decided against keeping it from you.'

'Hey, that was my first ghost introduction. I think I reacted pretty well considering the circumstances.' I pouted, quickly realising we had swerved drastically off the topic at hand.

'So, what do we do now, if she broke out of down there, I doubt she's going back willingly?' Beau answered my question with a vague and confused expression. I knew immediately what he was thinking.

'Believe me, there is no way she was getting a free pass through those pearly gates.' I chortled. I had no desire to be in Nanny Devlin's company. The thought of her spreading her bad juju vibes around our house made me cringe. I could only imagine death had fuelled her ghastly moods.

'I've kind of grasped an idea of the sort of woman Mrs Emile Devlin was and there is no way her getting to know me will help. One question. How is it your mother is nothing like her?'

'My Mum was adopted by '*The Devil Lady'* when she was eight. Her biological parents were killed in a head on collision. My Mum was the only survivor from a four-car pileup. To the outside world Mrs Emile Devlin was a devout Christian widow, with respectable prospects. She was unable to have children of her own. Her sour womb uninhabitable, I believe this was God's wish, a very nosey social worker did not. They placed my Mum in her care. To everyone around her Mrs Devlin was the perfect doting mother, but my mum spent her nights in a broom cupboard and her days scrubbing floors with a toothbrush. Luckily, when she was fifteen, dearest Nanny Devlin decided she was too much hard work and shipped her off to boarding school 'to make a decent woman' out of her, as she called it.'

'Emile seems to have a major problem with your Dad.'

'Yeah and a little heads up, *don't* call her Emile. My Dad made that mistake on their first meeting. She sees it as *discourteous and ill-fitting behaviour for a gentleman.* It didn't help that my Dad had shoulder length hair, ripped jeans and a leather jacket with matching black steel toed work boots. She was a bit of a religious nut. She had a pre-packaged idea from the 18th century of how people should be. Anyone who didn't conform to her crazy ideals should be hung, drawn and quartered in her eyes.'

'So, she wasn't your Dad's biggest fan then? She's consistent, I'll give her that.'

'I think if my Dad had been brave enough to eat her food, she would have happily poisoned him' I pressed.

'So that's a pretty concrete no then!'

'I don't get what she's doing here though?'

'She's just following your Mum about, criticising basically every move she makes.'

'So exactly the same as she did when she was alive then, what a surprise. Can she affect my Mum?'

'Nope. In order for a spirit to affect the living they have to have a connection with them, whether good or bad, they have to acquire a bond. It's clear that your Mum has left her in the past, right where she belongs.'

'So basically, as long as she doesn't find out what you can do, we can go on with our lives oblivious to her existence?'

'Yep.' The childlike cobalt glint had returned to Beau's eyes, which was projected through his smile - *my smile*. I stepped towards him, closing the space between us. Before I could follow through with what I was thinking my phone buzzed to life in my back pocket. 'Fame, I'm gonna live forever….' I glared at Beau.

‘I had nothing to do with that, I wouldn’t dare.’ He responded with his hands held up across his chest.

‘Cary.’ I fumed. He was going to get what was coming to him soon enough. 'One minute, I have to get this, its work.' I said glancing at the caller ID lit up on the screen. Beau’s face was gravely despondent as I accepted the call. He took a seat on the rusted three-piece French patio set under the flaking apple tree. As I listened to Luigi, I understood Beau’s expression. My face fell. For a moment, I forgot how to inhale, as realisation struck.

'OK...I'm so sorry. I’ll speak to you soon.'

'I can tell by your face that you’re angry.'

'Too right I’m angry Beau. That was my boss, his wife Claudette, you know the lovely woman we met at my work party. She’s in a coma. She collapsed. They said the brain haemorrhage had been waiting idly to burst. Mario had no idea. She’s dead. You saw something when you touched her hand didn’t you? Why didn’t you warn her?' He diverted his stare as I accused him harshly. My tone more thoughtless than I had intended.

'Grace, I did sense something was going to happen, but I had no idea where it would happen, or when. I can’t intervene every time I get a vision or a feeling. Do you know how much damage it would cause telling someone they were destined to die? I could feel that she was already past it, it had gone too far for her to be helped.'

'She isn’t a pack of mouldy potatoes! She is...*was* a person.’ I quickly corrected myself but felt immediately awful about it. ‘She deserved to know the truth! How do you know she couldn't have got help?' Playing the blame game really wasn't helping.

'Grace, knowing this about people, being able to see what I can see is soul crushing. I didn't ask for this, but that's life. It's my life. I need you to look at the bigger picture. What good would it do, ruining what time she had left?'

Love is hoped for, life is a trial, death is inevitable.

TWENTY-THREE

ꟸ

'What happened to you yesterday? It was like you vanished into thin air?' I mused.

'I had something to sort out.'

'Something?' I pressed.

'There was a problem with Gwen. She had a fall, I had to take her to the emergency room.'

'Oh my god, is she OK? What happened?'

'She said she lost her footing on the stairs.' His eyes traced the words on the menu. I got the impression he wasn't reading any of it.

'You don't believe her, do you?' I pulled the menu down from his face, beckoning his eyes to meet mine.

'No, I don't. Do you remember I told you that spirits can sometimes hurt people that are close to me? Well Gwen has been having some really bad cases of sleep paralysis lately, or at least that's been her excuse.'

'Sleep paralysis?'

'It's what doctors call episodes of hallucinatory sleep activity. I've had more than I can count and over the past month. Gwen's been waking up screaming. She's trying to protect me, but I know what's going on.' This was all suddenly sounding scarily familiar. I couldn't even keep track of the nightmares any more.

'What exactly happens...with this sleep paralysis thingy?'

'Well, doctors say it's when you have night terror dreams that feel real. They can cause marks, bruising, stuff like that. But they aren't just dreams. Spirits use people while they are asleep because they are at their most vulnerable, their most susceptible. If it keeps on like this, I might have to think about moving out. She keeps telling me she's fine, but I can't be the reason she's getting hurt. I won't be.' Beau's eyes were tear filled. I scratched my chest to relieve an itch, recoiling and doubling over as a sharp pain tore through my chest.

'What's wrong Grace?'

'I don't know.' I pulled on the neck of my top carefully, exposing the presence of four bloody scratches across my skin.

'Where did they come from?'

'I don't know.' A mix of confusion and panic washed over me. I got up hastily before he could fire an onslaught of probing questions at me and rushed to the toilet, knocking into patrons as I went. I pulled off my top hesitantly, addressing my reflection in the mirror above the sink. Bright purple, finger-shaped bruising on my arms appeared to protrude out of my skin. They were scar like welts and hot to the touch. The cavernous, crimson scratches on my chest were also gouged into my stomach. *How did I not notice them earlier, felt them on my skin? How did they get there?*

The harrowing intensity of my wounds made my head spin, whilst the macabre memories from the night before last came flooding back to me. *What was that incredible weight, that ripping sensation in my chest that taunted me?* I collapsed onto the toilet seat. The small room was spinning, my flashing memories a whirling blur of sick inducing confusion. *Beau shouldn't know about this, he's got enough on his plate,* I thought in a panic. For the time being, I would keep it to myself. I left the toilets, desperately trying to arrange a relaxed expression on my face. As I resumed my position at the table, Beau's concern had clearly not wavered.

'So, how did you get those scratches then?' He lent back on his chair with his arms folded as he astutely assessed my face, for any tell-tale signs of fibbing.

'What's this, an interrogation? I was playing rugby in gym class a couple of days ago and one of the other girls must have caught me. It doesn't hurt that much. It looks a lot worse than it is.' I lied and it wasn't a little white one. I was now deathly pale as I caught a glimpse of my reflection in the mirror fixed to the wall behind Beau.

'You don't take gym.' I clearly had to lie a lot faster and a lot better than I had been.

'No, I don't Columbo. Miss Ranger had one girl short and asked me to fill in. They were playing the championship game and she was desperate. Remind me to ask you for permission next time.' I rolled a smile in with the lie and hoped for the best. Being untruthful to others had become a little easier over time but lying to myself was impossible. I couldn't ignore that gut-wrenching feeling echoing in the pit of my stomach. I tried my best to shrug it off but for the rest of the day it lurked there, unrelenting and unmoving. It couldn't possibly be real. My senses tickled with the memories that I had tried so hard to banish.

Over the next few nights the delusional dreams became more vivid and harder to ignore. They were replaying the same horrendous scenario, as though I was watching a 4D re-run of a horror film. Except each time it still evoked as much dread as the last. The strong odour that I couldn't quite put my finger on, burned my nose and made my eyes water. The putrid aroma repeatedly gnawing at my sensitive gag reflex. The feeling of sodden rough denim scraped at my legs like cheese wire. The hand's that forcefully held down my arms were dirty, skeletal and calloused. The more I tried to piece together my dreams the more details I remembered.

Every time I awoke from these dreams two things were clear; two oddly white piercing eyes with minuscule black pupils and the cackling laugh that caused every hair on my body to stand on end. Asleep or awake these two facts disturbed me, infecting my every waking thought thereafter. Whatever or whoever it was that did this to me took a great amount of pleasure in it. His creepy whispers were inaudible. Whatever it was he was trying to tell me; I wasn't getting it. But it didn't take long before the dreams began to fade and with time, so did my wounds. I never completely forgot but storing them away at the back of my mind made life more bearable. Days turned into weeks and weeks into months. Life played out exactly as I had hoped, like an episode of the Brady bunch. Everything was delightfully perfect on the surface.

~~~~

There he was waiting in the pouring rain at the steps of the college, with the hustle and bustle of everyday life merging into the dull grey backdrop around him. He just smiled at
~~~~

me. I looked up at him as I approached the first step. He raised his hand and cupped my face, stroking my neck softly. There was that fairy tale moment again. Everything around us was silent. All except the faint hum of beautiful music cascading around us like a waterfall, melodically guiding us towards one another. The rain that was now creeping through to my bra was freezing. He pulled his coat open and invited me into the warmth.

'Why does it feel like forever since I last saw you?' I mused. *Wait. Did I just say that out loud?*

'I saw you yesterday Grace.' He pulled me in closer. I flung one arm around his neck and placed the other on his side near his hip. I gently traced my fingertips up his side. 'Hey!' He jumped away from me, exposing me once again to the elements.

'That never fails to make me laugh.'

'Yeah well it tickles like mad.' *What are the chances I could get away with doing it again?* He grabbed my wrist and came in for the kiss we had been building up to. Stealth wasn't one of my best attributes. Passion had been the forefront of our relationship and containing it was becoming even more difficult. I felt my feet leave the ground as Beau swept me up into his arms and suspended me there, his soft lips still on mine. Our tongues perfectly matching one another's determined strokes. His fingers danced up my neck and into my hair, tugging lightly at my messy tendrils. His skin heated and flushed beneath mine, I placed my hand on his rock-solid heaving chest that barely contained his pounding heartbeat. With my thoughts struggling for feigned PG rated composure and my body fighting the urge to hang on tighter, he lowered me slowly back to the ground.

I beamed with my eyes still firmly closed. 'Wow!' I uttered coyly, steadying my jellied legs.

'Right back at you gorgeous. Do you fancy skipping your classes today?' Beau asked with a cheeky grin.

'Beau, you wild child!' I exclaimed, feigning disapproval. 'Only joking, what did you have in mind?'

'There's somewhere I want to take you, and if you're very good, I'll even treat you to a burger.'

'You really know how to show a girl a good time!' I teased tugging at his collar.

'OK then, if you're *really* good and you give me another kiss, I'll treat you to lunch in a restaurant with tablecloths and everything.' I mulled it over for a moment as I attempted playing hard to get, even though the word yes was screaming in my head. Suffice to say, he didn't have to ask me twice. I met his lips with everything I had, settling into my number one favourite place to be; his embrace. I didn't know where we were going but Beau instructed me on route to stop at home to grab some warm clothes. What I had on was drenched and my feet were freezing. I dried my hair roughly and secured it under a hat, the curls frizzy and uncooperative but passable in my book. I tottered downstairs, trying not to trip over my clumpy Doc Martin's.

'Hey Grace, no college today?' *What are the chances I could make a break for it? Fat chance!*

'Urm...no Mum it's a training day, Beau's got something planned. I had to come home and get changed. So, I'll get going now, see ya.'

'Grace, come in here. Where is he taking you?' I strolled into the kitchen, dragging my feet petulantly. Sixty-eight-year-old Mrs Greenway was nursing a coffee at the table, her hair wound around curlers, step two in her getting her usual poodle perm.

'You look lovely dear.' Mrs Greenway lulled as she placed her mug on the table and headed over to the kitchen sink.

'What are you wearing Grace?' Mum demanded. Unlike Mrs Greenway, my Mum felt no need to disguise what she thought. Subtlety was not in my mother's vocabulary.

'He said dress warm.'

'Well at least run a brush through your hair, you look like Stig of the dump.'

'Cheers Mum. It's not that bad!' My reflection in the toaster sided with my Mum. It clearly wasn't passable. I pulled my hair free and ran my fingers through the wavy tendrils with some moose from my mum's workstation on wheels.

'Can I make one suggestion? Boots and leggings are great. But...'

'What's the suggestion?' I interrupted. 'I don't agree to anything you suggest until I know what it is. I learnt my lesson from the back end of the horse charity saga.'

'OK, well, I've bought you a new coat. I planned to put it away for your birthday, but today seems important to you. I want you to have it early.' Mum patted Mrs Greenways shoulder and made her way to the cupboard under the stairs.

'OK, can I see it first?' I tried desperately not to sound ungrateful but I knew my Mum too well. It was usually bright pink with fur or it had a montage of rainbow butterflies all over it. Those coats were the fuel for another year of mockery, but that is a whole other story that I will not be going into. Mum glided back through the doors with a large, clear dress bag. *Grey...a good start.*

'Are you ready?' Mum teased, ready to rip off the protective plastic.

'Yes Mum, I'm ready.'

'Right, if you don't like it, I can take it back, but I saw it and immediately thought of you.' She bit her lip anxiously. 'Ta-da!'

'Mum. It's gorgeous.' The stone marble colour, the oversized black buttons, the large lapels, the sweetheart neckline and the fact that it was knee length. It was girly but understated and utterly gorgeous. There was a black flower and stem detail sewn onto one side that coursed through the buttonholes, right on up to the neck. It came to just below my knees, falling longer at the back then it did at the front. The pleats added a bit of movement at the back and were secured by a detailed frog. It looked like a coat out of the 17th century and it fitted like a glove. The bell sleeves covered my hands with just my fingers in eye-sight. I was a five-year-old girl with a new princess dress; ecstatic didn't cover it! 'Thank you so much Mum, I absolutely love it, best present ever.'

'I'm glad you like it. So, you're sorted for your date then?'

'I guess I am. Thanks again Mum, I'll give you a call later.' I rushed towards the door buttoning up my new coat.

AWOKEN

Billie Jade Kermack

'Bye sweetie, have fun.' Mrs Greenway shouted out from the kitchen.

'Bye Mrs Greenway, your hair looks great by the way.'

TWENTY-FOUR

ജ്ജ

I ran to the car. Thankfully it was only drizzling. 'Hey hey gorgeous, looking good.'

'Thanks.' I replied confidently as the compliment tickled at the edges of my mouth.

'New coat?'

'What this old thing? It's actually an early birthday present from my Mum. So, where we off to?' I asked slotting the key into the ignition.

'I've got to make a quick stop at Gwen's and then I'll direct you.' Beau was in and out of Gwen's in about two minutes. He always looked great; on this occasion it was no different. His ever changing eye colour, which always allowed me to decipher his mood was at present a shimmering cerulean, the colour of a waterfall, against his cobalt button down shirt that he rolled up to his elbows and his fitted denim jeans, I couldn't stop my mind from racing to thoughts that were not so pure. Gwen stood at the door with only the top panel of the old barn door open and blew me a kiss. As he jumped into the passenger seat, shaking the rain out of his hair, he threw a large backpack onto the back-seat, it looking at home amongst the rest of the mess that I had amassed there. He unzipped the front pocket and took out a CD with a white label on the front. It read in bold black marker *For Grace*. 'Let's go' he said, pushing the CD into the old school stereo, that like the rest of my battered old Bob, was held partly together with duct tape.

'Hey, I like this.' I enthused with a hint of surprise as the first track began to play.

'Thought you might.' he grinned. We drove for a while, taking in the sights along the way. Every song I could imagine was on that CD. The ones that made me happy, the ones that made me sad and even the silly ones I thought no one else knew about. It was like Beau had made a soundtrack to my life, songs that represented treasured memories, hidden thoughts and secret feelings that I hadn't shared with anyone. 'We're here' he declared about half an hour later.

'Hyde Park?' I questioned confused.

'Yeah there's no parking today so we will have about a five-minute walk.'

'Hey Mr Vague, do you fancy filling me in on the itinerary for today?' After a short pause and a cheeky grin, I got my answer.

'No!' He remarked pointedly with no offer of explanation. We parked up and took the short walk hand in hand to the gates of Hyde Park. For as far as the eye could see along the never-ending stretches of London roads, tourists from all over the globe filled the streets in every direction, as they giggled excitedly at the anticipation of a new place and an undiscovered culture. Their wide-eyed expressions took in all that surrounded them. Beau tightened his grip on my hand and pulled me towards the huge iron cast gates that towered above us, leading into the park. Apart from the odd person walking their dog or feeding the ducks, the park was pretty much deserted. We strolled along the tarmac path hand in hand in silence as the light breeze lapped at my face. As though weighted with the world on his shoulders, Beau wrestled with the humongous rucksack he had perched on his back.

'So, what's in the backpack Dora?'

'That's for me to know and for you to wait and see. You'll like it, I promise.' I followed Beau's lead in silence, occasionally catching his glances. 'Here we go.' Beau gestured with open arms towards a massive oak tree deserted on its own in the centre of a field of freshly cut wet grass. The park was pretty quiet where we were but, in the distance, I could hear music and cheering. Beau opened his rucksack and pulled out a black sheet and a large tartan woolly throw. He laid the throw on the floor under the tree and secured the black sheet in the branches to protect us from any rainfall dripping from the leaves. He pulled out some Tupperware boxes and two plates, two sets of cutlery, two plastic glasses and a bottle of Cava.

'That's a Mary Poppins bag surely, how did you fit all that in there?'

'I'm a genius and don't call me Shirley.' He laughed. It took me a couple of seconds for the joke to fall into place. I clapped slowly congratulating him.

'Ha ha, very funny. Surely/Shirley, I get it. Don't give up your day job!' He continued to empty the rucksack. His iPod and speakers were next. 'You really have thought of everything haven't you? How did you prepare all this in the two minutes you were in Gwen's?'

'To be honest Miss Gracie I had this planned since yesterday, all I had to do was get you to agree.'

'I thought that kiss this morning was a little deeper then you'd usually allow' I chuckled.

'Well I had to make sure you'd come, it's a special day.' *Oh, Crap what have I forgot? His birthday, an anniversary? This is a perfect example of why I should start carrying around a Filofax!* 'What's so special about it, my birthday's not for another month?'

'No, but it is your Dad's.' I took a deep breath and fell to the blanketed floor on my knees. I sunk down, resting my back against the rough wood of the tree trunk.

'Why didn't Mum mention it? I can't believe I forgot, with everything that's been going on recently I completely forgot. How did I forget that?'

'Maybe your Mum didn't tell you because she could see how happy you've been lately.'

'Yeah I guess so. I just feel bad. I've never forgotten before, ever!'

'Well then it's lucky you've got me' Beau beamed.

'How did you know?'

'I read it on your Mum's calendar, the day you waltzed in like a rock star, wearing your dressing gown and kangaroo slippers.' He hushed his laughter with the back of his hand pretending to quieten a cough.

'Hey wait, what kangaroo slippers?' I said, knowing full well. *Damn it – goodbye last shred of dignity.*

'Oh Grace, don't pretend you weren't wearing them. I saw the slippers during your fame routine. I've got to say, I think I fell in love with you all over again when I saw your high kick.' He couldn't stop the laughter this time and fell onto the throw gripping his side. I slapped his leg. I hadn't missed his mention of the word 'love' but I didn't want to drive myself crazy analysing it, so I pushed it to the back of my mind for scrutiny at a later date.

'OK, OK, I have kangaroo slippers.'

'Doesn't it feel good to get that off your chest?' he teased through his laughing fit. The slap I landed on him was a little harder this time. Beau sat up and edged closer to me. We stretched out our legs as though we were sunbathing on a tropical white sandy beach in Hawaii. Although the reality was a world away from that day dream, it was pure heaven being anywhere with Beau. The rain started to pick up its pace and the grey shadow clouds drifted across the sky, masking any chance of a sunny day. Beau pulled me into his arms and ten minutes or so of silence passed with only the odd, soft sigh of contentment uttered between us. I gazed out onto the dusky ripples of the ashen pond and the cascading leaves floating on its surface. It was a perfect picture of art; proof of true, natural beauty. The fallen leaves, the beautiful neon greens and mellow gold's, blanketed the grass around us and danced in the breeze. Before long the cold drifted away, along with any desire to move from that spot.

'This is by far the sweetest thing anyone has ever done for me. Thank-you.'

'You're welcome, any time. As long as it's OK with you, could you tell me a bit about your Dad, what he was like?'

'Urm....yeah, sure.' We huddled together, closer to the tree, and I began my stories. It felt so soothing to talk about him out loud. 'My Mum told me that ten seconds after I was born, while he cradled me in his big arms, my Dad whispered in my ear that I wouldn't be leaving the house until I was twenty five and that I wouldn't be having any boyfriends until I was at least thirty.' The story that I had played out in my head more times than I could count brought a tear to my eye.

'Wow, he was that protective of you? I can understand where he was coming from though, I have this constant urge to be with you, to protect you, and it's hard to think about anything else sometimes.'

'I'd like to say my Dad would have liked you, but I think he would have maimed and killed you by this point.' After shared laughter and a short silence Beau readjusted himself, clearing his throat and sitting upright, tugging at the hem of his jeans tensely.

'What are you thinking Beau? I can tell there's something you want to say, so just say it.'

'How did he die Grace? I don't want to intrude but I get the strong feeling that you could do with sharing some of this stuff. You can trust me; you know that don't you?' I took a deep and reassuring breath. I hadn't talked about this with anyone, not even Amelia. I shut everyone out when it came to my Dad. I had nothing else left of him, so my memories of him seemed so private and sacred.

'He died from a brain tumour.' I had to force the words out as they scrapped at my throat and rolled uneasily from my lips. I could see Beau's regret at prompting some personal answers from me. I reached over and placed my hand on his. 'I trust you and I do want to tell you, I just need to do it at my own pace.' He nodded and smiled stroking my hand with his thumb.

'Take all the time you need. I'm going to open the Cava, toast your Dad properly.' The cork flew out with a loud bang and even preparing the glass under the neck of the bottle didn't stop the spray of fizzy wine flooding onto the grass.

'That reminds me of a story actually' I said. Beau passed me a full glass and we toasted. I sipped it and felt the tiny bubbles travel up my nose.

'So, what's this story then?' Beau prompted.

'Well, when I was eight, we were at a family barbecue celebrating my uncle's birthday. The job to open the champagne fell into my Dad's hands. Everyone stood in a circle around my Dad waiting to cheer. The garden was dimly lit with a large heater and these pretty flower detailed solar panel lights dotted along the stone walkway. My aunt was paranoid my Dad was going to break something so she ordered him to open it in the other direction, away from the house. My Dad did as he was told and turned to face the fence. Dad congratulated my uncle and counted down from five. The cork flew out of the bottle and it was suddenly eerily quiet. All that anyone heard was the high-pitched shriek of a cat. Dad had hit a bloody cat with the cork as it perched idly on the fence. The cat was OK of course, but it never went near Dad again and suffice to say he never got put on champagne duty after that.'

'You miss him so much don't you?' I didn't know why, but his question clearly upset him.

'So much, more than I could ever explain.' I replied sombrely as my gaze met with the ground beneath me. I picked at the frayed edges of the throw as memories of my Dad came flooding at me in their hundreds. *Why is this still so hard, why does it hurt so much to think of him?* A single tear teetered in the corner of my eye; this was the time. I had bottled this all up for so long, I felt the longing to share it all; with him.

'My Dad was ill for years before he died. He would constantly be going to doctors with headaches, unexplainable memory loss and impaired vision. They just sent him away with painkillers, and I'm not talking proper medicine like morphine. I think the strongest thing they gave him was over the counter paracetamol. It wasn't surprising he gradually became worse. We weren't told until it was absolutely necessary. So when I caught Mum crying and Dad would sleep for days on end, I demanded to know what was going on. Mum sat me down and as plainly and emotionless as she could tell me, she did. Her eyes said more than words ever could. They were wrecked with pain and sadness. From then I knew it was much worse than she was making out. I can remember that being one of the most horrific moments in my life. Anything pure or innocent I had experienced was quashed. My Dad soon had to be transferred into hospital full-time. He had gone completely blind in one eye and lost the use of his legs. We visited him every day and every day his condition deteriorated. The last thing I remember was Dad giving me and Cary a Terry's chocolate orange from the hospital on-site shop. I think he had sweet talked one of the nurses into getting them for him. We devoured it whilst Cary listened intently to my Dad's old band stories. That was the last time I saw my Dad alive.' I glanced at Beau, immediately concerned that I had shared too much. He nodded grave-faced, edging for me to continue with the ending to my story, the conclusion of possibly the most difficult time in my young adult life. For what was to be the end of my father and my childhood.

'He died that night. He had a heart attack and he was all on his own. No one should die alone. We went to visit him in the Chapel of Rest just before his cremation service. Mum couldn't stop crying. She was heartbroken. I on the other hand couldn't seem to cry. He lay there, so still, his face just didn't look the same, so pale and emotionless. I made up for the no crying of course. For more nights then I can count since his funeral I've buried my face into my pillow and cried myself to sleep.' I crumpled the dried sorrel coloured leaves from the floor in my hands as I dissected my life piece by excruciating piece, laying the deepest crevices of my soul bare to Beau. 'Time passed on, and so did everyone else. Nothing else had changed. We were just very different people. Things that bothered me in the past didn't seem to mean a thing. It took me a while, but I got back on track eventually and then you fell into my lap and brightened up my many days to come.' I took a deep breath and looked up into the tree. My lip trembled. I bit down on it hard, trying with great difficulty to calm myself and the emotions that were fighting to break free. *Don't cry, don't cry, don't cry!*

'You are such a beautiful person Miss Gracie.' he soothed with a warming smile as he pulled me in tight to his chest. 'I love you' he whispered softly into my ear.

TWENTY-FIVE

ꕥ

One for sorrow, two for joy,
Three for a girl, four for a boy,
Five for silver, six for gold,
Seven for a secret never to be told!

It was the first time Beau had told me he loved me and I had never believed anyone as much as I did him at that moment. The words meant more then he could ever know. After a while the rain stopped and the music and cheering, we had heard earlier sounded much closer. I sat up and along the path a hoard of women raced past us. It was a sea of pink clad smiling ladies of all ages, grouped together as their feet hit at the pathway. 'What's going on?' I nudged Beau.

'It's race for life today. All these women are raising money for cancer research.'

'Did you know this was going on today?'

'Yep. I wanted you to see that even though you feel alone you have so many people who share the same pain. You are never alone. These women are raising money so in the future people have a better chance at living.'

'You are just full of surprises.' I stood up and peaked round the tree trunk. The line seemed to go on forever. Attached to the backs of the runners were dedication sheets. *To my brother Manuel, rest in peace, 1986 – 2008. Shirley Hale, a brilliant mother, friend and wife. Grandpa George, miss you always, love Suzie. Nicky Thompson, fell asleep in 2002, we all miss you terribly.* 'It was then that I realised how right Beau was. I was not alone. The tears rolled down my cheeks individually, ending on the lapels of my new coat as I wiped my cheek with my sleeve. 'I don't know whether to laugh or cry' I said thoughtfully, a lump forming in my throat.

'What is it? Grace, I'm sorry if I've upset you.'

'That little girl's message was just cute is all.' I sniffled, sitting back down on the blanket.

'What did it say?'

'Cookies, you were a great friend and I would share my crisps with you always. Love you angel kitty.'

'That is pretty sweet' he replied softly.

'She was only about seven.'

'Did it help you at all, coming here?' Beau asked concerned, watching the tears fall down my face. I wiped my face furiously.

'It did, more than I could thank you for. My heart feels a little bit more complete, not entirely fixed, but no gaping holes to report at least.' He pulled my head into his chest and we relaxed into a slouch. 'My god, Beau, look at that.' In the distance, fluttering wildly in the wind and low to the ground, were magpies.

'One, two...six...seven...seven in total. I don't think I've ever seen so many in the same place at the same time before.' I beamed.

'Grace, I want to tell you something, it's why I've brought you here today. I don't want you to freak out.' There was a deathly silence as I assessed the worry on his face, trying to gauge just how concerned I should be.

'Spit it out then!' My chuckle was uncomfortable and his silence was now unbearable. Any flutter of playfulness disappeared from my tone as I sat up and put my hand on his, reassuring him with a warm smile.

'I've seen your Dad.' he uttered quietly, wincing while waiting for my reaction.

'That's not funny Beau!'

'I'm not joking, I wouldn't do that to you.'

'This is just cruel, why would you bring me here, get me to tell you things I've never told anyone, then throw that at me? Subtlety not in your vocabulary? You really are crazy!' A twinge of utter sadness, pain and disbelief all rolled into one settled in his eyes. I quickly snapped out of my rant. *What am I doing, I'm hurting him? Really hurting him and all he's trying to do is help me.* 'Beau, I'm so sorry, I didn't mean it.' I placed my hands lightly on his chest and prayed for his eyes to meet mine. I'd seen proof of his gift and my own experiences with the supernatural only fuelled my belief. How had it never occurred to me that he could maybe see my Dad? I felt foolish. You meet someone who can talk to dead people, your father falls pretty perfectly into that category, and you don't inquire as to his whereabouts. I was dumbfounded.

'I didn't want to upset you, I would never do that, but I thought you would want to know.'

'So, what you're saying is, my Dad has spoken to you? My Dad?' I fumbled around in my bag frantically and pulled out my purse. 'You've seen this man? My father?' I brandished the worn picture in my purse, waving it in his face irritably. It didn't matter how many times I repeated the words, they still didn't stick. I felt numbed, confused, astonished, explosive, heartbroken and angered all at the same time. I felt like a little girl lost.

'Yes, that's him.' He affirmed after glancing at the photo brandished in my hand.

'I'm going to need a little more than a *yes* Beau, I don't understand.' I sat up and moved my hand away from his sharply.

'Your Dad is here and he wants to talk to you. I know how cruel this sounds but you've seen my gift. I didn't want to tell you until you believed in what I do.' I shook my head in disbelief as the tears again began to cascade down my face and onto my coat.

'So my Dad, **WHO DIED**, the man who shuffled off this mortal coil, who took that journey down your magic bloody tunnel is here?!' I screamed in an uncontrollable rage. 'How long has he been here?' My tone was harsh and accusing.

'He has been around you since I met you. Not all the time but he thought, like me, that you'd handle it better...if you knew me first. I thought you had caught us when I was talking to him in that classroom.' He laughed but it didn't last as I continued to scowl at him.

'That was my father you were talking to? You have known this whole time? Am I just another person that you're trying to help? You've never loved me, you just needed to get another ghost off your back?' I could feel my heart shutting off, building a protective wall around itself as the misery enveloped me. I had let Beau into a side of me I had never shared with anyone, my misjudgement clawing at my insides.

'Listen...I know that this is really confusing and you know I would do absolutely anything never to hurt you. I love you more than I could describe. Yes, I saw your Dad first but I promise you, I fell in love with you, for YOU!' He took my hand in his and his bright eyes glowed deeply with concern as I allowed for his revelation to sink in. 'He's here and he wants you to know that he loves you.' My body grew stiff, the tears now unstoppable. 'I don't know how else to explain all this so you can get your head round it.' I got to my feet.

'I can accept what you're saying, I've had more experience with your world then even you know' I screamed. He looked at me puzzled, so I quickly carried on the sentence, calming my tone. 'You have to understand that when my Dad died I spent so many nights crying myself to sleep, agonising over what had happened, that over time I had to deal with it. I had to carry on. I think about him every day, but after a while you have to come to terms that he's gone and he's never coming back. Now you're telling me that he has come back.' Beau got to his feet and tried to wipe my face. After a short silence, Beau's message sank in. I had seen what he could do and above anything else I was sure he wouldn't lie to me.

'Can he touch me?' My question caught Beau off guard.

'It doesn't feel as strong as when I touch you but you could feel something there, a sort of cold presence. He strokes your hair when you're sad. He kisses your forehead sometimes when you're sleeping. He is there when you need him, just like he promised.' My lip trembled and my eyes stung. An overwhelming, agonising ache stabbed at my heart. *Why is he doing this to me? Why does this hurt so much?* 'I know you are upset. I am so sorry for that. I hate myself for making you feel this way. When you're ready, he has something to say to you.' I took a deep breath and nodded. 'He wants me to tell you that your prom dress was gorgeous. The blue one was definitely the right choice.' The salty tears were still there but they now trickled over my beaming smile. I put my head in my hands and tried to wipe my face. My emotions were like a tidal wave with every second and every passing thought they changed. Between the floods I couldn't help but laugh. *He is really here, he is with me always, he kept his promise.* 'Grace, are you OK?' Beau asked, hugging me tightly. 'Would you rather I hadn't told you?'

'No, of course not. I'm so glad you told me, it's just so hard to take it all on board. I can't lose him again.' Beau glanced into the empty space to the left of me. I reached my hand out, praying that my fingers would be stopped in their path. 'Can he hear what I'm saying?'

'Yes. Actually, an advanced ghost like your Dad has the ability to know what you're thinking. He's caught me out a couple of times.'

'Rewind!' I said. Shock and confusion no longer covered it.

'My Dad can do what?'

'Well, just like the living, ghosts can acquire gifts, talents, abilities. With enough practice they learn to harness them and in turn these gifts become a part of them.' He lulled, as though it was common knowledge. I suddenly became aware of all the ramblings in my head. I tried to use the smidgen of energy I had left to try and think of something worthy of a father's ears. *Hello brain, thanks for completely ignoring me.* One look at Beau's gleaming smile, chiselled jaw and heaving chest, stirred a memory that made even me blush. That particular memory was stored at the back of my mind for moments when I was alone. Beau kitted out in his black skinny jeans, baseball boots and no top. His rippling chest and strong arms, his mesmerising and enticing cobalt eyes deeply fixed on mine. *Awkward!*

I quickly looked at Beau, praying that either Dad's useful gift was on the fritz, or that he wouldn't depict in detail every embarrassing recollection that I had unwillingly just shared with him. 'Your Dad's telling me that it's OK, he's not mad. He's laughing actually.' Beau looked confused. I shot him a glance, grateful that only my Dad and I knew the truth. The fact that my Dad couldn't use a shotgun on Beau worked in my favour. It was a nice twist to my fits of tears. I couldn't stop giggling. 'He says to tell you you're on the right track, definite keeper.' It was clear Beau had absolutely no idea what message he was actually relaying. 'Oh one last thing, he says he loves you magpie and he's so proud of how high you're soaring.'

'Is he going?' I panicked.

'He'll be back, ghosts' sort of run on batteries. When they are emotionally drained it's like they need to recharge. Sometimes ghosts can recharge off the energy of others around them but you're completely worn out as well.' There was a lingering silence as everything around us swept off into a blur of random colours and shapes. I closed my eyes and felt a soft breeze hit my cheek.

'He's gone, hasn't he?'

'Yes, but not for too long. Now that you know the feeling you will be able to sense when he's around you. It's nice to see you so happy Grace.'

'Can all ghosts read minds?' The man from my nightmares crept unwelcome into my thoughts.

'Spirits can't go around reading just anyone's thoughts, they have to have a strong bond. Some spirits never connect with their next life enough to harness those sorts of abilities.'

'My Dad always believed that I could be whoever I wanted to be, do whatever I wanted to do and go anywhere I wanted to go. He made me feel as though anything was possible. No plan was too small, no dream was too far-fetched.' The picture of my father's doting face swept away that of the bad man's, making me smile broadly.

'What's so funny?' Beau queried as he shuffled closer to me.

'Whenever I cried my Dad always used to tell me the same thing. He would say I won't be able to promise you that I will be able to stop all your tears and sadness, but as long as you remember this, I will always be by your side, we will get through it together. Life is full of both happiness and sorrow, but the love I have for you will conquer all.' I finally understood his words.

TWENTY-SIX

ꕥ

Not usually a drinker; thanks to the horrific after effects of a tequila fuelled house party last June, I sipped at the glass of cava slowly, the bubbles tickled my nose, the cool liquid travelling down my throat a little easier than I had first thought it would. My head swam as I poured myself another glass. I was grateful to have something to drown out the emotion that flooded my brain. It wasn't long before the familiar sickly sensation settled in the back of my mouth. I don't think it helped that the cava was the only thing I had put into my body all day, food would have been a good call. I was emotionally drained and physically worn out. I put my head between my knees, breathing in sluggishly, trying desperately not to throw up. Beau grabbed me a Fanta out of his bag. 'Try some of this, you need some sugar.' He offered it to me, stroking my back rhythmically. I shook my head adamantly. I could handle this without a panic attack occurring, all I needed was to breathe.

'No thanks' I declined. It was an effort responding with a grin. I gave up halfway through and returned to looking at the floor through my legs.

'I think I should get you home.' He packed up the bag frantically, still keeping his eyes on me.

'I just need a minute, honestly, I'm fine...Beau.' Beau rushed to my side instinctively folding his arms around me. 'Okay, a Fanta sounds good.'

'A lot better, thanks.' I cooed between sips of the fizzy drink. Once the sugar had hit my system, I felt the pull of sickness settle, my stomach rumbling gratefully. I rested my head back onto his chest. I felt so safe in his arms, lulled by the comforting drumming of his heartbeat that mimicked mine, both beating Intune of one another. Everything in me settled. The calm with him forever my safe place. I turned to him on my knees, putting my hands around his neck. 'You're one in a million you know.' I pressed, reminding myself of the truth also.

'And I'm all yours Miss Gracie.' He moved in close and tucked my hair behind my ear. Moving the palm of his hand down my neck softly, leaning into my body, his lips now following the path of his fingers. My arms went limp, my body a slave to this man. His cool minty breath tickled at my ear. 'Love you always, with you always, miss you always.' He whispered, each word holding as much intent as the last. I could feel tears of happiness this time creeping down my cheeks.

'Ditto' I whimpered. He wiped the tears from my cheeks and in one movement pulled me up onto my feet.

'You have no idea how beautiful you are Grace, not a clue.'

'Lucky I have you to remind me then.' I giggled, pulling his face to mine, lightly tracing a kiss on his soft lips, the world beyond our bodies irreverent. It was now official, I loved this handsome, mind boggling specimen of a man more than I could have imagined, more than I ever thought one person could love another.

'I think I owe someone some lunch?'

'Definitely, I could eat a horse.' My belly rumbled loudly to second my point. We took the short walk to the park café. The winding brick path littered with used water bottles and pink confetti. Beau drew me in closer and put his arm around my shoulder. His hand still in mine as he lowered his head to kiss my knuckles. Standing proud outside the quaint wooden hut surrounded by potted plants of every colour was a soldier remembrance statue, beautifully crafted, the copper polished with care. As we entered a bell above the door rung, alerting the other patrons to our arrival. The windows were draped with orange tartan fabric, the table cloths made of the same material but grey in colour.

'I promised tablecloths.' Beau nudged as a young waiter showed us to a table in the back next to the floor to ceiling windows that looked out onto the greyish pond. A sea of trees with leaves painted all shades of green, gold and speckled crimson surrounded the café. He handed us a couple of menus and turned to serve another table of customers.

'Can I help you *sir*?' the petite, brunette waitress asked Beau flirtatiously. Her attention to the word sir making it almost sordid. *What am I, chopped liver?* I thought dropping the menu on the table. I shouldn't let it bother me I know, but it just does.

'Could we have two of your 78's please?' He replied, looking at me to see if I agreed with his choice. I nodded. I would have eaten anything placed in front of me at that point I was so hungry. He took my menu and handed them both to the waitress, glancing up at her when she didn't make an attempt to walk away. She was stuck in a thought process, just grinning at Beau dreamily like Alice in Wonderland's Cheshire cat, with absolutely no regard for me.

'Hi, could I have a strawberry milkshake as well please?' I questioned my ingrained manners as the word *please* hung on my lips distastefully. I had interrupted her, waking her from what I could only imagine was an X-rated fantasy involving a little too much of Beau.

'Oh, sorry, I didn't even see you there.' she said not so apologetically in her sweet Yorkshire accent. She scowled at me as Beau took my hand, his silent and gentlemanly way of showing every other woman affected by him that he was off limits. She scribbled down my drinks order and turned back to Beau. It no longer surprised me the effect Beau stirred in the opposite sex. Too much thought on the subject would send me crazy. 'Can I get you a drink with your food?' She smiled at Beau bearing all of her beautiful white teeth, fiddling her pencil in her loose pigtails.

'Yeah sure, I'll have the same please.' Expecting the waitress to take our order to the kitchen, Beau turned to me to continue our conversation. The waitress had turned to stone, or at least that's what I was secretly wishing had happened, she stood there for a further five awkward seconds before she realised what she was doing. She quickly strolled in the other direction, embarrassment tugging at her cheeks.

'Beau, I think you have some sort of super pulling power, women just seem to flock to you.'

'What can I say, when you have it, you have it.' He joked, flexing his arm muscles and kissing them like a prize fighter, or prize fool, the point was debatable.

'On a serious note Grace, the only girl I am interested in *pulling*, as you so articulately put it, is you. Most people just think I'm crazy.' *Cuckoo, cuckoo. How does he not see it?* I searched for any glimmer of immodesty, and of course found not even a glimmer. He genuinely hadn't a clue the effect he had on people. Men wanted to be him and women wanted to be with him.

'Well how about that waitress or all the other waitresses we've come into contact with? It's possible we eat out too much by the way.' I mused. 'That mousy girl in Blockbusters dribbles every time you step through the doors.'

'Well I've never noticed, and I think Mousy Martha actually has an illness that causes that dribbling.' I took a quick look around to see who was in hearing distance. Luckily by now the place was pretty much deserted apart from a group of rowdy teenagers all dressed in black with faces full of make-up, an old couple in the far corner holding hands and sharing a crossword and a balding business man on his laptop who looked stressed and in desperate need of a whisky rather than a steaming mug of tea.

~~~~

'What exactly is it you see?' I queried, pushing the chips around my plate. He swallowed the chunk of burger in his mouth hastily and gazed up at me. Always ready to answer my intrusive questions, he edged his chair closer to the table.

'What do you mean, what do I see?' He asked, lowering his tone as the Marilyn Manson tribute act picked up their rucksacks and guitar cases, bounding past us laughing like schoolboys towards the exit. I scanned around again for wandering stares, the restaurant now almost completely empty.
~~~~

'When they come to you, the ghosts, what do you see?' I whispered. He took a sip of his milkshake and cleared his throat.

'Do you remember when we first met? I wasn't what you would call...'

'Polite? Studious? Gentlemanly?' I offered.

'Ha, ha, very funny, I was going to say I wasn't very tactile.'

'Okay, yeah, you being a jackass jumps to mind.' I replied, his lips curling at their edges.

'Well there are so many angles to all this.' He hesitated for a second, reaching for his glass, his smile now deflated and horizontal.

'And...' I prompted, intrigued.

'I can get a feeling from someone by touching them. I can see their pain, in flashes in my head, sometimes I feel it as though it's happening to me. Your sadness and heartache were so strong, just sitting next to you I could feel it radiating from you. When you think of your Dad, even for a second, your subconscious is exposed and all the anger, pain and turmoil floods into me.' I looked down at his hand holding mine.

'So how come you can touch me now?'

'Well, you're more settled then you were when I first met you. All the good memories you have and the love you shared, outweighs the bad and traumatic things. Sometimes it creeps back, but it's still not as painful as it was.' His attempt to sugar coat the fact that my mere presence causes him pain had failed. The sudden pang of guilt hit me, making me retract my hand in response.

'Can you get feelings like that with everyone?'

'No, there's no warning, it just happens. I think it depends on the person and what they have been through. Until today I've never experienced that in the park.'

'What do you mean? Did I hurt you today?' I panicked. I hadn't even considered how having those interactions with my fathers' spirit would have affected Beau.

'No, nothing like that. I've experienced flashes a hundred times over of the grief that people go through, but not once, have I shared visions of happiness and joy. For that moment today, all of your feelings of delight washed through me. It felt wonderful.' For a second we enjoyed the silence. It calmed me to know that it wasn't all pain for him when he was with me.

'What do they look like?' My voice was now a little strained. I knew only too well what the red-haired spirit who visited me looked like, but without Beau, I had no idea for comparison. I had tried desperately to forget that night and pass it off as a terrifying nightmare, but it was just too real an experience. One that lurked at the back of my brain festering, preparing to pounce. Filling my senses with all that is Beau helped ease my fears though, which I was grateful for.

'Much like in life, everyone is unique. Sometimes I don't realise someone's a ghost, sometimes everything about them appears to be normal. If they don't know they have died, it means they hold on to their previous existence, appearing normal. Some people bring their inflictions, wounds and disabilities with them, as it was either the last thing they experienced or the only thing they knew. You have to understand, although some people leave this life peacefully in their sleep or in a hospital bed surrounded by family and friends, many are ripped from their lives so traumatically with no warning at all. They are confused. The trauma of the shift leaves them in a state of denial. They will shrug there last brutal and devastating memories off as a bad dream, a wild fiction, a product of their imagination. The longer they convince themselves of this, the harder it is for them to piece it all together. They can get very frustrated. That's where I come in.'

'So, when you help them...you know, figure out what they need to do...where do they go?' I felt myself drawing ever closer to blurting out my memories of the thin, red haired maniac. I swallowed deeply and took in a deep breath in a vain attempt to compose myself, I didn't want to share that with Beau.

'All I can see is a tunnel. Everything else around them, if there is anything else, is blacked out.'

'No bright inviting light then?'

'Not exactly, the darkness is what I see, but judging by their faces, the spirits see something entirely different. Just before they are completely engulfed by the darkness a slight glow surrounds them. There are no imperfections in the light. They are free from all physical and mental bindings that plagued them in life, they are restored. It is a true miracle to witness. To be perfectly honest, beyond that I don't have a clue. Once someone enters that passageway they don't come back. It's an end to this life but a beginning to a new one. Or so I like to think.'

'Where do you get the energy for all this?'

'This is my life. I can't switch it off and sometimes I wish I had never had it, but I have and I've learnt to deal with that.' A little smile raised the left-hand corner of his mouth as he dropped his head staring at his hands. 'I don't choose who I help, they choose me.'

'Are we always surrounded by spirits? Suddenly the thought of getting in my shower concerns me.' I chuckle.

'I like to think they have a discreet button that blocks them from seeing your intimate moments. But if I'm wrong at least you won't know any different.' He laughed.

'Surprisingly, that is not comforting at all!'

'Grace, spirits wander around after death with no concept of time. What feels like a day to us could feel like an eternity to them, or three years for us can feel like three days to them. There are no rules when it comes to time and death, it's just one of those unexplainable things. When you're born into this world you are learning everything for the first time, how to walk, how to eat and speak, jobs, skills, activities. When you die it is exactly the same, every detail you have learned in life slowly drifts into the background and it all becomes a haze. You have to learn how to do everything again. Some choose to good with their new beginning, some do not.' I dopily hung on Beau's every word as he trailed off memories of what I would usually describe as an unimaginable gore-fest, with mention of missing body parts and mutilated corpses. It didn't last long before he was melting my heart with stories of reunited couples, mothers finding their children on the other side. I pulled him towards me placing my hands behind his ears. The heat seared at my fingers. I pulled them to my lips to cool them down.

'What the hell is that?' I said. *How haven't I noticed it before?* Behind Beau's ear was a slightly raised white scar that trailed halfway down his neck.

'Let's just say that I had a bad experience involving an extremely emotional ten-year-old spirit and a massive glass candlestick holder.'

'It feels hot' I said, still tending to my burnt fingers.

'Yeah, when you come into contact with a spirit, they channel their energy and we feel it as heat. Glass and mirrors are conductors of spirits. It was a lesson I learnt the hard way.'

I started playing with the now cold chips on my plate again. I had in a round-about way directed the conversation to where it needed to be, in order for me to get some answers to some otherwise tricky questions. 'Are there bad spirits then?' I glanced at his eyes for a second trying not to make my feelings of dread apparent.

'Yes, unlike my ten-year-old spirit who was just venting some pent-up frustration, some spirits are evil and they are tremendously dangerous. They are not bound by our laws and moral ethics. Much like in life everyone has freewill. What they do is their decision and a bad spirit is definitely one you don't want to meet. Over time they learn how to affect us, to impose and alter our lives, and to ultimately fulfil their own sadistic fantasies.' I tried to fill the silence with a forced smile understanding only too well what Beau was telling me. 'Grace, because of how deeply I feel about you it's hard to push aside how aware I am of your emotions. Sometimes your pain overwhelms me. I feel so protective of you. I couldn't bare it if this affected you. You have so much unresolved heartache that you're dragging about and it kills me to watch you like that. To be honest, I'd have thought that today would have cleared that up for you, made you feel more at peace with it. I can't put my finger on what it is, but something is still lingering there, and I don't think it's your father.

'Beau, of course I feel better, you have given me something I never thought was possible and I will forever be grateful for that.'

'But?' He prompted.

'There's no but!' I replied defensively as the red-haired stranger flew through my thoughts sending a shudder down my spine. *Liar, Liar, Pants on fire! There's a massive BUT that you're keeping secret.* My inner bitch mused.

'Grace, you seem happier don't get me wrong, but I get the strong sense that something is bothering you, something you don't want to tell me.' He pulled my chin up with his soft fingertips and looked deep into my eyes. 'You know you can tell me if there is something bothering you, right?' He whispered gently, coaxing a feeling of warmth in my chest that was surrounded by the otherwise lingering cold exterior. The heat surged through my body slowly, pushing aside the feeling of dread and replacing it with contentment. All I needed to defeat my nightmares was to be with him.

'Honestly Beau, it's nothing for you to worry about' I lied again. I knew I should tell Beau what was going on and believe me it was hard restraining myself, but I also knew the very real truth that Beau would never stand by and watch this happen to me. The risk of losing him was far greater than the risk of me having another bad dream. I decided that whatever came my way, I would handle it. Alone.

'Grace, I want more than anything for you to be a part of my life. It took me such a long time to truly believe and recognize what was going on with me, it took a lot of convincing for me to trust what my senses were telling me, to ignore the damming thoughts of others. They all told me I was insane with an over-active imagination. I trained myself to hide my gift from others, it had only ever got me into trouble and I didn't need another reason to be singled out in a crowd. I know I'm asking a lot from you, expecting you to take it all on board so quickly, but unfortunately time is never on my side. I promise you, I will never let you become affected by what I can do.'

'To be perfectly honest I just see it as another part of you, an amazingly head spinning part, but a part of you all the same. I can't tell you that I understand fully yet, but I can promise you that I love everything about you.' I run my fingers lightly across his hand that rested on the table between us. 'Can I ask you something?' I continued.

'Sure' he replied openly as he took another slurp of his milkshake.

'Why me?'

'Why you what?'

'You've kept this secret for so long, how did you know you could trust me?' As each word left my mouth, realisation hit me. It didn't matter why he chose to trust me or why he decided I was the one he wanted to be with. The answer was in the fact that he did tell me. The fact that he let his guard down when so many people before had branded him a crazy liar. How much it must have taken for him to believe, that there was a reaction from me that he had longed for from someone, anyone, for his entire life. To wait to see if like so many times before he would be laughed at and ridiculed. Before I knew what was happening, I jumped into his arms and hugged him with more force then I think I ever had. I appreciated everything Beau had brought into my life, everything before him seemed so colourless, lifeless even.

'Well thanks for that, can I breathe now?' he chortled as I loosened my grip.

'Sorry, can't seem to keep my hands off you today.' My cheeks flushed, as did his.

'To be honest Grace, I didn't know whether I could trust you or not, but from the moment I met you, my heart seemed to change in its rhythm. Every time I was close to you, something in me yearned to be with you, to be the one who made you smile, the one who got to kiss those lips. You took my breath away and for my entire life, all I've had to go on is what my heart and my gut told me, reason went completely out of the window once I started seeing spirits. With you I finally understood what Wuthering Heights was about. How Rose and Jack could accept dying on the Titanic because they had each other and why Miss Piggy got so jealous when Kermit had other girls around.' I giggled as his smile grew. 'I was drawn to you and I was desperate to know you, for you to know me. I've never experienced that before and yet I recognised it.' I must have still been blushing as the warmth radiated from my cheeks making me reach for my drink.

'Beau, I can quite honestly admit, that I have never met anyone as emotionally confident as you are.'

'Don't be fooled, it's a relatively new trait. You have experienced love, happiness, joy, laughter, respect, consideration and understanding all your life. You've grown as a person because of it. I never had that until you and

Gwen. It just feels as though it's exploding in me. I'm finally catching up with the rest of humanity.'

'Well explode away because it's definitely a feature I love about you. It keeps things very interesting and me on my toes.' I could feel his warm breath hit my breastbone. His hands secured my wrists, lovingly stroking them as he pulled them up to his lips. Releasing one of my hands, I outlined with my fingers all of his chiselled features, continuing on to run my hand through his ruffled hair, letting it settle at the base of his neck; the place where all of his tension was usually held. The pulse of his heartbeat was relaxed but intense. His breathing ragged as my touch affected him. I love that I can prompt this reaction from him. His eyes locked onto mine. The outside world no longer our concern. I was a mess; my heartbeat was never one to relax around him. I would just have to get used to that. I closed my eyes tightly feeling Beau's fingers on my chin. As his lips met mine, I moved my arms around to his back. *I could do this forever*. He smiled in response to my unspoken statement. As the seconds passed the intensity grew. Any space between us was too much. We grabbed our bags, our coats and left the money for the waitress on the front desk. We shouted thanks as we catapulted out of the door hand in hand. Carefree and idly optimistic on our ever-changing futures, we jumped in puddles and raced through the park back to the car.

~~~~

I smiled at Beau and waved goodbye to him as he walked towards his front door, finally burden free of a secret, his shoulders relaxed, his face beautifully serene. The red eventide glow illuminated his chiselled features and his perfectly soft lips curled into the warm smile I had come to love. But how long would I be allowed to feel like this? How
~~~~

much devastation and heartache was yet to come? The damning but realistic notion that tomorrow may never come was excruciatingly painful and a thought I banished quickly. I never wanted to say goodbye to him and as the time drew closer and the sun begun to set on the houses, I could only think of the time we would have to be apart.

TWENTY-SEVEN

ꕥ

The nightmares had been gone for so long, but now they were back. The line between sleeping and waking was becoming thinner. My ability to function doing either seemingly impossible. I didn't know what was real and what wasn't. The bruises had faded and the scratches had healed, neither leaving any identifiable marks behind. *Why would they come to me again now? What could cut me so deep and not leave a scar?* Dreaming had become a chore and feeling dead on my feet was now a daily occurrence.

I arranged to meet Beau the next day. So far, I'd successfully, (or so I liked to think) made excuse after excuse for my declining sanity, but now I needed his help. That night I had planned; like every other, to attempt sleeping. Without realising it, exhaustion engulfed me quickly, the fear and panic following in waves not long after. This was not a repeat. The other dreams appeared as a re-run of that first nightmare, just as frightening and heart wrenching, but it was just relaying and filling in missed information. I had found a semblance of comfort in that fact. This however, was not a re-run and any comfort they may be hiding, was in short supply. He was no longer holding me down, but his recognisable reek of cigarettes, whisky and sweat still lingered in the air around me. His menacing cackle filled the space around me. My inability to move was thanks to the thick rope tied around my extremities securing me to a chair, the hope of escaping an impossibility. I had some kind of mask on my face, a moulded white plastic that limited my eyesight. I could see a wide metal door that reached from floor to ceiling, various locks, pulleys and chains keeping it secure. As I struggled against my restraints, I could feel a slimy mulch of leaves, rubbish, and what I assumed was rainwater beneath my feet. The pungent smell of damp clung to the walls around me, the stench almost visible as it invaded my nostrils. My surroundings had changed but I knew exactly who was coming for me. The sound of heavy footsteps squeaked towards me hesitantly, as their owner circled me. His amused cackle taunted me further, it becoming louder, clearer, the closer he got to me. Screaming was futile. New nightmare or not, I had refused to give this man anything that he wanted; my screaming and pleading being what fuelled his depravity most. I had learnt that the hard way. The blazing tearing from inside my chest was harrowing; fanned most by my stifled screams that had internalised themselves deep in my core. What I should have learnt though is that this man would prise my screams from me with whatever means were at his disposal, and true to his nature, he began executing a torture method that I had never experienced before. I felt like a dog's chew toy as my veins exploded, my blood pouring onto the floor around me, slash after slash he ripped my body open. He had my screams, every single one of them.

The pain, the smells, the noise - everything was amplified. I had my own front row seat to a 4D horror extravaganza. Only it wasn't make-believe and it wasn't entertaining. I couldn't block any of it out. After what felt like hours the tearing suddenly ceased. I writhed silently in pain; my screams now gurgled prayers for the brutality to stop. I caught my breath finally, silently praying for an intervention that could wake me up from this hell and pull me to safety. With a flash of light that stung my eyes, suddenly I could see him. A tall man with broad shoulders and the cautious movements of an ape. He looked a little grubby but not unkempt. There must have been a month's worth of dirt and blood embedded under his nails, his arms splattered with my contribution. His bright red hair was parted to one side and combed over neatly and slicked close to his head into a fifties duck-tail. His stained, discoloured denim jeans were soaked through with oil and mud. The bloodied white t-shirt he wore was barely in one piece, hanging off his dishevelled exposed body. His eyes were strangely mesmerising, devoid of a colour, just a small black pin prick on a snow-white background. They were filled with a lifetime of hatred that bore into me, tugging once again at my chest as his body recognised the damage it had done to me, as the pull increased, it didn't take long for the hatred in his eyes to vanish. In its place, a thrilled glint of pure depravity. He edged closer to me, gliding in mid-air, his boots scrapping through the wet leaves around me. 'Beau won't be saving you today sweetheart.' he whispered from behind me, His warm breath tickling at the base of my neck. My body stiffened in response. I was no longer planning my escape. I was frozen, the air around me glacial as my breath formed in clouds of white smoke before my eyes. It would not dissipate as it mixed with the stagnant air around it. Like the smoke from a cigar it lingered and stung my nostrils. *Will these breaths be my last?* I wondered. My fight to stay positive dwindling.

His tone was discerning and cruel as he enjoyed the sheer terror in my eyes. My legs and arms felt weighty, my fingers and toes twitching, screaming for a surge of circulating blood. I could hear the tremendous beat of my heart rush with every passing second. It drowned out his cackles just long enough for me to cry out Beau's name. If I had any word trembling on my lips as I died, I wanted it to be his name. I threw my head back as the pain circulated my torso and crept up my neck. I clenched my teeth and with every fibre not fallen prey to the torture, I mustered an ounce of sanity, trying to drift to a happier place in my mind. 'Beau' I cried again. An unstoppable fire ignited behind my eyes, the pain bludgeoning me from the inside, there was momentary darkness. 'Beau' I begged, my streaming tears extinguishing the flames.

'Crying for him will not help, you're here because of him.' He smiled ecstatically as what he had told me sunk in. The bitter, iron kick from the taste of my own blood trickled over my quivering lips as his onslaught of blows continued. My senses were a blurred mess of pixilated visions, all with a ruby red hue that shot through my mind as I attempted to detach myself from where I was. I could hear the sloshing of water in some kind of metal tin beside me. I turned my head not actually wanting to see what it was, but rather feeling compelled to identify my looming fate. The man stood tall over me, a naked lightbulb swinging on a long piece of flex above his head. With the large green petrol can in his hand and a sly grin plastered on his scratch-marked face I had all the answers I needed, no more guessing necessary. Surprisingly, amongst the horror and the sight of my now severely mangled body, acceptance and the idea of being no more, briefly fluttered forward; as it helpfully does when you are screwed to the point of no return. *This is where I would die. It will be over soon. Not much longer now.*

Quickly realising I wasn't reacting as much to his inflicted pain as he would have hoped for, his voice came at me again. 'Grace, I'm here to free you. I had never hoped for a more willing subject. After all the problems with Gwen I was about to give up, but then you arrived through the door. The love that stupid boy felt for you, that yearning devotion he projected without even realising it. It was all just too enticing to pass up. Christ, a blind man could see the affection you two have for each other. At first, I thought you wouldn't be susceptible, but Beau really hasn't taught you very well, has he? Instead of making sure you were protected, he's allowed you to stay this defenceless shell of a person. A puppy dog in a world of fiery dragons. This is going to be much more fun than I had anticipated. You are a lot more amusing then Gwen. She had way too much fight in her.'

With every step he took closer to me, the rotten reek of his stale breath intensified. Confusion and terror were blinding me. The only thing I could do was beg. He was right, I had no fight left in me; the mere mention of how Beau and I felt for one another kick started my drive to survive this, I refused to die at the hands of this monster. Acceptance of my dire situation was quickly taking a back seat to my desire to keep breathing. 'Look you don't have to do this; I'll give you whatever you want.' I pleaded, looking directly into those blood-curdling eyes, searching for any minute speck of compassion; even though I was pretty sure he didn't even know the meaning of the word.

'You don't get it, do you?' he laughed. 'I have exactly what I want...I have YOU!' I turned my head away from his glare and closed my eyes tightly. I tried to fill my mind with happier times. Memories of my Dad warmed me and slowed down my racing heart. Beau's smile, his kiss, how much I truly believed he loved me grounded me. Everything that I had in my life was so much more powerful than anything he could do to me. He ripped the mask from my face. The cold liquid splashed against my skin, flooding the floor beneath me. No amount of happy thoughts, reassuring memories or acceptance could save me now. The fear was too powerful and the agony too real. The emotional rollercoaster of it all the only reminder that I was still alive. The liquid doused my hair and my silk nightdress. It felt like thick tar as it trickled down my mouth and into my lungs. Then there was that scent again, that familiar but unrecognisable stench; the malodour of burnt human flesh. He was a twisted murderer and I was giving him every little bit of pleasure he desired. My weakness, my fear, my tears, my racing heart. I looked into his eyes, his shocking auburn hair alight against his pale milky skin. 'I'm not afraid of you.' I protested uneasily with an unmistakable tremor in my voice.

'Don't kid yourself, you are more terrified of me then you even know, even through the petrol I can smell it on you.' He wrapped his skeletal fingers around a lock of my hair, pulled it up to his nose and smiled. 'I've enjoyed the time we have shared together Grace, it truly has been more fun than I've ever had before. I almost gave up the last time, but I've spent a little time observing your weaknesses, I finally felt you were ready for me. You see, I'm no longer confined to the human body that held me prisoner and limited my power. It took me some time to realise my true potential. If I had known that being dead would allow me to have this much fun, I would have killed myself years ago. ' He circled around me, apparently plucking this nonsense from mid-air. I was not a person to him, just merely a disposable play thing for him to enjoy. 'It's time for you to go now Grace, but we can pick up where we left off again soon, I've got endless amounts of time. I've got a few other visits I've got to make.' He grinned cruelly, baring his off-yellowing teeth that were unusually long and thin. I screamed and struggled at my restraints. He pulled a gleaming hunting knife out of his waistband and raised it up to his lips.

"Shhhhhh."

The sound echoed around me. Then there, in his other hand, was the conclusion to my horrific nightmare, his explosive finale – my end.

He waved almost coyly before raising his other hand, holding up the lit match, it's flickering glow twisting his features. With a piercing scream the orange and yellow flames licked at my body. My once pink and supple skin now bubbling, puckering in response to the heat. I threw my head back and a noise unlike any other bellowed out of me.

He had won.

TWENTY-EIGHT

ꕥ

My body was vertical before I could even open my eyes, thrashing around on the floor of my bedroom whilst trying to extinguish the remnants of the flames that had licked furiously at my skin. The memory of them making the sensation all too real still. With the fire gone I took my time to inspect the damage. This time the bruises on my arms and legs were clear purple indentations from thick, tatty ropes. I traced the pattern with my finger, recalling the painful rubbing of the rope against my body, the searing heat emanating from my melting skin a close second. I shot up onto my feet for a better look in the mirror. Apart from the rope marks and the black rings that circled my eyes everything else appeared pretty normal, or as normal as anything could be in this situation. I ran my hands through the ratty tendrils of matted brown hair that were coated in a thick helping of petrol, remnants dripping down onto my top. *How could this come out of a dream? How can something make the transition between a dream and reality? Does this mean I can take something into a dream with me?* Knowing I had a machete handy next time I'm forced to endure that nightmare would be some comfort at least.

After an hour-long shower, two bottles of shampoo and the last of the hot water, I was finally rid of the petrol in my hair. Unfortunately, the reek of it still lingered over the aroma of my jasmine shampoo, I couldn't mask the marks that appeared around my wrists as easily. I got dressed quickly with little concern as to what I was wearing, as long as it did the job in hiding my secret, it would do. I tugged at the sleeves on my blue hoodie tucking the cuffs securely into the band of my fingerless black gloves. I threw my school bags over my shoulder, grabbed my car keys from the side table in the hallway and made my way out to my car as fast as my legs could carry me. My belly rumbled furiously. In my haste to sidestep any questions from my mother and get out of the house, I hadn't eaten breakfast. I buckled my seatbelt, turned the key in the ignition; the engine spluttering to life like an eighty-five-year-old chain smoker. I put the gearshift into reverse. Looking out of the windscreen, up towards my bedroom I noticed the billowing curtains that wafted open, disturbing the nets. Unsettled slightly I made my move to exit my car, my tummy rumbling again, protesting that I alleviate my hunger. As my foot hit the cobble stones of our drive, I stood motionless, fixed to the spot as *slightly unsettled* revved into third gear, dread now etched on my face. A pair of bodiless stiff hands clawed the edge of each curtain pulling them slowly back together. *I'll go hungry. No way, shape or form am I going back in there* I thought throwing my stuff into the back seat of my car. Whether it was stupid or sane; although I was sure I would be proved wrong eventually either way, I decided I would keep my dreams to myself. I shouldn't bother Beau; not at this stage at least. It was Gwen I had to speak to. The red-haired man had mentioned her, maybe if we could put our experiences together, we just might have a shot at doing something about it. I had no clue what was going on or who he was, but I had to hope that something could be done to send him back to where he belonged. I just really hoped I would live long enough to see it through.

~~~~

'So?' Amelia urged with a hyena smile and questioning wide eyes.
~~~~

'So what?'

'So, is it first base, second base, PREGNANCY!?' Everyone in the library turned around and began to stare at us intently, hanging on to our conversation with morbid curiosity, waiting with anticipation for the next sentence to leave my mouth. I pulled Amelia into the last row of the library by the strap of her handbag, which was thankfully deserted, I wasn't surprised, how often do you see college students making their own clothes and gardening? The self-help section never really got any foot traffic.

'Firstly, shush bigmouth and secondly, that's none of your business.'

'That means you've had a peck on the cheek and a friendly platonic hug.' Amelia retorted smugly.

'No, it doesn't, it just means I think you're bloody nosey.' As Amelia's face fell, I felt deliriously superior. I glanced at the list of the term's reading requirements, tracing my finger along the shelves looking for the matching reference codes. It was pretty pointless. The books were never where they were meant to be.

'Fine don't tell me, but don't come crying to me in six months when you realise, he's gay!' Amelia's controlling desire to know all had quickly turned into jealously and both I and Amelia knew that any shade of green was not a becoming look for her. I was enjoying her moody, frustrated silence but it took all of five seconds for Amelia to open her mouth again. 'Okay, I'm sorry Grace, I take that back, there's a pretty good chance he's not gay.' Her *sorry* felt terse, her actual statement only half-heartedly offered up in a bid to extract more information, trying to regain control of the conversation. I wasn't buying the particular brand of reverse psychology she was selling. 'Well a little advice anyway spoil sport, be good and if you can't be good, be careful. My Mum swears by it.'

'OK Doctor Phil, I'll keep it in mind.' I wouldn't. Amelia's Mum was currently on her fifth toy boy husband, each one younger than the last. Her top mottos were sending your divorce lawyer a very expensive gift basket at Christmas and becoming very good friends with your pharmacist. She popped the morning after pill like it was a vitamin. Amelia's helpful hint was discarded out of my head, much like the whole of year ten maths; before it had long enough to fester and breed, ultimately corrupting me. Who needs Algebra anyway?

'You really like him, don't you?' she teased as she poked at my arm repeatedly with her sparkly pink polished nails.

'Yeah I guess I do' I beamed sheepishly.

'Well then you need to be prepared for the inevitable, it won't be long before you succumb to his manly urges.' There were no words! Firstly, because her eloquently put point would usually just be described as *'doing it'* and secondly because she successfully used the word *succumb*. 'Grace, what are you staring at?' She fluffed her hair and pawed at her face making sure her three layers of make-up were still intact.

'Succumb? Manly urges?'

'Oh, I've started reading those Mills and Boon novels my Aunt Sally got my Mum last Christmas. They're bloody great. Patrice, the lonely milkmaid has just met Alastair, the handsome, always shirtless, brooding farm hand in the barn. Unfortunately, I fell asleep before I could get to the juicy bit. I got to the point where Patrice's *naked loins were burning with anticipation and yearning,* something was most definitely yearning.' she recounted dreamily as she stared off into the distance.

'So let me get this straight, while I've been studying the frightfully dull Ibsen, you've been getting all hot and steamy with a book about a desperate lonely milkmaid with no morals, who as luck would have it, has fallen for a rippling farm boy, who coincidentally, likes to roam around with his shirt off?'

'FARM MAN Grace, FARM MAN!' she emphasised defensively, once again extending her manicured finger like an unsheathed sword and jolting me in the shoulder.

'OK, calm down, Alastair the FARM MAN!' I accentuated every syllable just to annoy her.

'Right I'm off, have fun with Bill!' She turned on her heels and sashayed like a catwalk model towards a group of boys sitting around the computer tables, every single one of them doused in the early evening sun that funnelled through the large window behind them, looking like they had been dragged right out of an Abercrombie and Fitch advert. They made their way out through the glass double doors, their skateboards under their arms, Amelia and a blonde guy in a football jersey leading the pack.

'It's Beau!' I shouted at her before the doors could close, but by then she was already gone. The idea of taking the next step with Beau, or as Amelia put it, *'succumbing to his manly urges',* scared the life out of me. For me the idea was chilling. Actually, completely petrifying would be a more apt description. I definitely wanted to. I'd have to be deaf, dumb and blind to not want to. Whether it had crossed Beau's mind or not was a subject I didn't want to even attempt to decipher. I'd come to learn that Beau was different to every other guy I'd ever met. The moment his lips touched mine, my mind went blank, my thoughts dancing around whimsically like the pretty horses on a carousel. I was utterly powerless when it came to Beau. I had little control over how deeply I felt for him, and I was okay with that.

~~~~

A long week or so had passed since my last nightmare and I had relaxed back into a normal sleeping pattern again, except for the haunting flashback I got every time I filled my car up at a petrol station. I had pretty much been able to push the memories to the back of my mind, just long enough to get as much sleep as I needed to function on a daily basis, without causing concern. I had got my head around what had happened, planned to kick the creepy guys arse into oblivion and I'd made a date to go and visit Gwen. The task of telling Beau what had happened was looming. Lying to him was agonising. He had so much faith and trust in me, I constantly felt guilty. I walked up the drive cautiously looking for Beau's motorbike that thankfully wasn't parked up. It was now or never. I had to get this off my chest and Gwen seemed the perfect candidate to help me; or at the very least I hoped she could help me.

I reached out my hand to knock on the door but before my hand had met the rigid wood Gwen was there, smiling warmly as usual. 'Hello honey you're just in time, I've just made some tea.' She gestured to the living room inviting me in. The house as usual was very warm and the smell of freshly baked bread emanated from the kitchen. I walked towards the sofa anxiously fiddling with the belt loops on my jeans. 'Hey Grace, is everything OK?' It was hard not to notice Gwen's bandaged leg poking out from underneath
~~~~

her African print skirt. I wasn't OK and her injury didn't help to settle me any.

'Urm...yeah, I just really need your help with something.'

'OK, sounds ominous. Well no time like the present, what can I help you with?' Gwen took a seat in her armchair and waited for me to sit down.

'Right, I might as well just come out with it'

'Yes?' she prompted.

'Would you read my cards please?'

'Of course, honey, is that what you've been so flustered about?'

'Yeah, kind of.' I didn't know what I was seeing or what was happening to me. If Gwen could see it in her cards then I technically wouldn't have to say anything.

'Right, well let's get started then.' Gwen hobbled slightly to the dining room table and moved the full fruit bowl onto the dark wood dresser next to it. 'Grace, would you mind closing the curtains and turning off the lights please?' I did as I was asked quickly. The thought of Beau's surprised face popping through the door sent a surge of eagerness through me. Gwen moved the silky mauve shawl from the smaller circular side table onto the dining table, arranging it neatly; the tassels draped over the sides, falling onto the two chairs placed either side. Positioned in the centre of the table on the shawl was an oversized deck of cards. Gwen must have lit at least fifteen candles, all of them white and slender with their own ornate holders made of twisted silver. The largest display of candles was at the end of the table facing our chairs, an ornately designed holder that reminded me of a menorah. This holder held nine candles that shone brightly down onto the table, flickering light in every direction over the satin material. The strong scent of lavender wafted around me, reminding me of home as it tickled my nose. A large glass tumbler filled with water was placed next to the candle display at the end of the table. 'So, are we ready?' Gwen asked as she ushered me to my seat.

'What's the water for Gwen?' I inquired as she took her seat.

'It takes all of the bad energy out of the room and holds it in the confines of the glass. We don't want to pick up on any unwanted spirits while were channelling your future. Could get a little messy.' She replied nonchalantly as she relaxed into her chair. *Unwanted spirits – that's a joke!* He was always with me, whether I was awake or asleep, the memories of him ingrained in my thoughts.

'Right Grace, firstly I need you to relax, you look so wound up.' I tried to laugh off the statement that couldn't have been any closer to the truth. I shook out my arms and returned my gaze to the deck of cards. 'Well what I need you to do now is take the pile of cards in your hands and close your eyes. I'd like you to shuffle them any way you like and just try and get an overall feel for them. Think about the questions you want answered.' I closed my eyes and all I had to do was simple - think about what I wanted to know. As my mind delved deeper and deeper it became an onslaught of flashes. My Dad, Beau, the red-haired stranger. I couldn't separate or concentrate on any one image. *Screw it.* I gave up trying and hoped for the best. I opened my eyes and put the cards down on the table. 'OK Grace, now I'm going to spread out the cards face down on the table. I need you to pick out nine of them, whichever ones you feel most drawn too. Then hand them to me one at a time sweetheart, face down.'

'Right' I agreed. I waved my hand theatrically over the cards, channelling an old Debbie McGee special I had seen on ITV as a kid and picked each one at random. I didn't have a system. I didn't feel like I was drawn to any of them, it could have been a game of UNO for all the mysticism it was stirring inside me. Gwen placed the cards I had selected in three rows facing her. She picked up the remaining cards and put them down next to the shawl.

'Let's get started' she said as she reached for the first card I had chosen. 'OK....The Emperor' Gwen lulled. As though comforting a baby, her voice was relaxing and reassuring, at least a pitch lower than her normal voice. The experience was yet to unmask the problem of the red-haired stranger. With eight other cards glaring up at me I knew it was only a matter of time before my secret was out. My mouth was bone dry; my heart full of anticipation as it lodged in my throat. 'Now this first line shows your past. The Emperor is a man who is very headstrong, brave and visionary. He can be described as ambitious and you regard him very highly. He is like a hero for you.' As the words left her mouth, I knew exactly whom she was describing. I knew only too well what man from my past encompassed all those things - my Dad. I couldn't think of a response so I mustered a sincere smile. Gwen turned over the next card placing it beneath the Emperor card. Her face fell.

'What does that one mean?' The panic forged on as the death card glared up at me. My horror was evidently crystal clear.

'Oh, sweetheart no, this isn't what you think. It resembles change.'

'But you looked so worried. If it isn't what I think then...'

'No, it's just, it tells us that you need to let go of those who have passed on' Gwen interrupted. I had only just got my Dad back. Well, sort of. I wasn't ready for that to be it. I didn't want to feel like I did before. 'Grace, I know it seems redundant considering what Beau can do, but every end is a new beginning. Death shows us how destructive it can be to hold onto things, it's what sets us free from the past.' Although welcomed, her response lacked the understanding I needed, the understanding that only Beau could comprehend.

'Your next card is The High Priestess. OK, now this card is definitely you Grace. It represents an independent minded woman.' *Woman? When did that happen?* 'She likes her freedom of actions and choices. She is highly regarded, a warm and attractive young woman.' That word again. I imagined my mother suddenly, the bills, the killer mortgage, the school runs, the marriage, the giving birth - TWICE! For now, I was more than happy just being a kid.

'Are you sure that's me?'

'It may not describe who you think you are now, it's the past so it's who you were.' *OK- confused* I thought. 'It could also mean the woman you will evolve to be, it could be a mirror image of someone else from your past. Your past is a configuration of understanding and resolution Grace. So, you ready to find out about your present and your future? This is where the fun really begins.' I attempted to prepare myself for the revelations yet to come but I had a sneaking suspicion they would be as surprising as my past.

TWENTY-NINE

ഌ

'Well, well.' Gwen said as she placed her fingers on the Knight of Wands card.

'What does that one mean?' Curiosity gripped me. I edged my chair in closer to the table, scraping the legs on the wooden floor as I went.

'This represents a dynamic male energy in your life. He is forceful, extrovert and full of life. With him by your side he will inspire you to visualise yourself in a better place. He is optimistic and desires to explore life with you.' Our eyes met and our mimicked smiles stretched widely across our faces.

'Gwen, I think it's safe to say that that one definitely doesn't need analysing.' I chuckled.

The next card shocked me, it shouldn't have of course, if I was being honest with myself, it was exactly what I had anticipated. In a strange way this was the whole reason I had visited Gwen – the truth. The warm smile no longer licked the edges of Gwen's mouth. 'The Knight of Swords' she mumbled. 'This represents power by manipulation or force. This is a warning Grace, do not hand your rights over to this person so easily. Hard as it may appear, this is a great force you are threatened with. The desire you have to protect others, spurs him on further. It takes great courage to resist the hold he has over you but this is the only way you will succeed against him.' It was now clear why I was such a bad liar; my face gave me away every time. 'Grace, you know who this is, don't you?' Gwen's worry magnified as she cupped her hands securely around mine. I pulled my hands free from Gwen's and placed them on my lap. My inability to share this most obvious truth with Gwen blindingly clear, my emotions shutting off completely.

'No of course not, but he sounds bloody dodgy. What's the next card?' I prompted, ensuring I didn't make eye contact. After a short, uncomfortable silence filled with lingering suspicion, Gwen continued.

'OK, the last card of your present is...' The grave expression again washed over Gwen. It was becoming increasingly obvious that this red-haired man was invading more than my dreams. 'I will finish your reading Grace, but then I want you tell me everything...EVERYTHING, OK?' It was a demand disguised as a question. Her wide-eyed stare spoke volumes, warning me to forget about any lie I had begun to concoct. She placed the Tower card onto the table in front of me. The silence engulfed me as I waited for Gwen to speak. 'The Tower card is otherwise known as the Destroyer. Its aspects include fury, violence, ruin, rage and destruction. This card is here to teach us about courage in the face of hardship. You have to talk to someone, this wall that is holding you back, it can be broken down, but you need to release all the pent-up worries that are plaguing you. This is a test of your will, of your strength.' Gwen no longer spoke with her cheery tone and Disney-esque demeanour. I felt defeated and lost at that moment, I wanted desperately to share what was on my mind, to get it off my chest, but it just didn't seem that easy, my mouth refusing to comply with my brain's instructions. 'So, your present isn't as optimistic as we could have hoped for, but the Knight of Wands will help banish the destructive evil in your life. You have to be willing and open about the forces working against you. You have to be prepared for a new world of comfort and understanding. It will help see you through.' I took on board her advice, feeling a little more at ease than I had done ten minutes ago. My uneasiness wavered for a brief and fleeting moment as I sunk into her lulling words. I knew that the psychic inside her knew more than she was letting on, but I would take the specks of comfort where I could get them. 'Grace let's move onto your future.'

'I can only hope that's a little brighter. It's not like it's been all daisies and cotton candy so far.'

'Hush. And you can calm it with the sarcasm smarty-pants.'

'What the hell. Let's do this. Hit me with my future.' Gwen gave me a passing glance and turned over my seventh card.

'Now we're talking.' She yelled clapping her hands together. 'The Two of Cups represents a new chapter in an existing relationship. In this card we can see the mutual exchange of love, a heightened state of mind and a profound understanding of the emotive consciousness. It's a harmony in both mind and soul.' The feeling of trepidation eased; thoughts of Beau's face clear in my mind. However, brief it had occurred lately, my heart was now alit with the prospect of some good. 'We're on a roll.' The poker player buried deep inside Gwen jumped forward as she eagerly turned over the next card. 'The Eight of Swords explains a lot here. It represents frustration. You remain blindfolded by something that you are unable to explore. You cannot go to this place, however much you want to. Patience is the biggest virtue and with that comes greater understanding. Eventually you will see.'

'What do you mean it explains a lot?'

'Well, I see how you and Beau are together, I see the change in him since he has met you. You complete each other in a way that others try a lifetime to create. His gift will always make you feel like you're in a pitch-black tunnel, with a flash light that has run out of batteries. You can feel his hand on yours, but what he sees in the tunnel is not what you see.' I pondered the accuracy of Gwen's thoughts. *Question is, do I really want to see what he sees?* 'Shall we have a look at your final card then?' She pressed.

'Why not? I've made it virtually unscathed so far.' I laughed excitedly. The mere thought that Beau was present in my future, filled me with happiness, my fear of losing him always at the back of my mind.

'The Temperance. This highlights spiritual elevation, enlightenment, enhancing a gift that you possess and using it to its full potential. In order to develop a greater state of awareness you need to delve deep into your past, only then will you understand the present. If you place truth in your soul you will acquire the freedom you desire.' The words made their way in one ear and unfortunately left through the other just as quick. I was trying to analyse everything Gwen was saying, but on a whole, I wasn't doing a very good job.

'It's a good card then?'

'It's a very good card Grace. Your future shows great knowledge and acceptance, not just of others, but of yourself and how you have evolved. I don't know how far in the future it is, but something tells me you have a problem here in your present, which needs to be addressed.' Gwen placed my cards back into the deck and wrapped them neatly in the silk mauve shawl. 'I think it's definitely time for a cup of tea.

When I get back you can tell me what's been on your mind. I want the whole truth as well missy.' I moved towards the sofa waiting for Gwen to return. 'So, spill it then.' Gwen prompted as she handed me a mug of steaming herbal green tea and a couple of chocolate bourbons.

'It's hard to explain.'

'Try! I can see how much this is bothering you. Your cards clearly point out a problem.' I squirmed in my seat uncomfortably as she berated me to come clean.

'OK, here goes. Have you ever had a dream that you could swear really happened, like Freddy Kruger, Rosemary's Baby kind of vibe?'

'Start from the beginning, what happened in this dream?'

'Well, I was being restrained by this man. I didn't think much of it at first but the next day the marks were still there. I know I probably sound insane, but I can't explain it. I've gone over it a thousand times in my head and I still can't figure it out.'

'Have there been any dreams since that one?' As the worry on Gwen's face settled on the surface, the events that occurred seemed harder to shrug off as a nightmare. If she was worried, I definitely should be worried.

'A few others, I guess. The last time though everything was clearer, I couldn't move, I couldn't scream, the pain in my chest was agonising. The one thing that stuck with me is the sound of water dripping. All day it follows me. His shoes squeaked, like he'd been walking through puddles. That laugh, it was so intense, it scared me more than anything else I have ever experienced.' I took in a deep breath, my rushed words a flurry of information. I peered up at Gwen through my eye lashes, my head dipped towards the ground as I waited for her reply. Her gaze was fixed on the table, as though she was looking through the surface, oblivious to my presence. 'Gwen? Gwen? Are you OK?' I grabbed her arm to try and shake her back to reality. She returned to the now with a shudder, her back as straight as an ironing board. Her face pleasant but withdrawn, her small smile oddly unfamiliar.

'Grace, wait here, I need to show you something.' She hobbled off towards the stairs in a hurry. As though I'd opened a door in my head the faint sound of his cackling laughter sent a shiver pulsing down my spine. Within a second Gwen appeared at the foot of the hallway stairs carrying a silvery green box. 'Open it' she urged practically throwing the box onto the coffee table in front of me. She clearly didn't want to let loose whatever resided inside. To my surprise Gwen went to the side board, propped her cane up against the wall and pulled out a bottle of whisky and a glass tumbler. She filled half her glass with the copper liquid and took a swig. If I'm honest it was more of a gulp; a very long gulp. She raised her now empty glass to me as a silent offer. I shook my head declining her offer, resuming my concentration on the box as Gwen topped up her drink. I pulled open the lid with my eyes partially closed. If something was going to jump out, I was going to be ready! *Closing your eyes, good move Grace.* My inner bitch added sarcastically with two thumbs held up high. Inside the box was a chaotic mountain of newspaper clippings. 'What's all this?' I asked as my manic breathing began to calm. Gwen was silent. She handed me the article from the top of the pile and took another gulp of her drink.

'Today a community has been shocked by devastation as a loving and devoted employee of Brinton's retirement facility tragically drowned whilst saving the life of a severely disabled resident. Pensioner and War Veteran Fredrick Charles lost control of his wheelchair when the brakes failed him. The downpour earlier that morning had made the ramps slick. Glen Havers was the staff member in charge and the only one to hand as numerous staff members were at home, bedridden with the flu. As Mr Charles' wheelchair made its way down the slippery slope, Mr Charles, with no means to escape, ended up in the facilities communal swimming pool. Unfortunately, Mr Havers had never learnt to swim and as he took the leap that would inevitably lead to his untimely death, only one thing was on his mind and that was saving Mr Charles. We send out our deepest regards and sympathies for Glen's family and friends. We will report again shortly with the updates on this hero's story.'

'OK, so?' I questioned, failing to grasp the point.

'He was no bloody hero.' She spat through gritted teeth. Bloody was a strong word for Gwen to think, let alone say. I think the alcohol was starting to kick in.

'Don't you think that's a little harsh?'

'Grace, take a look at the next one.' As I picked up the cut-out piece of newspaper my heart sank. In big bold letters were the words. ***'Glen Havers, True Hero.'*** The shocking red hair took my breath away, those eyes, those teeth. His appearance in the photo may have lacked the same wickedness that he had in my nightmares but it was definitely him.

'What the hell?'

'I thought you might have that reaction. I was hoping he wouldn't find out about you.' she whispered uneasily under her breath. Her glass of Dutch courage in her shaking hand. 'He callously took the lives of others for his own sadistic pleasure!' The contempt she held for him rolled off of her tongue distastefully.

'He pushed you down the stairs, didn't he?' Gwen wouldn't make eye contact with me. I had my answer. I knew only too well the lengths Glen would go to.

'Gwen, this isn't your fault.' The growing sadness in her eyes was intense. I could literally feel her pain, the torment. Most of all I could feel the succession of relief. She had been trapped with this man inside her head for god knows how many years and now she had finally spoken his name. 'This story can't be right Gwen, surely a man who looked after and saved elderly people couldn't butcher and murder on his days off? Could he?'

'Right, now Grace, I'm going to tell you something I have never told anyone before.' I nodded, silently begging her to continue. If past occurrences were anything to go by, I knew this was going to be anything but a fairy tale bedtime story. 'When I was younger, back in my late twenties, I worked with Glen at the retirement home. I was a day nurse. I had previously been living with my sister but when we parted ways, which is a whole other story, I had to find a job and quick. A friend who I went to night classes with told me about this job. It promised easy hours and good pay. I never liked Glen from the moment I laid my eyes on him. From day one he made me anxious. There was something about him that just didn't feel right. A lot of the time, money and belongings went missing from the patients. Although everyone suspected it was Glen, nothing could be proved. On paper and in the view of our bosses he was a little peculiar, sure, but on the whole, he was a model employee. He got the work done. I went into my shift on the fifth of December, as I did every other dreary Monday morning. This Monday, however, most of the staff were out sick. I did my rounds as usual and as Mrs Parsons had died that previous morning, I figured Glen could deal with Mr Charles by himself. Instead of meeting out by the pool during Mr Charles morning walk round the grounds, as I usually did at 8:30am, I thought I could run an overdue assignment into college.'

'And that's when Glen drowned, I'm guessing.'

'Yes, Glen couldn't swim.'

'But why would he perform something so stupid if he couldn't swim?'

'Well Mr Fredrick Charles had been diagnosed with severe bowel cancer the previous month. He'd been given three months maximum to live. He had no living family and a very vast fortune from his young days in the stocks trade. Glen was determined he would make it into Fredrick's will, and if he didn't, there would be a very wealthy animal hospital over in Romford. It's all he could talk about in the canteen. He was obviously sure that I would be there to help him out of the water. Once he had secured Fredrick to the side of the pool grasping for dear life, he looked over to where I would usually be, but he was greeted with nothing.'

'Oh god Gwen.' I placed my hand on her cold still hands rubbing them ferociously, trying to help the blood flow again.

'He has blamed me ever since.' She sobbed.

'Does he visit you as well?' I asked, finding some solace in the possibility of sharing this fear.

'I can only hear him, but I would recognise that laugh anywhere, those shrills of pure evil.' We both shuddered in unison at the escapable memory, that had been burned into our subconscious.

'What can we do?' I pleaded.

'He seems to have a greater hold over you. The power and fear he can evoke in you will eventually be his downfall.'

'Can I ask Gwen, what is with the petrol can and the knife? I understand the squelching shoes and the dripping water but surly greed wouldn't push a man to those lengths?'

'Glen wasn't just greedy. After his death, when he visited me, he would tell me things and taunt me. It was only a year later I could piece it altogether and get an idea of what had actually happened before his death. Take a look at some of the other articles in there, in the red binder.' I delved down deeper into the box and pulled out a small red file that was hidden away at the very bottom.

THIRTY

ꕥ

'Another innocent young woman has been murdered at the hands of the elusive serial killer. He is yet to be named. He has left no evidence at any of the scenes, leaving the police baffled. They have a cold case which is in desperate need of being solved, as fear among the young women in this city soars out of control.

Rebecca Jane Seal was a twenty-two-year-old philosophy student with great prospects ahead of her. She was popular amongst her peers, constantly involved in charity work in her community. Her family and friends are said to be distraught at the news; at how someone so loving and giving could be snatched so cruelly from this earth.

Rebecca was found in a deserted alley in Camden on the stairs of a fire escape. Her body was discovered in the early hours on June 23rd by a couple returning home from a night out. They often used the alleyway as a short-cut home. Both were clearly traumatised by what they had seen that morning. Rebecca's body was severely disfigured. Her father identified Rebecca's body later that day by a birthmark on her right thigh. She had been beaten black and blue and tortured with what the police can deduce is a nine-inch hunting knife. She was then dragged to where she was later found, where the perpetrator set fire to Rebecca's lifeless body, a measure we believe the perpetrator is taking in an effort to make these victims unidentifiable.

We are pleading with the public for any information, no matter how small they may think it is. Were you in the

Camden area on the night of June 23rd? Did you see anything out of the ordinary? We hope to reassure our readers with some further developments in this case when we next come to print.'

'And they never caught him?'

'Of course not. To them Glen Havers never existed. They couldn't tie the two together. Until his death he was invisible. He was a recluse, quiet, always skulking about on his own. Here, read this one.' Gwen moved to the last insert in the red book and poured herself another drink. I considered taking her up on her earlier offer. 'It's dated six months after Glen's death.' She handed the dog-eared yellowing article to me, her hands still not completely steady.

'The police have now closed the case of the serial killer who roamed our streets and murdered the innocent. His spree of terror lasted two years, with more than fifteen innocent women laid to rest. The pattern of this particular serial killer had always been planned and date specific. It has now been six months and no one has seen or heard of any other cases. The police can only conclude that the perpetrator of these crimes has either been incarcerated or has died. We know that although the families of the young women taken so cruelly need closure, for other women who walk on these streets, we pray for the latter. A menace to society who clearly held no moral code or standing, who would kill as easily as he would make breakfast, we pray that this really is the last that we hear from him.'

'Gwen, why did you never go to the police with your theories after Glen had died?'

'How would I say I came about the information? The dead ghost of a murderer told me he slaughtered all those girls in cold blood? It's hardly a conversation I wanted to be having with anybody, let alone the police. They would have laughed me out of the station, or locked me up in some asylum. Do you remember that sister I mentioned?' I nodded. 'Well she had gifts too. They were so much more heightened then mine. She chose to try and ignore them, to pretend they weren't there.'

'Why would she do that?'

'Her husband didn't agree with it and she had kids. She didn't want them affected. School is hard enough without everyone thinking your Mum is a loony. She would know, we were teased constantly. Our Mum was a powerful psychic, but to most she was the crazy lady who lived in the big house on George Street. My sister died shortly after we parted ways, so I really did feel all alone then. I continued to work at my craft and did the very best I could with it. I've got so much to be grateful for, all my children, my grandchildren and now you and Beau.' She smiled as the words fluttered from her mouth. I had come to her with a problem so extraordinary, so unbelievable and she had supported me every step of the way. No wonder Beau loved her so much. I clapped my hands together before I began putting all the papers back into the box.

'So, I guess now the question is, how do we get Glen out of our heads and firmly out of our lives, for good this time?' I mused, a smidgen of hope clawing its way back into my soul.

'We're going to have to coax him into your head before we can get him out of it.' Gwen warned apprehensively.

'Why my head?'

'Well he seems to be strongest there. He can't get into mine which is why I can't sense him. We want him to think he has an unbreakable hold over you. I'm guessing Beau has told you about spirits and the variety of powers and gifts they can acquire.' I nodded along hesitantly. *Is it just me or does this idea sound worrying, terrifying even?* 'Glen has had time to manipulate those powers to his will. He knows that if he doesn't want to be seen he doesn't have to be. He can't risk us interfering. Beau's gifts are coveted, although he helps people to accept death and move on, there are many damaged souls that would love to take him out of business. Like a rotting apple, Glen has festered in your thoughts and dreams until it's impossible for you to get rid of him. Now he can get in and out whenever he wants.'

'That's why he seems to be getting stronger with every visit. He's definitely enjoying his new found sense of power.' I added.

'First things first Grace, I think you should talk to Beau about all this. He's away tonight but he'll be back tomorrow afternoon and if you want to come here, I'll have the paper clippings to hand.'

'What about tonight?' The dread had made its way back to my voice and it was hard to hide.

'I very much doubt he will be making an appearance tonight. They don't exist in the same time pattern we do.' she assured me as she put her arms around me. I got a full whiff of her musky Chanel perfume and the beads around her neck tickled my chest. 'Do you want me to call your Mum, let her know you've fallen asleep here? I will send you home in the morning.'

'Yes, please Gwen, just until I speak to Beau. I'll feel so much better once I tell him the truth. Actually, maybe I should call her, she'll only worry otherwise.'

'OK honey, use the phone in the hallway. I'll go and fix you some dinner.'

'Thanks Gwen.' I made my way to the hallway, picked up the heavy receiver, dialling the number hesitantly. My eyeline still drawn to the box of articles sitting on the coffee table. 'Hi Mum.' Her voice pulled me back into the present.

'Hey honey, is everything OK? I thought you would have been home ages ago.' I could hear the worry and sadness in her voice. I hated lying to her, especially with how far we had come, but this was for the best. The last thing I wanted was for her to know just how much trouble I was in.

'Yeah everything's fine Mum, I just felt a little unwell so I had some dinner at Gwen's and I fell asleep on the sofa.'

'What's wrong? Do you want me to come and pick you up?' The jangle of her car keys on the side table at the other end of the phone assured me if I had said yes, she would be in her car and on her way to me in an instant.

'No Mum, I'll be fine, I just feel like I've got a bit of a cold coming on, I think I'm going to stay here tonight. Beau's staying at a friend's house and Gwen's all alone. You've got that consultation, tonight right? Cary's still staying with Eloise, isn't he?' My attempt at faking strep throat was abysmal, so I coughed and spoke normally before she figured me out.

'Yeah, but only if you're sure, I don't mind picking you up on my way home.'

'Honestly Mum, don't worry about me.' I said it even though I knew she would worry anyway; apparently, it's a mum thing.

'Right, well I'll drop over some of your bits on my way out, then you can get comfortable and then I'll see you in the morning I guess.'

'OK Mum, I love you.'

'I love you too sweetheart.' It was clear that *drop over some of your bits* actually meant *come over to check out your story*. I giggled to myself as I put down the handset.

'Is everything okay with your Mum?' Gwen yelled from the kitchen as the kettle howled loudly and something sizzled in the frying pan, whatever she was creating smelt amazing.

'Yeah, all good.'

'Are you ready to go up?' Gwen asked from behind me. I nodded. Gwen escorted me up the wide carpeted staircase with a tray in her arms.

'Gwen, do you want me to take that?'

'I'm not that old yet Grace' she laughed.

'I meant because of your leg grandma.'

'Watch your tone.' she laughed. 'I will manage just fine.' I ran my hand along the hefty wooden banister and with each step I grew sleepier. Gwen opened the door to Beau's bedroom. 'I don't think Beau will mind. I think after a good night's sleep everything will seem a lot clearer.' She ushered me through the doorway with a nudge, following on after me, putting the tray down on Beau's pristinely made bed.

'Gwen, how did you make this up so quickly?'

'I have my ways.' she tapped her nose with her finger. Before I could come back with a snarky remark to make her laugh, she had her arms around my neck, pulling me into a hug. 'Everything will be OK Grace. If you need me, I'm just up the hall.' She went to pull the door closed behind her, a heartfelt smile on her face.

'Oh Gwen...'

'Yes dear?' She poked her head in the partially closed door.

'Mum's going to drop by soon with some of my stuff. If that's okay?'

'No problem, I'll leave the porch light on. I've got to finish off some stuff downstairs anyway. Night honey.'

'Night.' I replied sleepily on a yawn. The room quickly filled with the smell of the still sizzling bacon and eggs on the plate. I was hungrier then I'd realised. I climbed onto the bed and crossed my legs as I began to tuck in, for the first-time glancing around Beau's room, his half naked body no longer a distraction. I'd only ever really seen it in passing, when I used the toilet. The ornately carved, wooden, double bed took up most of the room, with two, small, identical side tables, one positioned on either side. The vintage music posters lining the far wall looked so old with their worn edges - The Clash, The Beatles and Muddy Waters. Now the Beatles I knew, Dad was nuts about them, but I was clueless as to the others. I myself was more partial to the musical stylings of Shawn Mendes or Kaleo, if I needed a side portion of gritty greatness with my day. There were a couple of shelves on the opposite wall filled untidily with books. His laptop was in the far corner on a blue metallic framed desk just under the window, white slatted blinds shielding me from the outside world. The small dark wood shelf over the bed had on it an old teddy bear with matted fur with a red velvet tie secured around its neck. Attached to its hand was a red jewellery box shaped like a rose. I debated for a second or too whether having a peek inside might have meant I was crossing a line, but I decided to call it inquisitiveness and have a look. *You're really going to go there? Rummage through his privacy? Don't say I didn't warn you.* My conscience was speaking loud and clear as I reached for the box. My desire to know what was in there winning the fight. There was a stunning gold and platinum heart locket pendant that had the word 'Reinca' engraved in swirly italics on the back. I had no idea what it meant though. The sturdy gold chain had four, different coloured, draping gems that sat idly, two either side of the delicate locket. Cradled in the bear's other arm was what looked like a handmade frame with pasta shells and glitter decorating the edges. Definitely not something I could see them selling in Tesco's. The frame held an old photo that was crumpled at the edges, its colouring washed out by light and age. A little boy and what I would guess was his mother sat on a large bucket chair, their eyes fixed on one another. Her stunning, long, scarlet coiled hair fell over her shoulders and covered her face as she held the little boy lovingly in her arms. The young boy, whose face could be seen more clearly, I had assumed was Beau. He had bright blonde curls, rosy cheeks and big, pale, blue eyes. Next to the frame was a small, rusting, purple Cadbury's tin. I had delved as far as I could. Yes, I wanted to know what was in the tin but

I could sense that whatever was in there, it was personal, deeply personal, and it clearly meant a great deal to him. It was a line I didn't want to cross. I didn't look inside. I took a bite of my toast and dipped it back into the runny egg. As I scanned the room, I recognised something that stopped me in my tracks. I put the toast back on the plate, edging towards the edge of the bed. Lying next to Beau's laptop was a chrome CD case, which for some reason seemed out of place. I didn't know why, but it seemed to shine a little brighter than everything else in the room; as though the light from above had singled it out. I put down my knife and fork onto the tray, my meal almost nearly completely demolished. I approached the desk and there it was; a CD of my Dad's music. *How did he get this?! Scrap that, where did he get it?* I took the CD over to the mini stereo that was on the bedside table next to Beau's bed. I felt the cover of the case, running my fingers over the edges, remembering when my Dad excitedly rushed through the door with it.

'It's finally here, our first printed copy! Something I will be able to tell Rolling Stone magazine about one day!' He beamed. His lifelong dream finally a reality. I moved the tray onto the floor and gulped down the glass of fresh orange juice. I jumped onto the bed and put the CD into the stereo eagerly. I plugged in the oversized earphones that hung from the bedpost, rested them over my head and pushed the play button. I reached over and cranked up the volume to the maximum, relaxing my head down onto the pillow as the soft beat of the drums of track one began. I pulled my knees up into my chest and covered myself with the brown sheepskin throw that was tucked pristinely at the foot of the bed. The sweet smell of Beau wafted up my nose as I took a deep breath in, this blanket the closest I would be able to get to him tonight. It would have to do. I had always listened to my Dad's music if I was upset or scared, it always made me feel at ease. Their indie, garage band tunes with powerful drum beats and edgy lyrical stylings had become

the only comfort I knew, until Beau walked into my life. With him came the realisation that there was a whole other world, even though I couldn't touch it or feel it, I now knew it was there. My dad was with me, he kept his promise. The music rung in my ears, the familiar melody sending me into a trance as I remembered his smile longingly. What I wouldn't give to his face again. It occurred to me that my Dad was going to miss out on so much in my life, my wedding, my children, my first house, the accomplishments I would make without him beside me, the times when I would need him and he wouldn't be there to hold my hand. I couldn't remember his voice anymore and the memory of his face was fading. Even with Beau's inside knowledge, it still felt like my dad was too far out of reach. *What will I do when I can't remember him at all?* For now, at least I had something to hold onto, a piece of him, a gift that I was grateful for. It was a chance encounter that I just had to cherish. Within minutes, with a tear in my eye and a smile on my face, I had drifted off into a deep sleep. The pulsing sound of my Dad's drumming was like a sedative; a horse tranquilliser but without the dodgy side effects. I was in a safe cocoon where sadness dripped away, the comfort of my surroundings lulling me into a peaceful rest

~~~~

I rubbed my tired eyes furiously, glancing at the clock next to me, the huge red numbers read 9:34. The coal black night flooded in through the blinds, whilst the shadows created by the moon and the swaying trees outside danced on the walls like playful children. The earphones were strewn on the floor and the faint sound of my Dad still playing the drums emanated from them. I switched off the stereo and threw on Beau's leather bike jacket that hung on the wardrobe door. The room was Arctic and with every step away from the warm bed I began to shudder a little more. If I hadn't needed to go to the toilet so badly, I would happily have
~~~~

snuggled back into the comfort of his bed for another twenty-four hours.

THIRTY-ONE

ഇ ര

I tiptoed speedily down the gloomy hallway, feeling along the pink rose papered wall for a light switch. I picked up the pace as my bladder threatened to explode. The frenzied need to not wet myself propelling me against the bathroom door and searching for the handle. When my hand finally curled around the cold steel, a feeling of pure exhilaration washed over me. After I'd emptied my bladder, which seemed to last longer then was humanly normal, I made my way to the white Victorian basin, turned the wrought iron fixtures until they hollered in protest; the pipework possibly just as old. I rinsed my soapy hands and grabbed for a pink stripped towel from off the rack. Calming warmth radiated against my cheek as the sun was rising, its rays hitting the circular stained-glass window from beside me. The shimmering colours created a rainbow effect that filled the room and sprung about wildly from walls to ceiling. I opened the door, the hallway either side of me at the end of my outstretched fingers were still draped in darkness. The wall in front of me however was illuminated by the golden shine that was projected through from behind me, my distorted shadow the only break in the light. The wall was swamped with at least fifty photographs, each presented in a sturdy, brown wooden frame. But as my eyes adjusted to the light, I realised there were in fact three frames that didn't match the rest.

The first print was sepia toned with frayed edges and a slightly blurry composure. The handmade frame still bore the marks of the tree it was cut from. There were two, beautiful, dark haired, pale faced girls, roughly seven years old, wearing matching lace dresses, an identical bow securing back the front of their hair. They stood in a wooded forest. Their mirror image faces were flooded with a despondent gaze. The fallen leaves covered every inch of the rest of the photograph, encasing their feet like quicksand. In the bottom right hand corner, scrawled in black ink, were the words '**Leaving Creston Lodge**' followed by a date '**1837**'.

The second photograph, closely positioned beneath the first was a black and white print secured in a scratched silver frame, time had tarnished its edges. *Are they the same two girls?* I mused. The girls were identical in each photo, the only thing that changed were their clothes and their surroundings. Their dresses here were now exquisitely draped around an exaggerated bell bodice. Their matching plush bonnet hats, secured with ribbons beneath their chins. They were standing on harbour docks, a colossal ocean liner positioned directly behind them, its vastness swamping the entire background of the photo. Scrawled in the right-hand corner were the words '**Clearwater docks**' followed by a date '**1873**', the handwriting on this photo the same as the last, the ink fresher though.

In the final colour photo there were the girls again. Their bright cherry hair, alight against their matching tan knit, cow–necked dresses that settled a little above their knees. They were sitting on a chipped bench that had been painted bright green, that same distant expression that plagued the girls in the other photos on their faces. Then there, in exactly the same place, scrawled in black biro were the words '**Oak Ridge Park**' followed by the date '**1964**'.

Glancing from one picture to another I couldn't tell the girls apart. Sure, their surroundings and clothes changed but the two young girls never seemed to change. *How is that possible? Maybe it's a photo trick.* With my imagination working overtime and my chilly feet turning into icicles I made my way back to Beau's bedroom. I put the headphones back on and restarted the CD from track one. I drifted back into a deep sleep easier than I had expected to.

~~~~

Relaxation and rejuvenation greeted me as I opened my eyes and acknowledged the new day. The headphones had worked their way onto the floor pulling the lead out of the stereo. Luckily for me the CD had finished. I kicked off the blanket energetically and reached down to get them. I hit the floor with a thud. 'CRAP!'

'Hey sleepy head' Beau beamed from the chair in the corner of the room behind me. My heart jumped into my throat as I greeted him with a frightened girly scream, my fingers grappling at the headphones and pointing them in his direction as though they were a weapon.

'Beau, what the hell are you doing here?' I shouted as I threw a pillow at him, using the momentary cover to flatten my chaotic hair. *Who said females could successfully multitask?*

'Well, you are in my room Grace,' he chortled with an inviting smile, whilst arranging the pillow comfortably behind his head, leaning back against it, that smile unmoving.

'Ha, ha, you know what I mean and don't look at me like that.'
~~~~

'Like what? I got back early and Gwen asked me to come up and wake you. I thought I'd take you out for some lunch.'

'Lunch?'

'Grace, it's a quarter past twelve.' I jumped out of the bed and rushed about like a headless chicken gathering up my stuff.

'My Mum's going to kill me!'

'No, she isn't, I spoke to her about half an hour ago.' I clearly wasn't listening to Beau. I threw my jumper on backwards, crouching down on the floor to retrieve my shoes from under the bed.

'Where the hell are they?'

'Looking for these?' Beau teased waving my baseball boots at me.

'Very bloody funny, give them back.' I held my hand out impatiently but I still couldn't help grinning at him. I grabbed my boots and dropped them onto the floor. I sat down on Beau's lap and he embraced me in his arms. I secured my arms around his neck, gently fiddling with his hair at the nape of his neck. 'I've missed you' I whispered. Leaning in as close to him as I could without actually allowing our lips to meet. The spark fizzled low in my belly, his bottom lip secured between his teeth making it throb a little more.

'I've missed you too Miss Gracie.' Everything about this man was clearly integral to my body functioning. My senses awoke to his presence, my skin demanding his touch as the hairs stood on end. *Kiss me* – the words were almost non-existent as they fell out of my mouth on a breath, more a plea than an instruction. With permission granted he stood up, pulling my body with his, my legs wrapped around his waist, my fingers tugging at the hair at the nape of his neck; insuring he couldn't break the hold. Even being this close didn't feel close enough. I pulled my hand around to cup his face, our mouths interlocked in the best kind of way. Needing to breathe I feathered light kisses on his face, hoping to settle the urge to rip his clothes off. It didn't work; never did. He lowered me down his body, my feet hitting the carpet.

'Let's go get some lunch, your treat.' He tugged at his full, ravaged lips, the sensation of me still lingering there.

'I don't bloody think so, it was your idea.' I chortled pulling on my boots and stuffing the laces into the sides. I put my bag over my shoulder and made my way to the door.

'I can't believe you're not even going to make the bed' he baited. I pinched his arm playfully, which made his smile grow.

'I thought I'd leave you something to do.' We made our way down the staircase still poking fun at each other and giggling as we went. I reached the living room and saw Gwen sitting at the dining table reading the paper. Her eyes met mine as she put down her cheese sandwich and her paper. *Oh god, I forgot. I've got to come clean with Beau.* After such a peaceful sleep I had completely forgotten everything that had happened the night before. As all the details crept forward, I took a seat next to Gwen.

'Hey, how about you two stay here for lunch? I just went shopping this morning, I'm sure you have so much to talk about.' Confusion washed over Beau as he glanced between Gwen and I.

'OK, is there something you need to talk to me about? You two look suspicious.' I couldn't look into those eyes; I didn't want to lie to him.

'Gwen, I noticed those photos in the hallway upstairs. Are they of your family?' I deflected.

'Nice try Grace.' she mumbled. Trying to change the subject with someone like Gwen who was always three steps ahead of me wasn't my finest plan I'll admit, but definitely worth a go. 'Right I've got to pop out for an hour or so, I'll let you two get on with it. I made some sandwiches and snacks for you, in there on the kitchen table.' Gwen grabbed her bag by the door and her keys out of the bowl on the side table. The door shut behind her with a thud. All of the morning's happiness leaving with her.

'Grace, what's going on?' Beau asked worriedly as he took my hand in his. I knew that I should tell him. Gwen had given me the perfect opportunity, but there was still something bothering me, like a pit-bull with a chew toy. What if I did tell Beau? He had made me a promise that he wouldn't let anything to do with his gift affect me. I didn't want to take the chance that he would leave me. I couldn't bear a life without Beau and at this moment, that was all I could think of. Sense and reason went out of the window when it concerned Beau. I would deal with this for a lifetime if it meant I had him by my side. With all this racing through my mind I said the only thing I could.

'Nothing's going on. I was trying to get out of Gwen what that surprise was you have planned for my birthday, but it was like getting blood out of a stone. That woman can definitely keep a secret.' I wasn't proud of it, but my heart and head agreed, advising me to lie, I would deal with any torture for this man.

'You are just going to have to wait until Friday. I promise you you'll like it though.' His smile was followed by a knowing wink. 'Well I'm going to have to love you and leave you, but I'll see you, tonight right?'

'Of course.' He leaned into me, his palm tugging at my waist, His lips softly met mine, a buzz of sensation making him jump back.

'What the hell was that?' The electric shock we shared glared at me with its *'you know exactly what that was'* look, as Beau rubbed his lips.

'Okay, better run.' I grabbed my bags from off the floor by the front door. I didn't want to be there when the penny finally dropped. I made my exit promptly, waving at him as I made my way down the drive. He stood in the doorway holding the door open with his foot still rubbing his lips with his hand, quizzically watching me jump into my car. 'Pop over later when you get a free minute, I want to show you something.' I yelled over the roar of the engine with a fixed false smile as I pulled away.

~~~~

As I ran for the door, I could already smell his aftershave. I grabbed the door handle and whipped it open without a word. The silence continued as I stood there like a lemon. 'Grace,' Beau said smoothly as he waved his hand in front of my face. I shook off my embarrassing daze.
~~~~

'Sorry, I was in a world of my own there.' I said as my jaw tightened uneasily. 'Come in!'

'So, Grace, what was it you wanted to show me?'

'Someone's a little impatient today, aren't they?' I teased.

'Rather intrigued actually.'

'Follow me.' I made my way to the stairs and Beau followed me eagerly as he removed his coat and hung it over the banister. 'Now, I've never shown you this. Saying that I've never shown anyone this.'

'Okay. Why are we standing outside a linen closet?' Beau inquired, desperately trying to peek around me to see inside.

'It's not...just wait and see.' I pulled the door to my darkroom/Mum's old linen closet open fully and led Beau inside. The bright amber light from the bulb attached to the far wall making every surface in the room appear orange. The deceptive size of the square room from the outside was exactly why I loved it. It housed three shelves on one wall that were cluttered with my camera lenses, photograph paper, boxed mixing fluids and a framed picture of me and my Dad. My workbench held the developing trays and the enlarging machine and even with all my equipment there was still space to swing a cat.

'Wow, this is amazing.' He glanced around the room as his eyes got used to the darkness. My prints blanketed the walls, some hung on string, strategically placed from each corner of the room above our heads as they dried. Beau wandered around looking at every piece of work I had lovingly produced. 'These are really great.'

'Thanks. These are what I wanted to show you, they were printed in a bit of a hurry but as soon as I saw them, I knew I had to show them to you.' I skipped over to the table resting against the far wall and muddled through at least a hundred prints. I passed a few to Beau as I kept searching for the others.

'These have come out great, if I do say so myself. You definitely capture my good side. Hey, hey, good looking' He lulled to his own image as he held his chin between his thumb and index finger. He turned to face the full-length mirror attached to the back of the door and struck a pose.

'Wow, big head, please remember this is only a small room and that ego of yours seems to be expanding with every second.' I glanced at his reflection. *Screw it, who am I kidding. He pulls off that pose with expert precision.*

'Ha, ha' he replied sarcastically as he crossed the room and put his arms around my waist.

'Here they are.' I turned around to face Beau and handed him the rest of our pictures.

'You look beautiful in these Grace.' I could feel the rushing blood pinching my cheeks a rosy red. Thankfully in the darkness Beau had absolutely no idea. 'Grace, is there a problem with your developing fluid? There are some smears or something in this one.' As he passed me the photo, I could feel a searing pain run up my arm and into my chest. My fingers flexed sending the picture floating in the air down to the ground beside my feet. I couldn't take my gaze from Beau, he riffled frantically through the pictures, this was the moment I was dreading, the moment where he would leave me. He would discover the truth and out my lies. 'And in this one. I can't make it out but it looks like someone's there. You see that?' He added quizzically. The stench of petrol began to fill the room making my head swim, my eyes losing the ability to focus. Without even glancing at the other photos I knew exactly who that was in the picture with us. 'This is a ghost Grace. Have you felt a presence or anything around you lately?'

'What do you mean? You're the one who can see them so how the hell would I know?' I retorted defensively; my legs just about ready to give way. The thought of him leaving me replaying like a bad record in my head.

'Breathe Grace, you need to breathe. Calm down.' he soothed, reaching over and taking my hand into his, the pictures now blanketing the floor.

'Maybe it's my Dad or something' I panicked.

'Grace, if it was your Dad, I would have seen him for myself. This is a ghost who doesn't want us to see him. If you know something, anything, you have to tell me!'

I sat on the stool next to him in silence and dropped my head. *What do I say? What could I possibly come up with to explain this? I know what I don't want to say that's for sure. The truth is not my friend in this situation.*

'Grace, the fact that this ghost doesn't want me to see him, and the fact that in every photo he is behind you, can only mean that he is attached to you.' Beau was right, in each photo, his presence became clearer, I couldn't see beyond Beau when I had looked at these photos. 'Look, he's leaving more and more of himself with you in each one. I've never seen it progress this quickly. Are there any more photos like this, of me and you?'

'Yeah, on the table.' Beau rushed to the table and recklessly raced through the photos. As the discarded pile grew, they began cascading onto the floor around me with the others. Beau frantically pinned the photos he had found onto the cork board secured to the wall. Once he was finished, I got up off the stool hesitantly. He was right. Now I could see something in the pictures. It was faint and grainy but there was no way I would ever forget that smirk, those grubby hands, or that head of russet red hair. *I have to come clean. If I don't tell Beau the truth now, he will work it out for himself and hate me – or leave me. Both situations I'd rather not explore.*

As I turned to him it was hard to control my words, before I could stop myself, I blurted out another lie. Fear had silenced my better judgement. 'I don't have a clue what's going on here.' I protested a little too eagerly. Beau looked at me intensely as he scanned my face for signs of a lie. Luckily for me I'd had quite a lot of practice lately. I had to find a way to tell him the truth, but this most definitely wasn't the way.

'Look Grace, I'm going to go and check a few things out. Try and keep busy and don't worry. I will sort all this out, I promise.' He kissed my forehead, fuelling my guilt, leaving the room running. I could hear his feet pound down the stairs as he picked up his pace. The front door thumped loudly as he pulled it shut behind him. The eerie silence enveloped me and with the second set of Goosebumps of the day creeping up my arms, I took it as a sign.

THIRTY-TWO

&

I made my way over to Gwen's to meet Beau for some lunch, as I veered around the corner and parked up outside, a sudden feeling of dismay washed over me. I quickly stifled my worry, climbed out of my car and locked the door. Within seconds of knocking a smiling Gwen greeted me. Her smile didn't warm me up as it usually did though, instead it left me a little confused as I readdressed my earlier feeling of trepidation. 'Come in sweetheart and I will put the kettle on.' she lulled through her plastered smile.

I entered the house and heard the door clunk behind me as she lowered the castle style bar lock. I made my way into the kitchen taking a seat at the large maple island. Gwen tottered over and filled the kettle at the sink. 'So, your legs feeling better then?'

'I suppose it must be.' She replied with her back to me. *Something's definitely off. Oh no, has Beau told Gwen about what happened in my darkroom? She knows I didn't tell him the truth.*

'Gwen, is it all right if I get on with my assignment while I wait for Beau?' *The school work excuse, good thinking* my inner bitch congratulated.

'Beau?' Gwen said with a questionable air of eccentricity in her voice as she turned to me. 'Of course, my lovely, you do that and I will make us some lunch.' My uneasiness lingered just below the surface, it piquing slightly as Gwen made her way to my side. I emptied the contents of my bag onto the island. *What is wrong with me? What did I eat yesterday?* My gut was now in an uproar.

'Have I told you how beautiful you are looking today? Such young, firm skin.' Gwen stroked my cheek with the back of her hand, which sent a shiver coursing through my body. My senses alert to an invisible danger.

'Gwen, are you okay?' I mused as my eyes met with hers. They appeared hollow, vacant somehow, any joy or comfort void from them.

'Yes dear, to be honest, this is the best I have felt in a *very* long time.' Her grin was now bordering psychotic. I turned around and once again focused my attention on my open literacy book. The back door whined as it shifted on its rusting hinges, a breeze wafting through the kitchen as he bounded in, stopping just shy of the alcove that separated the kitchen and the living room.

'Beau, what is it?' I exclaimed dropping my pen. His face was flushed, his breaths rapid as though he had been running, his eyes swamped with concern. But he wasn't looking at me. I glimpsed towards the reflection in the marble eighteenth century mirror that hung above the fireplace behind him. Gwen was standing over me, her face a contorted grin that reached from ear to ear, her eyes black and impossibly wide. I saw the eight-inch carving knife in her hand as the sun bounced off the blade. *What the hell is going on?* My body stiffened; my heartbeat as quiet as a mouse as her warm breath tickled my neck.

'What's your name?' Beau asked as he edged slowly towards us with his hands up in a bid to appear non-threatening.

'It's me, Grace.' I stuttered stupidly; my stare still fixated on the knife. Beau rolled his eyes as he took another step towards us. The poke from the knife that drew a trickle of blood from my throat stopped him in his tracks.

'I think he was talking to me my dear. I am Luan Lesney. You are Beau, I presume. We have been expecting you.'

'What do you want?' He added, trying to hide the looming anxiety in his voice.

'Well, I decided to take over Gwen's body. It really isn't as hard as you would think, what with being a spirit. There are only so many times being an invisible fly on the wall is entertaining. I am seriously bored with it. I heard through the grapevine that another spirit has been enjoying some alone time with your little princess here, thought it rude not to introduce myself.' *Great, outed by a ghost. Am I a homing beacon for the criminally insane or something?* 'Now that I've seen how beautiful she is, maybe entering her body could prove a little more fruitful then Gwen's. I don't know what it is but there is something just not right with this body. It's damaged, infected with god only knows what!' She laughed as she pulled my head around by my chin. For a split second I saw a flash of a different face staring back at me wielding the knife. A plain woman in her late twenties with raven black hair, the same piercing black hollow eyes assessing me. She had a large raised scar that ran over her eye and down her left cheek. She hoisted the knife away from my neck, making her way over to Beau. With very little effort, she chucked him across the room and into the bookcase, leaving him in a stunned heap on the floor, blanketed by some ruffled Dickens Classics. She turned to me leisurely, her movement fluid. *RUN, RUN, RUN!* This was my only (and too familiar) train of thought as she prepared to run at me. When Beau came to, I was playing a dangerous game of cat and mouse with the knife wielding manic in the Gwen suit, running circles around the centre console.

'Beau, what the hell is going on?' I yelled as he ran at us with a candlestick in hand. With one swift blow to the back of Gwen's head she was down, motionless on the tiled floor. I looked between the two of them, speechless and short of breath.

'Look, I will explain everything but we really need to tie her up before she comes around. Consider that nick on your neck a love bite. If I hadn't arrived when I did, it would have been a hell of a lot worse. Unless you were planning on getting filleted today?' I decided not to dignify his silly question with an answer. 'Go into the pantry, Gwen keeps some spare washing line cord in there, we can use it to tie her up.' I did as I was told, grabbing anything and everything that could possibly be used to restrain someone. It didn't feel like the best time to be unprepared. I rushed back into the kitchen dropping everything from my arms onto the floor.

'Really?' Beau mused as he held up a packet of strawberry laces from the pile.

'I panicked.' I huffed, watching Beau wrap the lengths of cord around her, securing her to one of the dining chairs.

The Gwen imposter gurgled as she came to. An onslaught of verbal abuse and profanities flying from her mouth. I didn't recognise the language, but with her stormy glares and her attempts to spit at us, I got a rough idea of what she was trying to convey. Her taunts felt much more frightening because I couldn't understand a word she was saying. I was wrecked with fear. Beau on the other hand seemed a little too nonchalant for my liking. 'Beau, I need to know what is going on here.' I demanded an explanation, reminding myself of my mother. Beau approached me, pulling me into his chest, his strong arms enveloping me. Relaxing into him was harder than it should have been as I was still very aware of the maniac plotting her escape behind me.

'Grace, firstly, I think there are a few things you need to fill in for *me*. Don't think I missed Mrs Ripper over there and her point about another ghost visiting you. I think we need to have a chat, obviously once we've dealt with all this.' It shocked me that he still had a small wry smile on his lips as he circled the room around to the sink to get a glass of water. 'And I want the truth this time.' he added.

CRAP!

'Secondly, this has happened before and I have every belief that it will happen again. This is the house of strange after all.' he chuckled. My glare soon stopped that. 'Gwen is like a portal and unfortunately the longer a spirit has been around the more tricks they pick up. Believe me, I have seen some shockers, this is only a three on the scale of freaky.'

'Well we can't just keep her tied up forever, what do we do now?' I asked as I edged a safe distance away from Gwen, snacking on the strawberry laces straight from the packet.

'Would you please Go and get Gwen's phone book, it's in the side table drawer by the front door. Look up Peterson, Michael Peterson.'

'Is that like Bond, James Bond?' I laughed; Beau nodded in our hostage's direction. *So not the time for jokes then. Address book, side table, beside the door.*

I fumbled about in the antique oak side table and finally found the flowery embossed book. I rushed it to Beau in the kitchen, the receiver from the wall mounted phone station already in his hand. This was quickly becoming the worst lunch date in history. Adding salt into the wound Gwen flashed me a sly smile, winking at me as she glanced at the gleaming, cold steel of the kitchen knife that was teetering on the sink dryer. I hurried towards the sink and threw the blade into the nearest drawer with a clunk, the noise grabbing Beau's attention. My panicked actions made Gwen cackle shrilly. I tried desperately to appear aloof, this made Beau giggle. His sniggering didn't last long though, the scowl I threw his way could quite possibly of broken glass. I may be new to all this supernatural stuff but mocking me was not helping to lighten the situation or settle my wrecked nerves. 'Where do I know her name from?' I mumbled, my head clearing.

'You find her name familiar Grace?'

'Yeah, but I can't put my finger on it.' Beau turned to Luan.

'Hey Crazy, where do you come from?'

'Why should I tell you? How about you loosen my restraints and we can all sit down with some coco and exchange histories.'

'Yeah, that's not happening!' He chuckled wide-eyed.

'Do you want me to gag her?' Beau offered, his eyes never leaving our guest.

'You are not coming anywhere near me with a gag, just because your little girlfriend here is a big sap! You not got the stomach for a little old ghost like me sweetheart?' She bated me, but no amount of teasing would rile me up enough to get within arm's reach of her. Cord or no cord, I wasn't stupid and I definitely wasn't risking it.

'Hi Michael, its Beau. Is there any chance you can make a house call? We have got one of *those* situations again, could really use your expertise...Yeah that would be great...Okay, I'll see you then...Oh, before you go Michael, we need some more sandstone and ground quartz. Gwen has run out and this spirit is a little unwilling to cooperate. She might need an extra little push.' There was a short silence from Beau. Then it hit me.

'That's it!'

'That's what?' Luan piped in. I quickly widened the space between me and the now interested spirit. The horrific ghost of the woman at Luan Lesney's cottage flashed before my eyes. I had been in her home, I had touched her things. Above all, I had seen her victims. She was the infection, a disease that encroached on people's lives and swallowed them whole. I would not be another fateful victim of Luan Lesney.

'OK, I will get the cooker on now, see you in twenty minutes.' Beau hung the receiver back up onto the wall mount and turned to face me. He made his way to the cupboards over the sink and pulled out an oversized clay mortar and pestle and a large silver cooking pot with hefty, twisted, black handles on either side.

'Good thinking, I am famished actually, how about some vegetable soup with homemade walnut dusted crusty bread?' Gwen chimed in as she licked her lips. I knew it wasn't Gwen, I knew she harboured a heartless killer, a witch, but I couldn't quite get past it. I had to understand she wasn't the sweet lady who made tea and crocheted, the nice woman who adopted children rather than murdered them.

'The only thing you will be eating is one of my old, smelly, running socks if you don't shut up!' Beau protested as he took what looked like glass herb jars from a locked cabinet above him.

For a second I actually prayed Beau was making soup as he grabbed a lifeless chicken out of the fridge. The fact that it had its head, legs and feathers still attached made my stomach turnover. Beau raised the very sharp meat cleaver in his hand above his head aiming for the poor chicken's neck, my hopes of lunch were squashed. He proceeded to drain the blood of the dead animal from its ropey feathered neck and angled it so he could empty it into the clay mortar. This was definitely not for soup! Luan beckoned me towards her.

'I know you, don't I? You have been to my cottage.' she said softly. *Did she just read my mind? Don't tell her anything. Don't let her get under your skin. Play dumb, you know nothing!* I told myself silently as my inner bitch dropped her gauntlet and cowered in agreement. In that instance I saw a flash of Gwen's panicked face morph into view, as her head shook uncontrollably and she fought to get free. I turned to get Beau's attention. 'Don't worry, your precious Gwen is still in here with me! Tell me, did you see my girls? I think you did.' She spat. I edged closer.

'What do you mean your girls?'

'You know exactly what I mean. I found in death what I was not able to find in life. I was ostracised for my gift, I was murdered because of it. More than once actually. Killing became easier once the living couldn't see me. They weren't the first, I doubt they will be the last.' I stepped back. Complete darkness filled her eyes like an inky black liquid and a smirk that tugged at the nerve endings in my throat settled on her face.

'Do you have no soul at all? What did they ever do to you?'

'You are barking up the wrong tree my dear, my soul is a beastly, detestable, swelling entity that enjoys sucking the life from innocent people. They see me at the end you know. I am the last thing that flashes across their petrified face as I steal their last breath.' With that Gwen's face disappeared completely. I was now seeing what so many poor souls had seen before me. Her callous, coal stare, her sneer drenched with sadistic loathing. Luan Lesney had been so many people's ending – she would not be mine!

Suddenly I gagged as the coppery iron stink of the chicken's blood that wafted in the air around me. I stumbled back to regain my composure. Halting as my back met with something very large. Although the bright sunshine invaded the room through the bay windows and Beau's protective arms were just a few steps away, I wanted, no, I prayed, I would turn around to nothing. I spun on my heels apprehensively. In front of me stood a mountain of a man, who towered above me silently. His bushy brows hung low over his hollow brown eyes; his glaring stare directed right at me. I screamed as every bone in my body shook uncontrollably with fright. Once I realised this was a mere man, (a bloody frightening man sure, but a man all the same) I excused myself and made my way up to the bathroom a little red faced.

'She's a bit jumpy, isn't she?' I overheard the large man boom to Beau as I climbed the stairs.

'She's a little on the fragile side, you know with the possession and everything.' Beau replied a little too cheekily. I splashed my face with warm water in the basin. I looked up and as the water dripped off my chin, I wiped it with a towel from off the radiator, looking intensely at my reflection in the cabinet mirror. 'Stupid, stupid, stupid! Well done, lets slap a little more crazy on an already bad situation.' I scolded my reflection. 'You have to calm down, it's all under control.' I tried to reassure myself in the next breath, failing miserably. *Talking to myself, great, now I can add insanity to the list. Wait a minute, I'm standing in a house with Casper the not so friendly ghost, Beau the chicken slayer and the wizard hulk man, who's apparently the go-to-guy when it comes to the supernatural. Nothing is under control; I didn't sign up for this. I stupidly thought a burger and a can of coke would be the highlight of my day. Boy was I wrong!* I inhaled a steadying breath and counted down from ten, feeling my heartbeat steady to a methodical pace. 'Composure, check.' I placed my hands out in front of me and they were now only slightly shaking. I rubbed them together furiously and then held them back out in front of me. 'Nerves, check.' I opened the medicine cupboard door with a creak and took out a small, white, plastic bottle. 'Thank God, painkillers, check'. My little trip to the bathroom had helped me to relax but as soon as I had headed back downstairs into the kitchen, that feeling of dread and fear washed over me again. *This is going to be one hell of an afternoon.*

'Hey guys, watch what you say, we have a child present.' Gwen smirked as she threw me a stare that caused my tibia bones to rattle. I reached out for the stool nearest me – I missed. Beau rushed to my side and encased me in his strong grip, pushing my hair away from my face once safe in his embrace.

'Are you OK? Do you want to go home? We can sort this out now.' He lulled, helping me to my feet.

'No, I want to be here. I need to be here.' I corrected in a hushed voice. I had experienced something that, although it fell into the category of out of this world crazy, I wanted to see it through. Beau was so relaxed; this was his world after all. While there are boys his age out there getting drunk and playing football, Beau had responsibilities to protect the people he loved. If I wanted to be a fixture in his life, I would have to come to accept the rules of his world.

'Do you want to help?' He uttered in a strangely upbeat tone.

'Doing what?'

'We need someone to untie her.'

'Bugger off...if you want a rendition of ding dong the witch is dead from a safe distance, I'm your girl. Untying the witch is a massive no no. I'd rather declaw Freddy Kruger.' I continued ranting incoherently. Beau pulled me back into the comfort of his chest, the place that seemed to soothe me instantly.

'Calm and breathe. I was only joking.' He teased. 'Bad timing, I know but I couldn’t resist.' He giggled and tensed up as he anticipated my right hook in his arm. I know he was trying to lighten the situation and like always, his smile did exactly that.

'I will be sitting over here, if you need me.' I pulled the metal bar stool towards the alcove leading into the living room. I parked it up against the wall. Have you ever passed a car crash on the motorway and although the numerous flashing lights of the ambulance alert you to a bloody crime scene, you can't help but slow down and take a look? Eerily compelling, that was what it felt like in the kitchen. I felt compelled to look at the Gwen/Luan hybrid, even though I knew it would only unsettle my stomach and threaten a matinee appearance of my breakfast. The chanting freaked me out a little as Michael the hulk man worked his magic on Gwen. I gripped the stool beneath me as Gwen's body twisted and contorted uncomfortably, the sheer agony present on her face. Her torturous screams echoed around the room, piercing my ears. The cord cut into her skin, which made her bleed. Her eyes glazed over and for a second, she slumped in the chair, her head hanging there sluggishly. With one quick movement, Gwen's head rose and her eyes were transfixed on mine. Her usually beautiful warm eyes were now completely black with no white visible at all. Her skin was deathly pale and appeared to have things moving beneath it. The things trickled and pulsated beneath her skin, making their way over her lips and down her neck. A shiver shot up my spine as she licked her lips, her evil grin aimed at me. There were no words as an icy stream flowed inside me, stiffening my muscles. The real face of Luan Lesney once again flashed onto Gwen's and before I could comprehend the situation, her head swung back and her body pulsated as thick black smoke poured out of Gwen's open mouth. The whistling, high pitched howl of the smoke polluted the now misty air around us, ringing in my ears. I threw my hands up to cover them as I watched on in horror, the blood from Gwen's wounds pooling into a puddle on the floor around her. The smoke collected and swamped the ceiling. The ash, the dust, the remnants of whatever the smoke was, floated towards us with a catlike movement. It made me edge my stool out of the way hastily.

AWOKEN *Billie Jade Kermack*

Then there was nothing left. Only an eerie silence, the stench of putrefied fish guts and my frantic heartbeat the theme tune for Gwen's exorcism.

THIRTY-THREE

ꕥ

Although life had gone back to normal and Gwen was safe, I still couldn't flush the face of Luan Lesney out of my head. Glen the red-haired psychopath definitely had a rival for world's worst nightmare. 'GRACE! GRACE! COME ON DOWN I'VE MADE YOU BREAKFAST!' Mum hollered up from the kitchen. I had no desire to move from my bed. It was the first Friday of no school. I'd always been lucky my birthday fell on the last week of October. Half time meant lie ins were pretty much the standard for me, mooching around the house in my PJs all day whilst watching Friends re-runs were also notable perks. My Mum spent each and every year trying everything she could to mess with my natural order. Lie-ins, PJs and sofa surfing, for some reason bugged her.

'MUM PLEASE, JUST A LITTLE WHILE LONGER.' I begged, muffling my yell with my cover over my head, seeing even a peak of daylight would mean I wouldn't be able to fall back to sleep and I was dreaming of him and that smile, that was a gift all of its own.

'Grace, get your butt out of that bed!' She was now standing beside my bed, her fingers already gripped onto the edge of my bedding. I groaned with every little bit of energy I had. Mum quickly whipped the covers off from around me, exposing me to the cold air that slapped my thighs.

'MUM, SERIOUSLY!' I screamed tight lipped, trying to force a little smile, hoping she would reconsider her actions and give me back my covers. I may not be able to fall back to sleep and dream of him, but that wouldn't stop me from thinking of him.

'Dream on Grace.' She teased with glee.

'I wish you'd let me Mum!' I held my pillow tightly over my head but that still didn't drown out my Mum and my mouth full of delicate lace was making it hard to breathe.

'Don't get smart with me Grace, it's time to get up. Amelia and everyone are downstairs. I thought I'd throw you a birthday breakfast party, considering you're apparently too old for a real birthday party.'

'Oh Mum, you shouldn't have.' I retorted caustically.

'It's my pleasure honey.' Her comment laden with sarcasm. Arguing was futile!

'No, you're not getting it Mum, I really wished you hadn't.'

'Look, no more arguing, I'm your mother and I know what's best. Now get washed and by the looks of your hair I suggest a hat is needed, we don't want you ruining the pictures. If you are not downstairs in five minutes, I will bring everyone up here to wish you a very happy birthday, got it?' She smiled at me as she hurried out of the door, closing it behind her with my cover securely stuffed under her other arm. I kicked my feet on my bed repeatedly, like a toddler having a tantrum, and then made my way to the bathroom, dragging my feet under protest as I went. *Oh god, has she invited Beau? No-one knows about us. Amelia is going to throw a bitch fit!* If this had occurred to me earlier, I wouldn't have been so determined to stay in bed. As I approached the kitchen, I desperately tried to think of an explanation that might clarify Beau's presence, and that was only if everyone didn't know already. They had all had forty-five minutes to gossip while I was upstairs. With how perfect it was going between us I really didn't want it to be public knowledge. It may sound selfish but having him to myself made it feel that much more special. I didn't want to share it with everyone and I certainly didn't want to share him with anyone. A pang of relief washed over me as I edged across the threshold, glancing around the kitchen and seeing Amelia, Jack, Morgan and Cary perched at the kitchen table. For a brief moment I relaxed, what a fool. I turned on my heels quickly as water spluttered violently out of the faucet, there at the sink was Louisa. 'I'm so sorry.' She gushed to my mum, patting down her clothes where the spraying water had caught her.

'Don't be silly, it's just another thing I've added to the list of *To Do's* that seems never ending.' My mum replied handing Louisa a tea-towel from off the cooker. Louisa was guarding a large pink box, wiping it with the tea-towel, chatting animatedly to her mother who was sitting on a chair beside her.

'Finally, Grace, we've all been waiting for you.' My mum announced, everyone in the room now quiet, their eyes fixed on me. 'Did I tell you Louisa's Mum makes the best cakes?' She chimed in, clearly trying to explain their presence. My mum had no idea that I had been in their company not so long ago. I strolled over to the large pink box and inside was a beautiful cake draped in white icing, delicate marzipan red roses dotted its entire circumference, the piped cursive message - ***Happy 18th Birthday Grace,*** in bright pink frosting, not a single line crooked or out of place; I can't even write that well with a pen.

'That's gorgeous, thank you so much.'

'After what you and your friend did for us, it's the least I could do.' Louisa's mother beamed whilst reaching out to take my hand into hers affectionately.

'What did you do Grace?' My mum's confusion was clear in her voice, I didn't even need to look at her face. With my brain a sludgy mess, I fought to find a suitable answer to her question before Louisa jumped in excitedly.

'Grace and her friend found some of my Dad's papers hidden in the car. We thought that all was hopeless before Grace knocked on our door.'

'Sweetheart, you didn't tell me.' She cooed securing a strand of my hair behind my ear. Her simple act of care felt strange somehow, as though that gesture was reserved for only him.

'To be honest Mum, I completely forgot.' I grinned awkwardly, the lie leaving a sour taste in my mouth. 'Soooo, what's for breakfast then?' A change of subject couldn't come any sooner, the mere mention of my very helpful *friend* still hung dangerously in the air.

'We have homemade pancakes with syrup and yogurt, fresh fruit smoothies, bacon, sausages, basically everything you could think of.' My mum beamed proudly, gesturing her oven-gloved hands towards the banquet filled table. I took a seat with everyone else who were already engaged in their own titillating conversations. The banners and streamers that blanketed the ceiling draped the entire length of the kitchen. The cheesy my little pony plastic tablecloth and matching paper accessories dotted around the table, instantly transported me back to my eighth birthday. Both Morgan and Jack were sporting the matching pony party hats.

'I would have worn a hat with it being your birthday and everything, but I just got my hair done. So, well you know.' Amelia chimed in, winding her fingers around her bouncy curls, making sure each lock was still perfectly in place. We all scrambled for the food and started piling up our plates. Without even noticing it, much to my surprise, I had begun to enjoy myself. The drum of the chatter subsided to a low hum as we all devoured the spread. Amelia gave it a good attempt with two tablespoons of yogurt and three strawberry's; making sure their size and weight were exactly the same. I'm not kidding, scales were used. Unfortunately, my good mood had blind sighted me, leaving me unable to foresee what would happen next.

'Oh Grace, I called Beau to invite him this morning. He said he had to take Gwen for a check-up though. He said he'd pop round to pick you up a little later for your surprise.' She reeled off the information nonchalantly whilst fiddling with a packet of birthday cake sparklers; the dotted tear here line clearly more of a concern for her than the now dead silence of everyone else in the room around her. The very public exposure, of a very private matter, would forever and always be what people would remember from this day and I had my mother to blame.

'What the hell is going on Grace? I knew nothing about this...this Bob.' Amelia jumped in, clearly the ten seconds of someone else getting some attention had bruised her ego.

'Amelia, we have actually talked about him, in depth if we're going into specifics. It's not a big deal anyway and his name is not Bob its Beau!' I retorted defensively through clenched teeth. Suddenly wishing I had protested with my mother further and stayed in bed.

'OK, sorry! Touchy much? So, who's Bob?' She queried to no one in particular. I rolled my eyes, letting her stew on her thought. My eyes darted towards Jack. He was numero uno on my list of people I would need to placate, when the news of my relationship with Beau hit the masses.

'So, you and Beau huh? Can't say I'm surprised, a girl falling for the mysterious new boy. It's pretty much the tagline of every rom-com going. How well do you actually know him though? Maybe you don't know what you're getting yourself into, for all you know he's seeing other girls, dealing drugs, robbing old ladies or something along those lines.' He spat his cross examination at me sharply without pausing for air.

'Jack, been on a crime watch binge again? Not that it's any of your business, but over the past few months we have got to know each other pretty well.' I remained calm and collected, biting my lip to hold back any anger his words had stirred in me.

'Six months and you haven't told any of us. I thought you'd started getting a little distant, but I had no idea this is what you were choosing to do with your time.' Jack barked across the table. His second attempt to derail me. His bitter drenched words were laden with unresolved spite.

'Firstly Jack, I don't understand why you care so much and secondly, at what point do I need to run my love life past you?'

'Fine, I'll just let you make your own mistakes.' he sneered, picking violently at the remnants of a pancake on the plate in front of him.

'Thanks Dad, that would be just tickety-boo!' I retort, my tone rife with caustic indignation. I resumed shovelling crispy bacon into my mouth with little care to how uncouth I appeared. The uncomfortable silence that now rained over my birthday gathering soon drifted to one side as the low hum of chatter started up again.

'So, Beau is your Mr LBW then?' Amelia whispered as she smothered a slice of toast with butter. 'Why didn't you tell me?' she asked as she reached for the jam.

'To be honest there wasn't much to tell' I answered quickly on a mumble.

'Right, well, what's the gossip on him picking you up tonight then? Do you know where he's taking you?' She squealed enthusiastically as she jumped up and down in her seat, clapping her hands together like a performing seal. I couldn't help but laugh. The awkwardness, that a moment before had hung on the coat tails of the mere mention of Beau's name dissipated quickly, as I resumed enjoying myself. I made a point of not looking in Jack's direction as I could sense his disapproving glare was still firmly fixed on me. 'What's so funny?' She asks.

'Nothing.' I grinned. 'I don't know where Beau's taking me. He said it's a surprise.'

'Oh Grace, you know what this means don't you?' She beams, her eyes alight with exhilaration.

'What is that smile for? Whatever you are thinking - NO!' I reacted worriedly. She had that all too familiar look in her eye and in that moment my protests were pointless. I knew exactly what she had in mind. I didn't like it; but then I don't think I had a say in it anyway.

'MAKEOVER!' she screamed animatedly clapping her hands once again, her Aquarium floor show entertaining at least. Everyone but Jack glanced over giggling at Amelia which she soon joined in with. Jack had a face like thunder, the creases in his forehead aged him by at least ten years as he sat arms folded across his blue tank top, his mismatched yellow stripped shirt poking out around his neck. Fortunately, his scowl was only noticed by me. I wasn't about to let that spoil my day; it was my birthday after all. After the happy birthday sing song and the hugs and kisses, everyone started to leave. Jack wouldn't come anywhere near me, but Morgan assured me he'd *'kick Jack's arse six ways from Sunday'* if he kept up his stupid behaviour. I saw everyone to the door. As I re-entered the kitchen the vibe had noticeably changed, Mum and Amelia were standing by a stool near the island; my mum's hairdressing bag sitting on top of it. They both grinned from ear to ear. Clearly Amelia's idea of a makeover was a universally well-liked plan, my mum was on board, I would have absolutely no chance of getting out of it. 'You have got to be kidding.' I whined, tugging at my hair. 'There is no way.' I held up my hands as they both chose their weapon of mass beautification. Amelia wielded an already hot pair of hair curlers, my mother ready and waiting with her cutting scissors. I may have believed in my words wholeheartedly but my small smile was relaying a different message. Okay so I didn't want to get out of it. I wanted to be the best me I could be for this man and enlisting the help of two woman in the know couldn't hurt.

'Grace, how about you leave all the technical stuff up to us.' Amelia interrupted grasping my arm and pulling me towards the stool with enough force to leave imprints of her manicured talons in my skin.

'This is completely against my better judgement, but on this occasion, I will let it happen. Two rules though!' I turned to my mother, authoritative finger at the ready. 'Firstly, NO CURLS!' Mum nodded silently. Amelia unplugged the curling iron and placed it onto the side. 'And secondly...' I turned to point at Amelia. 'No pastel coloured eye shadow or anything that makes me look like a clown, think <u>SUBTLE</u>!' I emphasised; my eyes wide.

'OK, OK, stress much? Can we get on with it then?' Amelia cooed impatiently, blusher at the ready.

'Go for it.' I smiled as my Mum swung the black gown around my shoulders and secured it. After about an hour of spraying, cutting and primping, I felt myself starting to doze off as the warmth of the hairdryer hit my head.

'All done. I'm now passing the reigns over to my beautiful, extremely talented assistant.' My mum announced as she unplugged the hairdryer and curtsied as Amelia passed her, her makeup bag already open and in hand. Amelia stalked my way now armed with a pot of foundation, an application brush twitching excitedly in her hand. After another half an hour of preening, poking, dabbing, smoothing and accentuating, I was apparently ready to face the mirror. *Why am I so nervous? Duh, you loooovvee the boy and you don't want to look like an 80's throwback* my inner bitch added as an apparent attempt at comfort. I walked uneasily into the hallway, the feeling in my legs slowly returning. I looked into the large mirror next to the coat rack but kept my eyes closed tightly. I didn't know what to expect. Well if I'm honest I expected my rules to fall on deaf ears and the reflection in the mirror would show a half clown, half Cher mix breed. Luckily and quite astonishingly, this wasn't the case. The soft brown eye shadow and the light stroke of liquid black eye-liner framed my otherwise tired eyes, brightening them. A thin layer of cherry scented lip gloss sparkled on my lips and my usually pale skin had a subtle, healthy, golden glow. My hair had never looked in such good condition. The loose shiny chocolate tendrils that fell down my back and around my face had more life and bounce then I ever imagined possible. I looked like a totally different person. I hardly recognised the girl staring back at me. I may not have recognised her but boy did I like her. As I walked back into the kitchen it was impossible to mask my happiness. Amelia and my mum gave each other a geeky, celebratory high five.

'Now all that's left Grace, is the perfect outfit.' Amelia was clearly in her element as she took the stairs up to my room two at a time. Her wedge heels threatening to give way on each bounce.

'That's all you girls, I wouldn't have a clue. I'm going to get tidied up down here.' My mum walked to my side and leaned in for a hug before I could follow Amelia upstairs. 'You look absolutely gorgeous sweetheart; you'll knock him dead.' Her words were low, sincere, a tear teetering in the corner of her eye. The idea of my Mum using the word dead and Beau in the same sentence made my stomach somersault. She kissed me on the head and sent me upstairs to get ready, wiping her eye free of the built-up moisture as she waved me off. Amelia was already rummaging around my wardrobe as I entered my room. No rummaging was the wrong word, assaulting was more fitting. 'I'm sure I sorted you out with more clothes then this on our last shopping trip.'

'You did, it's just a lot of them weren't to my taste, sorry.'

'Well unless you want to wear a vest and pumps on your special date tonight, I'd show me where you've stored everything else. Give me the good stuff lady.' Amelia ordered; disapproval clear in her tone. After what seemed like forever, we finally had an outfit. A pair of strappy blue wedges that I would usually never wear and a heart necked, black knee length strapless dress, a blue flowered design embroidered up one side. I approached the full-length mirror on my wardrobe with an unmoving smile etched on my face. My heel work still needing a little finessing, but for the first time in so long, I felt fantastic. As we made our way downstairs the doorbell chimed twice and my heart jumped into my throat. My ankle snapping awkwardly as I fumbled on the last step. I shooed Amelia, who was still tugging to loosen my wavy hair down across my chest, into the kitchen with my Mum. Strolling towards the door, nervously patting down my clothes, I stumbled again in my heels a little as I reached for the handle. I shrugged off my unease as the door swung open. 'Hi Beau.' The Dog whistle chime of my voice made me want to slap myself in the face. Nervous was an understatement. He looked H-O-T hot and a 10/10 on anyone's scale. His trademark denim drainpipe jeans, crisp white, collared shirt and dark blue fitted suit jacket made him look relaxed and effortlessly stunning.

‘WOW, Grace, you look fantastic, I mean...WOW!' Beau lulled wide-eyed. The outfit, the hair and the makeup obviously did its job. Beau seemed to be finding it difficult to get his words out. *Perfect.*

'Thanks. Do you want to come in?' I offer, my nerves and his compliments playing havoc with my psyche.

'Yeah sure, that would be grit...sorry great.' He laughed. Silently cursing at himself. 'Not that you need it, you were perfect before.' He added as he stroked my cheek. I had honestly never met someone who knew exactly what to say and when to say it. I put my foot in my mouth on most occasions.

'So, I'm just going to say bye and then we can go.'

'Okay, can I use your bathroom quickly?' I nodded my reply. As I watched him ascend the stairs two at a time, his converse clad feet a lot steadier than mine, I hobbled uneasily into the kitchen and pulled the sliding doors closed behind me. Feeling like I could finally take a breath.

'Right, I think I'm ready.'

'Have you got your keys...your phone?' Mum asked frantically as she slipped into parental mode.

'Yes Mum, got it all, I even checked twice.'

'Have you got your three P's?' Amelia jumped in. I dreaded to think what these three P's were but once again my curiosity got the better of me. Rookie move on my part clearly. I glanced over at Mum worriedly and she looked back at me with the same concerned gaze. Our eyes soon grazed back towards Amelia. 'Purse, perfume and...'

'And what?' I exclaimed in an attempt to rush her as she lingered on the final word. I heard the bathroom door open at the top of the stairs.

'PROTECTION!' She mouthed, desperately trying to avoid the glares of my disapproving mother.

'Right that's it, shut up before he hears you. Is it your main goal in life to embarrass me Amelia?'

'Better safe than sorry.' Amelia added sheepishly as she dug fruitlessly out of the imaginary hole that surrounded her and opened the kitchen doors. As Beau's foot hit the bottom step Amelia flushed a bright crimson colour.

'You must be Amelia, I'm Beau.' Beau extended his hand politely towards her and smiled. His effect on the opposite sex kicking into gear. Amelia could only giggle and flick her hair playfully. In all our years of friendship, I had never seen Amelia speechless. She was my best friend but I still couldn't help roaring with laughter inside as she stood there dumbstruck like a love-struck teenager, her big, innocent, puppy dog eyes transfixed on my gorgeous, lean man. You'd have thought I had just introduced her to Bon Jovi. After a long, somewhat awkward silence and a few concerned glances from a confused Beau, Amelia realised what she was doing, or what she wasn't doing to be more precise. After making sure the flies on his jeans weren't still open and he wasn't introducing too much of himself, he realised it was Amelia who was acting out of character. 'Is she OK?' Beau asked me quietly through gritted teeth so not to offend her.

'I'm perfectly fine' Amelia protested a little too eagerly. 'Sorry about that, I was in my own little world for a moment there.' She babbled fretfully. She extended her hand out to shake Beau's, her prim and proper manners awakened. 'And you must be Brad, Bob, Bill, BEAU!' She screamed. Her hand was now an inch from his face. Crippling nervousness was not a good shade of pink for Amelia and I think she had now come to terms with how mentally challenged she had come across.

'Well, you got there in the end.' He added kindly, patting her on the shoulder, a move that was more caring than condescending.

'Urmm....I've really got to go.' She was already edging restlessly backwards like a cornered kitten. 'Beau, it was really, really great meeting you.' Amelia fanned her face and tugged at her collar. She took a deep breath, patted down her clothes and without a backwards glance, she quickly stepped out onto the front step and pulled the front door closed behind her with a clunk.

'You really have some...SPECIAL friends Grace.' Beau was finding it difficult to keep a straight face.

'Special is not the word, that was pure insanity. I'd love to say I didn't enjoy that but I would be lying!' I emphasised giddily.

'I'll wait for you outside Grace. Lovely to see you again Mrs O' Callaghan.' He mused to my mum who was now filling the kitchen doorway.

'Now Beau, I've told you before, please, call me Catherine.' Beau reached for the door and turned.

'Noted, Mrs.... sorry Catherine.' He corrects. She nods her approval at the kind young man desperate to make a good impression, remembering fondly memories of my father picking her up for their first date.

'Right, try not to drink too much, but also remember to have fun.' She kissed my forehead lightly, those tears once again teetering in her eyes, a fresh Kleenex in her hand, ready to dam the inevitable waterfall once we left. She quickly sniffed and barricaded the tears back, wiping my forehead where I can only imagine sat a ruby red lipstick stain. Beau grabbed my hand and waved goodbye as we practically ran down the path.

'Where's your bike. Did you want me to drive?' I asked, suddenly realising these shoes probably weren't driver friendly.

'No this is your ride for tonight.' He gestured towards the pristine, baby pink Cadillac that was parked up underneath the oak tree at the end of the drive.

'Are you kidding? How did...I mean, I didn't know...What are?' Any and every sentence evaded me.

'Is there a full sentence in there somewhere Miss Gracie?' Beau grinned, once again voicing my thoughts in that magical way he did. I was speechless. It was absolutely stunning.

'I didn't know you could drive?' I blurt.

'Yep, I just prefer the motorbike. It's easier to get through traffic. I thought for tonight you deserved to go in style.'

'And where exactly are we going?'

'Grace, do you really think I would stumble at the last hurdle and ruin the surprise.'

'It was worth a try. This must have cost you a small fortune Beau.' I gushed as I ran my palm over the polished bonnet in awe.

'Not at all, I did a favour for someone, luckily for me he owns a vintage car dealership.'

'Do you mean a ghostly favour?' I whispered behind a cupped hand.

'Yep' he replied ever so nonchalantly.

THIRTY-FOUR

ℰ⊃ℭℛ

The uneven cobble path beneath our feet made my job of walking in skyscraper shoes even harder than I had imagined. I gripped onto Beau's arm, ready to dig my claws in if the floor was swept away from me. Cinderella had her enchanting evening but I don't remember anywhere in that fairy tale a part where Cinderella ended up arse over head in front of her prince charming. We strolled through a budding white rose covered archway, all my worries dissipating as my grip loosened. 'This is stunning Beau.' I was in awe. Oversized, Romanesque, pillared candles dotted the entire stretch of the winding grey gravel path. There were three extremely large, white, canopied tables on the far right of the stretch of grass, which were illuminated dimly by white fairy lights, draped behind a silvery mesh curtain backdrop. The tables were swathed in luscious crème and ruby silk cloths, laden with an exquisite array of foods, most of which I couldn't even name. The choice to take Spanish 101 would have been helpful here. The numerous bottles of wine that occupied one of the other tables definitely didn't resemble the £4.99 bottles in our local Co-Op. There was nothing ordinary about this date. I don't know if there would ever be anything ordinary about this beautiful man either. Sitting on the stretches of neatly cut grass on either side of the winding path were couples. I'd say about fifty so far if I had to guess. They were all facing north relaxing on blankets. 'This is one major picnic Beau. I don't think you know how to do something normally.'

'It's a picnic with a twist.' He grinned as he reached for his trusty Mary Poppins rucksack.

'How did you even find this place, it's absolutely breath-taking?'

'Oh Grace, you haven't seen anything yet.' His words were heavy, his lips dangerously close to my ear as he took my hand in his and lead me down the snaking path. As the gravel crunched beneath my cork heels and the lights danced on the windows of the towering buildings that encased this wonderland, I couldn't help but beam. Any other expression at that point in time would have been impossible. The world around it stood still; sadness and fear ceasing to exist. I gazed up at Beau, feeling his hand in mine I realised that although this setting was perfect, unlike anything I had ever seen in real life anyway, it wasn't the location that made me feel so held in a moment. It didn't make the world a better place or stop time. It didn't continually make my legs weak and my heart skip a beat - he did. 'Wait here, I'll be one minute.' He instructed, running towards a deserted patch of grass just left of the path, the area canopied by the tendrils of vivid emerald leaves from a willow tree, tiny fairy lights intertwined around the branches. A tree almost exactly the same as the one in front of Gwen's house, another coincidence I suppose. He pointed at the reserved sign hanging from the tree and smiled. Beau opened his rucksack pulling out a red tartan woolly throw, he laid it onto the ground beneath the tree and beckoned me to sit next to him. He removed his suit jacket and placed it on the edge of the blanket. 'Would you like to take a seat my lady?' Beau mocked in his best aristocratic butler impression. The sentiment and his voice making me swoon.

'Why thank you Jeeves.' I played along as I took my seat and stretched out my legs. Silently thanking Amelia for the heels when I noticed what they did for my legs.

'This is a lovely surprise Beau; I couldn't have imagined a more stunning night. So how did you get such great seats? No one else has their own tree.' I note glancing up at the reserved sign hanging above us. Beau signalled into the distance. My eyes followed. 'Is that Mrs Dayton, our dinner lady?'

'She's my trusty insider. She's not actually a dinner lady at all. She's a reporter doing a piece on college life. Apparently, the biggest secrets among teenagers are shared with their friends in the cafeteria. Anyway, her company had the scoop on this event and she got me tickets.' Without the frumpy apron, matching hairnet and those teddy bear patterned slacks, I could definitely see Mrs Dayton in a new light. Her crisp black waist coated two-piece suit and pink bell sleeve shirt slimmed down her frame and elongated her legs. She did not resemble the Mrs Dayton I knew on any level.

'I don't believe it. So why the free tickets for you then?'

'I helped her out with something.' I clearly looked bemused as he cracked open a bottle of chardonnay with a pop. 'A ghost thing.' He added as way of explanation. It was becoming shockingly clear that spirits where around us all the time and Beau was their go-to guy.

'Is that why she always gives you extra chips at lunch?' I smiled.

'No, that's just because of my dashing good looks. Obviously. I am a man with many contacts.' He boasted sardonically as he ran his hand through his hair like a suave James Bond. He couldn't keep his pose up for long before he started grinning. 'This is only the beginning Grace. I have a lot more planned.' He lovingly stroked my cheek, as always leaving me wanting more. He turned, pulling a slim box decorated with pink butterflies, lined with gold edging, secured with a large cerise bow, from behind his back. As I ripped at the bow excitedly, but carefully, I could feel Beau's anticipation radiating from him as he eagerly waited for the bow to float to the ground and his gift to be out in the open. I didn't miss the nervous bite of his lip either. I delicately unwrapped and pulled out the bound papers that lay in the pink tissue. The front page read: **Superboy and Miss Gracie.** As I flipped over each page Beau's pencil sketches came to life. I could finally see how he saw me. The enticing young girl with long brown hair, her aversion for sarcasm, love of fast food and converse trainers, her quirky attitude; it was me. 'Beau this is fantastic. Where did you find the time to do all this?' I beamed.

'I wanted it to be ready for tonight, so if I get an F on my DT coursework you know why.' He laughs.

'I'd apologise but I love it. Thank you so much. Enjoy that F.' I cooed as I read on, my eyes unable to leave the page.

'Why is it Super boy and not Superman?'

'I thought it was a bit big headed to call myself Superman, so I changed it a little.' He shined. Every one of our encounters, our lunches, being at Gwen's, he'd remembered every little detail. He'd left out all the ghost stuff of course, but that was a secret I was happy to keep to ourselves. The depiction of me in my pyjamas strutting about the kitchen was a page I skipped past pretty quickly, Beau's attention to detail made me cringe.

'How did you know what dress I was going to wear?' I pushed the comic towards him, which depicted in great detail Mum and Amelia getting me ready for my birthday date with Beau.

'Oh, well I had a little inside help with that one.' He smiled broadly.

'My Dad?' I whispered, as a tear teetered on my eyelid, ready to roll down my cheek.

'You didn't think he'd miss your birthday, did you?' Fearing that our moment with the spirit of my father in the park was all a figment of my imagination, I had tried to push it to the back of my mind. Little did Beau know; he had already given me the best gift anyone could ever give another person. I flipped over the last page and there was Beau, encased within the draping leaves of the willow tree with me by his side. I held the comic in my hands, the kiss the characters were sharing impossibly deep, even in a black and white sketch. 'I was hoping that this is how it would end.' I gushed, a breath hitching in my throat as Beau leaned in towards me. The space between us diminishing quickly.

'Me too.' He lulled. I could have drowned in his sparkling ice blue eyes as they spoke wordlessly to my inner desires. His fingers caressed the nape of my neck, his other hand resting on my bare thigh. He snuggled into my neck comfortably as though it was the only place he needed to be, his lips softly grazing my skin. That familiar wanting rush of lust and desire pulsated in my chest, tickling the depths of my stomach. My core arguing to be closer to him. Our lips met and a twinge of adrenaline surged through me. I wrapped my arms around his neck and pulled his body into mine. Where it rightly needed to be; deep did not even come close to describing how connected I felt with Beau at that moment. Devoted was a word that felt more appropriate. We spent the next hour gorging on some of the most delicious food I had ever tasted, every colourful bite cooked perfectly, unknown spices dancing over my tongue. With the consumption of far too much food and two glasses of smooth red wine for me, we scooted down the tree, our backs now flush with the blanket beneath us. The dark amethyst night sky was dotted with fiercely twinkling stars as far as the eye could see. I lay in Beau's arms, contentment filling me. I fiddled with his shirt buttons, gazing up above, simply enjoying where I was and who I was with. A moment of complete serenity engulfed us. For a man who always seemed so sure of himself; so confident, his eyes suddenly betrayed him, a smidge of vulnerability, his innocence shining through, causing my heart to beat a little out of rhythm. He tightened his grip around me and sighed, brushing my hair from my face, resting his chin on my head. On a long sigh he pulled my body in closer to his and skimmed my cheek softly with his warm hands.

'Would you like to dance?' Beau stood up and offered me his open hand. I sat up to a sea of people who were all swaying hand in hand, circling each other tenderly. The mellow breeze was filled with the scent of fresh seafood that reminded me of being on a Riviera on a remote tropical island, or at least what I could imagine that would be like. The closest I had come to fancy seafood on a tropical island was breaded crab sticks in Clacton. An attractive olive-skinned woman with jet black hair ornately draped down her back, her body swathed in a long sleeved, delicate gold and black lace gown, stood proudly on a make shift stage ahead of us. Her melodic soprano voice abated any feelings of stress within the crowd. The song journeying through the whimsical back beat of a cello, a piano and a violin. I took Beau's hand and followed him to dance. I placed my hands around his neck, enjoying the advantage these shoes gave me. The air lapped at my bare shoulders enticing me to move in closer to him. I trembled as his fingers traced little circles on my lower back. The song ended and as the other couples around us stopped to applaud, Beau and I couldn't take our eyes off of each other. I peeked up from under my elongated lashes into his eyes and as his hand ran slowly down my side over the zip of my dress my breath hitched in my throat; everything around us blurred into a colourful haze. His arms tightened around my waist and with a soft jolt, my feet no longer sat in tune with the ground as they swam giddily in mid-air. My lips touched his, igniting that familiar spark again, that accustomed crescendo in my heartbeat present, ultimately stopping me in my tracks, drowning out the world around me.

'I want to dance all my dances with you.' I professed. The words a spoken thought. I fell back to reality and as my feet touched down on the spongy grass, I rested my head onto his chest and closed my eyes. I could quite happily have stayed in this moment forever.

~~~~

I climbed back into the confines of the car and rested my birthday present on my lap. On the road again, the tarmac running for miles beyond the black night sky behind us, I closed my eyes tightly, contemplating just how perfect the night had been. It felt as though it had been whipped off the screen of a romantic movie, an endless and poetically fantastic dream. Every young girl's fairy tale.

'Grace, are you tired?' Beau asked as he secured my loose hair around my ear, running his fingers affectionately down my face to prolong his touch.

'Nope...' I began, attempting and failing to quieten my broad smile. I turn towards him.

'Beau, what's happened?' I cried out in horror. The smile that I thought would remain etched on my face for the rest of my days, highlighting how extremely perfect my life was, was suddenly replaced with a look of sheer dismay. The
~~~~

streaming pool of crimson blood dripping down onto his shirt was so vivid. He quickly read my concerned expression and cupped his hand under his nose. Beau swerved the car into the rest area, slamming on the brakes. The headlights from the car set the twisted branches of the trees in front of us ablaze. The street lamp above us highlighted the extent of the problem. Beau rested his head onto the steering wheel and took a few deep breaths. Worry soon morphed into panic as he began hitting the steering wheel powerfully in a rage, before he looked up to face me. 'What's going on? Beau, you're scaring me, is there anything I can do?' I passed him a crumpled tissue from my borrower sized clutch bag. Fiddling in the catastrophic mess that I'd call a glove compartment to find another. Beau held his hand to his nose, gripping the bridge of it with his fingers and swung his head back as he desperately tried to stop the continuous flow of blood that poured over his lips. He returned his head to the steering wheel. I reached out to him and his shoulders tensed. I retracted my hand sharply. After a short silence Beau lifted his head and looked at me. His eyes were glazed over and the colour had completely drained from his face. 'Okay, you're really creeping me out now, spill it!' I pressed, not knowing what else I should do.

'I'm sorry, that's not my intention at all, it's just difficult to explain.'

'Well I've come this far with you, a few more surprises can't hurt.'

'Grace, I told you what I can do but I didn't want to scare you, give you too much information at once. I mean everything with your Dad, Gwen...' Glen had warned me that Beau hadn't revealed everything. But why wouldn't he tell me?

'Just spit it out!' I ordered as I held his now free hand, ignoring the splatter of blood that crept up his arm and through his shirt. *Do I really want to know? I think a few more surprises could definitely hurt me if I'm going on past experiences. Why is it that all good has to be haunted by the bad?* By now, as though a tap had been turned off, he began wiping his hands and face onto the cuff of his shirt. A tinge of red still marring his otherwise beautiful face.

'Spirits aren't the only things I can see.'

'Okay... and?' I pursued anxiously.

'There are these things called Shadows. They are ferrymen of sorts.' I listened to him try and explain, likening it to a Harvard scholar explaining quantum physics to a toddler. I could hear him talking, but the words just didn't seem to make sense. 'When someone is in great danger, or when there is going to be an accident that will cause the deaths of many people, a Shadow will linger before the person is due to die. The shadows make Jason Vorhees look like the Easter bunny. They want the souls of the living, their life force. Their aim is to evoke tangible fear in their victims, their souls that much more desirable. A feeding frenzy is more like it.

'Do you see these Shadows all the time?'

'They don't like to be seen and they especially don't like what I can do. They deliver the recently deceased spirits somewhere. It's their job to acquire people's essences. It's like a sick pawn game, the more they get, the more rewards they receive. I kind of put a speed bump in their plans.'

'Beau, what are you telling me, if it's fairly normal that you would see them why do you look so shook up?'

'I've had a lot of these nosebleeds, however uncomfortable and painful, they are a sign of sorts, a warning of what's coming. There is a shadow very close and it's so strong I can barely think straight.'

'What can you do, there's no one around for miles, how would you find out who it is that it's attached to?' I glanced up and down the deserted country lane, very aware that something depraved and baying for blood was lurking in the darkness around us. The reeds whistled in the wind, the crickets singing in the silence. The full moon now hid behind a mass of grey clouds, the hollow whipping sound of the branches of the trees drowning out everything else. The familiarity of my uneasiness was crippling. I tried my best to banish the sinking sensation in my gut. 'Beau, we need to get out of here, it's giving me the creeps.' The chuckle that left my mouth was false bravado laden with distress and he knew it.

'It's you Grace. They want you and I don't know why. This is all my fault.' His voice was sullen and lifeless. He wiped his nose again, hurrying to turn the key in the ignition, the engine roaring to life A frozen, hollow, flush of air swept over my bare shoulders. All the hairs on my arms stood to attention, my stomach firmly settling in my throat. *Is that them? Are they coming for me? Don't panic, we can sort this, I'm sure of it.* I tried desperately to reassure myself but failed at every juncture. 'I think I feel them, and I think this isn't the first time they have been around me. I've felt them before.' My voice trembled, every note sticking in my throat.

'I'm so sorry.' Was all he could say as a tear slid down his face and hung on his lip before he banished it with his blood-soaked sleeve. *That's all he can say? Is he serious?* My inner bitch snarled in an understandable panic. Beau could barely look at me. His eyes were fixed on the winding road ahead. That familiar penny drop moment hit me as hard as a brick this time and my inner bitch was speechless. I knew what he had said, I knew it must be serious, but it just wasn't registering in my brain. After what felt like hours my ability to speak returned. My mouth was dry and my body was still unresponsive as I stared out onto the endless murky coal road ahead of me, the breeze lapping affectionately at my tear stained cheeks. 'Where do they take the spirits?' I whispered uneasily.

'I don't know.' Beau replied dejectedly, still concentrating on the road alone, punching the car into fourth gear in frustration.

'What do you mean? If one of these things is after me, I need to know where they're planning to take me.' I yelled as we pulled up outside Gwen's house, his foot stamping on the brake pedal throwing me forward against my seat belt.

'Grace, I can't see what the Shadows see, just like I can't see what spirits see when they crossover into the light. I don't know where the Shadows go, but I'm pretty sure it's nowhere good. They are full of darkness. They are ten steps of sadism and cruelty above Miss Lesney. They choose who they want, it's all preordained, I don't know how to stop them. They do not favour people who are destined to fulfil a life of immense goodness, someone who will in the future help on a huge scale to tip the balance in favour of good. They want a world that's filled with iniquity, death and destruction. I told you that this would hurt you, I should never have let this happen. They want you because of me, it's my fault. I should have walked away when I had the chance.' The finality in his voice was heart-breaking. He was beating himself up on a whole new level. His knuckles flushed white as he gripped tensely at the steering wheel.

Throwing his head back the angered roar that he expelled into the air was almost animalistic.

'You need to calm down, we can sort this, just like everything else!' The conviction in my point was lacking. All I wanted to do was cry. For a moment, however brief that it was, he wished we had never met, my soul withered in response to the thought of not having him in my life.

'You don't get it! They find it difficult to identify and hone in on someone with your level of decency, honesty and purity, someone with that much heart. Good people are embedded with a shield of sorts to protect and hide them. I've never felt one with this amount of strength and determination though, it's like it has got help, and something or someone is weakening you.' The wicked face of Glen Havers and his crooked, evil smirk flashed through my head. The truth bubbled up inside me, fighting to break free of my lips.

'Grace, do you know something? You have to tell me. Please.' He begged, his eyes now firmly on me.

'I didn't want to worry you. I really didn't think it was important. Gwen was trying to help me and he got to her. I didn't know how to explain, I thought you'd leave me.' I whimpered desperately gasping for air.

'Let's go inside and you can tell me everything.' Beau drew his eyes away from mine coldly, walking ahead of me up Gwen's drive. I followed behind like an ashamed puppy that'd just be told off for peeing up the neighbour's tree. I entered the door sheepishly and full of fear, Beau closing it behind us with a thud. This was going to be anything but simple.

AWOKEN *Billie Jade Kermack*

Hello backbone, ready to stand up and lay everything bare? Who am I kidding? I'm an absolute coward!...

...I can't lose him - not now.

THIRTY-FIVE

ꕥ

‘Gwen there’s something that needs sorting out and I don’t know how far along its gone, or how dangerous it is exactly.' Beau explained to Gwen as he glared back at me disapprovingly, pacing the same stretch of floor repeatedly.

'Beau, don’t be so hard on her.' Gwen tried to reason as she moved towards me. After a short silence Beau stopped pacing and turned to face us.

'You’ve known all along, haven’t you?' He accused; his scowl now shared between the two of us.

'I haven’t known the whole time. I thought it was important for Grace to tell you herself.’ She stated in her defence.

'I can’t believe this Gwen, you of all people know how dangerous this is! The Shadows won’t give up until they have her!' Beau cried out. His usual air of coolness was now an empty shell of anguish, worry marring his beautiful face.

'Shadows? I had no idea it had got to that Beau, if I had, I would never have let it get this far.' Gwen’s face was no longer solemn and understanding but, in my defence, I didn’t have a clue about the Shadows either. Unfortunately, this little fact was of no comfort to me. The look of dread from both Gwen and Beau as they exchanged knowing, fretful stares made me more than a little uneasy. 'Right, well, Grace, does Beau know EVERYTHING?' Gwen emphasised, raising her eyebrows like only an adult could.

The air was humid and as Beau and Gwen gawked at me, I felt like a five-year-old being told off by her parents. The full moon shone brightly through the living room bay windows and an unexpected sense of calm took over. It was quickly pushed aside by an unearthly sense of impending trouble that plagued me as the realisation of what I had to reveal hit me hard and fast like a ten-tonne brick. *Any chance, just for once, we can change that brick for a pillow? I feel the headache too you know!* my inner bitch snarled with a cold compress to her forehead. I turned to face Beau.

'Do you want the long version or the short version?' I asked, knowing full well that they were both pretty bad.

'I want to know everything!' He pressed. I thought that by not telling him, I was saving him some heartache, but I hadn't; if anything, it was worse. It's like when your Mum has a go at you for doing something and then ends the argument with, *I'm not angry at you, I'm just disappointed.* I should have told him, I should have followed my heart and asked for his help, why did I let things get this far? Beau and Gwen moved towards the fireplace, whispering in hushed voices, I realised I had to take a good hard look at myself. Beau knows this stuff, it's been apparent from the beginning, his whole world is ghost related in one way or another. *Why don't I just tell him? It's like trying to tell a butcher how he should dissect a pig. There's a good chance he knows and I don't. Beau knows this stuff inside and out and all I've done this whole time is lie to him. What if he thinks it was all a lie? He told me once that I was the first person in a long time that he trusted and I've ruined that.* As all these thoughts rushed through my head. I felt as though I was Alice and with every sentence that left my mouth about Glen, it was forcing me further and further down the rabbit hole. *Damn, where's the cuddly white rabbit when you need him?*

After what seemed like forever, but was actually about two and a half hours, I had recited every point, however minuscule it may have been, of every grave encounter I had had with Glen. I had reeled off every little detail that I could remember, including the bad and the downright awful. My body had not relaxed the entire time, my shoulders in knots, but at least Beau no longer looked at me as though he wished I had never existed. His eyes were soft, his expression pensive. He sat quietly in the armchair, drawing his elbows to his knees and lowering his head into his hands. He looked completely deflated, like a tree wilting in winter. All the life just fell out of him. I had finally covered everything and as the last words left my mouth, I finally understood what Beau was saying. Once I had condensed everything, I realised how shocking it all was. Gwen rushed to the kitchen, I nervously joined Beau by the fireplace.

'I know I didn't let you in. I didn't ask for your help and I should have. I thought I was doing what was right. I wanted to hold onto you so desperately. I see now that instead; I have pushed you away further by not being open and honest. I should have told you the truth. Beau, I am so sorry.' The tears fell, as did his stare. *What have I done? How could I have messed this up so epically?*

'Hey, you two, I've sorted something out but I can't get everything together until tomorrow.' Gwen said softly. She couldn't have been more evasive, but I was very aware that I was in no position to argue for more of an explanation. My eyelids were slowly getting heavier, the expositions of the evenings gathering making my head throb. I stood up, climbing off the sofa and made my way over to the front door. Gwen stopped me as I passed the kitchen entrance and gave me a much-needed hug. Her small arms fighting to cocoon me. I could have fallen asleep there and then. Warmth and love radiated from her. I gave her a little wave and flashed as much of a smile as I could muster, which really wasn't a lot. I took my coat off the peg and reached out towards the door handle.

'Grace, you know I love you, don't you?' Beau whispered in my ear from behind me, his warm breath grazing the soft spot below my ear. The barrier of restraint I had poorly constructed around my crippling emotions to this point was now breaking away; my fear, my love, my remorse flooding out of me in waves. I turned and fell into his arms, into my safe place. My coat dropped to the floor as I wrapped my arms around him. It occurred to me in that moment that I should remember everything I could about him, the smell of his aftershave, the feel of his fingers on my skin, the wobble in my unsteady legs under his touch, the adoration in his eyes reserved only for me. I never wanted any of this to be just a memory, I wanted to be able to hug him as much as possible, whenever I wanted, for the rest of my life. The tears streamed down my cheeks, dripping onto his bloodstained shirt. As he held my head to his chest, running his fingers through my hair, I could hear his heartbeat thump in his chest and suddenly, for that couple of seconds, I was oblivious as to the situation at hand. I was lost in him and grateful for it.

'I love you too, so much.' I whimpered breathlessly into his chest.

'I think I should get you home.' Beau approached the door, picking up my coat as he passed me, the lack of his touch leaving me empty. I frantically wiped my eyes, thankful that I was nowhere near a mirror. I did not need to see what a mess I had made of my makeup. I grabbed a tissue off the side table, licked it and rubbed furiously under my eyes. Not ideal, but it would have to do.

~~~~
~~~~

AWOKEN *Billie Jade Kermack*

The hot sun beamed through the drawn curtains as the mood in the room tensed with every passing second. Gwen laid out a crocheted, rainbow coloured blanket in the centre of the living room, Beau pushed the furniture out to the four corners. With a space cleared, Gwen placed a large, mauve, satin cushion with tassels on the blanket and started arranging imperfect, ornate, white crystals in a circle around it. Gwen held the last crystal in her hand and beckoned me towards her. 'Grace, once you're in the circle and I put the final crystal in place you will not be able to leave it.' Gwen handed me a long cylinder glass jar filled with white shards.

'What's this?' I asked.

'It's rock salt. Once in the crystals you need to make a circle of the salt around you. It's for your protection. I will tell you exactly what to do from there. We will be able to make contact with you up to the point of the spirit's entrance. From that point on you will have to use every bit of energy you have to fight him. Now, I need you to trust that we will not allow any lasting harm to come to you. I've explained to you before what our aim is. You just have to keep in mind all the love that the people around you have for you and the love you have for them. That is the strongest thing you have, your weapon of sorts.' The distress was blindingly clear in my face. Beau came towards me and held me at arm's length, the worry lines on his brow furrowed.

'You can do it Grace. I'm just sorry I got you into all this. If I could take your place I would.' He pulled me into his arms and kissed me – I mean really kissed me. For a second I blushed. Then the dawning realisation that it could very well be our last hurtled me into it, to the deepest crevices of my love for him. Gwen cleared her throat and Beau released me. I hung there in the comforting feeling for a brief and fleeting moment. I entered the circle tugging at my now red puckered lips, his force almost instantly missed as they tingled. I centred myself on the blanket. 'Grace, give me your right hand.' I did as Beau instructed but for some reason, I couldn't divert my eyes away from Gwen's solemn face.

'Ouch! What the hell...' I yelled; my eyes now firmly fixed on Beau. The double-edged knife in his shaking hand was dripping blood, my blood, onto the floor, a few centimetres shy of the crystals. Its black handle was battered and partially wrapped with a cream material. I could see a crescent silver moon either side of a silver circle engraved on it. The sharp blade was discoloured and now painted vermilion along one side.

'I'm sorry.' Beau's words were barely a whisper.

'Right, Grace, I need you to...'

'Hold on a minute. I need you to answer a few questions.' My hand was sore as I cradled it. The blood oozed from my sliced skin, droplets hitting my jeans.

'Grace, do not get your blood on the floor. I know how confusing this all is for you but you needed to be in the circle before we cut you. We don't have much time here.'

'Funnily enough I was more intrigued to find out WHY you cut me.' It was clear to everyone in the room that I was not a happy bunny. It felt like getting prodded and poked with weapons was now part of my weekly schedule. Apparently if I didn't shed some blood there was something amiss. Beau placed the knife carefully onto the table beside him and crouched down at my side, but still at arm's length.

'The Athame has been passed down from coven to coven for about the last three hundred years. For this ritual to work I needed to cut along the life line on your right hand. I know it hurts.'

'Really smart arse?' I snapped. Beau lifted his hand, palm out. There were three, neat, healed scars that matched my cut.

'Believe me, I know.' He mumbled. His sadness momentarily overriding my pain.

'Look, we need to get on with this. Grace, I will answer all of your questions once we are done with all this, but for now you are very vulnerable. We need to secure you in the circle to begin.' Gwen's words should have been comforting but they weren't! She passed me a chunky pair of industrial sewing scissors.

'I don't have to cut anything off do I?' I was only half joking as I counted Beau's digits. A sigh of absolute relief came out as I noted the tenth, his pinkie finger. Beau also noticed my panic and an amused smile formed in one corner of his mouth. He flexed his fingers out in front of him and wiggled them playfully as proof, reading my mind in the way that only he could. Gwen put down the final, almost transparent crystal to complete the circle. Beau's serious face was back now.

'Grace, you will need the scissors to cut off some of your hair. We can't do that for you and it must be done once the salt circle is complete. Now shake the salt out evenly in a circle around you. Make sure there are no gaps it has to be a continuous line.' I did as Gwen instructed with my undamaged left hand.

'Wait, why does this seem so familiar? I think I would have remembered doing this before. I can't shake this feeling, like Deja-vu, or something less insane.'

'John Hurt? Kate Hudson?' Beau chimed in.

'The Skeleton Key.' I mused almost internally.

'Great film!' Beau said, briefly forgetting the intensity of the situation at hand.

'But that's all made up, it's not real. Right?'

'There are times when entertainment gets it right. In this case they came very close. It was the red brick dust that messed it up.'

'Am I going mad?'

'Probably. You would be amazed how close people have come to getting it right, and after we get you through our present little challenge, I will reveal all.'

'Okay, what's next?' *Back to business.*

'You need to put your palm onto the north, east, south and west of the circle. In that order' Gwen advised.

'Geography was never my subject Gwen.' Beau smiled and walked around the circle. I placed my left palm where he instructed for North.

'No, your other hand.'

'Really? This is going to pinch a little isn't it?' I asked. Beau held up his scarred hand again as a response.

'Okay, been there, done that, I get the picture.' I snapped.

It didn't pinch. Oh no, *pinch* was not the word. Acidic lemon juice in the eye felt like a more apt description. I wiped my salty wound on my top once I was finished, glaring at Beau.

'Now sweetheart, cut just a little chunk of your hair and scatter the strands over the blood and salt. Once you're done, I need you to lie down, head facing north. I know it's hard, but you really have to try and relax. I need you to bring him to you. Remember his face, how he made you feel.' Her eyes were fraught with concern. Little did she realise this was the easy part; I saw his face every time I closed my eyes. The feeling that he evoked in me remaining with me always. Suddenly the fear of the unknown sent my heart racing. I did as I was told and watched Gwen as she closed her eyes and began to chant.

'Nomay Rentay soo folan, Nomay rentay soo folan, Nomay rentay soo folan.'

I felt trapped, bordering claustrophobic. It was as though I was in a Perspex box filled with water, unable to make contact with the outside world. The air rippled around me, drowning out the voices outside the circle. The barrier was officially up.

'It's all going to be OK, I love you.' Beau mouthed as he reached for my hand suddenly remembering he couldn't and dropping it down beside him. I fidgeted uneasily and tousled the tassels of the cushion through my shaking fingers. Gwen was still chanting with her eyes closed but I couldn't make out what she was saying. I started to feel queasy, dazed, and lightheaded.

'Close your eyes and clear your mind.' It was Gwen's muffled voice but in the same moment it wasn't. Her eyes were no longer closed and no longer a beautiful deep brown but instead a glazed pearly white. *Let's get this over with!* I shut my eyes tight as Gwen had instructed, letting my mind wander back to that first terrifying dream. The sensation of falling at a great speed through the air made my eyes fly open again. Everything around me outside of my little box was moving in fast motion, but what was in my mind was painfully slow. My body was at war. I saw a swirl of colours and shapes, my senses flipping about wildly on a rollercoaster ride with no visible end. The stabbing, uncontrollable pain in my forehead, was worryingly, the only part of my experience that made me feel human. The cuts, the dreadful stench of petrol, the tearing of the skin around my wrists and ankles as the ropes tightened and my desperate pleas for freedom; every horrific and painful moment Glen had subjected me to played out in my head. No longer a memory or a flashback, I endured the strangely bearable pain as I fell aimlessly in and out of consciousness, dragged helplessly between the two worlds of the living and the dead. In a flash I found my way back to reality, but everything had changed! The sun had vanished and now only the dim lights of candles filled the room, creating snaking shadows across the ceiling that appeared to have a life of their own.

I came out of my dream state a few times and although it only felt like I had closed my eyes for a few minutes so much had changed so quickly. I could no longer hear anything outside my little box. The only thing that didn't change was the look of pure dread on Beau's face, no matter where in the room he was, his expression never changed. He feared for me, for my life. Once stood by the roaring fire, another on his knees beside me, and lastly as he paced around beneath the alcove. *What had I got us into?*

The smell of Gwen's rosemary incense burning on the dining table filled my nose briefly and although it was strong enough to take my breath away, it was soon shoved away by the familiar sickly scent of Glen's overflowing petrol tin that lingered all around me. My sight was dwindling and my eyes felt heavy, the yellow flames of the candles in Gwen's dining room flickered violently, turning a misty blue colour. I soon found that I couldn't open my eyes any more. *Am I dead? Am I gone now?*

As I glided from one world to the next, my insides suddenly felt as though they were grappling to force their way out of my body. With every breath I took, my chest began to burn. The searing heat was rising up through my throat and into my mouth where a scream should have voiced my pain, I could only muster a petrified gurgle. My organs flared and tugged inside me. My heart speeding up as it tried to keep pace. My blood boiled beneath my skin, it coursing aimlessly through my fragile veins. In that moment I wished for death and welcomed its arrival with open arms.

Then there was nothing.

I must have passed out – *Thank god.*

BEAU

As I watched Grace lying there, writhing in pain, desperately trying to detach herself from whatever he was doing to her, all I wanted to do was take her in my arms, to wipe the streaming tears from her eyes and to take her as far away from there as possible. Surprisingly I was able to hold onto some of my sanity. *What would taking her away do, the damage is already done. They will find her, no matter where she goes, or where she hides. I'm meant to protect her.*

The minutes ticked away, her back arched, her limbs flayed and contorted, tears rolling down her cheeks, I couldn't help but chastise myself for arriving back into Gallows Wood all those months ago. I was nothing but a parasite in her life. It felt as though I had been watching her go through this for days. Her body convulsed and began to spasm uncontrollably, her cries for help, splintering me at my very core. Her cries were piercing, heart wrenching and although muffled by the barrier between us, for me, still crystal clear.

The frightful torture of her body soon calmed, Jolts of pain now making her appear sluggish. It was becoming clear that Grace was losing control. She was slipping away into a consciousness that not even I could understand. It wouldn't be long before she could draw him in and bring him out. Now all we could do was wait. After a while Grace became eerily still, almost statue like. You had to pay close attention to even catch the rise and fall of her chest.

The wind no longer forced the tree branches to pelt against the windows and the bright flames of the candles no longer flickered, it was as though all the air in the room had completely vanished. I knew that something was wrong but it's not as though these rituals were a daily occurrence for me. I had seen a catholic exorcism when I was about five or six, but that was my only means of comparison and Gwen had already told me that it was completely different. Without warning, the blood started pouring from my nose and as it hit my shirt, I plugged it with my hands.

'Here's a towel, try not to get any in the circle. We don't want him having a connection with you as well.' Gwen urged.

'How did your night go? Was Grace surprised? I wish I could have seen her face. I still can't believe I finally get to be a part of her life.' His voice rung cheerfully from the kitchen.

'Beau, who is that I can hear?' Gwen asked with a worried glance at Grace's body.

'He's back. It's Grace's Dad!' I panicked. James glided into the room, making lightwork of travelling through the wall separating the kitchen and the living room. His broad smile fell, replaced suddenly with a horrified wide-eyed expression as he looked on at his battered baby girl.

'What is going on? What have you done to her?' He roared accusingly.

'Mr. O'Callaghan, she has to do this. I'm so sorry, I never meant for this to happen.' My voice shook, his hands trembling, his frustration clear as he longed to help his daughter.

'I trusted you to look out for her, you promised you would protect her!' James seethed, tears forming in his eyes.

'Mr. O' Callaghan. I am Gwen. I can hear you but I cannot see you. Grace is in good hands. I am so sorry you had to witness this but she will be okay.' Gwen's words fell on deaf ears as Grace's father knelt at the side of the circle, dumbfounded and forced to watch the horror unfolding before him.

'What have you done to my baby girl? You listen here boy, if anything, and I mean ANYTHING happens to her, you will have me to answer to!' His words hit me with more force than I thought was possible from a ghost.

'Mr. O' Callaghan, you have to calm down. I know how much this must be worrying you, but you will flat line with all this emotion. If you have to go and recharge, who knows how long you will be gone.' I watched as a grey glow, speckled with black, heaved its way out and away from Grace's father. The build-up of pure rage in him dissipating slightly.

'Please sir, you have to calm down. This is how you help her.' I yelled, trying to break through the emotional wall that James had bricked up around himself. Although ghosts have no need to breathe, Grace's father was panting. Laboured and angered spurts of air left his mouth as his chest instinctively heaved, the rage returning to his face as he reacted at her battered body still writhing on the floor at his feet. For a split second you could almost forget he was dead.

GRACE

Suddenly, as though all the blood had departed my limbs and rushed to my head, there came another surge of pain. It was like an electrical current had shot up my spine and stiffened my entire body, causing my arms and legs to contort, stretching to their limit. It was excruciating, if I had wished for death at that moment, I would have been pleading for it wholeheartedly. All I could see was darkness, a pitch-black sea that offered no reassurance of my impending plight. The pain in my spine alleviated momentarily, setting my limbs free. The minute sense of hope that flushed across my face was short-lived. The absence of the agony just the calm before the storm. A bloated fullness pulsated in my head, like being on a plane at 14,000 feet with the cabin pressurised. All I could hear was the dull drum of my own panic-stricken heartbeat, the beats quickening in response to the growing pain.

I tried to distance myself, to go somewhere else in my mind, somewhere far away from the agony. It wasn't long before my Mother's mind over matter technique finally started to take effect. Wherever I was, the darkness began to slowly lighten, the pounding in my head calming to a dull thump of a small hammer on concrete. *Drip, drip, drip.* I looked out into the wavering blackness, suddenly glad that I couldn't see what was ahead of me.

'What the hell is going on? Help her! Do something!' It was Beau. There was no sign of him and he sounded a million miles away but I was sure it was his voice. I had obviously descended into the cavernous dwellings of my mind to where I was supposed to be, but this offered up no reassurance. As the dripping hit the floor again it was much louder. His red hair shadowed the reflection of what I assumed were wet walls either side of him. I instinctively screamed out as loud as I could. It didn't take me long to realise that no one could hear me or my desperate cries for help. I was stuck in a world that was foreign to me and as I remembered my body lying on Gwen's rosewood floorboards and that patchwork blanket, I realised that wherever I was, it was nowhere good.

I can hear him, his distressed cries to help me. What is happening out there? My body – what is it doing?

The strange sensation of feeling completely separated from my body made the floor spin beneath me. I had lost my connection with the real world, a world that until now, I had taken for granted. I implored with every inch of my soul that I would touch down in that real world very soon, or at the very least; be expelled from this horrific hellish ordeal I had willingly entered into. I prayed I'd find myself deserted on a plane of existence unbeknown to Glen. He stepped closer to me; each move he made unhurried. Glen had me right where he wanted me, clearly feeding off my fear as with every step towards me, his repulsive grin grew. His evil smirk and callous bright white eyes had me mesmerised, blinding what little hope I had left. I couldn't hear Beau any more. I was finally alone.

THIRTY-SIX

ꕥ

BEAU

'Beau, I want answers now! Wait, what's happening? Is she OK? Help her!' He screamed. His presence was unexpected, but I couldn't worry about James right now. I selfishly didn't have the time or the energy to placate him as I watched the love of my life struggle under an invisible force.

'I don't know. Gwen, Gwen, GWEN!' I almost didn't recognise the shrill begging of my own voice. Grace's bare arms were no longer a flushed delicate pink. Scrawled in elongated italics, carved deep into Grace's skin were words, letters formed before our eyes. They appeared agonisingly slowly as each cut pierced her skin. Blood trickled to the floor beneath her as Gwen rushed back into the room.

'Oh no!' Her hands flew up to her mouth as Grace's body reacted silently to every cut. Her mouth wide, her screams non-existent. 'He is testing us. He wants us to pull her out of it, but we can't. Beau, grab a piece of paper and a pen. Over there, in my cabinet. We need to write this all down, it may help in the long run.' James paced the floor back and forth, his feet making no impact on the ground beneath him, wincing, as he glanced every so often at his mutilated daughter.

'I can't just stand here and do nothing. I will make you pay if she doesn't pull through this! If you love her you will fix this.' James ordered, not taking his wide eyes from mine.

'I do love her, more than I could ever describe and I will get her through this, if it's the last thing I do. This really wasn't how I wanted you to get to know me.'

Death to her, death to them. Family bonds, sweet blood. She's not the first, not the last. Father, you have lost them both. Innocence invites me, torture compels me. Thy will be done.

The words made no sense, they told us nothing. I threw the paper and pen across the floor. Her skin was raised painfully around each ragged slash. 'When did he get so preachy?'

GRACE

'Well Grace, what a pleasure to see you again, it's been a while.' His tone was eerily chipper, as he juggled the blade between his hands. 'By the look on your face, I'm guessing you had a little chat about me, with my good old friend Gwen. I thought once it had occurred to you to ask for her help it wouldn't be long before she figured it out. Showed you her treasured little box of newspaper clippings aswell did she?' As I went to answer him, he raised his bony finger to my lips. 'That was a rhetorical question, I really couldn't care less!' He smirked, pushing his knife into the leather holder attached to his belt, turning and placing the petrol can on the floor next to his grubby walking boots. I attempted to speak, my first word a mere squeak as he glared at me, letting me know that all he needed from me was my silent attention. "To be perfectly honest Grace, I didn't think you'd hold out on your own as long as you did. I underestimated you. I thought you would have gone blubbering to the town psychic a lot sooner. I'm really impatient when it comes to getting my own way, as Gwen has probably told you already. She has made me wait years for this, but then it occurred to me. I have an eternity to play with. I can take my time and really plan my future.' It sounded as though he was applying for his dream job as the words rolled off his tongue, an optimistic glint appearing in his eyes. 'Dragging it out might actually be more fun.' Glen hissed as he pulled the six-inch hunting blade out again from its sheath, running his dirty finger over the sharp side without flinching. His blood trickled down to the tip of the blade and onto the floor. Each drip sounding like a soft chiming as it made contact with the metal tin.

'You won't get away with this, Beau WILL save me.' I protested, believing with everything in me that what I was saying was the truth.

'Less of the interruptions.' He warned. My plastered bravado only proving to frustrate him. 'Let's get to your part in this little tale.' He hissed, pointing the bloodied blade at me, the tarnished steel mere inches from my face. He cackles, as the fear he so sorely desired settles back into my eyes.

'Wait a minute, dragging what out exactly?' I mustered shakily; my eyes still fixed on the knife.

'Well killing Gwen of course.' He exclaimed jovially. I literally couldn't speak, spluttering incoherent sounds in response to his statement. 'Oh Grace, I can tell you're confused, so let me explain. Since my death, I have been waiting for someone to come along who could help me.' He pointed the shiny steel at my face again, signalling my part in his sadistic little stage show. 'Someone I could shamelessly manipulate without their knowledge, possibly a little girl in love.' He teased. I tried in vain to edge the chair backwards as the rope tore into my skin. He ignored my attempts and continued to spit his little story at me. 'Beau was clearly off limits, he could see me coming a mile off. I depended on your unwavering devotion for him. I knew you wouldn't want to tell him about our little rendezvous. Once Gwen realised the signs of when I was near, her *'little accidents'* just weren't as much fun.' His air quotes that accompanied his words 'little accidents' just made him look petty. 'The amount of kids that came in and out of her house you'd have thought one of them would have been of some use to me, but unfortunately, Gwen had thought of that already. I can only attach myself to someone once they are asleep, when their guard is down, this is when they are most susceptible. Of course, they have to believe as well, so I have Beau to thank for preparing you on that one.' His smile is broad, the twisted remnants of his depravity lingering at the edges. 'Once her foster children grew up, she encouraged them to move as far away as possible, so it was pointless working on them once they had left. Gwen kept her psychic abilities to herself, the thirty or so hex bags she planted around their bedrooms to ward off evil meant I had no chance. If I never smell that vile mixture of wolfsbane and rosemary again it will be too soon. Frightfully appalling stuff!'

With these out of character, gentlemanly phrased words, Glen seemed to wander off into his own thoughts for a second, which conjured up a much-needed glimmer of hope - it was short lived. 'I can't wait to see Beau slap that smug look off your face. He will get you and he will send your crazy arse back to hell, where it belongs.' I screamed, finding my voice. His glare was hollow as his fists rained down on me. My eye throbbed as his knuckles tore into the skin protecting my cheekbone. The crack silencing me as my head bobbed backwards and forwards, like a dashboard retriever statue.

'What did I tell you about interrupting? It really is terribly rude.' He smoothed down his tatty clothes, wiping his face free of my blood with the back of his hand, doing little else but smearing it around. 'Where was I? Oh, I know.' He said excitedly before continuing. 'Then one summer morning in you walked. I sat silently at the foot of the stairs ready to give up, but then occurred in me, once I saw that revolting doe-eyed look on your face, that little glint of adoration that flashed on your face every time you looked at Beau, I knew then, that I had finally found my partner in crime. Whether you were a willing participant or not, you were my way in. I gave you the time you needed to believe, but I knew with your unwavering feelings for Beau, it wouldn't take much.'

It was my fault, all of it. He never wanted me, he didn't care what happened to me, as long as I could get him in the door. My thoughts hit me in a blind panic as my stifled tears mixed with the blood from my fresh wound. 'But wait, how exactly are you going to get Gwen? They wouldn't have sent me here if they didn't have a plan?' I prompted brightly, hoping I had burned a huge hole in his sick plan. I coughed and spluttered, spitting out my now detached left incisor onto the floor at his feet.

'Christ, did Gwen not explain anything to you? In a few moments, after I've tortured you of course, you and I will return to your body, except you will be the spectator and I will be the host. Don't look so panicked, I'll take good care of your body while I'm using it. After all, being a teenage girl is all new to me.' He chirped hungrily. I tried desperately to shove the *tortured* part of his speech to the back of my mind.

'What do you mean, while you're using it?' I panicked. Any vague sense of relief would have been excellent at that moment but as Glen reeled off his plan with a huge sense of pride, I could only feel one thing - irreversibly rigid and uncompromising fear in all its grandeur. I was a puppet and Glen knew only too well how to pull my strings.

'Well I thought I'd go home and meet your family. I never liked school, so that will have to stop.' He babbled on ever so nonchalantly, as though he was noting down his weekly shopping list.

'Don't you think someone will notice? Beau? My Mum? Someone will know it's not me.' I protested bleary-eyed.

'Once I'm rid of your little boyfriend and my dear friend Gwen, I really couldn't care less who notices!' He seethed. I opened my mouth to speak, but within a millisecond Glen was already up to my face. He pushed his filthy finger to my trembling lips as my body numbed with dread. 'Now Grace, I can see you probably have a question or two, but this isn't a lecture with a Q and A session. I will talk and you will not. You have seen what happens when you interrupt me.' He stated lazily, grazing my cheek to second his declaration. He raised his knife and pushed it to my throat, the pressure of the steel constricting my windpipe. I quickly nodded in agreement like an obedient child. 'Now, Gwen, being the predictable bitch that she is, will be ready at the moment we both come out of this daze. Expecting a battered you and my weak spirit of course, she will remove a crystal and then use her funky heathen magic to compel me for all eternity into the depths of hell, or at the very least, store me in a jar until she finds someone who can. As you can probably guess, I am not a big fan of this plan. Her overall desire is to damn my soul to hell for an eternity. I don't much like hot holidays so I doubt I'm going to like going there second time around. Been there, done that, got the hot poker scars to prove it. Now, I have found a loop hole that I intend on taking advantage of.'

The immense enormity of his life destructing plan didn't faze him. I quickly realised that he would hurt and destroy anyone who got in his way without a second thought. He paced around me slowly, effortlessly, retightening my hands and feet with the red rope with just a directional flick of his fingers in the air as he cockily continued on with his speech. 'You see it isn't just me that would benefit from all of this. I believe you have been acquainted with the Yamen or maybe you just know them as the Shadows.' My mouth dropped. I knew exactly who they were and I knew exactly what Glen was about to say. 'They caught wind of my little plan; it appears they would be rather happy if I could get rid of your prince charming Beau. Once I am in your human body, I can kill whoever I want, they see slaughtering your boyfriend as a huge favour. Two birds, one stone!' His eagerness and twisted fondness of everything relating to the butchery of another human being sounded more like terms of endearment rather than statements of malicious intent. This only caused my heartbeat to thump faster than I'm sure would be medically normal. He enjoyed my suffering, relishing the power he had over me. As the last speck of hope dwindled, a realisation hit me like that all too familiar brick that had accompanied me ever so closely these past few months. 'You want Beau, not me?'

'Wow, you catch on fast.' He mocked. 'Think of it like a game of mousetrap; there are nine or so steps to conquer before the final hurdle, you my dear, are one of those steps, your boy, is the hurdle.' I felt sick. The tears rolling down my cheeks as I fought to calm my breathing. Refusing to give this man anything that he hadn't snatched from me under duress, I wiped my cheeks furiously with my bound hands, the rough rope grazing at my brutalised face. I composed myself as best as I could and swathed a courageous facade over my fear.

'Aren't you forgetting something Glen? I'm protected by the crystals. No one can get in or out without Gwen letting the protection spells down. As soon as they see I'm not me or that I haven't dragged out your disgusting, pathetic excuse of a spirit, they will banish you. Don't worry too much, I hear Satan welcomes back previous residents with a happy slap on the back.' My eyes beckoned his, I refused to back down. I couldn't believe my cockiness. I was in a parallel world with a man who was wielding a knife and promising to torture me for fun. I swiftly shut my mouth once I saw his grin morph into an angry grimace. In a fleeting second, my composure and strength slipped away.

'Oh, you poor, misguided, little girl. How do you think the Shadows coax unwilling souls?' He cackled. My face dropped, my stomach plummeting into my intestines as that debilitating feeling of dismay returned. 'Shadows are endowed with a great power, the power of misdirection, of trickery, the power to alter one's appearance, their personality, their speech. It's only for a short time, but hopefully, it's long enough for me to get out of your little charmed circle. I will look like you Grace, I will talk like you and after the many tiresome months I've had to sit and watch you and lover boy, however sickening it will feel, I will clone your every soppy word to him. Thanks to Gwen, I've had a lot of time to practise my craft.' His cackle tickled uncomfortably at my body; the stomach-churning noise almost visible. A ballooning hollowness filled my chest. I couldn't move and I couldn't speak. At that moment I looked down at my hand. I swear I could feel Beau holding it. I could smell his aftershave coursing through the air around me. There was no way I was staying there to rot for the rest of eternity, staring into that darkness with only Glen's face to remind me of my fate. A waft of Beau's aftershave caught my nose again. I closed my eyes tightly, lovingly picturing the face of the beautiful man that I love, the man that allowed me into a world that he called his own. I am his and he is mine.

'You can sense him, can't you?' Glen whispered from behind me. Dragging me from my self-affirming trance. 'Let's get this party started!' He cheered loudly with a celebratory slap to his knee. I may have been locked in my idea of hell but it was only too clear we were in Glen's impression of pure heaven. He held up his knife, glancing at his reflection in the rusty blade. He ran his tongue over his stained yellow and black teeth, brushing his contorted stick like fingers through his neat, duck tailed, russet mane. He started to stroll towards me, that glint in his eye poisoning my thoughts, my bones shuddering in response. 'Now all we have to do is get their attention.' The words danced through his smirk as he danced around in front of me, shaking out his arms and legs as though preparing for a race. With his body now calm, his legs parted, his eyes now fixed on mine, he raised the knife above his head, the gleaming tip of it, directed right at me. 'I've been looking forward to this.'

BEAU

By this point it was too quiet. As I leaned in to hold her hand, for a brief second, I thought I saw her smile. This did not last. 'Grace. Grace, can you hear me?' I hadn't even realised I had started crying. Everything in me was pleading that she would answer me.

'Beau, I think you should step back sweetheart.' Gwen urged softly, counteracting that by forcefully grabbing me by my shoulder and tugging me backwards. In that same second Grace's body began to twist and warp, her shrill screams thunderous. Suddenly, from out of nowhere, bloody wounds began to puncture her torso, they sliced at her flesh, ripping her clothes, spilling blood onto the blanket beneath her.

Each strike frenzied and out of control. Gwen held me as tightly as she could, the fact that I couldn't break free of her small, frail frame meant that she was using magic to assist her efforts. I fought on, compelled to help Grace, to put a stop to her cries of pain. Grace's ordeal was nowhere near over and Glen made sure that I knew it as he continued to butcher her. Gwen no longer needed to hold me in her arms, her magic had built up a forcefield that kept me prisoner from my girl. All I could do was helplessly watch her suffer. She fought tirelessly to free her arms and legs from invisible restraints, gouges and bloody scratches on the skin around her wrists appearing out of nowhere as they ate at her flesh. I couldn't fight something I couldn't see. I pushed at the barrier that separated us, feeling it waver under my body. Gwen pulled me by my shoulder to face her. 'Beau you can't interfere; you will do her more damage than good. He's doing this on purpose. If you wake her now, there is a chance, she will be stuck in there with him, forever.' I got as close to the circle as I could without disturbing it, my compliance and understanding disintegrating the now redundant barrier.

'Grace, I don't know if you can hear me, but I want you to know, I'm sorry. I should never have put you in this position. I would give anything to stop this.' I whispered, tears still pricking at the corner of my eyes. Talking to her was the only thing I could think to do. The pain continued for her whilst the heartache continued for me. Thick crimson blood began to trickle from her mouth, coughs and wheezes signalling her fight tipping its edge, she had just about had enough, anymore and he would surely kill her.

'It's nearly time sweetheart, almost there.' Gwen lulled on bended knee beside me, her eyes closed, her voice quiet but powerful as it reverberated in the air through the barrier of the crystal guarded circle. 'We have to prepare Beau, it's time.'

GRACE

Photographs of smiling girls against mottled blue backgrounds – school class photo I think – flashed before my eyes as I fought to keep them open, the swelling from Glen's assault stabbing at my face. The young girls, late teens or early twenties I would guess, looked similar, with their long brunette tresses and big eyes, their beautiful faces alight with hope for their futures. I didn't recognise them, but I felt compelled to look at them. Glen's shrill laughter echoed in the background behind me. The agony reverberating around my body begged me to close my eyes. In that second, I felt Glen's cold dead hands on my chin, forcing it up so I could look at every picture of his handywork that flashed up in front of me, the realisation of my future now clear.

'Oh Linney, she was one of my favourites. Does she look familiar?' I shook my head lethargically, the humming of pain vibrating up my spine. 'I can't believe you don't see the similarities Grace. You both have those same stunning, big, azure eyes.' He stroked my face affectionately, my stomach retching up towards my throat in response.

'You really are bat-shit-crazy!' I spat through my fat-lip; pronunciation of my r's slightly hindered. I looked at the picture projected Infront of me as he waited impatiently for me to comply. Except for the obvious similarities of hair and eye colour, I couldn't see what he was getting at. Any energy I had evaded me. The succession of pictures continued, as did the recurring theme of young women with dark hair and blue eyes. Whether I wanted to look at them or not, I had to, the sharp nudge of his dirty blade jammed into my body if I even attempted to give in to my impending unconsciousness kept me awake. Then the pictures changed; I didn't need his knife to keep me awake now. The images came in parts, sections of a larger picture, like random puzzle pieces that were a bit out of focus. A leg, some hair, a woman's eye, they were all haphazard, but as the puzzle began to come together, it all clicked into place. They were pictures of the same women I had seen before, but now they were all dead. There was zero hope in these photos. Their butchered, violated, burnt and bludgeoned bodies lay exposed. The blood, the sadness, the pure brutality that covered their bodies tugged at my chest. Glen did that to those women, he was the one to blame. Those women died at his hands and he wanted me to know exactly what I was in for. 'They deserved it, each and every one of them.' He chuckled proudly with a sigh, now using his knife to clean the dirt from under his nails. The last picture I saw was of Linney's funeral, the woman he had previously noted as one of his favourites. A gathering of guests, huddled around her headstone, amongst the masses of flowers that covered the surrounding grass. A tear fell down my cheek; a tear that felt more prominent than all those that he had dragged from me before that point, this tear was for her. *How could someone be that evil?* I lowered my head and closed my eyes, solemnly pondering everything about my life that I would miss. Glen soon continued on with my torture, if anything his little slide show seemed to have given him a new lease of life. His strikes were now determined, unrelenting. The carnage of it all excruciating, each slice of my skin felt deeper and persisted longer than the last. There was a look of sheer ecstasy in Glen's crazed eyes as he pushed the blade into my stomach. With every thrust of the blade it forced out a gurgled scream, the blood frothed up my throat as air and fluid tried to escape the confines of my ravaged body. He pulled at my chin to meet my sluggish gaze.

'Grace, that fear on your face echoes a lifetime of hurt and suffering that good old Linney felt. She was in your position once. Luckily for her, I didn't get to spend so much quality time with her.' He pulled his dirty fingers through my hair, bringing the blood-soaked tendrils up to his nose, inhaling my scent. 'Those long striking brunette locks, those mesmerising eyes. I haven't seen you smile Grace, but I'm guessing there's a possibility that that's comparable as well. I most certainly have a type.' He thrust the knife down deep into my shoulder, his breath hitting my neck, his spine-chilling chortle ringing in my ears. 'Your father seems to have a problem protecting those that he loves. I see the other side and how he worries for you.' He teases as the searing pain begins to burn fiercely within me.

My gut feeling guided me tiredly to the conclusion that as my eyelids grew heavy and the rich taste of iron stained my skin, the scent lingering in the air around me, it wouldn't be long before I passed out - or died. Sadly, that gut feeling wasn't exactly being very decisive as I swept head first into a stupor that merely heightened the excruciating torment in my body. By the glories of God, he suddenly stopped.

'This is goodbye Grace.' He said casually looming over me. He sliced down my cheek amongst the rest of his brutal handy work with one of his grimy fingernails, it stung just as much as the bitter steel blade of his knife. Gwen will mend your wounds, but my mark will always be there as a reminder. A token that will be with you for an eternity Grace. I promise.' I closed my eyes tight, picturing Beau, Gwen, my Mum, my Dad and even Cary. I would have given anything to be with them. Then he was gone and I was finally alone. My mind and body ravaged to a point I was sure I could never return from.

'NOW!' Gwen shouted to Beau. Her voice echoing around in the darkness. With one quick movement my eyes flew open, the connection to my body feeling distant as Glen had described. Above me was a full-length image of myself,

AWOKEN *Billie Jade Kermack*

Glens glower emanating through my eyes. Before I could get my bearings, they let the mirror go without a second thought. The glass came hurtling towards my already brutalised body, my hands shooting up to protect myself. All I had now, was that darkness.

THIRTY-SEVEN

ᘓᘐ

'Beau, you collect the pieces. It's time to bring Grace back.' Gwen called frantically, beginning to chant in Aramaic as I fell in and out of consciousness. As I looked on into the darkness, I suddenly felt a pull, as though hospital resuscitating paddles were bringing me back to life. With each jolt my heart thumped louder and the ropes around my wrists got tighter. I was stuck helplessly between two worlds. Currently bound, a prisoner in both. I began to cough and wheeze. In a moment I felt someone's arms around me. I screamed and tried to get away with what little energy I had left. I held my eyes together tightly, refusing to look at him.

I would die in Beau's arms without a second thought, his smile a substantial runner up prize that I would be proud to receive, but here, in the darkness. *I will not die here, I will not live for the rest of time in the dank, dirty confines of Glen's thoughts. I would never stop struggling against him.*

'Grace, it's me, open your eyes, it's me.' He beckoned. I knew that voice. I stopped fighting it, opened my eyes and gazed up. Initially the soft light was blinding. Then there he was. It was Beau. I was back. I couldn't stop the tears, they came in their thousands, heart tugging sobs, with the relief that swamped my chest, I didn't think they would ever stop. I gripped at him, praying that my senses weren't teasing me. The pain began to ease and although my clothes were still ripped and bloody, my wounds were slowly healing, right in front of my eyes, like magic; one by one the gaping holes that once bore into my flesh were moulding back to normal, like play-doh. I glanced between Beau and the disappearing wounds in amazement. 'It's Gwen.' He breathed as he pushed the sweat sodden hair from my face. His body not leaving mine, even as I moved beneath him assessing the pain that elevated from my body. I glanced up, squinting under the light of the candles, faced with Gwen who was chanting with her eyes closed, her hands floating purposefully around me, the invisible bubble containing me, finally popped. The wonderment and shock that Gwen's power stirred in me ceased, leaving the room baron of energy, my eyes pooling with tears. 'How did you know it wasn't me?' I blubbered in a panic, my body relinquishing any hesitations and resting into Beau's embrace.

'We knew what his plan would be, the fact that he hated Gwen so much meant that he didn't anticipate what a talented Witch she was. Gwen knew she could heal your wounds, well most of them anyway.'

'What do you mean most of them?' I patted at my body frantically for any sign of lasting damage, my muscles although free from wounds still sore.

'Well, that black eye you're going to have for a little while, those rope marks will heal eventually and that cut on your cheek won't completely vanish.'

'Why not?' I whined, alarmed and terrified with a lump in my throat as I pawed at all the wounds he had noted.

'Gwen knew Glen's fascination with knives and fire. He was predictable like that, but once a ghost touches you with their hands, that mark cannot be erased. But don't worry, the black eye will fade and the slit on your cheek will scar, eventually.'

'Great, so he was right. I'm going to have to live with him for an eternity.'

'Having a scar to remind you won't be that bad. In that darkness you experienced, that loneliness and fear you felt, is where Glen will be, forever. I will make sure of that.' He lulled; determination rife in his explanation. Gwen stopped chanting, her body falling towards us onto the floor, her now brown eyes tired, her skin an opaque grey as the life that seeped out of her travelled towards me, pulling me safely away from death and back to life.

'Sweetheart, are you OK? I'm sorry I couldn't tell you what the plan was, we couldn't risk him getting it out of you. We needed the element of surprise for this to work. You were so brave and we are so proud of you.' She cupped my face and gave me one of her warm smiles, supporting my weight as Beau got to his feet.

'So, where is Glen now?' I squeaked nervously, fearing my safe return was all a mirage that Glen had concocted to mess with my head.

'He is now in the mirror. Mirrors are a portal between our world and theirs. Have you ever looked in the mirror and you could swear you saw a glimpse of someone behind you? That's a slither of vision into their world. He won't be getting out of there, I promise you. Back in the day it used to be common practice that when someone died in a household, they would cover all the mirrors, so the soul could not get trapped within it.' With those words Gwen tucked my hair behind my ear. I realised I hadn't even noticed the twenty or so mirrors dotted around the room covered with sheets and bedclothes. 'More mirrors the better.' She chuckled light-heartedly. The exertion of laughing proving difficult for her as she steadied herself on my arm, her breathing out of sync.

'But the mirror is shattered. You're telling me he's still there, in the pieces?' Even though Glen wasn't there by my side, I tucked my hands and feet into my body to get away from the mirrored pieces shimmering on the floor around me, my very real fear that he would reach out and suck me in there with him, was a feeling I wouldn't be able to easily shake.

'I will get it to its original state and store it somewhere safe. Other than that, there is no way of getting rid of him, or at least, no other way that I have discovered yet. The Shadows are the only beings that can destroy an evil spirit and for some reason they're not ready to get rid of Glen completely. Give me some time. Where there's a will, there's a way. I'll get rid of him eventually.' She smiled broadly sounding very Stepford wives as she hurried over to the kitchen, her energy almost completely restored. Beau knelt down by my side with a glass of cold water in his hand. The cool liquid set about dampening the burning in my throat, it was welcomed. I watched as he set the empty glass onto the coffee table, grabbing his black hooded sweatshirt from off the armchair and proceeded to wrap it around my shoulders. In one fluid movement he lifted me up into his strong arms; his muscles bulging beneath his white t-shirt. I could have stayed there forever. I could feel his reassuring heartbeat under my hand as I stroked his chest. My head snuggled into his neck. That is what kept me holding on, the once distant hope of being in Beau's arms again. I had truly never felt so safe; clasped tightly in my favourite place.

'I think we could all do with a cup of tea.' Gwen mused, as she set about returning the furniture to its rightful place. Her attempts to centre the heavyweight coffee table respectable after everything she had just endured. The shattered mirror sat in a pile on the floor in the corner of the room. The shards glistening under the iridescent light of the table lamp as Beau carried me across the room, my arms tightly secured around his neck, my legs crossed across his arm. Beau lowered me onto the sofa and I couldn't help but wince in pain. The visible wounds may have disappeared, but every muscle in my body was still aching. It felt as though someone had been sadistically chipping away at my bones with a sledgehammer. The truth wasn't too far away from the thought.

'Grace, you need to relax, you should take it easy for a bit. I'll call your Mum and say you're staying here.' I watched Beau intently making his way to the phone table, rubbing the back of his neck as he went; stress still present across his troubled face. Something felt different between us, something I couldn't quite put my finger on; but something I could feel as strongly as the bulging black eye on my face. Before I knew it, I was fast asleep, my head burrowing into the large sofa cushions fluffed beneath my aching head. For so long I hadn't realised that I wasn't actually sleeping. I was waiting for Glen, for the nightmares, for me to be honest with Beau, for Beau to realise maybe I really wasn't worth it. For the longest time all I had been prepared for was the possibility of the bad in my life becoming an inevitable reality. Now I could actually face sleep, all senses calmed, my body relaxed, my mind no longer strangled by torment. Sweet needed rest. When I came around a good four hours or so later, my sight was hazy, all the furniture was now back in its rightful place, not a speck of shattered glass to be seen, anywhere. The dim light of the Tiffany butterfly lamp on the TV bench stung my eyes. I rubbed them furiously, begging them to come into focus. I clamped them shut for a second and willed them open again a second later, everything finally clear. Despite the colossal weight that seemed to be holding me down, I fought against it and got to my feet shakily, like a baby deer on its first walk after birth. 'Beau?' My voice was low and raspy. I coughed, realising instantly that I had aggravated my sore throat; invisible needles scrapping at my gullet. With every word that left my mouth I winced again. 'Beau!' I yelled in a clearer, yet still husky tone. Beau came rushing in from the kitchen with a pitcher of ice water and a pint glass, sitting on the coffee table to be close to me. He put the jug and glass on the table beside him. As the ice hit the sides of the glass a shiver ran through me. 'Are you cold?' He grabbed the tweed blanket from the back of the sofa and put the back of his hand on my forehead taking my temperature. The inviting warmth of his hands soothed me instantly. 'You don't seem to have a temperature.' He dropped his hand down to stroke my face, staring deeply into my eyes for the briefest of moments. He turned grabbing the glass off of the table and dropping his eyes to the floor, the lack of contact with him setting my internal heating to cold again.

'What's wrong?' I reached over to take his hand in mine. The necessity of having his body close to mine was more important than food and fluids.

'It's nothing. You look a lot better.' He smiled, tugging his hand free. His claim of *nothing* clearly a lie, as I note his tell; his teeth gripping at his lower lip. 'I rang your Mum and told her you were feeling a little unwell and that you had a fall. She'll be here soon to pick you up. She mentioned something about a McAllister wedding party.'

'OK.' I couldn't think of anything else to say. I didn't want to go home; I didn't want to be anywhere but with him. Beau's attempts at emotional distancing was making me feel dreadful and uneasy. Things had never felt so bitter between us before. The pounding in my head forced me to see reason and the thought of my bed was so tempting. I convinced myself that whatever had to be said between us could wait until tomorrow. I closed my eyes, drifting easily back off to sleep, with Beau by my side. We had triumphed through everything, we had to be grateful for that.

~~~~

Ring, ring. Ring, ring.

'Hiya Catherine. Yeah of course that's not a problem. She's been resting on the sofa; I think she'll just be happy to get into bed. OK. I'll call you in the morning. OK drive safe. Bye.'

'Gwen, was that my Mum?' I asked groggily, the ringing still echoing in my head.

'Oh Grace, I thought you were sleeping. Your Mum is stuck in traffic and she doesn't think she's going to get home until the early hours of the morning. She's got Cary sorted and she said she'll see you first thing tomorrow. If it's OK with you sweetheart, you are more than welcome to stay here tonight.' Gwen lulled. I nodded finally and smiled briefly, the only response my battered body and frazzled brain would allow. Beau lifted himself out of the armchair across from me, whisking me up into his arms again, taking me upstairs without uttering a word. I rested my head lovingly against his chest. The thought of a warm bed and Beau by my side was the only thing that filled my mind. He placed me on the edge of his bed before jumping across the mattress and lying down. He kicked his baseball boots onto the floor, stretching out his arms and placing his hands between the pillow and his head. I followed his lead; my movements a little less enthusiastically and once in place he pulled the blanket over us both. His deftly fingers traced feather like curls down my spine as they made their way
~~~~

down to settle on my waistband. The tingling sensation continued throughout my back, long after he had nestled his hand snugly in my back pocket. I rested my hand on his chest and fiddled with his shirt collar, running it through my fingers. My hand settled with the lulling drum of his heartbeat beneath it. With his free hand he cupped mine and gently stroked my fingers, intertwining them. *This is my forever, right here, with him. He completes me.*

However beautiful and compelling this scene was, there was a sense of hesitancy that plagued his every touch. My eyelids felt heavy and my body began to succumb to my exhaustion. 'Why did this happen to me? What did I do to deserve this?' I whispered without thinking as a stab of pain vibrated against my ribs, I gasped as the heat spread like fire through my abdomen.

'Me, that's why this happened to you. I promise you Grace, you deserved none of this. All of this is my fault, I swore I would never let my gift hurt you, I failed.' He testified. His guilt a wound as present as those that marred my body. Crippling sadness crept onto his face only to flitter away once he realised, I'd been staring. It was quickly replaced with a loving yet empty smile. I fell asleep shortly after with the weak glow of his wall lamp shining on my face. His words stuck on repeat in my head.

~~~~

If I was confused the night before, it was becoming alarmingly clear that the morning wasn't offering up any relief either. It took me a few seconds to work out where I was. Even with the warm sun blistering through the window, I still felt cold. I had huddled myself into a ball and moved to the far-left side of the bed, ensuring that with every little stretch, the blankets still covered me. My left eye
~~~~

was barely open and with what little sight I did have I could see the purpling lump on my cheekbone. I reached over and Beau was not resting beside me as I had expected. I took a deep breath in, my head buried in his pillow, the scent of him relaxing me immediately. I flipped over onto my back, stretching out my arms and legs, occupying every inch of the bed. The sound of rustling paper beneath my fingers pulled my focus. I sat up and the second I saw my name on the piece of folded yellow paper a pang of worry jerked at my insides. Beau's delicate handwriting seemed to elevate off the page, each word ingraining randomly and out of sequence in my brain. The car-crash that was this letter held me motionless; my attention fixed. The splash against the paper alerted me to the fact that I was crying, my salty tears stinging my skin as they made their way across my open wounds.

My dear Gracie,

I will never be able to explain to you how hard it was watching you go through what you did last night. The weeks that you have spent feeling afraid and alone breaks my heart. I know that what happened to you was my fault. Without my gift, without this world that I forced onto you, you would never have been put in that position. As you lay sleeping, all I can see is the pain I have put you through. I make you vulnerable and this will not stop while I'm around. I want you to know that you will forever be in my heart and in my thoughts. I love you more than I could describe and you have to know that I'm doing this to keep you safe. I will not call you and I will not write to you, I will not put you at risk. I want you to take this chance to live your life. Whether I am by your side or not I will forever cherish the time that I spent calling you mine.

Love you always, with you always, miss you always.

Beau x

I glanced over to the open wardrobes that were completely bare. His laptop gone, his memory shelf above my head stripped of everything except for a set of photobooth pictures of the two of us. I grabbed the photos and slid them into the back pocket of my stained jeans, the blood now completely dry and almost brown. I wiped my face on my sleeves and rushed to find my stuff. I had to make him stay. I ran around the room trying to find my shoes. One was strewn across the computer chair and the other was nowhere in sight. I dropped to the floor with no second thought to my poor knees and like Cinderella's glass slipper, my mangy old baseball boot gleamed from under the bed. *How much of a head start did he have? Is he on foot, a bus maybe, what about a plane?* While still trying to get my shoe on, I grabbed my bag, hobbling towards the door, I threw my jean jacket on, bumping into the door frame as I went. My body pulsated with adrenaline with every step I took as it tried to drown out the now emotional pain that engulfed my every limb. I passed Gwen on the stairs and she shouted bye as I whipped through the front door, having very little thought for anything other than him. I ran for the bus, unable to swat the image of Kings Cross train station out of my mind, the surrounding shops, the queues of people getting their morning coffee from Starbucks. The clapping of the destination boards constantly changing. The train times rang in my ears. It was deafening. *Angel at 5:10, Clapham on the over ground due now, Walthamstow central has a 10-minute delay.*

I willed the bus to sprout wings and get me to the train station in a hurry, not only to find Beau, but to hopefully calm the relentless travel announcements ringing out in my head. I followed my instincts to the letter, running amongst an excited crowd of tourists through the high carved pillars of Kings cross station's entrance. The noises calmed, for a split second everything became clear. Once again, I could picture Beau's face, but as quickly as it had come to me it had disappeared. I ran through the bustling station bumping into people left and right, urgently trying to settle my concentration in one direction. The hordes of people, the controllers over the loudspeaker, it was impossible to focus. I closed my eyes and tried to settle my mind. The neon lights of the Gate 12 podium flashed through my head. I couldn't explain it, but that oddly reassuring gut feeling had seemed to be all I had guiding me. I had nothing else to go on.

'Gate 12 will be closing in four minutes so please make your way to the platform with your tickets ready.'

The announcer roared over the speakers above me. This couldn't be a coincidence; in big yellow print I could see gate 12 at the other end of the station. I ran as fast as my legs would carry me, my tortured muscles protesting. 'Beau, wait, please Beau. Wait!' I shouted across the vast space. Everyone turned to stare at the spectacle, nothing was going to make me take my eyes off him. He turned to face me but he wouldn't look at me. 'Beau, please don't leave, I don't want to be here without you.' I pleaded out of breath and probably a little louder than was necessary, everyone continued to stare at us and I couldn't care less.

'Last call for Gate 12.'

'Grace, I really have to go.' He stroked my cheek softly, those beautiful blues drawing me in, then turned to face the platform. He handed the ticket to the attendant and did not turn back. As quickly as he came into my life, he left it. He walked away without another word or a backwards glance and that day I died inside. As I watched him board the train, I felt helpless and alone. I was lost for words and any gut feeling I had once had to reassure me now only evaded me.

'Please, don't leave me.' My begging was almost non-existent, my voice small, the grief swallowing me up from the inside. *Do I really want to chase him down and make him say something I don't want to hear?* I stood there for what felt like a lifetime. The bustle of commuters passed me by but all I could see was him leaving me, all I could hear was his voice saying goodbye. His aftershave covered my shirt and as it filled my nose I cried, tears that I thought would never cease. I watched Beau's train depart the station and felt my heart and soul leave with it. As the other couples and loved ones around me took advantage of their last chance to say goodbye, I realised how cruelly my last chance had been ripped away from me. I eventually wandered through the station in a silent stupor with my eyes fixed on the floor. I didn't realise until I got home and sat on my bed that I still had the note from Beau clutched tightly in my hand, with the ink of his final words printed on my palm. I threw my bag on my bed and as I approached my desk there was a little gold box with a card sitting idly behind it. I opened the envelope cautiously as my tears hit the card with a thud.

'Grace, I wanted you to have this.'

Inside the box was a St. Christopher's medal on a long gold chain. As I turned it over, the engraved words that would forever make my heart fall, caused a flood of tears to pelt against my shirt.

'Love will conquer all.'

AWOKEN *Billie Jade Kermack*

THIRTY-EIGHT

ജ്ഞ

Dear diary,

That deep dark hole that I lived in after I was forced to say goodbye to my Dad, that place where you are all alone and everything around you is blurred, that lonesome place where your heart is broken and your soul lies in tatters destroyed on the floor, that is where I am now, and there is no luminous white light guiding me to an exit. My father always told me live, laugh, love; a motto he swore would get me through life. I have to tell you living is hard, laughing is impossible and loving left on a train and could be an eternity away right now. Of course, life will go on, it has to, but I know now that I will neither live nor laugh as I once did and as for loving, it hurts way too much. I honestly don't think my heart could take it. I've loved and lost and as my life moves on and things around me change, that loss still cripples me - forever saddens me. I know I cannot change the events that have occurred, but I do know that with every scrap of energy I have, I must hold dear the fact that there was a time when I did love, there was a time when I did have a full and rich heart and there was a time, which feels like a lifetime ago, when there was a man - a very special man - who made me feel complete.

I miss you more than words could say Beau. I will not yet say goodbye.

Sleeping was becoming more of a nuisance. When I could sleep, I dreamt of Beau, when I couldn't sleep, I thought of Beau. *What was he doing? Where was he? Was he thinking about me? Does he miss me?* I put all the pictures and mementoes that reminded me of Beau in the box he had wrapped my comic in; that stunning night in the park. I stored it away under my bed, my ever-growing feelings of distress and longing its only friends. The holidays went by and with every passing day the hours and minutes merged into one. Most days I'd sit in my room and idly gaze out of the window with only my thoughts for company. It didn't make much sense to do anything other than think of him. The kids that would fly their kites and the sound of the annual charity football game on Grove's field; life passed me by and I cared very little about any of it. My iPod became my only comfort and I couldn't remember the last time I had had a proper conversation with anyone. It worried Mum of course, but what could she do, apart from send me to the nut house (which for the time being would stick firmly as option B)? She decided it was better to leave me to work through it. Surprisingly Cary agreed with Mum and he didn't bother me either.

Beau's letter was now crumpled, discoloured and torn on the fold lines. I knew the words from memory. They had run through my mind more than a thousand times. I still traced my fingers over the words as I tortured myself repeatedly, in a strange way the anguish had slowly become a comfort. It was proof that he did exist and he had left. I couldn't fool myself into believing it was all a dream as the words jumped at me from the page. I ran the St. Christopher through my fingers hoping that some of Beau's strength would rub off of it. I couldn't let it go. I wouldn't let it go. Three months had passed since I last saw Beau and I could still close my eyes and picture him in that station like it was yesterday. I had no appetite and eventually I couldn't even be bothered to get dressed. I'd roam around my room in my pyjamas sitting at that same bay window looking out onto the world that refused to stay still, its occupants and their lives racing by me so quickly. The leaves on the trees no longer looked as green and the sun never beamed as brightly. Nothing seemed to function as well as it had with Beau by my side. I was a sheep amongst the wolves and nothing that I did could save me from myself. Yes, I was slowly destroying myself, but on some level, it scared me to not think about Beau. Of course, I wanted to stop hurting. The memory of his smile was heart-breaking enough, but I always worried that if I didn't hold on to that pain, remember his face, his hands, his smile, then what would I have left? What if I forgot someone who was such a big part of my life? Someone who bridged that gap between my world and my fathers'? He'd given me something that people only dream about and as surprised as I was, I think he loved me too. I guessed we would never know for sure the mystery surrounding Beau. *If a broken heart is all you get for falling in love, why risk it?*

~~~~

Over the next couple of months, I was just as miserable as I was right after Beau had left. Except now I had hair where there shouldn't be and I was in desperate need of some sunlight. Slightly pale was an understatement. I just couldn't seem to find the energy to do anything. I discovered a new level of self-pity and once again the tears fell on a regular basis. After a particularly bad night (and I'd had quite a few) I woke up looking like I had squared off to Rocky Balboa, and LOST! I took baby steps at first; going to the shop for some milk, meeting Gwen for lunch, eating dinner at the dining table with Mum and Cary. It wasn't long before I was back in the swing of life. I was still sensitive about it all and Amelia liked to tell me that I was '*a right moody cow at times*' but I loved her honesty and like everyone else, she knew just to steer clear of the Beau
~~~~

conversation. I owed part of my recovery to Red Bull. *'A mild caffeine energy booster'* was an understatement. I don't think I would have even got out of my bed at all if I hadn't had a family size pack of those handy.

'Go time in ten kids.' Mum hollered up to us from the foot of the stairs. I grabbed some clothes out of my wardrobe, stuffing them into my holdall. Bournemouth was meant to be pretty chilly so in went the hooded jumpers and woolly socks. I grabbed the butterfly decorated box from under my bed and without glancing inside like I usually did, I shoved it into my holdall, covering it with my clothes. It had become clear shortly after Beau had left that he was impossible to forget. In company I masked it well and tried to put a persona on that would satisfy those around me, but if I slipped, even for a second, his face would creep to the forefront of my mind and that debilitating sadness would again course through me. Mum had a bridezilla to contend with that weekend and unfortunately Cary and I had the pleasure of accompanying her. I think she was still a little worried about leaving me alone. I love her but she kept giving me the *'you're still fragile'* speech, which had really started to bug me and managed to only remind me of my situation. Yeah, I was sad but I wasn't a bloody vase. I could probably have benefited from a little show down, vent all that pent-up emotion I had stored up. The day was still young and stuck with Cary in Mum's car for five hours on the motorway could prove destructive. On her head be it! I think the last time me, Mum and Cary all went away together was when Cary was still in nappies. I can still remember fondly that Winnie the Pooh dummy that forced silence. Absolute bliss.

'Grace, get a move on I'd like to get going at some point today.' Cary yelled obnoxiously through the door with a smirk. *Bugger cleanliness in this house. Silence is definitely next to godliness,* I laughed to myself. I unplugged my iPod from its charger and threw it into my bag as I headed for the door, remembering seconds later to also unplug the charger from the wall and pack that also.

'Mum, are you really sure you want me to come? I don't think this is going to be the easiest of road trips.' I glared at Cary who was fastening his seatbelt next to me.

'Grace, you're not too old for family trips and I think it will do us all good to get away.' She beamed at me softly with her puppy dog eyes. As usual I backed down without a fight. I had very little energy to smile so an argument I could probably never win was pointless. I popped on my seatbelt, praying sleep would steal most of my journey. 'So, no one wants to sit upfront with me then?' Mum queried, looking at us in her rear-view mirror.

'You never let us have the front seat?' Cary trumped confused.

'Well it's not like you two are babies anymore.' Cary and I observed one another hesitantly, as though we were cowboys in a Clint Eastwood western reaching for our pistols, we unclipped our belts tentatively, watching each other's movements like hawks. 'Shotgun!' I exclaimed, but before I knew what was going on, Cary was settled in the front seat with his belt already fastened. I smacked him on the back of the head and relaxed back into my seat with a crafty smile plastered proudly on my face. Cary turned to face me and stuck his tongue out triumphantly. Before I could remember how old I was, I stuck my tongue out right back at him.

'Maybe I was wrong about you two not being babies' anymore.' For the first time in forever Cary and I shared an understanding smile, a sweet and loving smile that surprisingly made me want to hug him rather then hit him. I managed to restrain myself. It didn't take long for me to revel in the fact that Cary had nabbed the front seat. Mum was a chatty driver with a catalogue of stories; these trips are the very reason I learnt to drive and passed my test first time. I pulled my earphones up over my ears from around my neck as my mum began to tell Cary about her days as a die-hard Wham fan. I picked an old-school rock playlist on my iPod and cranked up the volume to the max, silencing the outside world. My smile was unmoving as I saw Cary descend into the once holy front seat with his head in his hands. My phone shuddered in my pocket making me jump; The Beach Boy's Good Vibrations ironically filling my ears.

Hello sweetheart.

I hope you get this. Texting really isn't my thing but I know you're probably busy, so I thought this would be easier. If I'm honest, I'm seriously technically challenged. I saw your mum last week and she mentioned you were looking for a job. I've pulled a few strings and there's one going at the hospital with me. It's nothing great, but it pays well and its great hours. Let me know. Also - and I debated whether to tell you this - but I have finally heard from Beau. He is fine, but that was all the message said. I thought you would want to know.

All my love – Gwen xxxx

After about an hour and a half of driving, with Kaleo's back catalogue blasting through my iPod, my thoughts stumbled to Beau's message to Gwen and the excitement raised from my new job prospect; I chose to concentrate on the latter, allowing thoughts of Beau to sit too long in my mind just filled me with sadness. The rain was relentless as I rested my head against the window, even with my music on I could still hear the calm pelting as it hit the steamed glass. Before I knew it, I had dozed off. I woke suddenly to the sound of honking. I had no idea how long I had been out of it, my eyes lazy as the car spun. A searing pain ran through my neck as I was thrown forward and to the side, only to be saved uncomfortably by my awkwardly placed seatbelt, but not before my face made contact with the window. I threw one hand to my face, the other to my neck, the car jolting me about in my seat like a dodgem, propelling my iPod out of my grasp, thrusting it into the windscreen. With the car now completely still, its hinges creaking, the smell of burnt rubber from the tyres coming in wisps through the heating slot, I reached for my seatbelt, still half asleep and in a daze; it was jammed. I opened my eyes trying desperately to be alert, but failing miserably, as my eyes struggled to focus. I fought off a sense of worried confusion as my surroundings became clear.

'Hey mate, ever heard of Specsavers?' My Mum's voice was hoarse as she slammed the car door shut behind her, the movement of the car as a result making me wince.

'What the hell is going on?' I screamed still cradling my face.

'Hey sleeping beauty, great time to take a nap.' Cary remarked bitterly as he rubbed his arm furiously.

'Why have we stopped?' No amount of massaging my neck was relieving the burning sensation throbbing beneath my skin. 'Where's Mum going, is she OK?'

'She's gone to check on the old couple in front of us.' Once free from my belt after a couple more jabs at the button I edged forward, my body protesting the movement, a sharp pain raging up my neck. The line of cars stretched for as far as the eye could see, disappearing in the distance where the motorway curved. Every car from what I could tell had some form of damage, whether it was a battered bumper or a blown tyre. Thankfully it was no longer raining, the low early afternoon sun now shining down on the cars, throwing off beams of blinding white light from the still sodden tarmac in every direction. With the traffic silenced, the lapping waves of the clear blue sea could be heard as they beat against the crumbling coastline to the left of us, we couldn't be too far from the hotel.

'Owww. Mind much?' I retorted curtly as Cary prodded at the deep cut on my lip, blood dripping down onto my white Ramones t-shirt, the familiar scent of iron filling my nostrils. It was only a little bit of blood but it stung like hell. Flipping him off, receiving the same gesture from him in return, I sat back in my seat and opened my window, grateful for the soothing salty fresh breeze that danced across my wounds. I gazed at my reflection in the rear-view mirror and dabbed at my broken skin with the sleeve of my red tartan shirt from the footwell. The small concave scar on my cheek below my fresh scrape – my present from Glen - was an unhealthy reminder of just how bad I could get hurt; this little scratch was superficial in comparison. Before I could open my door, Mum sat back in the car with a wad of tissues cradled on her face. They were a bright crimson and soaked right through. Suddenly any and all pain that I may have been feeling dissipated. 'Mum, what happened? Are you OK?' I fumbled around grabbing a towel out of my holdall and passed it to her.

'My airbag didn't deploy. Apparently, there's been an accident up the road, just past the bend. An ice-cream truck and an oncoming car. The Parsons just about swerved in time and missed colliding with the car in front of them...'

'Wait, who are the Parsons?' I interrupted. This was too much information to take in all at once.

'Sorry love, the old couple in front. Luckily, I pushed on the brakes in time, but before I knew it, we were slammed into from behind, there was nothing I could do.' She stressed. Only my mum could get into a fifty-car pile-up and end up adopting a couple of geriatrics.

'Mum, you did everything you could and we're all safe, stop panicking.' Cary chirped as he put Mum's old bloody tissue in a used Tesco bag that he'd rescued from the glove compartment. Steam whistled out from under the bonnet of our car, grabbing our attention. My mum stuffed some more tissue against her bloody nose and rested her head on the steering wheel in exasperation. We were going to be stuck here for a while.

'Grace, Cary, are you both feeling OK? Are you in shock?' Mum stressed again, ignoring her own obvious wounds as she tipped her head back against the seat rest pinching at the bridge of her nose.

'We're a little battered Mum, but nothing we can't handle.' Cary nodded agreeing with me as he rubbed his wrist. I leant forward to pick up the remainder of my crushed iPod from under the handbrake. 'Well my iPod seems to have taken the brunt of it.' The screen was dented and there was something loose inside; an iPod shouldn't rattle. 'Well we are all alive, that's what matters.' I said a little too cheekily as I threw my destroyed iPod into my holdall in a strop.

"Always look on the bright side of life, da dum, da dum, da dum, da dum!" Cary's unhelpful rendition of Monty Python's classic hit just made me miss my music that much more. Without it, there was no escape from his voice. Mum

and I shot him identical glares. The heat in the car rising. He quickly ceased his singing and resumed gazing out of his window.

'Mum can you turn the radio on, maybe we'll find out what the hell's going on.' I pressed. Half an hour later we were none the wiser and I was ever closer on the verge of strangling Cary. After the numerous heated phone calls Mum had made to a representative named Clive at the AA, it was pretty much a waiting game. It didn't take long for boredom to kick in and my mind to wander, which is something I definitely didn't need. Three hours and forty-seven minutes later exactly, with no iPod, no air conditioning and the blazing hot sun beating down on us, I began to lose what little of my sanity I had left. The idea of reading my book was the best I could muster; anything would do to keep my mind busy. The crazy notion that I could even attempt to concentrate long enough to get through a novel was squashed, as I remembered the book was perched on my bedside table at home with the bookmark still stored between pages five and six. This is where the novel had lived for the whole six months that I had owned it. I would swim the length of the Atlantic at this point, to have that book in my hand, a crisp cold glass of Jacob's Creek and some Beatles tunes filling my headphones. I sighed longingly, admitting defeat as Cary started up a conversation with my Mum about the history of trigonometry. As we approached the fifth hour the road began to clear, a flurry of cars and trucks that had very little or no damage manoeuvring around us to hit the motorway at speed again. The sun was now unbearable and we were on our last bottle of water. Clive from the AA cheerfully assured us he would have someone out to fix the car within the hour. The first hour came as did the second. We kept positive that the third hour was the lucky one but as the minutes ticked by our wavering hope subsequently drifted away. *Hello fourth hour!*

What seemed like a mirage in the distance crept up slowly from behind us. We were one of three cars still left on the side of the motorway, the rest of the car owners clearly members of other service companies. We could hazily make out the big yellow letters AA. My heart literally leapt for joy and I uttered a long-awaited sigh of relief. By this point, I don't know if I noted, we were in our fourth hour of waiting and the chirpy demeanour of Ted, our Irish AA service man who pulled up to our car with a toothy smile stretched from ear to ear, was neither amusing nor welcomed. Ted misread our annoyance, completely side-stepping our obvious frustrations, his smile never wavering, even when my mother practically threw the cars log book at him. His choice of response surprised us all. 'Right there's an Englishman, an Irishman and a Scotsman...' Ted said jovially with a skip in his step.

'I'm going to stop you right there buddy!' I eased Ted away from my Mum who was now seething with impatience, her top drenched in dry brown blood that had been stiffened by the sun, her lack of patience almost visible in the air Infront of her face. With my help and Mum's expression, Ted soon realised his effervescent leprechaun routine was not needed. We needed a mechanic, not a clown! It took a further forty minutes to check everything over, change the front tyre and to fiddle with something under the bonnet that Ted assured us had just come lose, the little comparison he made between that and an old Steve Maqueen film was lost on me, I had officially lost the will to listen to anyone; even my own thoughts were starting to grate on me. In no time at all we were doing sixty MPH, back on our way to Bournemouth. I rolled down my window until it creaked in protest, the cool air lapping affectionately in my face, whipping my hair back and soothing the burning on my swollen cheek. I closed my eyes, breathing deep, filling my lungs to the point of exploding. I could now see the unruly dipping and diving of the masses of seagulls circling above us, the faint

AWOKEN *Billie Jade Kermack*

thundering of the crashing hillside waves soothing my tired brain.

THIRTY-NINE

ꕤ

I woke up the next morning with a fat lip, a roaring headache and as it had done since the day, I met him, Beau's face was seared into the forefront of my mind. I joined Cary in the breakfast room and grabbed for the nearest pot of coffee. Mum was already off doing her duties and sorting out her client's ever-growing bridesmaid clan. The tiaras were all bent up in the accident, so Mum was out at eight that morning looking for replicas so as not to enrage the one they called Bridezilla, well we called her Bridezilla; to her guests she was Penny. We sat through breakfast silently. Cary had his beak perched in the pages of a James Joyce novel which was bigger than all the books I had ever owned combined. I figured looking out of the open floor to ceiling bay windows at the beautiful, golden view was a lot more relaxing then trying to start up a conversation with my little brother. After breakfast I parted ways with Cary and our absolutely riveting conversation, or lack thereof, and made my way into town. Cary had begrudgingly agreed to meet Mum upstairs in the bridal suite, so she could keep an eye on him. Cary hadn't listened to Mum and stayed exactly where he was – this was a dangerous game he was playing. My sixth sense of knowing all impending dangers involving my mother and her wrath made me instantly wary, but as I wasn't going to be on the receiving end of her anger, I wished him well and carried on with my day.

'Hey dude, good luck, I think you're going to need it.' I beamed. Two steps shy of the balcony exit I heard my mother's frantic heels tapping against the waxed floors of the foyer, her yells of his name shrill and commanding. I exited with my camera bag slung over my shoulder as fast as my legs could carry me, grabbing a banana from the breakfast bar by the window as I made my way out to the automatic glass door, leading onto the 4-acre wide back garden. The hotel staff were setting up a marquee for the matrimonial festivities that were now mere hours away from kick-off. Without a backwards glance in my brother's direction, my mother again repeating his name in that way that only a mother could, I snuck away unseen. Next stop – the town centre. Apparently that unusual patch of belting sun yesterday was it for our British summer, the good old English rain was officially back in full force. I pulled up the fur-lined hood on my duffel coat and took a stroll along the deserted pier front. I snapped away on my camera, the roaring grey ocean interrupting my frame every time the tide struck the rocks at the water's edge. An old couple sat silently on a peeling green painted bench. Clearly enjoying the comfort of each other's warmth, no need for anything else, their years of love elevated through them in a moment when their hands touched. As the orange and red infused sky began to stretch out above me, the amusement arcade lights popped to life; the strobes of colour a distorted reflection in the pools of rain, on the gravel beneath me. A fleet of sterling white clouds hung low in the sky and as they illuminated everything beneath them, a feeling of unscathed happiness roamed through me. It was the first time in a long time that I allowed myself to think that maybe, just maybe, everything would be okay, that I would be okay.

My mouth was watering as I stepped inside *Mel's Chip Emporium.* Hearty portions of crispy battered fish that still smelt like the sea lined the chest heaters, thick cut chips smothered in onion vinegar and salt thrown into newspaper that had been folded expertly into funnels. My belly grumbled angrily, grabbing the attention of the robust, auburn-haired woman in the queue ahead of me. I suddenly felt like a complaining child as she looked down her nose at me with one of her disapproving eyebrows raised high on her wrinkled forehead. My phone began silently vibrating in my pocket, severing the odd tension between us.

'Hey Mum.'

'Grace, are you OK, I haven't heard from you all day?' Her voice was squeaky and panicked.

'Yeah, Mum I'm fine. How did the wedding go?'

'So far, so good. Everyone's hair has stayed up so I fulfilled my end of the bargain.' She chortled. Without even needing to see her I could hear as her shoulders relaxed, her worry finally dissipating. The faint beat of a Michael Jackson tune in the background - Billie Jean I think - conjured up images of fancily attired men and women circling the dance floor, pulling out their best 80's grooves. My mother on the other hand would more than likely be in a corner, swaying along to the music in her long mauve dress and matching shoes, her purple beaded John Lewis shawl draped annoyingly over her shoulder as it clinked against her champagne glass.

'So, all's going to plan then?' I prompted. My mother had never been one for weddings, not since my father died anyway.

'Everyone's loving it, even Cary's having a good time. It seems Mrs Rutherford is a PTA member at that school he's trying to get into. It is also extremely likely that Cary may be a little smitten with her daughter Imogen. I haven't been able to prise them apart all night.' Mum seemed in high spirits, which was nice to hear, the fact that Cary was getting some action from a girl surely could only make him less annoying.
'Do you want salt and vinegar on your chips sweetheart?'

The gruff, southern English accent came from a short, balding, stout man from behind the counter.

'Urhh...yes please and some ketchup in the corner if you have it please.' I smiled politely before he bent over and checked the top cupboard on the far wall. Thankfully the flash I got of his stained yellow boxers and hairy back didn't put me off my chips.

'So, I hear you have dinner sorted then honey.' My Mum yelled down the phone as George Michael's song Faith echoed amongst a crowd of cheering in the background. 'Look, I'll let you eat, but if you need me, or you want to chat, if you need absolutely anything at all, just call me. I'm hoping the fresh air and change of scenery will help you forget about...I love you honey.' She professed, quickly correcting her thoughts with a momentary pause at the end.

'Love you too Mum' I smiled with a lump in my throat. I knew who she was about to mention and up until that moment; for that day at least, I hadn't thought about my heartache. I took my newspaper wrapped bag of steaming chips and headed out the door. The sour vinegar stung my nostrils as the cold sea breeze lapped affectionately at my face. I could only have been in there ten minutes but already the street lights along the entire stretch of the white wooden pier were alight, illuminating the edge of the beach. The now full moon was glowing low in the sky as its reflection danced on the soft calm waves. I strolled down towards the beach front with my chips in hand. Finally finding a spot close to the water's edge, which didn't take long as the incoming tide was only a few metres out from the street. The drenched, murky beach in either direction of me, that seemed to go on for miles, was completely empty, not a soul to be seen. I pulled up my hood and zipped up my Parker. I untied my sodden baseball boots and removed my socks, strolling along the beach barefoot, clumps of sand forming between my feet and collecting between my toes. The tide lapped against my bare ankles, the tinkling sounds of raindrops hitting the waves stirring a feeling of complete serenity within me. A calm that I hadn't realised I was missing drummed quietly inside me. The fog of heartache had momentarily subsided, everything seeming clear. I slumped down onto the sand, the chimes of the amusements now far enough away for me to hear the lapping water as it hit my feet, still devouring my salty chips; my only source of dwindling heat. The wet sand soaked through my trousers and the rain pelted against my coat, but I was happy here, I didn't have to plaster a fake smile on my face or pretend that I was okay when I wasn't. I was better off alone. I didn't know why, but the thought scared me. I rested my head on my knees, closed my eyes and prayed, to whoever or whatever there was out there that could possibly alter the lonely fate that I was clearly destined for.

FORTY

ഇ

In bursts of quick-fire explosions, the street lamps behind me on the boardwalk sprinkled glass onto the pebbled pavement below them. The shards glittering like diamonds in the light of the now high-flying full moon. Instinct and an uneasy feeling in my gut brought me quickly but unsteadily to my feet. The delicate tapping of rain on my coat and the familiar scent of iron in the air sent my mind racing. I wiped the blood from my nose with the back of my hand. It looked almost black in the darkness. I couldn't stop it. I panicked, my hands trembling wildly. The dead eerie silence enveloped me, only the soft howl of the sea breeze could be heard. Then there, looming above me, stood a shrouded stranger. The harsh blows that the stranger rained down on me felt oddly calming, painful yes, but detached somehow. A crack in my cheek sent a pulsating throb vibrating through my head. I didn't see it coming, but the flow of balmy liquid creeping over my eye and down my face alerted me to my fate. With my vision clouded and my heart racing I turned to run, but my feet were two steps behind my brain. The stranger pushed me face down into the sodden sand and it stung as the gravel particles embedded in my wounds. I pleaded for my life, whimpering around my disjointed pleas, they were unanswered, the weight on me unbearable.

Fight, Fight, FIGHT! The words were alarmingly clear in my head, like those neon temporary road signs warning you to take a break or beware of animals crossing. I willed my outstretched fingers to find something, anything to help me. Eventually reduced to tears, the clumped sand sifted through my shaking hands. Nothing. Then I saw them. The deserted street that had not so long ago been filled with the laughter of excited children and the echoing rainbow lights of the amusements, now held nothing but pain and fear, nothing but death. Spirits, hazy grey forms, lined the long street as far as the eye could see in both directions. Men, women, children. White, black, Asian. Young and old. Beaten, bloodied, ravaged. I didn't know them, but as their eyes bore into me, I knew their torment, their anguish. They wanted something from me, something I couldn't give them. The odd detachment I had walled up around me to block out my agony settled without me realising as another blow from something metal popped my shoulder out of its socket. A feeling of utter dread tugged at my now fragile heart and sucked the air from my lungs. I had nothing left to give. I had stared death in the face more times than I cared to recount, I didn't know how much more I could physically or mentally handle.

The cooling sea water lapped at my twitching bare feet. The crimson flow of blood seeping from my wounds, curdling into the soft waves, a memory of painting in art class when I was five or so suddenly jumped into my head and drew me in. I had a red puff ball dress with yellow daisies on it. My long mousy brown hair was secured neatly in two French plaits and shone brightly beneath the golden sun filling the room through the large double windows. The sweet smells of strawberry jam coated biscuits and milk from the snack table wafting around me. My hands were small, pale and pink. I flexed them out in front of me. Blues, reds, greens, purples, oranges; the paints ran together and in between my fingers. An innocent, elated smile spread widely from ear to ear for a moment, a very brief moment, realisation of my situation only too happy to trample my thoughts of happier times. Stagnant reality challenged the settling memory and dragged me back kicking and screaming into the dark. The otherwise barely audible sound of my heart was now deafeningly clear, as it panicked to supply my veins and organs with the blood they desperately needed.

My eyes fluttered as unconsciousness, or more likely death, threatened to take me. Without warning an odd sensation took a one-way route around my body, firing synapses, barking insanities in my now worn out brain. *Goodbye liver. Spleen – going so soon? Kidney on the left – fancy giving your brother over there a kick start? Hey heart, you may want to calm down, all that exercise can't be good for you!*

One by one they gave in, buckling under the pressure of my mangled body. It suddenly felt as simple as flipping on a light switch. It was an oddly foreign but calming feeling of acceptance. My mind had given itself over, but as I glanced down, my body was still fighting, writhing to succeed for that last ounce of vital energy, that last glug of needed air. I watched the blood drip tiredly from my veins, bleaching the congealed grey sand beneath me a bright vermilion. Each laboured intake of air tried desperately to flourish in the now dusty crevices of my chest, but it only licked at the hollow space like white hot flames. Dying wasn't the hard part. I'd never known giving up to be so easy. Knowing I had allowed Glen to beat me however, was soul shattering. I had just about enough energy left to roll over and face him, but I would do it with as much feigned composure as I could muster. My artificial stability was fleetingly brief, my body knotted and exhausted. My tormentor, the person towering over me, admiring their work as I lay there choking on a concoction of blood and salty tears, wasn't who I thought it would be. He was not Glen. He was not even a he at all.

Her voice was a sickly-sweet surprise. A whisper laden with unfiltered anger and hate.

It wasn't supposed to end like this.

It would mean a great deal to me if you could leave a review. Thanks. All the best.

Billie Jade Kermack lives in London with her family and pet dog Sherlock. She currently works as a makeup artist for films and TV. *Awoken* is the first novel in its series. She is currently writing *Ascend,* Book Two in the series.

Book trailers for *Awoken* by *Nothin or Double Films* can be found on YouTube.

Follow her on twitter at: @BKermack_Awoken

Instagram - billiejadekermackauthor

www.facebook.com/BJKAwoken